# Porn Money &
# Mummy
## Wannabe

# Laura Barnard

Nicola,

So lovely to meet
you!

Love + Laughs

Laura Barnard

6   6   6

Published in 2016 by Ingram Sparks

*This book is dedicated to my Grandma Breda Harty who was always the best story teller. She's been my inspiration in so many ways and I will miss her greatly.*

# Chapter 1
## Poppy

### *Christmas Day*

'Darling!' My Mum screeches as she swings the door open to me, Ryan, and Grams, Ryan's Grandma; a half-drunk bottle of wine in her hand.

Jesus. It's only 11.00. Please don't let this be a repeat of last Christmas. She got so drunk she decided it would be funny to piss in the garden. Only, the emergency light went on, and the neighbours saw everything and complained. So then she decided to shit in an envelope and post it through their door in protest of her 'right to do whatever she wants in her own garden'. Needless to say, they weren't invited to the next neighbourhood watch meeting. They were the subject of it. Thank God they moved.

She grabs Grams and kisses her on both cheeks. 'Hi, Grams. Lovely to have you here.'

She looks at my joke red Christmas jumper. Ryan and I decided it would be funny to wear the tackiest ones we could find. Mine's got a Christmas tree on the front which lights up when I press my right boob. Ryan's one says 'Merry Christmas you filthy animal'. A quote from one of our favourite Christmas movies; *Home Alone*.

'Darling, what on *earth* are you wearing?' She looks over me in disgust. 'A baggy old jumper? You look like you're wearing a sack. Why?'

Ryan smiles knowingly at me, his chocolate eyes dancing with amusement. 'Actually Meryl, we just wanted to - '

He's interrupted by Mum. Of *course* he is.

'Stop! Are you telling me what I think you're going to say?' Her face nearly explodes with happiness. 'You're pregnant, aren't you darling?' She jumps up and down, spilling some of the wine, grabbing me into a hug, crushing me against her monster breasts. 'Not that I'm over the moon about being a grandmother *again* while I'm still in my forties,' she smiles.

Forties. I can't help but snort. Who is she trying to kid?

'No, Mum!' I snap, nipping this in the bud before it gets out of hand. Again.

You see, whenever anything happens in my life, Mum thinks it's me trying to tell them I'm pregnant. Literally, from the minute I got married. I called her from my honeymoon to remind her to water my plants and she started whooping and hollering all over the place, telling me it was earlier than expected, but she was still over the moon. By the time I got back, the whole gang was out with a banner saying congratulations. My mother just doesn't understand the concept of being wrong.

'I mean it,' I say as sternly as I can. 'There is *no* baby in here.' I point to my stomach.

Ryan smiles sadly and wraps his arm around my waist. That smile makes my heart ache. You see, we *have* been trying to get pregnant for nearly a year, but I haven't fallen yet. It wouldn't be so hard to deal with if everyone would stop asking me when they're going to hear the pitter-patter of little feet. Unless you have a bloody crystal ball, I have no fucking idea! But I have to pretend like we're just 'enjoying each other for now' and act horrified at the idea of dirty nappies.

We follow Mum into their new house just down the street from us. It's smaller than the last house, but still absolutely gorgeous. Not that Mum hasn't completely ruined it with her idea of interior design. The kitchen diner at the back of the house was completely modern with clean lines and shiny cabinets. Only Mum decided to get Jemima, my niece, to pick the theme. There's *always* a bloody theme. It's The Lion King theme. That's right. It might actually be worse than her previous Moroccan/under the sea themed house.

The dining room chairs are covered with zebra printed velvet, the table covered in a camouflage cloth. Jazz, my best friend, who conveniently ended up with my brother Ollie and had the beautiful Jemima, badly painted a mural of every animal in the zoo onto the wall next to it, with mosquito nets hanging from the ceiling. There's a small bamboo hut in the corner which Jemima uses as a play house. Giant elephant sculptures stick out of the wall holding candles from their tusks. A small sofa which looks like it's a jeep is nestled into a corner. There's even a stuffed giraffe wearing a top hat. Every single thing is animal themed from the kettle to the sugar pots. It honestly looks more like a child's bedroom than a kitchen/diner. And it's all currently covered in twinkling fairy lights; flashing so quickly I'm surprised none of us has had a stroke.

'Are you okay?' I whisper to Ryan as Mum gets us some wine out of her enormous wine fridge. Most people's wine fridges aren't bigger than your average fridge/freezer.

'Course, babe,' he smiles, kissing me on the end of my nose.

I scrunch my face up, pretending he's annoying when really I find his affection totally adorable. God, I love him so much. I just hope to God I can give him a baby.

'Hey, bitches!' We turn to see Jazz running towards us for a cuddle.

She's wearing what looks to be a Christmas tree dress. It's bloody awful. Off the shoulder green velvet which goes out at the hips to just above her knee. She's attached ornaments to it with what looks like sticky tape, and she's got light up earrings.

'Jazz, what the hell are you wearing?' I snort, giving her a quick hug.

'I'm a Christmas tree.' She rolls her eyes. 'Duh!'

I snort out a laugh. 'Where's my little Jem stone?'

She rolls her eyes. 'She's in the sitting room. You know how she loves it in there.'

The front room theme was again designed by Jemima. It's Cinderella themed. Although I join in with everyone taking the piss, it's actually my favourite room. It's so girly and beautiful. The walls are painted a cool blue with an over the top crystal chandelier hanging from the ceiling. The sofas were specially made to be Cinderella carriages with wheels and gold detailing

7

making you feel like you're in some sort of pod. She has pretend mice holes painted onto the skirting boards and mice placed randomly around. A canvas saying 'A dream is a wish your heart makes' is above the fireplace. The rest of the room is decorated with ornate white mirrors and small horse sculptures. There's even a pumpkin footstool. It's ridiculous, but I bloody love it.

I'm surprised Jazz, Ollie and Jemima have managed to live with my parents for so long, but I'm sure Jemima having a Disney house helps.

'Uncle Wyan! Uncle Wyan!' Jemima screams from the hallway, running towards him. Her long blonde curls bounce after her. She's growing up far too quickly. She's nearly three already.

Ryan's face lights up, and he scoops to pick her up just in time for her to run into him.

'Hey, trouble,' he smiles, poking her in her tummy. 'Merry Christmas!'

'Merry Cwistmas!' she sings. She turns to me. 'Auntie Pwoppy! Father Cwistmas came last night!'

'No way!' I gush, greedily taking her from Ryan's arms. She's always so warm. She smells of biscuits today. I could eat her. 'What did he get you?'

'What didn't he get her,' Jazz mumbles under her breath.

She said Ollie went a bit mad this year.

'I got a choo-choo train. And a Disney pwincess. And some makeup.'

'Makeup?" I exclaim, horrified. There's no way Ollie would have bought her makeup. She's three years bloody old for god's sakes.

She grins, nodding in delight, her eyes as big as saucers.

I look to Jazz. She smiles devilishly. 'Mummy wrote a letter to him explaining how she loves stealing mummy's lip glosses and how Mummy's ones are very expensive and not for children.'

Ollie walks into the room, wrapping his arms around Jazz's waist from behind. It's so cute how smitten he still is with her. Thank god they're all over the awkward will they/won't they phase.

'Yeah,' he says raising his eyebrows towards Jazz. 'Me and Santa are going to have to talk.' He finishes it by getting in a quick squeeze of her boobs while Jemima's not looking. Gross.

Mum hands us our wines. I take a large glug.

'I didn't tell you, darling. Guess who's pregnant?'

Oh great. *Another* pregnancy story.

'That Michelle that used to live next door to us. Forty she is!' she cries as if she might as well said she's one hundred. 'Not even planned. Thought she was going through the menopause apparently and then surprise! It's a baby.'

'Great,' I drool sarcastically.

Jesus, even a forty-year-old can fall pregnant that easily. Like it's that bloody easy. Like you just sneeze and go, *oh I'm pregnant!*

She smiles hopefully at me. 'Are you, at least, getting a little broody, darling?' I avoid her gaze, shifting awkwardly from foot to foot. 'Just, I keep seeing little booties, and I can't wait to spoil a grandchild.'

'What about Jemima and Hazel?' Ryan points out. Hazel is my brother Henry and his wife Abbey's daughter, who is beyond adorable.

'Oh, of course,' she waves dismissively. She cradles Jemima's head and bends down to kiss her cheek. 'They're my little cherubs. But it'll be different when my own daughter has her own baby. More special.'

I roll my eyes.

Dad appears, still in his pyjamas. 'Plus it would be great to have a boy in the family again.'

Great. So I'm not just being pressurised to have a baby, now they want a specific sex!

'No such nonsense,' Mum snaps. 'I brought up all of those moody, smelly boys. Constantly trying to clean jizz out of every blanket they ever touched. I'm finally getting my own back with my own pack of girls.'

'Eww. Mum!' I shriek, images of my brothers whacking off into blankets invading my mind.

'What?' she shrugs as if she hasn't just said anything gross.

There's a knock at the door. Dad goes to answer it. I wish I could. Anything to get away from this conversation.

'Anyway,' Ryan says, clapping his hands together. 'What time's dinner?'

I smile at him gratefully. He's so used to handling her now.

'I don't know,' Mum says, chugging back her wine. 'I really should check on the turkey.'

That's weird. I can't smell it cooking. It's normally the first thing I notice on Christmas morning, but all I can smell are those cinnamon scented candles.

'Merry Christmas, everyone!' Auntie Beryl sings as she enters, wearing a sparkly red dress that's two decades too young for her.

I have to do a double take when I see a slightly balding man in his sixties with her. Who the hell is this dude? He's dressed in tartan trousers and a worn green blazer.

Mum looks over at him in undisguised horror.

'Beryl, who on *earth* is this? I realise you may feel bad not having a date, but there's no point picking up hobos off the street, darling.'

Ryan and Ollie spit out their beers. Jazz and I grimace and try to hide behind a playing Jemima. Why must she always embarrass us?

'He's not a bloody hobo, Meryl, you rude cow!' Beryl shrieks back, her face red with fury. 'This is Simon. He's my new boyfriend.'

The poor guy is mortified; his cheeks are puce. I *have* to save him. I jump up and extend my hand.

'Lovely to meet you, Simon. Please ignore my mother.'

'We do,' Ollie agrees, nodding his head in a hello.

'Where on earth did you meet him?' Mum asks as if he's not there, her mouth still gaping open in shock. 'At the homeless centre?'

He might be scruffy, but he in no way looks homeless.

Beryl links arms with Simon and gazes up adoringly at him, ignoring mum's rudeness. 'We met online.'

Online? Wow, so people actually do that. I'd never trust it. I mean, he could be a woman for all she knows. Although, with his stocky build, I doubt it. He would have been one hell of an ugly girl.

He sneezes, so bloody loudly that everyone in the room stops to stare at him. That must be a joke sneeze. Surely no-one really sneezes that loud.

'Bless me and save me!' he shrieks, pulling out a hanky and blowing his nose like a trumpet.

What a bloody nutcase. Jazz looks at me with wide comical eyes, and we instantly burst out laughing, so hard my stomach aches.

Looks like it's going to be one hell of a day. I excuse myself to go to the bathroom so I can calm myself down. I don't want to openly laugh in the guy's face. That would just be rude.

I look in my knickers. No period yet. Not that I'm even bloody hopeful. I'm due today, and I'm bound to come on. That's just my life. I sigh, looking around the room in dismay when I suddenly spot a giant turkey in the bath. I jump so high off the toilet that I fall badly and end up hitting my jaw on the side of the bath on the way down. Aagh, fuck that hurts! Why the utter fuck is there a turkey having a bath right now? Am I imagining this? Am I really drunk right now? No, I've only had two glasses of Prosecco. Not that it takes much these days.

I pull my knickers up and run downstairs as fast as I can to find mum. I pull her away from Auntie Beryl.

'Mum, why the hell is there a turkey in the bath?' I hiss in disbelief. I can feel a headache coming on along with my aching jaw.

'Oh, you found him then,' she chuckles.

'Just tell me why,' I demand massaging my temples.

'Well, darling,' she twiddles with her long costume necklace. 'I forgot to defrost the thing. So it's been in a hot bath since this morning. I'm sure it'll all turn out fine.'

'WHAT?'

'Oh, darling,' she cackles, rolling her eyes at me as if I'm adorable. 'I do wish you'd stop worrying so much.'

# Chapter 2
## Poppy

Three hours later we're eating a burnt roast dinner. A burnt roast dinner with fish fingers. Yep, the turkey didn't make it. After him having a bubble bath for another hour Mum tried to get him in the oven. It seems she didn't consider the size, as this one didn't fit at all. Only my bloody family.

But funnily enough, it's not a huge disaster. Jemima and Hazel are over the moon about having fish fingers. I watch as they play dollies. Jemima is, of course, in charge and telling Hazel exactly what she must do. The girl's so bossy; if she weren't so cute, you'd think she was a right little know-it-all.

'I need to speak to you,' Jazz whispers in my ear.

'Why?' I ask. She sounds serious.

'I just do. Come on.'

She drags me out into the freezing garden and lights up a fag. She still has one now and again when she's stressed. And from the way she's puffing on it now, I'd say she's stressed as fuck.

'So come on,' I say shivering, wrapping my arms around myself to stop my nipples from falling off. 'Before I freeze to death, tell me what the hell's wrong.'

She takes another slow inhale of smoke, her mind completely elsewhere. 'Ollie wants another baby.'

My mouth drops open as my stomach plummets. Okay, that is not what I thought she was going to say. In fact, I would have bet money that she'd say bloody anything other than this. He wants another baby? My brother wants *another* baby when I just want one? How unfair. What a greedy little shit.

'What did you say?' I ask eventually, realising Jazz doesn't know we're trying. I must try my best to come across as a supportive friend.

'I told him what I've told you. I don't want another child. Jemima is more than bloody enough for me. I just genuinely don't have any bloody desire to do it all again. It's like we're just getting our lives back and he wants to fuck it all up again.'

'And how did he take it?'

She blows out a puff of smoke. 'He just rolled his eyes and smiled. He totally thinks he can change my mind. Like a quick flash of his dick and I'll be begging to reproduce with him. What a dickhead.'

I laugh. At least we can both agree on that.

'Anyway,' she looks closely at me, her brows drawn together. 'Are you okay, babe? You don't seem yourself.'

Shit. It's noticeable. I straighten myself up and force on a cheery smile. 'Nah, was just fancying turkey is all.'

We both burst out laughing. The Prosecco's definitely loosened me up.

'Come on,' she grins, linking arms with me, 'let's go back to the madness.'

This is why I'm so glad Jazz is part of the family now. I don't have to face these events alone. Not that having Ryan isn't fabulous, but sometimes you just need your bestie with you when you're dealing with your mother.

We walk into Simon sneezing ridiculously again.

'God bless and save me!' Another trumpet-sneeze into his handkerchief. Eww, I hope that's not the same one.

How can Beryl stand him! He goes off every two bloody minutes!

My brother Richard and his girlfriend Grace have arrived. She insisted on going to her parents' house first for an early dinner. She's dressed in the most revealing black mini dress ever. The plunging neckline is so deep it's almost to her navel, showing off her fit to burst breasts. Not that I'm jealous. Much. It's far too much for the dinner table. Although, if I had a killer body like that, I might just dress like a slut.

Annoyingly enough everyone loves her. Mum and Beryl are always cooing all over her, complimenting her outfit and her hair. Yeah, yeah, she's bloody perfect. I get it. Henry is staring at her boobs, very obviously; so bad that Abbey elbows him in the ribs while shooting him a warning look with her eyes.

Grace hugs everyone but bypasses me. She always 'accidently' forgets me. It pisses me off no end. I hate the way she can just insert herself in my family and make me feel uncomfortable in my own parents' house. That's Mum's job.

'Where's Dad?' Richard asks as he hugs me like a stranger he's just met. I look around for him.

'He was here a second ago. I'll go and look for him.'

Anything to get a break from the madness.

I go into the sitting room but he's not there. That's weird. Could he have gone out? I creep upstairs, strangely feeling like I'm intruding. Unlike the other house, this isn't the home I grew up in. I tiptoe closer to mum and dad's room and find it slightly ajar. I can hear sniffling. I peer through to find Dad sat on the bed crying. What the hell?' My Dad never cries.

'Dad?' I ask stupidly as I open the door.

He quickly wipes away his tears and straightens up. 'You scared me, Poppy pocket,' he utters, trying to force his voice to sound cheery. It doesn't work.

I rush forward and sit on the bed next to him.

'Who the hell has upset you?' I demand, rage filling me up. Whoever it is, I'll kill them. Especially if it was Grace. God, I'd love it if it was Grace. Any excuse to smash her face in. That woman just brings out the violence in me.

'It's nothing,' he shrugs with a smile. 'I'm just being silly.'

Silly. What the hell could he be being silly about? He's balling like a baby.

'Is it the turkey? Are you upset that we had to have fish fingers?' If I'm honest, I'm a little bloody upset.

'No,' he laughs, wrapping his arm around me. This is weird. Dad hardly ever shows affection like this. Not that he's not a loving father, but we've not got that type of touchy-feely relationship. 'I just...'

'You just what?' I order, shrugging him off. 'Just bloody tell me.'

14

He looks down, as if ashamed. 'I...I found a lump.'

My world shatters around me as I stare back into his scared blue eyes.

A lump? A fucking lump! What is he telling me? That he thinks he has cancer? Has he gone to the hospital yet? Bile starts rising in my throat at the possibilities.

'It's probably nothing. I've booked an appointment for Monday. I'm just a little...' he looks away, embarrassed.

'Scared?' I offer, attempting to swallow down my own panic. He smiles shyly. 'Dad, there's nothing to worry about. It's probably just gristle or something.' I sound far more confident than I feel.

I feel sick at the thought of this lump. This lump that could be cancer. That could rip my life apart and leave a big gaping hole where my dad's love used to be. I feel emotion brewing in my chest and I swallow it down. I need to be strong for him now. He doesn't want me blubbering all over him. That's not going to help anything.

'Why don't we go back downstairs?' I suggest with a forced smile. 'They'll come looking for us soon.'

He nods. I hold out my hand and he takes it appreciatively. Now I look at him closer I see that he looks tired. His skin is sallow and his eyes surrounded by dark circles. I hope to God it's just from worry and not something more sinister. I lead him downstairs and back into the kitchen/diner.

'Ah!' Richard says when he sees us both. 'There you guys are.'

Everyone's crowded round him and Grace as if they're about to make an announcement. Oh god, are they getting married? I really don't know if I have the energy to pretend to be happy for them right now.

Richard looks at Grace with adoring eyes. Lucky for him she looks back just as happy. She's finally found someone to love her as much as she loves herself.

'Grace and I are getting married,' he announces with a flourish.

I fucking knew it. She's going to be my actual sister in law. An official part of this family. This is a disaster. Everyone rapturously applauds like they've just declared world peace or something.

'In February,' he adds as if it's no big deal.

The room quiets down immediately. What? In February? That's a bit bloody rushed isn't it?

'Are you *mental,* darling?' Mum asks him, quite serious.

'No,' he grins. 'We're very serious. We've picked 6th February as our date. We're only planning a small wedding.'

'Small wedding my arse!' Auntie Beryl shrieks. 'Why on earth would you want a small wedding? This is a celebration, is it not! And why the hell so soon?'

'We just don't want to wait,' Grace says, squeezing Richard's arm her gold bracelets jangling.

'And...' Richard grins back at Grace; so happy he could burst. 'We're going to have a baby.'

My stomach hits the floor with a thud; my arms begin to tremble and I feel light headed. She's pregnant? No. Grace, of all bloody people, is going to have a baby. And before me. How could she? What a bloody bitch.

Everyone gasps in shock before screaming their congratulations. Everyone except me. I didn't think it was possible to feel this devastated and jealous at the same time. Why is it Grace seems to have everything handed to her on a silver fucking platter? She's not only got the looks but now she's getting what I want more than anything else in the world. A baby to call her own. She's not even maternal.

I find Ryan in the crowd. He looks back at me; that one look tells me everything. Of course, he's happy for them; like I am deep down. Deep, *deep* fucking down. But he's also disheartened. It obviously wasn't planned, yet she's fallen with absolutely no problem. He must be regretting marrying me. He could have had Grace and have a baby of his own by now.

I feel the tears slide down my cheeks before I realise I'm even crying. I hastily wipe them away and force a smile. Simon sneezes again.

'God bless me and save me!' Trumpet blow into the handkerchief.

Jesus, someone just shoot him and put him out of his misery.

The doorbell goes. I take my opportunity to run and get it. I swing it open to find friend Izzy, and her boyfriend, Michael. She has me to thank for that. I took a job working for the very famous film director Michael Sworsky a couple of years back and introduced them when he needed a personal trainer. I don't know how he fell for her; well, obviously I do. She's bloody gorgeous with her Italian skin, long brown wavy hair with honey highlights and minuscule waist. What I meant is she can be seriously bossy and annoying about keeping a healthy diet and exercise programme. Sometimes I just want to eat my jaffa cakes without being bothered. I didn't even realise they were invited. I kiss them hello and invite them in.

Apparently Izzy already knew both about the pregnancy and the wedding plans. I suppose Grace does count her as her best friend. Grace finds me re-filling my Prosecco glass.

'Oh, hi, Poppy,' she says as if she's shocked to see me at my own mother's house on Christmas day. 'Did you just get here?'

Is she bloody serious?

I glare at her. 'No. I've been here the entire time,' I say with no humour in my voice.

'Oh. It's just that you haven't congratulated me yet.' She rubs her completely flat stomach while also managing to show off her big round sparkly engagement ring. How did we all miss it when she first came in?

It's hard to be happy for someone who has what you want. And is a complete cow.

'Congratulations,' I say through gritted teeth. 'I'm so happy for you.'

She smiles smugly. 'Are you not trying yet? With you being thirty this year, I'd have thought you'd be in a hurry.'

Does she know I'm trying? Is it written across my face in felt tip pen? Am I putting out 'trying' vibes?

'Well, some of us want to enjoy each other while we can,' I smile snarkily. 'We like to plan things. Not just fall pregnant and then have a shotgun wedding.'

She glares back at me, pissed that I have an answer for her. Ha! That got you, bitch. For a second her glare is so intense, I worry she's going to launch herself at me and wrestle to the death.

'There's *nothing* shotgun about *my* wedding,' she growls. 'I'm very good at keeping your brother happy and right now he wants a child. If I were you, I'd pop out a sprog pretty quick before Ryan gets bored of you. He's sure to come to his senses soon enough.'

That's what I'm worried about.

'Oh, why don't you fuck off, Grace?' I'm without any wittier comeback and I hate that.

Mum swoops in just as Grace's face turns murderous. 'We okay here, girls?'

We glare at each other with so much contempt I'm sure it's radiating from both of us. Mum grabs hold of my arm and starts pulling me away.

'No-one likes a girl that punches a pregnant woman, Poppy,' she hisses in my ear. 'Especially when that person is carrying your niece or nephew.'

'Whatever,' I snort. Very unladylike of me.

'Let's go and talk to Izzy and Michael, hmm.' She drags me over there before I get a chance to refuse.

'Hi guys,' I smile before hiccupping. Maybe I *am* drunker than I first thought.

They all start polite chit-chat, but I can't concentrate. All I can think about is Grace being pregnant. What a bloody lucky bitch. It's not enough that she's insanely gorgeous, but now she's creating a new life. Who no doubt will be just as beautiful. Oh god, Jemima's third cousin won't be my child, it'll be theirs. That's so bloody sad. I wanted them to be as close in age as possible so when they grew up, they could go clubbing together. By the rate I'm going Jemima will be able to babysit mine. And that's if I'm lucky.

Auntie Beryl soon joins in on the chit-chat. My phone starts ringing, one of my best friends Lilly flashing up. Ugh, great. We met when we were both PA's at the same firm. Our friendship went from work colleague to actual friends after she took some diet pills one day, farted and accidentally shit herself. I hid her in the toilet and went out to buy her a new skirt and tights.

She was extremely grateful and we've been good friends ever since.

I show my flashing phone to Jazz who grins. 'Yeah, good luck with that.'

I begrudgingly answer, knowing she'll keep calling until I answer. Our Lilly is nothing but persistent.

'Hey babe, you okay?' I ask.

A loud squeal comes down the phone. 'I'm better than alright! Alex and I have finally set a date!'

'Oh, really.' I even *sound* uninterested.

You see we've spent the best part of two years discussing her wedding. I'm pretty sure Lily likes the idea of a wedding far more than the actual reality. I mean, was I this annoying when I was getting married? I must get three phone calls from her a day already. Matron of honour was the worst decision of my life. Not that I could say no.

'Well! Don't you want to know?' she encourages.

'Of course,' I giggle, forcing myself to get excited.

'This April! Can you believe it?'

'Shit. You realise that's only four months away right?' I try to reason.

'Well, we've got such a good idea of the kind of wedding we want now. We wanted to tell our parents first. But now there's nothing stopping us from planning the best wedding ever! So we're going to have to have more regular meet ups to plan everything.'

'Really? I mean, we just had one last week.'

'Exactly.' I can imagine her nodding into the phone. 'I'm thinking with the wedding getting closer we need to meet at *least* twice a week.'

'Wow.'

'What?' she snaps. 'Are you saying I'm being unreasonable, Poppy? Because I really don't think I am. This *is* the most important day of my life.'

'Of course. I wasn't - '

'Because if you're not up to the matron of honour job, my cousin Kathleen could easily step into your shoes. Or converse, or whatever it is you wear.'

She's actually gone mental. Bridezilla is too calm a word for her.

'No, of course I am!' Why am I fighting for this? 'I'm just tired, that's all.'

'Good. I don't want to sound like a bitch, babe, but you're not pulling your weight. I really need you. You're up to it, right?'

I gulp down the panic.

'Of course. Anyway, I've got to go. Bye.' I quickly hang up before she scares me anymore.

When I start to zone in and listen, I realise that Mum and Auntie Beryl are having an argument.

'I'm just saying,' Auntie Beryl says bitchily to Mum, 'that if Michael were to cast anyone, it would *obviously* be me.'

'With that honker on the end of your face,' Mum sneers. 'I don't think so. I'm sure Michael would want someone far better looking.' She smiles at him. He looks back in terror.

'Well then it definitely won't be you,' she snaps back, red lipstick on her teeth.

'Ladies,' he attempts, holding his hands up in defeat. 'I'm sure you'd both be fantastic.'

'*I* definitely would,' Beryl says arrogantly.

'Oh, wind your neck in, Beryl. No one wants to hear your shit,' Mum snaps. 'You couldn't even find a man without begging online, like a whore.'

Wow, that escalated quickly.

'How dare you!' Beryl snaps. 'Just because your husband is too scared to leave you. God knows he puts up with enough of your shit!'

'Don't swear in my house!' Mum roars back, her face red and puffy. 'There are young ears here!' She looks over towards Jemima, who's asleep in Ollie's arms.

How much wine have they had?

'Ladies!' I shout over both of them. 'Is there really any need to have such a domestic on Christmas day? Especially as we're celebrating Richard and Grace's engagement and baby news?'

Both their faces turn to ecstatic smiles.

'You're right, darling,' Mum smiles, putting her arm around me.

'You are,' Beryl nods. 'Why are we fighting when we should be busy planning a wedding?'

Grace turns around, clearly having heard them.

'Oh, Graaaaaace,' Mum sings. 'We have a wedding to plan!'

'I'll get the book,' Beryl says excitedly.

Grace's face contorts into barely concealed horror. Ha. At least you have to put up with the chuckle brothers you snide bitch.

## Chapter 3
### Poppy

*New Year's Eve*

Ryan's stressed as we set up for our New Year's Eve party. I don't know why he even agreed to it. He's turned into such a house-proud maniac since we moved in. If people are coming over, he'll notice a spot on the ceiling that needs re-painting or a little stain on the kitchen floor. Then he'll set about racing to make everything perfect. It's beyond annoying. Especially when he's shouting at me to 'get the crisps, Poppy!' Chill out, dude.

I get that he wants everyone to see he has a nice place, but it's not like we're even having loads of people over. Just our normal little gang for cocktails, a bit of dancing, and to watch the fireworks on the TV. But who am I kidding. Last year it ended with Izzy vomiting in the pond and Jazz declaring it was over with Ollie. They were only disagreeing over what was better: McDonald's chips or Burger King chips. But you know Jazz. She can be a *tad* dramatic.

I'm so tempted to tell Ryan my exciting news, but I don't want to raise his hopes. But...well I'm pretty sure I'm pregnant! I still haven't come on, meaning I'm now six days late. If anything, I'm normally early. Plus, I'm peeing more than normal, and my boobs are *so* sensitive. I haven't managed to do a test yet because of the Christmas madness. And, I'll admit that I'm scared. I don't want to find out I'm wrong. At least this way I can live in my own little fantasyland where I'm going to have a bouncy baby in nine months.

∝∽

At first, it's just a few extra people. Jazz and Ollie bring their friends, Rachel and Adam. Then Lily and Alex bring their mates Jess and Pete. Izzy calls while on the way to say that Michael staged a last minute read through of a script and could he bring the cast? So, it's sort of turned out to be an unofficial company New Year's Eve do. If Michael hadn't brought cases of champagne with him, I'd have been pissed off. Then it seems to have spiralled from there. Throughout the night, people ask if their friends can join us as they're at shit parties. So somehow we have a house full of people.

Grace has been bitching that with all of the extra bodies she's too hot and is worried it'll hurt the baby. Get a fucking life. And it's not like I can just get drunk to block her out. What if I *am* pregnant? I need to keep the potential baby safe. But it's bloody miserable being sober on New Year's Eve. All I can see are people having fun, chugging on champagne.

By eleven thirty Jazz is shitfaced, and I'm desperate to know if I'm pregnant. I manage to escape upstairs to the bathroom and am about to shut the door when she spots me and forces her way in. She puts down the toilet seat and sits down on top of it.

'Can you believe we're going to be thirty this year?' she asks in disbelief. Her eyes are wide as if she honestly can't believe it.

'I know.'

It *is* bloody shocking. I still feel like the same eighteen-year-olds that met at Uni, but here we are. I'm a married homeowner, and Jazz is a mummy.

'Scoot over. I actually need a wee,' I say, pushing her off and opening the toilet seat. It's annoying that she's here; I'd be able to do a quick test if she wasn't.

I pull down my knickers and let out the wee, feeling massive relief. Too much water. It goes straight through me. I wipe myself and see blood on the tissue. Then I look in my knickers and see blood there too. My world falls onto its side. My period. Of *course* it's my period. I'm not pregnant.

My heart sinks into the pit of my stomach. I was a silly bitch for even thinking I was for a second. It's pretty clear by now that there must be something wrong with me. But what? Are my tubes fucked up? Did I drink too much alcohol in my life? Do I have a deformed vagina? What the hell is it?

Not that I can ask Jazz any of this. I have to act normal.

'Oh no,' she says seeing my knickers. 'Just come on, babe? Do you have a tampon anywhere?'

'Yeah,' I shrug, sorting myself out.

'Babe this year is gonna be a big deal for us. You know I'm inheriting my money on my birthday. I'm gonna be fucking rich!'

I know this; she tells me every time she gets drunk. Her Dad had it written in his will that she'd have to stick to a strict allowance until she turned thirty. Then she inherits her father's fortune, her Dad's porn empire money. It's scary how much money she's going to get. I do wonder whether it'll change our relationship. We've always been more or less on an even keel, even if Jazz has always lived beyond her means.

I try to focus on what she's talking about and not how I feel right now. Not the crushing disappointment weighing heavily in my heart.

'You'll still talk to your poor friend, right?' I joke.

She grins and pats my head. 'Of course, babe. I'll always need a maid, right?'

'Ha ha, bloody ha,' I drool sarcastically.

'I mean it though, babe.' She grabs her glass of champagne and hands me my glass of water.

I grab her champagne out of her hand, and down it in one. If you can't beat them, join them. And right now I have a lot of sorrows to drown. Seems like a good time to get shit faced.

'That's the spirit! This is gonna be our year!'

People begin shouting from downstairs.

'TEN, NINE, EIGHT.'

Shit. Have we been chatting for half an hour? We both race downstairs to find everyone.

'SEVEN, SIX, FIVE, FOUR, THREE.'

I get to Ryan just in time, pressing myself against his strong chest. I need his comfort right now, even if he doesn't know what it's for.

'TWO, ONE, HAPPY NEW YEAR!' everyone roars.

I look up into Ryan's beautiful face, placing my palms around his jaw to treasure the sight of him. He beams down at me, his eyes full of love and devotion. If only he knew. If only he knew that there's something wrong with me. That I can't give him a baby.

'Happy new year, baby,' he whispers into my ear. 'It's gonna be our year.'

I let him kiss me, and I kiss him back with as much passion as I can, as tears run down my cheeks. I only hope to God he's right.

But in the meantime CHAMPAGNE! Let's get this party started.

### 2.36am

So what if I can't get pregnant? Who wants to get pregnant anyway? Then you can't drink booze and be awesome like I am right now. I'm pretty sure I can only breakdance and do the splits when I'm this drunk. I mean, I know I'm currently icing my vagina with a bag of frozen carrots, but it was totally worth it to see the look on Ryan's face. He looked so fucking impressed by how sexy I am. He *totally* wants to fuck me tonight. Even now, all pretending to be concerned and threatening to call my mother. What a silly Sally.

'Pops, I'll ask one more time. Please drink the water and eat the sandwich.' He looks down at me with a frowned forehead. God I love those forehead wrinkles. I want to rub my nipples all over them. He'd probably like that. I'm *such* a sexual being. Who knew there was a little sex bomb in here the whole time?

'Come on, Pops,' Lilly says, rubbing my back.

I push her off. Why is she rubbing my back? I'm totally fine. Why are people trying to control me?

'Stop crowding me, Lil! I'm fine.'

'Eat the fucking sandwich, Poppy!' Ryan explodes.

'Woah,' I breathe out. 'Babes, where's all 'dis anger coming fwom?' I look back to Lilly. 'He needs to take a yoga class,' I laugh. 'Am I right? Am I *right?!'* I explode into giggles. I'm *so* funny.

Jazz comes staggering over to me. 'Babe,' she claps, a big stupid smile on her face. 'That split! You were unreal!'

Finally! Someone who gets me. She slumps down next to me and embraces me in a cuddle.

'Remember babe. This is gonna be our year. I'm gonna be rich, and you and Ryan are gonna carry on living in married bliss and probably pop out a couple of kids.'

I look up to Ryan frowning down at the both of us. If only it was that fucking easy.

'I'm serious.' She grabs my cheeks. 'Here's to two thousand and fucking sixteen!'

# Chapter 4
## Poppy

*Thursday 21st January 2016 - Jazz's Birthday Party*

Red blood. *Everywhere.*

Why does this have to keep happening to me? That Mother Nature bitch must be laughing her arse off. What a cruel cow. What better way to remind me that I can't get pregnant? Make me bleed for seven days. Great. Just *great.*

You see, Ryan and me have now been trying for exactly a year, and each month my period is just a cruel reminder that something must be wrong. It's not normal to have to wait this long. I know it's not. But it's not like I've been able to ask people's opinions on it as Ryan has me sworn to secrecy. Even Jazz doesn't have any idea.

But I have to pull myself together quickly. I can't break down in these toilets and sob 'WHY ME? WHY GOD, WHY?' Nope. No matter how hard I might want to; I have to get back to the party. Jazz's thirtieth to be exact. This is a happy day and it's not going to get ruined by a bit of blood. Or a lot of blood in my case. Jesus, why am I so heavy sometimes? Is that normal? I know we shed our womb lining, but fuck, mine must be thicker than the line on the borders at Calais.

I take a deep breath and wash my hands in the sink, checking my mascara hasn't run. You can do this, Pops. Someone chucking their guts up in another cubicle makes me jump. Ugh. See, it could be worse. I could be her right now. It does sound like she's rather ill. Obviously had too much of the free champagne. Maybe I should stay and make sure she's okay. The flush goes and my mouth drops open when out walks Grace. Shit. She looks rough.

Her usual olive skin is blotchy and she's desperately trying to comb down her erratic hair with her hand. She spots me and quickly glares back, obviously furious that I've caught her looking anything but perfect.

'Shit, Grace, are you okay?'

'Fine,' she snarls back immediately. She leans over the sink and it's then I can see that she's sweating a lot.

'Let me help.' I go into the cubicle and get some loo roll and begin running it under the water.

'I don't need your help,' she snaps.

I ignore her and pat the back of her neck with the tissue. 'Stop being stubborn, Grace. You're carrying my niece or nephew in there. It's purely a selfish act.'

That makes her smile for a second. She actually looks beaten down. The sad thing is that I'd give anything to trade places with her.

She snatches the tissue from me. 'Whatever.' Then she turns and flounces out of the toilet like nothing ever happened.

Yeah, you're totally welcome! Bitch.

I take another deep breath, more to stop myself from following her out of here and strangling her to death, and then head back into the posh Landmark Hotel ballroom. Its imposing marble pillars, large windows and chandeliers make me feel inferior in comparison. Just one barren woman at her mate's party.

It's absolutely stunning and would be a lot better if Jazz hadn't got her ideas in. In contrast to the posh, almost regal building there are pink feather trees, glittery purple table cloths and a cirque de solei women hanging from the ceiling on a piece of fabric. Jazz's old friend from Ibiza is on the DJ decks, pumping out tune after tune of old school garage. Normally I'd be on the dance floor screaming *'I LOVE this song!!'* but I just can't fake that kind of enthusiasm.

It's an extra celebration as tomorrow she's loaded. She finally gets the rest of her Dad's fortune after sticking to what she would consider a 'poor budget'. Or, you know, most people's mortgage payment a month.

Not that anything will change. I look around at all of these rich, beautiful people who apparently know her. I might have met a handful of them in the twelve years I've known her. Oh, well. Time to hit the bar and drown my sorrows.

I stumble and fall into someone. I look up to see a beautiful guy about our age. He's all tanned skin, beaming white teeth and designer suit.

'Sorry! Apparently I can't even walk,' I murmur, more to myself.

'No problem,' he laughs back. Wow, that's a posh laugh, more like a horse neighing. 'Wait, you're that Poppy aren't you?'

He knows me? I quickly scan my brain back to see if I've met him before when I've been ridiculously drunk. Who am I kidding? As if I'd remember.

'Yeah, that's me. Have we met?'

He smiles condescendingly. 'No, of course not.' He seems sympathetic towards me. What the hell is up with this dude? 'I'm Jazz's *old* friend Jeremy from boarding school.'

'Oh,' is all I can offer. Never bloody heard of him. A line appears between his eyebrows.

'This must be a hard night for you.'

Huh? Wait, can he see that I've been crying? Are my eyes still red-rimmed? I thought it was too dark in here for anyone to notice. Does he know I'm trying? No, of course he doesn't, you idiot.

'No. I'm fine. Why would it be a hard night for me?'

He sighs and rests his hand on my shoulder. I look down at it in confusion.

He gives me a lopsided grin. 'Knowing that after today Jazz won't be in your life as much.'

'Sorry?' I blurt out, sounding far more hurt than I should be. Is this guy serious?

'You've done a great job looking after her. But it's time she came back to us.'

Who the hell is this dude? Oh, I forgot. Jeremy the jack arse.

'You sound like a cult,' I smirk. 'Who the hell are you? The Chelsea massive?'

'I'm from Chelsea,' he nods seriously, not getting the joke at all. I expect tumbleweed to float by before he does. 'I mean, you don't honestly think that Jazz is going to stay hanging around in St Albans when she could be back living in Chelsea and living it up with friends who can actually *afford* to keep up with her.'

Is this guy for *real?* Am I on a hidden camera show? No one's shouting out surprise yet.

'Of course she will!' I snap. 'This just shows that you know absolutely *nothing* about Jazz. She'd never move back to Chelsea to hang around with you planks. She's more than happy with her life at the moment.'

He smiles. God, I hate that arrogant smile. If we weren't so public, I'd be tempted to kick him in the balls.

'You keep telling yourself that, honey.'

He saunters off, sipping his pathetic girly cocktail. What a tosser. And how wrong could he be? I mean, yeah, things will change slightly. Of course they will. Jazz will have more money obviously. She won't have to worry about money again. Her and Ollie will probably move out of Mum and Dad's house and go on a shit load of holidays, but it's not like she's going to dump her old best mate.

A flash of bright red hair stumbles into me.

'You alright, Lil?' I ask amused. She can barely walk she's had so much free champagne.

'Bloody spiffing, darling!' she shouts in a fake posh accent. 'One does like to drink with the peasants!'

I roll my eyes. She's so going to enjoy Jazz coming into her money.

'Look.' She reaches into her handbag and pulls out some loo roll. 'I nicked their loo roll! Had to have a memento of my time here didn't I!'

I look into her handbag and also notice a champagne glass, six packets of roasted peanuts and a pink bottle of champagne.

'Shit, Lil! You didn't need to take all this!'

She grins sloppily; her lipstick smudged under her lip. 'Sssh!' she covers her lips with a finger. 'What the barman doesn't know won't hurt him.'

Shit. Did she steal it?

'Oh crap,' she babbles, looking past me.

'What?' I follow her eye line to see a hotel manager and a barman chatting while pointing at her.

'Gotta go, Poppy Wops.' She steals a glass of champagne from a passing waiter, downs it and then runs off in another direction.

My neck is suddenly pulled to the right. I look round to see Jazz hanging off me, paralytic, dressed in a leopard-print floor-length dress.

'Babe, is this the best fwucking party or what?' she slurs, chugging on a pink bottle of champagne.

I smile victoriously. There she is. My drunk bestie.

'Best party ever,' I nod, appeasing her.

'And tomorrow I'm fucking rich!' she shrieks, thrusting the bottle up into the air.

I roll my eyes. How could I bloody forget?

'Our friendship won't change though, right?' I ask like a pathetic insecure girl.

'Fuck off, babe,' she laughs. 'As if I'd ever trade you in for a newer model.' She taps her nose. 'You know too many secrets.'

I laugh. She's bloody right. I could take her down with the shit I know. I just hope to God she's right about this.

# Chapter 5
## Jazz

*Friday 22nd January*

'Babe, time to wake up,' Ollie says gently.

He knows not to piss me off in the mornings. Especially the night after my thirtieth birthday celebrations. He shakes me slightly through the covers. What the fuck is his problem? If he touches me again, I'm going to put him in a headlock and give him a Chinese burn.

I feel rough. Oh God, don't tell me now that I'm old I'm going to start suffering from hangovers? That is far too tragic. I open my eyes under the cover. I don't think I'm ready for direct sunlight yet. Ugh, my head feels as delicate as glass.

'Come on, babe. We need to get going soon.'

Ugh. The thought of getting up. But then I do want to check myself in the mirror. See if I've developed any horrible wrinkles overnight. If I do, I'm calling up a Botox doctor immediately and asking him to inject all of the fucking poison in the world into my face. Then I smell my veggie sausages cooking. Damn that Meryl. She knows my weakness.

I roll out of bed, only to land on the floor with a thud. Ollie laughs at me.

'Babe, you're a mess.' He leans down and then goes into a press up over me, hovering his sexy as fuck face next to mine.

He leans on his forearms and picks up a tendril of my hair that I'd dyed pink. 'I'm not sure this is really your colour,' he grimaces.

'Are you saying my mid-life crisis looks silly?' I joke back, trailing my hands down his back and feeling his super soft skin.

'I'd still do you,' he grins. 'You know; if you begged.'

I laugh and hit him in the chest. 'Not likely.'

'Oh yeah?' He lowers his lips to mine, so close I can feel his breath before he abruptly gets up. Way to leave me hanging. 'But we've gotta go and see your solicitor, remember?'

I grab the back of his neck and force his lips back down onto mine. I kiss the fuck out of him until I pull away and his sad little puppy lips come with me, desperate for more.

'How could I forget? Today I get rich and become your sugar momma.'

He frowns; his angry boner pressing against my stomach.

'You're cruel,' he moans as I push him out of the way. I need to get me some veggie sausages.

After devouring Meryl's amazing veggie fry up (God bless that woman) and an hour car ride we're finally at the solicitors in Chelsea.

'Now, I just need you to sign a few papers and then the money will be transferred into your bank account immediately,' the stern looking guy in the suit says.

I can't help but feel disappointed as I sign them. What a bloody anti-climax.

'So...I don't get one of those big cheques or anything?'

Ollie smirks and covers his mouth with his hand. Obviously trying not to openly laugh at me. I don't think it's a ridiculous question. I mean, it's not every day that you inherit a bloody fortune, is it? You'd think they'd have at least decorated the office in some streamers and had champagne on ice for us.

'No,' the suit says. 'No lottery-style cheque, I'm afraid.'

I frown and jut my bottom lip out. Totally unfair. We leave ten minutes later after him babbling on about being responsible and considering my investments. As soon as we're out of the glass doors and onto the street, I smile. I finally have money again.

'So, Miss Moneybags, where to next?' Ollie asks with a grin, taking my hand in his.

This really is my perfect day. Strolling down Chelsea, hand in hand with the love of my life. I can't wait until this is my life every day. No worries. No money struggles. Just being able to enjoy my life.

'I think we'll start at the estate agents.' I can't wait to move here. Be back in London. I breathe in the polluted air. It's like no other. 'Look, there's one over there.' I start dragging him towards it.

'Woah,' Ollie argues, pulling me back to him. 'We talked about moving, but I just assumed we'd want to stay around by my Mum and Pops? You're not honestly suggesting we move to Chelsea, right?'

I frown at him. Poor, Hertfordshire boy. He has no idea.

'Of course I am, babe. We have the money now. Why on earth wouldn't we want to move here? All my friends are here; it's the best place in London! Plus, amazing schools for Jemima. It's got everything we'd want.'

'Apart from all of our family and friends,' he snaps staring at me as if I'm mad.

'We have loads of friends who live here,' I counter. Why is he being so dramatic?

He rolls his eyes dramatically. 'No. *You* have loads of friends that live here. I know no-one.'

'So I'll introduce you to people. What's the big deal?'

He sighs, shoving his hands in his pockets. 'Maybe I don't want to be introduced to your swanky, stuck up mates. Maybe I like my life the way it is now.'

'What? Living with your Mother? Are you *insane?*'

'Hey! Don't start bitching about my Mum. She might be crazy, but she's done a lot for us. A lot for you.'

I hate being reminded of how much Meryl helped me when I was suffering from post-natal depression. The truth is that I know without her help, I could be at the bottom of the Thames right now. I had no idea how to look after Jemima and she just came in, took control and completely saved me from myself. More than my own Mother ever has. But still, I hate feeling that I owe people things.

'I'm sorry,' I say begrudgingly. 'But come on. Let's, at least, look at some of these houses, yeah?'

He looks at me intently for a long time before answering.

'Okay. I'll look. But I mean it Jazz. I'm not going to be bossed around by you just because you've got more money now. We're equals or we're nothing at all.'

Jesus, drama much? Why did Meryl have to raise such drama queens? It's exhausting.

'Of course, babe,' I smile, pecking him on the end of his nose. 'Now let's go and buy a house!'

I hear him sigh behind me as I stride purposely over the road.

# Chapter 6
## Poppy

*Monday 25<sup>th</sup> January*

'So,' Ryan says, nuzzling against my neck. 'What do you want for your birthday?'

I stare at him confused. My birthday? My birthday isn't for another four months.

'You're a bit of an eager beaver aren't you?' I giggle as he rubs his morning wood over *my* eager beaver.

'Well, apart from the obvious.' I hear the smile in his voice as his lips tug on my earlobe. 'You want that all the time anyway. What else?'

'Well, aside from a baby I can't think of much else I want.'

He stills next to me; the tension in his body evident. I've said the wrong thing. Of course I have. Stupid idiot. Why the hell did I have to bring up the baby issue? Now he's going to go all self-conscious.

'I'm trying my hardest, babe,' he says, his voice low and earnest.

My heart breaks for him. Why am I such a thoughtless bitch?

I pull him away from my ear so I can look into his eyes. They're troubled beyond belief.

'I know you are, babe. I'm sorry. I didn't mean it to come out like that. Only...'

'Only what?' he demands, looking for answers in my face.

Oh god. I've been meaning to broach this subject for months now, but this is so not the right way to do it.

'Only it's been a year now and...' I look down, so I don't have to see the disappointment in his eyes. 'And I think we should see the doctor.'

'The doctor?' he asks, his face scrunched up in horror. 'Why? Do you think there's something wrong with me?'

'No! Of course not! I...well, I think it might be something to do with me.' I look down at the floor, ashamed at the possibility.

He grabs my chin and forces me to look at him. 'Why would you say that?'

'It just seems more likely that it would be me. You're normally perfect, and I'm just some scatty bitch who falls down a lot.'

He stares out of the window for a long time. I stroke his biceps reassuringly. 'But, babe, what if it *is* me?'

'So what if it is?' I ask with narrowed eyes. 'Do you honestly think that would change anything between us?'

It's his turn to look away. 'Of course it would. You'd blame me for not being able to give you a baby.'

'Just like you would if it turns out to be me!' I counter.

Wow. I didn't realise I had that outburst in me.

'You know I wouldn't,' he smiles kindly, stroking my hair back from my forehead.

I sigh, drained by the whole situation. 'Well, then why don't we just find out? Then we can cross any bridges we have to, once we know.'

'Okay,' he nods slowly, swallowing hard. 'Book the doctor's appointment.'

I look at my watch. I really need to get up so I can go to the doctors with Dad. He's having a scan. He could have cancer for all we know.

'Talking of doctor's appointments.'

'It'll be fine, babe,' he says soothingly, 'I'm sure it's just a benign lump.'

'Yeah, I'm sure,' I nod, averting his gaze. I don't want him to see how nervous I am.

What happens next will determine our future, one way or another.

Dad and I sit in the waiting room of the hospital. I'm only here for support. He had the scan about half an hour ago. They said it's likely they'll know straight away if it's cancerous. It's just annoying he had to wait so long for the appointment.

'And you're sure you couldn't read their reactions?' I ask him; sure they would have reacted if it was cancer.

'No,' he shrugs not giving me any eye contact. 'They just told me to wait and someone would come and chat to me.' He's jumping his leg about like a madman.

'But were they smiling or were they avoiding eye contact?' I persist. He'd make a rubbish detective.

'I don't know, Poppy,' he snaps his mouth set in a hard line.

Wow. I don't think Dad's ever snapped at me before.

'I was busy trying to get my testicles back into the privacy of my trousers.'

Eww, thank god he didn't make me go in with him. I'd like to think we're close, but that doesn't mean I'm okay with seeing his junk.

'I'm sure it will be fine.' I bite my lip so hard I can taste blood.

Of course it will. Right? My Dad can't have cancer. He just can't. These kinds of things don't happen to people like us.

'Mr Windsor?' A tall, balding man with spectacles calls suddenly.

My heart starts racing. This is it. This is when we're going to find out if this is just a stupid cyst or if this is something that's going to change our lives forever. I clasp Dad's hand and smile as reassuringly as possible. He smiles back weakly, his eyes weary.

We stand, both seeming to be on unresponsive jelly legs, and walk into the small consultation room. It smells of pine cones in here. Has he been using a leftover Christmas candle? Because someone needs to tell him that vanilla would be more settling.

We sit down on the green squeaky chairs, which seem to make farting noises every time I move. I stare expectantly at the man in front of me shuffling papers, trying to read any possible body language that might tell me what I need to know. His face remains passive. Does he honestly have no idea the kind of suspense he's building right now? It's worse than the six-chair challenge on the X Factor?

'Well?' I demand, not so politely.

Dad raises his eyebrows at me, no doubt reprimanding me for being so rude. 'What she means to say, doc, is, what's my prognosis?'

Prognosis? *Ooh*, doesn't he think he sounds posh. Where the hell did he pull that word from? Someone's been reading the dictionary.

The doctor takes a deep breath and looks Dad square in the eye. I hold my breath.

'When we're looking for a cyst we normally find a lump filled with fluid. However, your lump was more solid.'

'Which means...?' I ask, begging him to hurry the fuck up. You'd think he'd have had training in this.

'There's a chance that the swelling could be a sign that it's cancerous.'

The floor might as well have been taken from underneath me. Cancerous. It *is* cancerous. Does that mean he has cancer? Will he need an operation? Will he need chemo? Shit, is it too late? Is it terminal?

'Of course, we'll need to run some more blood tests to see if we can identify any markers in your blood.'

I turn to stare at Dad. He looks completely normal. Like he hasn't just been told the most confusing news ever.

'So is it cancer or not?' I press, desperate for some kind of clarification.

'I still can't say for sure. We'll know more after the blood tests.'

'But...' I swallow down the panic attempting to escape in the form of vomit. 'You think it most likely is?'

'I don't want to speculate,' he says avoiding my gaze. Dad's still just sitting there staring blankly back at him.

'You can't say something like that and expect us to just leave. What exactly is the probability of cancer?'

He shuffles some more paper and coughs. 'If I'm being truthful...it's looking likely. But, there's no need to worry yet.'

'No need to worry? Are you fucking insane?' I stand up and start pacing the room. 'So, what if it is cancer? What do we do?'

I need some kind of action plan. I need to know exactly what's happening.

'We'd take a biopsy to make sure it was cancer. However, that would mean taking the entire testicle.'

'Entire testicle?' Dad gasps.

Finally, he speaks! Talk about a man's balls and he'll sit up and pay attention.

'Do you really need to take the entire testicle?' he asks again.

'This is all speaking figuratively of course. But we would, as this kind of cancer can spread so quickly.'

His face drops just like my hopes of a normal life. This is it. Our family has been hit with the big C.

# Chapter 7

*Monday 25th January*

From: Poppyisawesome@hotmail.com
To: Lindadavis4321@gmail.com
*Hi Linda,*

*Sorry I haven't been in contact the last couple of weeks but what with Christmas and New Year's, it's been crazy! Grace and Richard decided to announce that not only are they getting married, but they're also having a baby! We're over the moon to be an aunt and uncle again.*

*I also got the bad news that my Dad has cancer. Well, likely has cancer. It's all very confusing. I obviously don't have to tell you not to repeat to anyone as you don't even see anyone, but it's shaken me to the core. I just can't believe that my Dad, my strong Dad that brought me up, could have this horrible disease. But we're waiting for an official diagnosis.*

*How was your Christmas? I hate to think of you spending it alone, especially with you staying clean for so long. If I could just get them to see that…but you know I can't. I've attached a few pictures of us over the holiday, as I know you like to see him in whatever way you can.*

*All my love*
*Poppy x*

I know what you're thinking. And yes I'm a terrible human being. I'm still talking to Linda, Ryan's mum. Ryan's ex-druggie mum that totally broke his heart. Twice. It's just that when I saw her at our wedding, I looked into her eyes and saw vulnerability. I just saw a woman who wanted to see her son get married. Yes, there's a load wrong with her and yes, she hurt him, but I just can't help but want to believe that people can change. I always want to see the good in them. And Ryan says he loves that about me. So in a roundabout way, he can't really blame me...right?

It started when I sent her a few pictures from our wedding. She sent the sweetest reply, thanking me profusely. Then she mentioned that although she never expects to be in Ryan's life again, she'd love if I'd send her the occasional picture so she could see him living his life successfully. How could I turn that down?

And she's come on in leaps and bounds according to her. She's got a job as a cleaner and is in a flat in Hendon. She's never asked for money, and she's never asked to meet. That in itself tells me there's no harm in it. Well, you know, unless Ryan was to find out. I'm really trying not to think about that. I dread to think what he'd do.

## Jazz

So I've managed to get Ollie, Poppy and Meryl to come along and see an amazing house in Chelsea. I saw it online and just fell in love with it. Yes, it is a *little* expensive, but it's Chelsea! If it were cheap, any old idiot could live here. And I want the best for my Jemima. She deserves to grow up with the entitled life that I had. Not eating supermarket branded Rice Krispies.

'This is it!' I squeal, looking up at the cream bricked townhouse.

We start walking up the concrete steps to the black shiny front door.

'But...it's a terrace,' Ollie says, his brow creasing in confusion.

'Duh,' I snap. 'This is Chelsea. They're all terraces.'

He folds his arms across his chest; a hard look spread on his face.

'I'm just saying do we want to spend money on a house that's a terrace?

Wouldn't we prefer a detached?'

'Detached would be fabulous,' Meryl butts in, beaming at the idea. 'No noise from the neighbours.' She points to the house like she's looking at a hovel. 'Here you're basically on top of each other.'

I roll my eyes. They have *no* idea.

'Let's just go in, shall we?' Poppy offers forcibly. I smile gratefully at her. Thank God somebody's on my side.

The estate agent, Rick, opens the door and shakes my hand so hard I think he's trying to pull it out of its socket. Way to look over-eager.

We walk into the stunning sitting room, with natural light streaming through the huge bay windows. Its high ceilings take my breath away. All white, crisp, fresh, and edgy. There's a huge TV over the modern fireplace. I can just imagine myself here snuggled up with Ollie watching a film. It's *beyond* fabulous.

'Wow,' I breathe out, my heart fluttering so loudly in my chest I feel it might turn into a butterfly and take off on its own.

The estate agent is rattling on about the usual. 'Subject of substantial refurbishment, yada yada yada.' But I'm too busy looking around. There's a glass floor at the back of the room, which leads to an office and the stairs to outside. I practically run downstairs to see the rest of the living accommodation.

There's an enormous kitchen, all black and white chrome. At the front of the house, there's a cosy cinema screening area. At the other end is a huge dining room table in front of bi-folding doors that lead into the garden, as natural as if I live here. I'm too busy gushing to even look at the others. I find myself walking into the garden.

It's small, as they all are here, but it's modern and has enough space for a small table and chairs and a grass area for Jemima to play around on. Plus there's a big tree in the middle. I can imagine Jemima playing in the shade of it while I get my tan on. I love it. I've never before felt pulled to a house.

The others finally catch up with me. The agent looks hopeful. He might as well be rubbing his hands together in glee. Probably already working out his commission.

'Miss Green,' he says clearing his throat, 'as I was just telling the others here you've yet to see upstairs. There's five bedrooms, all with their own en-suites and a media surround sound system which is included.'

I really don't need to hear any more. This is it. This is our new house. I can feel it in my bones.

'We'll take it,' I grin, taking Ollie's hand. He looks back at me horrified. A flash of anger passes through his eyes.

'What? We bloody won't!' he barks, throwing my hand off his.

I look down at my deserted hand. What is he doing?

'Huh?' I look back to the agent, embarrassed that he's being such a little bitch causing a scene like this. 'Please just give us a minute.' I drag Ollie away from him. 'Are we even seeing the same house here?'

'Yeah,' he nods, still seeming completely unimpressed. 'You might be in a dream world right now, but what I see is a terrace house with a tiny garden and broken up living space. It's just not practical for what we need.'

I stare at him completely at a loss.

'Yes it is! And anyway I'm the one who's home all day.'

He looks hurt, his shoulders sagging. 'And what you really mean is, it's your money, right?'

My head retracts as if he's slapped me. Where the hell has this come from?

'That's not what I'm saying at all.'

He rubs his face wearily. 'But it's what you're thinking. I mean, you haven't even told me how much this place is.' His eyes radiate hurt.

'The amount isn't important,' I say vaguely, not wanting to tell him the price. He might freak out.

'Well, how much is it?' Meryl asks, having clearly eavesdropped on our conversation. Why can't she just mind her own business?

The estate agent looks at his board before answering. 'A steal at just under five million.'

I watch as Poppy, Meryl and Ollie's faces drop in shock. Okay, so maybe it sounds bad when you say it out loud. But it's *totally* reasonable for what you're getting.

'Five million for a fucking terrace?' Ollie spits in disgust. 'Jazz, you *have* to be having me on.'

Poppy places her hand on my shoulder. 'It does seem a lot of money, Jazz. And maybe you shouldn't rush into it.'

I shrug her arm off. I hate how condescending she sounds. I know what I want.

'I'm not rushing into anything. I've found the house of my dreams, and I'm not letting anyone get in my way.'

'I can't fucking believe this,' Ollie snaps, pure hurt radiating from his contorted face. He backs away, before fully turning and leaving. Meryl runs after him. Bloody mummy's boy.

I swallow and turn back to the agent. 'Start preparing the paperwork. It's mine.'

## Poppy

### *Thursday 28th January*

Shit. I really can't believe that Jazz is still going ahead and buying that house. Five bloody million! How ridiculous. I don't think I'd ever be able to part with that kind of money, no matter how much I had. I'm just too tight deep down. Not even that deep down really.

According to Mum, they haven't spoken since, and that was five days ago. I hope Jemima's not picking up on the bad atmosphere. They really need to sort it out. It's no use having a mansion of a house if your mum and dad are splitting up. But I do get that she wants to move back to Chelsea. Even though I'll miss her being so close, I get that she wants to be near where she grew up. That's one of the reasons I feel so comfortable being back in St Albans.

I'll just miss her being so close. I mean; am I upset that she's so eager to move so far away from me? Okay, maybe a little bit. Am I afraid that she's

LAURA BARNARD

going to drop me and start hanging around with her old mates? Of course not.

Because right now I have to focus on Ryan and me. I push the doctor's reception door open and find him already waiting for me, dressed in a navy suit and white shirt. God, he looks delicious. Is it even possible that he's getting better looking as he gets older? It's so unfair. I'll probably age like a prune next to Mr Gorgeous.

'Hey, babe,' he says, wrapping one arm around my waist, pulling me into him and nuzzling my neck, before planting a quick kiss on it.

I swoon, my breath leaving my body as if I've been winded. It still surprises me when he does things like this. Like he still can't get enough of me. Especially at the moment. We've been having so much sex that I was sure he'd be bored of me by now. Apparently not. It makes me feel like a wild vixen that can't be tamed.

'Mrs Poppy Davis?' an Indian doctor calls from a room.

God, I never tire of hearing that. Mrs Davis. People look around as if to check who is being called. I take Ryan's hand in mine and walk proudly towards the doctor's room. I always get the same looks. Women, registering how hot Ryan is and then looking at me wondering how the hell I snagged him. Hell, I don't even know myself! Anyway, time to get serious.

We close the door behind us and sit down in awkward silence. What is it about the silence in doctor's rooms? It's like they're designed to make you feel uncomfortable straight away. The amount of times I've come in here and totally forgotten what I was here about, only to babble on about a mole or something I'm not even worried about. I'm sure they do it deliberately to keep the traffic of patients going.

'What can I help you with?' the doctor asks looking at us both with disinterest.

Ryan looks to me. I suppose I'm the one saying this then. Great.

'Well...we've been trying to get pregnant for a year now and...' I fiddle with my hands in my lap. 'Well, we haven't...you know, got pregnant. So I just wondered if there was something wrong.'

46

He starts scribbling down something wildly with his biro. Typical doctor. Can't make out a bloody word.

'And how often are you having sex?' he asks, completely straight-faced.

'Woah,' Ryan laughs awkwardly. 'That's a bit personal isn't it, doc?'

'I'm afraid I need to know.' Still no emotion on his face. Maybe he's just had Botox.

Ryan again looks to me. This is mortifying. I rack my mind.

'Maybe two or three times a week?' I offer, not looking him in the eye. 'Not every week. But it's hard, as my cycles are irregular.' I cringe at having to talk about my periods in front of Ryan.

'That was my next question,' he nods.

'Cycle?' Ryan asks, completely bewildered. 'You don't own a bicycle, Pops?'

Oh, bless him. My cute, clueless husband. I smile knowingly at the doctor.

'My period, babe.'

He squirms uncomfortably in his seat. 'Oh, right.'

God forbid I bleed. Sorry I'm a woman.

'Okay.' He scribbles some more on his sheet of paper. 'I'm going to send you for two blood tests. One seven days before your period is due and one on the day you come on your period. I'll also ask you to complete a urine test and send it back to the surgery so we can rule out chlamydia.'

'Chlamydia!' I shriek. What the fuck is he talking about? He thinks I'm riddled with a sexually transmitted disease? 'I'm not a tramp you know! I haven't slept around at all.' Then I remember my one and only one-night stand with that idiot when I first moved into Ryan's. 'Well, I might have once, but we totally used a condom.'

Ryan balks next to me, visibly cringing into his chair.

The doctor doesn't even flinch. Probably used to far worse.

'Please don't misunderstand, Mrs Davis. I'm not insinuating anything about your previous relationships. It's just procedure. Chlamydia is also going to be ruled out for Mr Davis during his sperm test.'

'Sperm test?' Ryan gasps, affronted. 'I thought it was far too early days for that?'

'Afraid not, Mr Davis. And to be frank, you have to get used to a lot of embarrassing questions if you're going to be referred for further tests. You'll be tested for every sexually transmitted disease, including HIV.'

'Shit,' Ryan mutters, looking down at the floor. Real graceful, Ryan. 'And *are* we likely to be referred?'

'Yes,' the doctor nods. 'Even if we find no evident problem we'd still have to check everything else. Plus, with your wife's irregular cycles, your chances per year could be halved already.'

'Oh my God,' I utter. I am not hearing one piece of optimism coming from him. Why couldn't we have a happy doctor?

This is really happening. Up until now I've been kind of thinking that I've been over-reacting, but having him telling me to my face like this makes it so real. It's kind of scary.

'And what *could* it be?' I notice I'm shaking, and the back of my neck is sweating. Do I even really want to know?

Ryan looks at me, eyes wide. I realise I must sound hysterical, but fuck, I *am*. This is some scary shit. What if they find out I can't ever have a baby?

'Please, Mrs Davis,' the doctor says in mollifying tones. 'The main thing is to try and remain calm.'

Is he crazy?

'Calm? How the fuck can I remain calm when you're telling me I might never be able to have kids because I have chlamydia or HIV? I mean, how the fuck am I supposed to act?'

Whoops. I possibly shouldn't have sworn at the doctor. I'm so unladylike sometimes. The poster behind his desk, reminding patients they won't tolerate abuse, glares at me.

'Poppy,' Ryan hisses. He leans over and places his hands on my shoulders as if to try and shake me out of it.

'I'm sorry,' I sniff, feeling a pulling on my throat. Oh fuck. Do not cry. Do NOT cry like an absolute little bitch. Mothers are supposed to be warriors who protect their packs. 'I just feel stressed out by it all.'

'Totally understandable,' the doctor nods. 'But you must try and work on your stress levels. It doesn't help.'

Is he insane? How can I not worry about the future of my fertility?

'Yeah, I'll work on that,' I scoff sarcastically.

He opens a drawer. 'Take these with you.' He gives me and Ryan a urine bottle (both for different reasons I'm guessing) and me, two blood test sheets to show reception. This is really bloody happening.

We walk into the reception glum-faced and bump straight into Richard and Grace looking sickeningly happy. What the hell are they doing here? Maybe we can duck out without them seeing us. I grab Ryan's hand.

'Ryan?' Grace says, her eyes lighting up like she's just seen Jesus Christ walk on water in front of her.

'Hey, guys,' Richard says, wrapping his arm around Grace protectively like she's a trophy or something. I bet she loves it. 'What are you doing here?'

Oh my god. Why the hell would he ask such a private question? It's not like we're in a shopping centre and we can say 'oh, just needed bread and milk.' And if front of all of our bloody neighbours who I just know are eavesdropping. The inquisitive bastard.

'Err...' I turn to Ryan, who's bright red.

Crap. I don't think I've ever seen him red. If he's red, I've got no chance. My cheeks already feel like they're on fire. Think, Poppy, bloody think of an excuse. All I can think of is my blushes blending into the other.

'Hang on,' Richard whispers, his eyes lighting up as if he's just twigged on. Please, God, don't tell me he's guessed. It'll be hard to lie to his face. 'Don't tell me you're here for the same reason as us?'

I look at Grace, my eyebrows furrowing.

'You guys are pregnant too?' Richard grins, practically jumping up and down on the spot.

Oh my god. My stomach hits the floor with a thud; my arms begin to tremble, and I feel light headed. He thinks I'm pregnant?

'This is awesome!' he continues. 'Our kids will be in the same year at school.'

This is horrendous. The floor suddenly feels unsteady.

Grace begins rubbing her completely flat stomach. 'Not that they'll be in the same school for sure. We're already considering paying for private school.'

Of course she is.

I look up to Ryan with a forced smile trying to ask what we should do. He's smiling too, but I can see the devastation in his eyes. I silently beg for him to tell them the truth so that I don't have to. I don't think I'm strong enough to speak right now without bursting into angry tears at the injustice of life.

'We're not pregnant too,' he replies, his voice low and grave.

Richard's face falls. 'What? Then what the hell are you doing here together? And halfway through the working day?' He looks between both of our faces, searching for answers we're not willing to give. He narrows his eyebrows. 'Wait, one of you guys isn't seriously ill, right?'

Oh my god. Now he's thinking I've found a lump or some serious shit like that. No, that's our father.

'No!' I shriek, so loudly that everyone in the waiting room turns to stare. I cringe, my head shrinking into my shoulders. 'Nothing like that. We were just here for...for...' I *literally* cannot think of one single thing. I look to Ryan for help, desperation in my eyes.

'For...' he attempts, also clearly at a loss. 'A...' he looks down at the pee pot in my hand. I should have hidden it. 'Chlamydia test?'

My eyes widen so far and fast I'm worried they've actually ripped my face apart. He said *what now?*

Richard and Grace's jaws drop onto the floor, both subconsciously taking two small steps away from us. He's said I'm being tested for chlamydia!

'Wow,' Richard says, wringing his hands together in a painful, awkward silence that I'm sure will go down on record as the worst moment in time.

I can't believe Ryan said that. Of all the fucking things he said, it had to be that! Why? Now my brother is going to think we're both riddled or something. And who will they think gave it to who?

Grace glares at me in disgust, her lip curled up like she just smelt gone off fish. It gives me some comfort that she looks ugly like that.

'Well...I hope that goes well,' Richard nods awkwardly, backing away slowly.

'Wait,' Grace snaps, her hand up in the air. She turns to Ryan. 'Does this mean I should get tested too?'

Oh my god. And just when we thought it couldn't get any worse, we all have to be reminded that my husband has slept with Richard's fiancé. Sure, it was years ago, but it doesn't change the fact that they were intimate. By the look on Richard's face, I'd say this is news to him. Uh-oh.

'Why would...' he trails off, as he puts two and two together. I can practically see the cogs in his brain working. 'You guys? W...when?'

Ryan runs his hand over his hair and grasps the back of his neck. 'Rich, it was years ago. Before I even met you. Or Poppy.'

'Right, right,' Richard nods, clearly not okay with it while desperately pretending to be. He turns to me, anger flickering in his eyes. 'You knew this Poppy?'

Woah. All of that information and he's blaming *me* for this?

I nod. 'It was just a quick shag though.' I relish in Grace feeling used. Which she was. It's not my fault Ryan used to be a giant manwhore. He changed when he met me. Although I still have no idea how or why. I'm hardly Gisele, whereas Grace could pass for her sister. But apparently sometimes girls like me get lucky.

'You don't have anything to worry about,' Ryan retorts, his head down.

At least he's put their mind at ease. Grace looks relieved, but then her eyebrows shoot up like she's just realised something.

'Wait? So it was Poppy that gave it to you?' Her eyes are lit up in pure delight.

Oh my God, of course that's what she'd think.

'No!' I snap. 'It definitely was *not* me!'

'Look, let's just go,' Ryan says, trying to usher me out of the waiting room.

'No!' I hiss. 'I'm not going anywhere until you tell them it wasn't bloody me.'

How can he imply it was me when he's the one that dumped us in this shitstorm? The selfish bastard.

'Well...' he looks to them apologetically, 'we still need to get the results anyway.'

God, he's right. One of us *could* actually have it. Neither of us has even been tested before, and we're already tearing each other apart over who's fault it is. And this is just over chlamydia. What will it be like when we find out it's one of our faults we can't have kids? Like I'm barren. Will we turn on each other again? Will this relationship even survive that?

'Anyway.' I swallow down the lump in my throat. I really just want to go and hide under my duvet and have a good cry. 'It was lovely seeing you both, but we've got to get going.'

Ryan grabs my hand as we walk silently towards the car. I wriggle my fingers out of his grasp. I'm so mad at him right now.

'I'm sorry,' he mumbles apologetically.

'Don't,' I bark. 'Just don't.'

# Chapter 8
## Jazz

### Saturday 30^{th} January

Having money again is beyond incredible.  I realise now how much of a pauper I was living like before.  And the worst thing about being poor?  Having to rely on other people to help you.  And I've really relied on Meryl the last few years.  If it weren't for her, I wouldn't have got through my post-natal depression.  I just know it.  So I'm taking her shopping as a thank you.

I wish I could fly her straight to somewhere fabulous like New York, but with Jemima, everything's that little bit harder.  So we're stuck with Brent Cross.  After we've had our final fitting of our bridesmaid dresses and said goodbye to Grace, I tell her we're hitting the shops.  Meryl's really into her clothes, but I know that Douggie has told her to stop spending money on numerous occasions.  This way he doesn't have to worry.

We speed through the shops like a whirlwind.  We head straight to Fenwick's as I know it's one of her favourite shops.  I pick up a gorgeous navy blue summer dress and hold it against her.

'This is gorge.  Why don't you try it on?'

Her criticizing eyes assess it.  'Not my style,' she snaps, pushing Jemima onwards in her buggy.

Is it me, or has Meryl got the arse?  She seemed fine at the fitting.

'Really?  My treat,' I smile cheekily.

A blank, scary expression rests on her face.  'Thank you very much, Jazz, but I don't take charity.'  She pretends to look at another dress even though it's three sizes too small.

'Meryl, it's not charity. Jesus, it's just a small thank you for everything you've done for me the last few years.' Why can't she see that?

She smiles tightly. 'That's very thoughtful of you, darling, but it's really just not necessary.'

Wow. Talk about burst my happy bubble.

How can I get her to shop with me? It's no fun on your own. Ah, I know! I've got just the thing.

'Okay, but how about we pick up some outfits for Poppy?'

Her eyes light up with a devilish glint I don't think she's even aware is there.

'Fabulous idea, darling! That girl needs a makeover. The jeans and t-shirt combo is getting on my last nerve. Why can't she just dress like a girl?'

She actually looks like she's expecting an answer from me.

I grimace apologetically. 'Err...she just prefers to be comfortable I suppose.'

'Nonsense,' she barks shaking her head. 'Comfort is for children. Beauty is pain. She should just be grateful we're not putting her in corsets these days.'

'O...kay.'

'Right,' she claps her hands together, a new steely determination on her face. 'Let's get started.' She abandons the buggy and starts walking through the aisles. I struggle to keep up with her. 'Oooh, I just know this would look fabulous on her.' She picks up a pink summer dress covered in flowers.

She couldn't get further away from her taste. I grimace. Poppy would run a fucking mile. How do I put it without offending her?

'It's...err...' I try not to visibly squirm. 'I don't really think it's her style.'

She narrows her eyebrows at me before thrusting the dress back onto the rack.

'Fine, you don't want my help. Fine by me.' She crosses her arms over her chest making it clear it's anything but fine.

Oh, God. She's so easy to offend sometimes. Sorry Poppy. Please forgive me for what I'm about to do.

'No,' I shake my head, picking up the dress again. 'You're totally right.

That *would* suit her.'

'Really?' she asks pursing her lips together like a child wanting attention.

'Really.' I pick my credit card out of my purse and hand it to her. 'Let's go crazy.'

Her eyes light up, giddy with glee. *Finally,* I've got a shopping buddy.


An hour later we're laden down with bags. Why didn't I think to hire some sort of shopping assistant in advance? I asked and apparently they don't supply that kind of thing here. How ridiculous.

We're just queuing up in John Lewis to buy one more thing for Poppy. Something I know she'll actually like. Limited edition jewelled converse. She'll lose her freaking mind when she sees these bad boys.

'Anyway, Jazz,' Meryl says carefully, twiddling the shopping bags in her hands, 'I've been wanting to talk to you.'

My back straightens immediately. I'm *so* not in the mood to be told off right now.

'About what?' I ask vaguely looking to the front of the queue. And I haven't even done anything. Have I?

'Well...are you sure you want to move to Chelsea? I mean, it's terribly far away.'

Oh God. Just what I need. A lecture about how much better St Albans would be.

'Has Ollie been bitching to you? Because if he's got something to say about it, he can say it straight to me rather than going crying to his mummy.' We've barely kissed and made up from his tantrum at the house viewing.

Her face softens. 'Jazz, he needs someone to talk to,' she smiles sadly. 'And anyway, this isn't just about Ollie. We're used to living with Jemima. Having her taken away from us so you can move that far would break my heart.'

I suppose I can understand that, but enough with the emotional blackmail.

'Besides, with how much you're going out at the moment, it would be handier to have us babysitters just down the road.'

With how much I've been going out? What the hell is she talking about? Is she now choosing to bitch about my nights out? How dare she. I mean, yeah, of course I've been out celebrating. Who wouldn't? I'm filthy rich.

'A few nights out is no big deal, Meryl,' I counter avoiding her judgmental eyes.

'I'm just worried about you, love.' The corners of her eyes wrinkle. 'It's going to start affecting Jemima. Partying all day and not getting up until midday is fine for now as you've got me to do the nursery runs, but what about when you move that far away?'

Is she insinuating that I'm a bad mother? Because it took about a million bottles of wine for her to raise her kids.

'I'll get a nanny,' I snap. 'One that doesn't interfere with my personal business.'

'A stranger?' she shrieks as if I've just said I'll throw her into a paedophile ring. 'You'd rather have a *stranger* look after her than her own grandmother?'

Again with the bad mother stuff. Making me feel guilty for everything I do.

'Just butt out, Meryl,' I scold harshly. 'I mean it.'

She reacts as if I've slapped her round the face. Oh god, I suppose, in hindsight, I was a *bit* cruel. I keep forgetting all that this woman has done for me the last couple of years. Without her, God knows where I'd be. The woman's been more of a mother to me than my own ever has. But that *still* doesn't give her the right to tell me how to live my life.

'Where's Jemima?' Meryl asks suddenly, pushing people out of the way.

'She's right here.' I look down to the buggy that she was holding onto two seconds ago, but she's not there.

A fresh swoop of fear goes hurling through my body. I look around, desperate to find her on the other side of me, but she's not. Oh my God, where's my baby? Meryl's frantic now, screaming out her name, but all I can do is stare. Goose pimples break out over my shoulders, and my feet feel numb as if frozen in place. Where the hell is Jemima?

I leave the buggy and the bags and force my feet to move.

'My daughter!' I yell in a strangled voice to anyone who'll listen. 'My daughter's gone missing.'

The woman behind the desk speaks into her radio. The shutters close down immediately. Wow, that was quick. But what if she's wandered out of the shop? What if she's trying to get back inside but now she can't, and some predator takes her? Vomit rises in my throat. I push it down. I've no time for that.

'Open the shutters!' I scream as I run up to them, pounding my fist on them. 'She could be on the other side.'

'Madam, this is procedure,' a member of staff tells me. 'The highest possibility is that she's still in the store.'

'But what if she's not?' I scream, at my wits end. 'What if she's out there?'

'We've alerted the entire Brent cross security. Right now there's a total lockdown of the shopping centre, and we have everyone searching for a child. But now I need a detailed description of her from you or, if possible, a photo. Our security are going back through the store footage right now.'

My head is spinning. 'Err...yes.'

I reach into my wallet and pull out her pre-school's photo. I love that photo. Her hair looks like a pineapple I'd pulled it so high on her head. Next to it is her baby photo from when she was only six months. It's her passport photo. God, what have I done? I've lost my baby. Tears sting at my eyes, but I force myself to hold it together as I hand over the photo.

'Thank you,' she nods, taking it from my shaky hands.

Meryl's at my side. 'What have we done, Jazz? How could we have been so reckless? Douglas will kill me.'

'Douglas? What about bloody Ollie?' I gulp imagining having to tell him I've lost his daughter. I push the thought away, too horrific to even consider. 'I can't think about this right now.'

'You're right,' she nods, placing her hands on her temples. 'We need a plan.'

Well, I'm all out of ideas. All I can think about is how this is all my fault.

'I've got it,' she says brightly. 'I'll stay here and liaise with the manager, and you go and look for her.'

'Look for her? Where the hell do I look? This is John Lewis! She could be anywhere over three floors.'

She scrutinizes my face. 'Well then you better get a move on,' she barks.

I turn on my heel and run.

I run through all of the aisles of clothes calling her name, but she's nowhere to be seen. Just lots of people, staring at me and whispering. Obviously inconvenienced that they can't leave the shop and whispering what an incompetent mother I am. Selfish bastards.

'You could help me look you know!' I yell at them.

I feel frantic, my whole body shaking with adrenaline I had no idea I even had. I'm just walking around blindly, only aware of the panic coursing through my veins. I slow down and lean against a wall. Okay, Jazz, just think. Where would she have gone? What does she like? Ooh, she loves trying on my shoes. I sprint towards the shoe section already feeling relieved. She'll be there stumbling over in high heels. God, if she's there, I'll never shout at her for trying on my shoes again.

I reach the shoes, but she's not there. The place is deserted. It's like a bloody ghost town.

Fuck!!

I run around the whole level, passing handbags, perfumes, and jewellery. I get my hopes up when I see the children's area with furniture, clothes and toys. But I can't find her. This is bloody hopeless. I slump down onto the floor in the furniture department, sobs escaping from my chest.

A ball of guilt is growing inside me, a guilt that stabs at me every time I realise how hopeless this is. How this is going to ruin everything forever.

The manager finds me after a while. She looks apologetic. Shit, they still haven't found her. What the fuck am I going to do?

'Miss?' I nod; already weary. 'The good news is that she is somewhere in this store. Our video proves she hasn't left. We're just trying to trace where she went right now.'

Oh thank God. If they're right, there's still some hope of finding her. I mean; they have to find her, right? Unless there's some psycho in the toilets right now shaving her head and changing her clothes so she can pass as their son. God, at times like this I wish I didn't have such an active imagination.

A snuffle sort of sound makes me turn to my right. What was that?

The shop lady smiles sadly at me. 'Is there anything I can get you while-'

'Shhhh!' I hiss, throwing my hands up in front of her.

I listen again, desperate to know I'm not crazy and hear the snuffle sound again. Almost like a snore. I wander around, desperately trying to find it. It leads me around some of the children's bedroom furniture.

My heart soars when I see something under the covers of a child's bed. Please, God, say it's her. I rush over and pull the covers back to find her snoring loudly. Relief warms my frosty heart. My precious baby!

'Jem!' I say through my tears. I push her wild curly hair out of her eyes. 'Baby, wake up.'

She stirs slightly before opening her groggy eyes. 'Mummy, I'm tired.'

I laugh, tears streaming unrestrained down my face. 'I know baby. Why didn't you tell me before you found the bed?'

She pouts. 'You and Nana were arguing.'

Oh my god. She knows we were arguing. This is all my fault. If we hadn't been snapping at each other, she wouldn't have wandered off.

'We were just having a discussion, baby. Come on, let's go home so you can have a proper nap.'

Chapter 9

Poppy

## Monday 1st February

By the time I get to Leavesden studios the following Monday morning I've *just* about finished ripping Ryan a new arsehole. By yelling at him, obviously. I'm not into any kinky shit like trying to fuck him up the arse with a strap on. Hey, if people are into that all power to them, but it's not for me.

He tried to grovel, bringing me cup of tea after cup of tea and he even baked me banana bread. Damn that beautiful man knows my weakness. So I've forgiven him, for now. But if it gets back to my Mother, I *will* murder him.

Even though I wasn't sure at first, I actually love my job here. When Charlotte came back to work, and I could no longer be Michael's PA, I was devastated, but he had other ideas. He put me in charge of the runners. Although it was a nightmare at first, I eventually learnt to kick their arse. Within a short space of time, I've managed to work my way up to Crewing Assistant, which I absolutely love. It basically means that I train the runners and match them to suitable jobs on films. I rota when films will need specific people and who can be put in there to do it. I had no idea a job could be so fulfilling. To think I could still be back taking shit from my old boss Victor makes me realise how far I've come.

I've just finished putting in a new runner for the new action movie being filmed next year when my phone rings. Home flashes up. A sinking feeling develops in my stomach. This can either be Mum getting nervous about Grace and Richard's wedding or Dad with his blood test results. Either way, it's not good.

You can do this Poppy. You're an adult. I gulp down the panic, take a deep breath and press answer.

'Hello?'

'Poppy.' It's Dad's voice, and he sounds tired. Defeated. I know before he even has to tell me.

'What is it? Did you get the results? What did they say?' I can feel myself holding my breath, my heartbeat racing. Just in case I'm wrong. Hoping I'm wrong.

There's a long pause where all I can hear is my own heartbeat hammering in my eardrums.

'It's bad news, Poppy Pocket.'

My eyes burn, and my chest squeezes like the devil himself has hold of it and is refusing to let go until I give in and cry. But I can't cry. God damn it, I knew it was coming. If I'm really honest with myself, I knew. But hearing it out loud. Knowing its real and all of this isn't some strange long realistic nightmare. A tear escapes out of my left eye.

But I still want it clarified. I need to hear the word.

'Wh...What did they say?' I ask, my voice high-pitched and wobbly. I'm really struggling to hold it together, but I have to for him.

He sniffs, and it breaks my heart into tiny pieces. My Dad's broken, and I can't fix it.

'They said...something about markers in my blood and it being confirmed as cancer. They want me to come straight in Monday morning to have my testicle removed.'

'Oh my god.' It's not helpful, but it's all I've got.

'I know,' he sniffs.

'But you're going to be fine,' I nod, trying to convince myself. 'Have you told Mum yet?'

'No. She can't know.'

Is he for fucking real? Does he honestly think he can go through this without Mum knowing? She's like bloody Miss Marple. I'm surprised she hasn't sniffed this shit out already.

'You can't be serious.'

'I am Poppy. It's Richard's wedding this weekend. You honestly think it's a good idea to have her crying every two seconds throughout it?'

He is right. Plus she'd get terribly drunk and tell everyone, and the whole wedding would be ruined. It'd turn into more like a funeral than a wedding.

'Okay, okay,' I huff. 'But first thing Sunday morning you tell her, okay?'

I selfishly want my mummy to hold me so I can have a good cry about it. I don't like all this pretending to be strong.

'I promise, love.'

Shit. My Dad really has cancer. I never thought this would happen to me. I know people always say that, but I truly didn't. This is a horrible story you hear about someone you know, not something your own family goes through.

I root around in my bag for a tissue, so the others don't notice my tears. I spot the wee pot. I still need to do that wee sample so they can rule out chlamydia. Me having that would really be the cherry on top. Now is as good a time as ever. Take my mind off my Dad and my life crashing around me.

I look closer at it and quickly realise there's no way I'm going to be able to aim and piss directly in it. I'm going to have to pee in a cup or something and then pour it in carefully. I rush to the small communal kitchen and search the cupboards. I pick out a mug, thinking it will be less obvious.

I take it into the toilet and try to think of gushing water and not my family's impending doom. Waterfalls, tinkling sounds, anything to get me going. I eventually pee (half over my hand) and take the mug out with me to wash my hands thoroughly. I place it on the side as I hear a chain flush and another woman from the building come out of her cubicle. Crap. I thought I was alone. I politely smile as I dry my hands.

'Ooh, you must be thirsty,' she says chirpily, staring into my cup. 'And apple juice, you healthy thing. I just can't stay away from that damn coffee.' Ugh, she is far too happy.

I smile, really not wanting to get into conversation with her. I had planned to transfer it in to the pee pot here, but I'll just have to take it with me now. How annoying.

All of a sudden she starts coughing loudly. Coughing so loud she's making a right show and dance. 'Need...need your drink,' she says in between coughs. She reaches her hand out for my cup.

She must be joking.

'Oh, no. Um...I have a cold sore. Have some water.' I start running the tap for her, but the bitch looks like she's dying or something. She's going bright red, and her eyes are watering. What the fuck is happening?

She grabs the mug, but I'm stronger. She pulls it towards her, but I yank it back, careful for it not to spill.

'Give...to me,' she coughs.

'No! Get your own!' I shout back.

She must think I'm insane. Not wanting to give her some of my 'apple juice'.

'Just GIVE it to me!' she gurgles. In a moment of weakness she manages to unclasp my hand from it, and before I can grab it back, she's gulping down my pee.

Oh my god. This *cannot* be happening. She's drinking my piss. It's beyond gross. Although maybe she won't notice.

Her eyes widen in horror before she spits it out in a spray all over me. *Nice.* Now I'm covered in my own piss. I wipe my eyes.

'What the hell kind of apple juice is that?' she demands, her eyes wide as saucers.

Well, it's not like I didn't try to tell her. I wipe my own pee from my face before replying. 'It's...it's err...from Somerset apples.'

'Well, it tastes vile! Goodness!' She storms out without even a thank you. You're welcome, you crazy bitch! Oh well, at least I don't have to see her every day. She must be working on something else.

I quickly wash my face and then transfer the remaining wee into the pee pot. I wrap it in tissue and put it in my handbag before making my way back to the set as discreetly as possible. I stand next to Greg checking the schedule.

He suddenly turns to me with a confused expression. 'Can you smell piss?'

Oh my God. I should have found some perfume. I smell like the homeless.

'Err...no?'

My phone rings in my pocket. Saved by the bell. I look at the screen, Mother. Oh my God, what if Dad's decided to tell her now?

'Hi, Mum,' I answer, for once glad to hear from her, even though I've repeatedly told her not to call me when I'm at work.

'Hi, darling! How are you?' I go to answer, but she's already started talking again. 'I need you and Ryan out this Friday night. We're having a little dinner before Richard and Grace go their separate ways before the big day on Saturday.'

My heart sinks. Great. Dad hasn't told her. I have to watch all of my family swooning all over Grace and Richard when our Dad has just been told he has cancer and has to endure it all before his op.

'Oh, okay.'

'7.30pm darling at Ristorante Al Caratello and do me a favour and wear some makeup. Grace always looks so glamorous next to you.'

'Gee, thanks.'

'You know I only say it because I love you, darling.'

At least, I'm not having some last minute shotgun wedding like a slut.

'I need you looking nice. We're meeting Grace's parents for the first time.'

Ah, we're *finally* going to meet them.

'Don't you find it strange that we haven't met them before now?'

'Not really, darling. It's saved us a lot of potentially boring conversations. That's why I'm dreading Friday. What if they're total bores?'

'They have Grace as a daughter. I'm pretty sure they're used to a fair bit of drama in their life.'

'Anyway, I'll see you then darling,' she says clearly not listening to a word. 'And remember lipstick. There's bound to be celebratory photos.'

'Bye, Mum.'

# Chapter 10
## Poppy

*Friday 5th February*

By the time I arrive at the restaurant that Friday I'm an hour late. I only went and came on my period, didn't I! So I had to call the doctors and get the emergency blood test they said I'd need. I always hate speaking to those bitchy receptionists. They basically made me tell them what it was for, and I know they don't have the right to demand that. They probably go home at the end of the day and laugh their arses off about all of us and our health issues. Like I said; bitches.

Anyway, now I have a bruised upper arm right before the wedding. Great. Everyone's going to be asking questions.

I walk in to everyone already sitting at a long table in the corner eating various forms of spaghetti and pizza.

'Thanks for waiting for me,' I say sarcastically.

Ryan gets up with a grimace. 'Sorry, babe, but we were all starving. And we couldn't make Grace wait.' He means because she's pregnant. How could I forget? He lowers his voice to a whisper. 'How did it go?'

'As good as a blood test can go,' I whisper smiling weakly.

'It's your own fault for being late darling,' Mum says, waving her wine glass around erratically. Great, so she's already smashed.

I finally notice what I assume are Grace's parents from their olive skin and dark hair. I know they're from Spain but aside from that nothing. Her mum is not at all what I had imagined. I expected someone completely gorgeous and glamorous, but this lady looks cute. She must be in her early sixties, with perfect curled short dark hair. You can see that she once possessed Grace's beauty, but her brown eyes are surrounded by creases, and her neck has lost all elasticity, resembling a turkey.

'This is Grace's mother,' Mum says, clearly taking the hint that Grace wasn't going to bother introducing me. 'Carmen.'

Carmen nods at me but doesn't stand or offer me any kind of handshake.

'And this is her father.' I look across at her dad. He's an intimidating man with grey hair and a matching beard, but contrasting jet-black eyebrows. He's got a few lines under his eyes, but apart from that he's got great, glowing skin. He's dressed in a smart navy suit, with an open light blue shirt underneath, unbuttoned so low you can start to make out his chest hair.

'This is Alejandro.'

He again nods, seeming no friendlier than his wife.

'Order yourself something, Poppy,' Auntie Beryl says eagerly. I notice Simon's with her again.

'Aaaaa-chooooo! God bless and save me.' God, he's annoying. How does she stand him?

I look over the menu, aware that whatever I pick, Mum will comment on. Plus, with Ryan watching, I stupidly feel like I should order something super healthy. Let him know that I'm really keeping my body in tip-top condition so I can carry his baby. I know it's ridiculous, but that's how self-conscious I have become.

'Err...I'll have the Caesar salad,' I say to the waiter. He nods.

'Wait!' Ryan shouts, gesturing for him to come back. 'Pops are you sure? You normally love the pizzas here.' His eyes are asking me questions like 'why are you being so weird?'

Weirdly I feel better now I have his permission. I'm basically reverting to a beaten wife in the fifties. Where's the feminist in me?

'Oh, go on then!' I laugh. 'I'll have the chicken pizza.'

The waiter nods. 'My colleague, Max, will now be taking over your table. I hope you enjoy your meals.'

'So,' Mum says smiling tightly, 'what were we talking about?'

'I can't remember,' Richard says openly yawning.

A black waiter comes over. 'Hello, my name is Anton, and I'll be your new waiter. Please let me know if you need anything.' He sounds far more helpful than he seems. His whole demeanour says 'not bothered', from his sleepy eyes to him leaning on one hip.

'Some drinks,' Carmen says, downing her wine and shaking her glass at him rudely.

'Of course,' he nods, plodding away slowly.

'What is it with these Negros and their lack of can do attitude?' she says with a cruel laugh.

My mouth drops open. Ryan spits out his drink. Simon sneezes again. Hold the phone, did she seriously just say *Negro?* Richard's eyes look like they might bulge out of their head. Grace looks down at the table.

'Sorry?' Richard says, obviously praying that he misheard.

'I'm surprised the blacks even have jobs they're so lazy,' her father remarks.

Oh my God. They're total bloody racists!

Everyone just stares at each other in shock. Well, this got awkward real quick. I really want to say something, but I just can't think of what to say. I keep opening and shutting my mouth, but nothing comes out. I'm better to just keep my mouth shut. Hopefully, it'll be the last remark of the evening anyway.

An hour and fifty minutes later, and I still haven't eaten. The others went ahead and ordered desserts, seeing as it was taking too long. I'm beyond starving, and I really don't understand what's taking so long. I mean, yeah, every table is taken, but we've been here before loads of times. The service is normally spot on. Plus, it means I've been subjected to Grace's parents' talk about 'the problem with Jews.' Jazz actually tried to jump across the table and attack them over it. When Ollie held her back, she took Jemima and left.

I'd like to say I can't believe Grace has such hideous parents, but the truth is that I can. The apple doesn't fall far from the tree.

'This is really beyond ridiculous,' Mum splutters, outraged that she hasn't had her ordered wine yet. She ordered it a whole...ten minutes ago. That, to my Mum, might as well be two years dry. 'Excuse me!' She clicks her fingers at our waiter.

I hide my face. I hate when she clicks her fingers. I mean, does she honestly think people are going to go out of their way to help when she's just clicked her fingers at them? It makes me cringe. Plus any excuse for Grace's parents to be racist.

'Yes,' he says through gritted teeth, his shoulders tense.

'What on earth is going on?' Mum shrieks. 'We've been waiting for our wine for ten minutes!'

'And,' I interrupt. 'Um...I hate to be a pain, but I ordered my food like, nearly two hours ago. Do you think it will be ready soon?'

'Do I have a crystal ball?' he snaps, making me jump. 'The kitchen is overworked.'

'Okay, sorry,' I mumble, shrinking in my seat.

'Don't apologise, Poppy,' Auntie Beryl argues. 'His response was rude and unjustified.'

'Agreed,' Simon nods, taking a handkerchief out of his pocket. 'A-CHOO! God bless me and save me.'

God, Jesus, this sneezing loon is not going to help our case.

'We are very busy tonight if you have not noticed,' the waiter says; hand on his hip like a diva.

'Typical,' Carmen snorts under her breath.

Richard suddenly stands up. 'My pregnant fiancée hasn't had her dessert.'

Grace strokes his arm like he's a trophy. She looks over to the waiter. 'My blood sugar,' she says her puppy eyes on. 'And I'm getting married tomorrow.'

'All of this is not my problem!' he shouts, turning and throwing a chair back onto the floor before walking away.

Shit.

'Well, that escalated quickly,' Ryan says with alarmed eyes.

'Way to live up to your stereotype,' Alejandro laughs. 'Show some violence.'

How can these be real people? They're awful.

'I say we don't pay,' Mum announces, Beryl nodding furiously.

'We can't just not pay,' I try to rationalise. 'Most of you have had a main meal already. That will be totally illegal!'

'Illegal smeaggal!' Mum scoffs. 'I'm sure there's some sort of act in place that says we can refuse to pay. Poppy, bring the car around and get ready for a quick getaway.'

'You have to be joking.'

'Do I look like I'm joking?' she snaps, warning with her eyes. She turns to Grace. 'You go with her. I don't want my pregnant daughter in law to be getting trampled the night before her wedding.'

Can't we ever just have a normal family meal?

# Chapter 11
## Poppy

*Saturday 6th February*

Today, the monster that is Grace is marrying my brother Richard. She'll be my sister in law. How horrific.

We're all slightly exhausted after the ordeal that was last night. Me, Grace, Ryan and Richard managed to get away in the car only to then be called by Dad and told Mum and Auntie Beryl had started a brawl in the restaurant. We had to go back and restrain them both. Mum had the waiter in a headlock while she lectured him on politeness. Slightly ironic. It didn't help that Grace's parents were doing monkey impressions. It was horrendous.

By the time we managed to calm things the police had arrived. Mum shouted, 'thank God, the service here is criminal!'

And having to deal with Grace's racist parents. No wonder she didn't want us to meet them until the night before the wedding. Thank God it was our friend Tom, who let them off with a harsh warning. It was still not what we needed the night before.

They've chosen to get married at The Vederterra hotel. The priest wouldn't marry Richard again, after he married his now ex-wife Annabel there. Something about church rules. How stupid. He didn't ask her to be a two-timing bitch. Either that or the priest saw that Grace was the devil in sheep's clothing and ran for the hills.

She didn't choose me as a bridesmaid, even though I was guilted into having her as mine. Like I care. Especially when I saw the gold, sequined monstrosity she'd put the others in this morning. It has puffy sleeves and a huge poufy skirt. I think the eighties were the inspiration. I have a feeling

Mum and Beryl had something to do with it.

I'm waiting in the aisle for it to begin. I say aisle, more like in one of the gold chairs decorated with pearls and black feathers that the hotel has placed around this room, so it looks legit. I'd hate to get married in a place like this. Don't get me wrong, it's lovely with its cream walls and strategically placed fairy lights, but it's just got no soul. I'm glad I was able to get married in a church after all. Not that I've been since. Shit, I really should. Maybe that's why I can't get pregnant. Could God be punishing me for not attending? But then if that's true I don't want a baby. I'd rather keep my free will then be blackmailed into it like that. Oh, what am I saying? I'm so desperate I'd sell my soul to the devil.

This place just feels cold. Much like the bride. Even the hotel I chose was brand new after Dad's firm re-decorated, it still had character. Not that the garish gold and black theme has helped at all.

The harpist starts playing the wedding march. I hate to admit it, but it sounds wonderful. I'm shocked she chose something so classy. I was half expecting Take That to blare out of the speakers. Not that I wouldn't secretly think that was awesome.

Jemima and Hazel begin walking down the aisle, dressed in matching white poufy dresses with a gold sequined sash. They have white roses in their hair, which from Hazel's scratching, I'd say she finds uncomfortable. She's got her hand shoved in her mouth, her sign she's nervous. I smile at her brightly which seems to perk her up a bit. They're just so adorable. I wonder if there's an award for cutest kid? I should totally enrol them in child modelling. We could be sitting on a fortune.

All of a sudden, Jem stops walking, her little forehead creasing. She looks down at her legs. I follow her eye line. Oh no. Is that...wee trickling down her leg? Oh no, she's bloody wet herself. Down the aisle.

Jazz is starting to walk down, completely oblivious to it. I grimace at Jemima. The poor thing looks like she's about to burst into tears, her eyes welling up with water. Before I have a chance to react she hikes up her dress, yanks down her knickers, steps out of them and comes heading for me.

71

Horrified gasps fill the room. This couldn't be more embarrassing.

'I wet my knickers, Auntie Pwoppy,' she says loudly for everyone to hear.

Luckily they all laugh raucously at her cuteness.

I can hear Grace shouting in the corridor 'what is everyone laughing at?' The not knowing is probably killing her.

'That's okay, baby.' I smile, bringing her into our side.

I get the baby wipes I've learnt to carry with me since she was born, out of my bag and wipe her down. I'm annoyed at myself that I never thought to bring some spare knickers.

Jazz walks past, and mouths 'thank you'. God, she looks ridiculous in that dress. Once I've cleaned Jemima up I put her onto my lap for a reassuring cuddle.

Izzy's next down the aisle, then Grace's cousins, Sara and Ana. They all seem to be able to miss the puddle of wee, thank God. Then Grace is at the doorway.

Wow. She looks incredible. Her white dress, which she has the cheek to wear, looks amazing against her honey skin. Her dress is princess size big with what looks like layers of tulle material. On top of that is a bodice covered in crystals. Kim Kardashian eat your heart out. You can't tell she's pregnant at all. Even though, everyone knows already.

Her hair is scooped up off her face showing off her long swan like neck. It's twisted into a bun, with curls softly framing her face, her cheekbones as razor sharp as ever. I hate to say it, but she looks unbelievable. And I'm jealous. How awful am I? I'm jealous of Grace. Obviously not of her marrying my brother. Eww, that's gross. I look up to him at the front. It's hard to take him seriously in his gold sequined waistcoat, but he's beaming at her. No, I'm jealous because she's carrying a precious baby in that tiny tummy. Okay and maybe I want her boobs too.

She glides down the aisle like a heaven sent angel. She notices the wee, the horror impossible to hide on her face, and edges her dad away from it. Only when she straightens up again, her long flowery train drags through it. Uh-oh. The bride smells like piss. Jazz looks at me with a comical expression on her face.

The registrar starts welcoming everyone and rambling on. I swear; we must be at the age in our life where everyone is getting married. I feel like all I do nowadays is attend them. I could possibly recite this all by heart and marry them myself.

BEEP BEEP BEEP

What the hell is that? I turn towards the noise. Shit, someone must have left their phone on. Everyone starts nervously ruffling through their bags, checking it's not theirs. Grace looks like she's willing to murder whoever it is. I check mine as discreetly as possible.

'Please turn that phone off,' the registrar barks. But it's still going off.

BEEP BEEP BEEP

Thank God it's not mine. Grace would have definitely used it as an excuse to punch me in the throat. I try my best to follow the noise. It's definitely behind me. A few people a couple of rows back are staring at an old man. It's my great-Uncle Herbert. It must be him. Shit, he's hard of hearing.

I place Jemima down and stand up to get his attention.

'Great-Uncle Herbert! Your phone!' I shout at him.

He leans forward as if just catching that I've said something to him.

He nods as if he's understood. 'Three o'clock, dear,' he shouts back.

He thinks I'm asking the time?

'No! Turn off your phone!'

'Three o'clock!' he shouts back as if *I'm* the deaf one.

I run over to his aisle, pushing people out of the way. If I don't stop this soon, Grace might pummel him to death with her bouquet for ruining her day. I search his pockets for his phone.

'Poppy, why are you trying to take my jacket off?' he shouts in my ear.

Jesus, did I say hard of hearing? I meant deaf as a fucking post.

It's only then that I realise; it's his watch alarm. I start stabbing at it randomly, and it eventually stops. I sit down next to him, my heart racing, and sigh in relief. Grace is still looking like she could spit feathers. And glaring at me like it's *my* fault. I glare back. It's not like I set this up you stupid bitch. I've just saved the day. *You're welcome.*

People keep turning round to stare at us.

'Nothing to see here people, nothing to see!' I shout, shooing them away with my arms.

Ryan smiles back at me holding a laughing Jemima. Yeah, thanks for the support guys.

The registrar clears her throat and goes back to waffling on. I count down in my head the time until she asks if there's any lawful reason why they shouldn't be joined in matrimony. I hate this bit at the best of times. It's always the time when I sneeze or giggle, or just do something generally as stupid. It makes it worse that its Grace and I'd secretly love to ruin her day. Well, if the toddler pissing in the aisle and the old man's alarm clock hasn't already. Here it comes. My heartbeat starts racing and my neck feels sweaty, strands of my hair becoming instantly damp.

I sit on my hands in a bid to stop them flying up in the air. Who knows when you're going to have an arm spasm? I press my lips together and bite my tongue until it feels like it may bleed.

'If any person here present knows of any reason why these two should not be joined in matrimony speak now or forever hold your peace.'

Ryan discreetly looks over his shoulder at me with a smirk. Cheeky bastard. My Mum also looks, warning in her eyes. I'm starting to feel offended.

The registrar looks around as if expecting to find someone. Just as she nods and takes a breath to speak again, I hear a bang. There's a commotion up front. I stand up and look towards the chaos. Izzy is lying on the floor with her eyes shut. Shit.

I rush over, my ears throbbing with shock to find her passed out on the floor. What the hell happened to her? Jazz is leaning over her.

'Can you hear me, Izzy?' she repeats over and over again.

I push her out of the way and begin tapping her cheeks. Nothing. I look at Grace, who seems mildly concerned. I can see it's just an act. She's furious that people are stealing her thunder.

'Izzy you're ruining the wedding,' I hiss into her ear.

Just like that, her eyes ping open. Bless her. Just the thought of spoiling Grace's day is enough to rouse her.

'She's awake!' Jazz shouts to everyone like she's just unleashed Frankenstein. I think she intends on being reassuring. 'She's awake.'

I drag her arms up to sitting and throw her over my shoulder in a fireman's lift. Damn, the bitch is heavy. It's true what they say, muscle is heavier than fat. I stumble down the aisle with her thrown over my shoulder and run from the room.

As soon as we're in the corridor I place her down on the floor. Her eyes are still sleepy. Jazz comes running out behind us.

'Izzy?' I shout, attempting to bring her round. She's still so out of it. I look up to Jazz. 'Should we call an ambulance?'

'I'm fine.'

We both look down at Izzy, who's trying to sit up already.

'Jesus Izzy, you gave us a fucking heart attack. Are you okay? Do you want a drink or something?' I offer.

'I think I need sugar,' she says in a quiet voice, attempting to take deep breaths.

'I'm on it,' Jazz shouts already running towards reception. 'One doughnut coming up.'

Izzy rolls her eyes. 'A piece of fruit would be better.'

I raise my eyes to the ceiling in annoyance. 'It's probably all of this healthy eating that made you faint! You need to eat more.' All she does is munch on fruit, nuts and seeds. She's not a bloody squirrel.

She pushes me off and goes to stand. 'I eat loads, thanks very much. I don't need processed sugar to mess up my insulin levels.'

I grab her arm and help her to stand properly. 'Whatever, Izzy. You need to take it easy.'

'I'm fine,' she snaps again. 'I'm just tired.'

'Why are you so bloody tired? Probably because you're always exercising, even when you're not with clients.'

She opens her mouth as if to tell me, but quickly shuts it and re-thinks. 'No reason.'

'Don't bullshit me, Izzy,' I snap. 'What's going on? Are things okay with Michael?'

'Of course they are,' she retorts sulkily. 'I just wish there wasn't so much bloody pressure on our relationship.'

'What do you mean?'

Jazz runs back down the hall, stopping her from opening up.

'I could only find a croissant and a banana.'

Izzy's eyes light up like a kid at Christmas. 'Banana please!'

It's official; she's beyond help.

The reception is a hell of a lot calmer. Well, it has been. I seem to have been the only one noticing the guitar player taking full advantage of the free bar. He was drunk, two beers ago. His songs have gone from being upbeat and perky to depressing. Plus he's sweating profusely. Under his shirt are damp patches. It almost put me off my dessert. Almost. I mean it was strawberry and chocolate cheesecake. I could probably eat it off the floor if I'd have dropped it; it's that yummy. It sometimes scares me what I'd be willing to do for desserts.

I turn back to Izzy, who's at our table. 'You're sure you're feeling better now?' I ask.

The thing with Izzy is that she never wants to be any trouble. She could be dying of Ebola, and her last words would be, 'I'm fine, honest.' I decide to keep a close eye on her.

The reception is ridiculously over the top and disgusting. The tablecloths are gold with a black runner. There's a huge clear vase in the centre of the round tables with white roses and dramatic black feathers falling from it. I mean; it's not my taste. Especially with that enormous cake. It's actually bigger than me; a giant magical kingdom made out of cake. It kind of looks like the Disney castle, but I doubt that was her inspiration. Probably more that she sees herself as a queen. It's covered in black, white and gold flowers, with the top of the castle completely covered in edible gold glitter.

*'I'm dying tomorrow, but kiss me today!'* The singer croons, playing strings on his guitar that sound nothing like a song. God, he really is drunk. He's finally getting some stares from other guests.

Ryan raises his eyebrows to me. 'This guy? Is he serious?'

Jazz bursts out laughing. 'I think he's *very* serious. What is he trying to sing anyway?'

*'It might be the last chance to have a roll in the hay,'* he sings.

'Isn't this terribly depressing for a wedding? Should someone tell him?' I ask in all seriousness.

*'But you broke my heart, so I can't grant your wish.'*

'I swear I know this song,' Izzy says, her forehead creased in concentration.

*'So I turn with a swish, I'll never warm you again.'*

'I know it too!' Ollie shouts, suddenly excited.

Jemima claps on his lap excitedly. 'Daddy knows it!' she giggles.

Ollie nods. 'Yeah, isn't it that song with the British guy.'

'You're gonna have to be a bit more specific than that,' I joke, rolling my eyes.

'You know, the one that married the hot American. Called their kids after vegetables.'

I roll my eyes. That could be anyone. Besides, this sounds like a totally made up song. I think this guy is just mental.

Ollie scoffs. 'Can't he sing something upbeat, like *Nelly's* 'Hot in here'? We danced to it at your mum's birthday party last year.'

She pulls a face. 'Vaguely,' she shrugs.

I look to the little makeshift stage. The guy is actually beginning to cry. Jesus, this is a disaster.

Mum's suddenly behind me, squeezing me on the shoulder forcibly. 'Poppy, you *have* to stop this.'

*'Never warm your cold, cold heart again.'* He chokes on his tears

slightly, letting them fall down his cheeks.

I scoff. 'You do it!' Why the hell am I always depended on to save the day?

She lowers her voice to a deadly whisper. 'I'm the groom's mother. It wouldn't be right. But you could have a word with him.'

I look back over at his tear stained face.

'He looks like he's having a breakdown. It might not be safe for me.'

'I mean it, Poppy,' Mum continues, pulling my chair back and basically throwing me towards the stage.

I climb the stairs at the side of the stage slowly, like I'm scared of startling a rare bird. I mean, if he's had a psychotic break he could try and slit my throat with a butter knife for all I know. I can't believe it's always down to me to rescue these ridiculous situations. Especially when my awkwardness normally makes it worse. You'd think they'd have figured that out by now.

I tentatively tap him on the shoulder. He stops playing abruptly and looks up to me, his sweaty forehead shiny under the lights.

'Yes?' he sniffs, wiping his nose with the back of his hand.

Damn, I should have brought him a tissue. That would have got him on my side. Made him see I'm sympathetic.

'Hi,' I wave weirdly. 'Sorry to interrupt, but...well, we've noticed that the music has got a bit depressing. And we wondered...well, actually my mother wondered...if perhaps you could speed it up a bit. You know what I mean, right?'

God, I didn't even understand that. How on earth is this emotional cripple supposed to?

'Sure,' he sniffs, a forced smile on his lips. There's something in his eyes that seem dead. I'm starting to think this guy is a psychopath.

'Thanks.' I do a weird bow before running back to my table.

'Well?' Mum asks me with anxious eyebrows.

'All sorted,' I smile, hoping to God that it is.

*'I hear you're sleeping with the special girl I love...'*

Oh no. He can't seriously be attempting to sing that new song in the charts. He is. Jesus, he is. But please god let it be the censored version.

*'And I wanna say FUCK YOU, ooo, ooo, ooo.'*

'Oh my God,' Ryan utters in disbelief, standing up. 'I have to stop this.'

I stand up with him and start to follow him to the stage. 'Be careful,' I warn, squeezing his strong biceps. Any excuse really. 'He's not in his right mind.'

*'I guess I wasn't rich enough to keep that bitch, so I wanna say FUCK YOOOOOOU, ooo, ooo, ooo.'*

'Mate,' Ryan shouts over the guitar. 'Stop playing! This is *totally* inappropriate.'

*'And fuck you too!'* he sings back at Ryan.

Ryan's shoulders tense and I know he's pissed off to the maximum. He climbs the stage to get closer to him and attempts to take the microphone from him.

'Let go!'

He falls off his chair and is no longer able to play the guitar, thank God, but he's still not letting go of that mike. The whole reception gasps in unison.

'Fuck you, Sandra!' he shouts into the microphone. 'I loved you, and you slept with my brother, you bitch!'

Oh my god, this guy is unreal. Can't he see through his grief that he's ruining a wedding? Not that I'm not secretly pleased its Grace's wedding. I'm evil like that.

'Give me that,' Ryan shouts again lunging for it.

The guy pushes him hard. He stumbles back onto me, his body weight hitting me like a double decker bus. If I wasn't wearing these stupid heels, I might have had a chance. But oh no, this is me we're talking about.

I feel the heel snap and myself falling backwards off the stage. I fall, landing on the side of the food table. It stabs me in the kidneys before I'm thrown to the floor. I look up, dazed, to see the whole wedding staring at something above me. I go to look up, just in time to see the giant wedding cake fall down on top of me, the weight of it completely winding me. Great. Just fucking great.

'What have you *done?*' Grace screams, running over to me. Not offering me a hand or anything, just looking at her broken cake.

I wipe as much icing from my eyes as possible and lick my lips. My God, it tastes amazing. There's only one way I can crawl out of this, and it's with being cocky.

'In my defence, what a yummy cake! Good choice, Grace.'

She screams in frustration before turning on her heel and running away. Ryan's at my side in a second, along with the gang, asking if I'm okay. At least *some* people care about me.

'Yeah,' I nod, wondering how on earth I'm going to get rid of this cake. I mean; will normal shampoo get rid of it? Can I just pop home quickly now for a shower or is that bad form at a wedding?

'Pops, I told you heels from Primark aren't going to last that long,' Jazz tells me off with a worried look on her face.

Izzy's already attempting to take cake out of my hair. God love her.

'I couldn't afford a new pair, okay?' I snap, pissed that she's picking this very moment to pick on me.

'I've told you; I've got money now. I could have bought you a pair of bloody shoes.'

There she goes, throwing her money around again. It's really beginning to get irritating.

'I don't need your charity, Jazz! I can buy my own bloody pair of shoes, thanks very much.'

'You *just* said that you can't,' she says back calmly, looking at me as if I'm an alien.

'I can! I just don't need you throwing your money in my face like it's going to save everything. I'd still have fallen.' I can't help but sound bitchy. I'm not even mad at Jazz; I'm just mad that I have cake in my hair, and she's the closest person I can shout at.

Mum finally comes rushing over to me with a sour, sad expression painted on her face.

'Oh, Poppy, darling. You really can't do one family event without causing a disaster, can you?'

Blaming me. Of course she'd blame me. Not the nutty guitarist that seems to have escaped unharmed.

'Oh shut up, Mum,' I shout, standing up and running to the toilets.

## Jazz

'Can you believe Poppy?' I moan to Ollie as soon as she's gone. 'What's her bloody problem?'

'She was covered in cake,' he counters, raising his eyebrows like I don't get it. 'In my experience, that's not the best time to diss her shoes.'

I glare back at him. 'I didn't diss them.' Well...not exactly. 'I just don't see what her problem is.'

If someone was offering me Prada over Primark, I'd have bitten their hand off.

He looks sad for a second. 'Her problem is that you've changed.'

'Excuse me?' I snap, so shocked I can feel my eyes bugging out of my head.

Izzy swiftly picks up Jemima and takes her away from what she knows is going to be an almighty fight. Well, on my side. This guy is losing. Izzy's such a champ.

He sighs, leaning on one elbow on the table. 'You have to admit that the money has changed you. It's changed all of our relationships with you. There's nothing worse than someone trying to throw money at you all of the time.'

How can he see money as an insult? And have they all been talking about me?

'I wasn't throwing money at her. I was just offering her my help.' What's wrong with them all?

He locks his blue eyes with mine. 'Be honest with yourself, Jazz. You weren't. Offering help would have been taking her to the bathroom to help wash it out. Not dissing her shoes and offering to buy new ones.'

Ouch.

God, I hate that he actually makes sense. It makes it so much harder to be mad at him.

'Okay, so maybe I'm wrong,' I begrudgingly admit, crossing my arms over my chest.

'Lucky for you, I still love you,' he winks cheekily, wrapping his arm around my shoulders. 'In fact, play your cards right and you might get lucky tonight.'

I roll my eyes sarcastically, even though a thrill of excitement dances through me.

'A girl can dream.'

## Poppy

Ryan walks into the ladies toilets like he owns the place. It's beyond sexy. Especially in that navy suit that fits him like a glove.

He sees me leaning over the sink and smiles apologetically.

'Pops.' He walks over to me and pulls me into his chest for a hug.

'But I'm still covered in cake,' I protest, not relaxing into him.

He looks down at me with amused eyes. 'So now I'll have cake on me. We can match.' God, he's so sweet. What did I ever do to deserve him?

I sigh and relax into his strong chest, his muscled arms around my waist.

'I'm sorry I'm such a loser,' I sigh.

He pushes me back, with a horrified expression on his face, his eyebrows to the sky.

'Pops, don't ever say that you're a loser. So you fell? So what? We're all used to it. In a way, if you hadn't, we'd have been worried. There would have probably been rumours that the marriage was doomed because of it.'

I smile, despite feeling shitty. His poor suit is now smudged with the remains of icing. There's even some on his chin. I really want to lick it off.

'So you love me regardless?'

'Of course,' he smiles, leaning in to lick some cake from my chin. Tingles run down my spine. 'Now let's go out there and start the dancing off.'

How did I ever end up with this dream man?

'Unless you'd like a quick shag here?'

'I'll take the second option.'

# Chapter 12
### Poppy

*Monday 8<sup>th</sup> February*

I woke up yesterday morning feeling a lot better about Dad and his whole cancer thing. Well, actually I woke up in my next-door neighbour's flowerbed and found I'd murdered three of her garden gnomes. Whoops. I'm going to have to get her replacements.

Anyway, as I was saying, Dad promised that he'd tell Mum on Sunday. The relief that now Mum knows is unreal. If she would have found out any other way she would have skinned me alive and left my remains for Ryan to find. She really is that vicious.

Dad texted me last night and asked me to take them both to the hospital today for his op. So as I beep outside their house at ten am I'm feeling a little bit jittery. She's bound to bombard me with questions about how long I knew and ask all of the same questions she's no doubt asked Dad yesterday. I've had six cups of tea so I feel ready for her.

Dad runs out wearing his thick black coat with the scarf Mum attempted to knit him last year. It can't even be described as a scarf really, more like a tie, it's so thin. Plus it has large holes in it. There really is no point in wearing it as it keeps in no heat, but he loves to make her happy. He jumps into the car, warming his hands on my pathetic car heater.

I look towards the front door, which is shut. What the hell is going on? 'Where's Mum?'

'She can't come,' he babbles quickly, not looking away from the heater.

'Why not?' I ask, narrowing my eyes at him, telepathically telling him to look me in the eye when he tries to lie to me.

He continues to look at the heaters. 'Her programmes are on.'

He must think I'm thick as shit.

'Cut the crap, Dad! Why didn't you tell her?' I shriek. I'm half tempted to march in there and tell her myself.

He looks down at the floor. 'I just couldn't Poppy. She got a call last night from an old friend whose husband died. She was all cut up about it, and I just couldn't add to it.'

That's annoyingly understandable. I sigh, indicating to pull out. 'I *suppose* I can see how that was hard for you,' I admit begrudgingly. 'But you still should have told her.'

He smiles back at me smugly. 'There's no need really. After this operation, it'll all be over.'

Is he *serious?* He can't be that naïve...can he?

'What if you need chemo? And are you forgetting that you'll only have one ball left? I'm pretty sure your wife is going to notice, don't you?'

Eww. I physically shiver at the idea of them having sex.

He smirks. 'We aren't that intimate these days; truth be told. Since your mum went through the menopause...'

'Eugh! Stop!' I shriek, almost crashing into a cyclist. 'I don't want to hear about the ins and outs of your sex life. I'm happy to think you've only had sex four times. Only to conceive us all.'

His mouth twitches. 'Well, you did ask, love.'

I shake my head, hoping the images of Mum and Dad having sex someday get erased. Bleurgh!

'So how are you going to explain you being away in hospital for the next few days?'

'I've told her I'm going to visit my friend Tom who's just had a heart attack. Said you were dropping me at the station.'

I growl in frustration. 'So you still involved me in the lie? If she finds out, she'll bloody kill me.'

My stomach starts doing back-flips. I hate lies. Especially when my

Mother is involved. I'm just not someone who sneaks around easily.

He sighs and looks out of the window at the fresh falling rain. 'I wouldn't have done it if I didn't feel it was necessary, Poppy Pocket.'

I sigh. I can see why, but I'd need Ryan with me if I were going through something like this.

'But you have to tell her afterwards, right?'

He looks back at me with a sad smile. 'Let's discuss it afterwards shall we? There might not be any need to worry her.'

'Dad!'

'It's my wish, Poppy!' he barks, making me physically jump.

Wow, this cancer is not looking good on Dad. He never speaks to me like this.

'I'm sorry,' he admits on a sigh. 'I'm just nervous and I don't think you should be worrying me more than I already am right now. You said you'd come to support me, so I expect you to support me. Otherwise, you can drop me off at the nearest bus station.'

I roll my eyes. The drama llama. 'You've been hanging out with Mum too much.' He knows we're almost there too.

'Thanks, Poppy Pocket. I owe you one.'

One? More like a bloody million.

## Jazz

I've been at home all day looking online for inspiration of how to decorate the new house. Poppy should have never introduced me to Pinterest. I'm so bloody excited! My very own house! And okay, maybe I've let Jemima run mad with the toys. And maybe I haven't even bothered taking my dishes and cups all the way to the sink, but I've been busy. And okay, majorly lazy too, but whatever. I'm too rich to clean up after myself. Ooh, that's another thing to add to my to-do list; hire a cleaner. You know, along with washing myself today.

The door bangs shut and I hear Meryl's heels click along the wooden floor. I'm happy to carry on hiding in the sitting room. I just know she's in a bad mood even from the way she's walking. Jemima's napping and I really don't want to have to deal with people today.

I hear her loudly sigh. Oh God, I really hope she doesn't kick off. She hates mess. I think cleaning her house is the only thing stopping her from being a full-blown alcoholic.

Better I just get it over and done with. If she wants to whinge, she'll find me anyway. I drag myself off the sofa and walk into the kitchen.

I force myself to smile. 'Hi,' I say brightly.

She turns, her eyes possessed. Wow, I didn't expect her to be *this* mad. I'm almost imagining steam coming out of her ears.

'Have you honestly been here *all* day and you've not cleaned up after yourself *once?*' she shrieks in pure disbelief, her face scrunched up.

I roll my eyes. Jesus, she can be dramatic sometimes.

'It's just a few dishes, Meryl.' I shrug. 'I'll clean it up later.'

Her eyes bulge out of her head in rage. 'No, *I'll* clean it up now. It's always me cleaning up after everybody,' she hisses under her breath.

Well, she has me there. She *is* always tidying up, but still. She's just so bloody impatient when it comes to these things. I'll clean it up, just later. I hate having to work to her schedule. This is why I can't wait til we're in our new place. I can just relax.

'Try not to be so dramatic, Meryl. I said I'll clean it later and I will.'

She turns back to me, her eyes wide with a fury I've never seen from her before. It makes my own eyes widen in fear.

'Dramatic?' she screams, visibly shaking with temper. 'Am I really being dramatic because I don't want to live in a dirty squat? No, you haven't even SEEN me dramatic!'

Woah. I've unleashed a beast.

'Ok, calm down,' I snap rolling my eyes and crossing my arms. She always makes me feel like a teenager. I hate that about her.

Her face and neck turn bright red in rage. Okay, wrong thing to say. I start to slowly back away.

'Calm down? Calm fucking down? I'll show you what really dramatic is!' She picks up a dirty mug. 'I suppose we might as well just get rid of mugs if we can't keep them clean.' She smashes it onto the floor, the last remnants of tea spilling onto the tiled floor along with the shattered pieces.

My eyes nearly bulge out of my sockets. What the hell is she on?

She picks up another and smashes that one too, it crashing into tiny pieces.

'Meryl, stop!' I scream. 'I'll get a maid if it makes you happy!'

She picks up a cereal bowl and smashes that too, remnants of Rice Krispies all over the floor. She's fucking insane!

'Oh, that's your answer for everything. Throw money at it. My name's Jazz and I'm *so* rich I don't have to do my own dishes! And it's not like we actually do them. We HAVE a dishwasher!!' She picks up a plate, throws the toast in the sink before launching it over my head. I duck just in time for it to smash into the wall behind me.

'Meryl, stop!' I yell at the top of my lungs. This is some scary shit.

'Why should I, huh?' She starts opening the cupboards and throwing everything she can find on the floor. She's going to be left with nothing if she carries on.

Jemima starts crying on the baby monitor. Great, she's woken her up. She hates being woken up. Now she'll be in a horrible mood all day.

'You've woken Jemima now. Well done,' I say bravely, quickly regretting my words.

Her face twists with hurt. 'Oh, well I wouldn't worry about that. Soon you'll be in your new house miles away, and Jemima won't even remember my name!'

I roll my eyes. 'It's Nana. It's really not that hard,' I snap sarcastically. 'And maybe she'll be better off if you're starting to act this crazy.'

I turn on my heel, desperately trying to ignore the devastation in her face as I storm upstairs.

## Poppy

Dad looks up at me from his hospital bed, wearing that horrible white and grey gown. I wonder if they wash them in between patients or throw them away? I hope they're disposable.

He's going to be taken into surgery any minute now, and I could vomit from anxiety. My stomach is lurching violently like I'm at the top of a rollercoaster expecting to fall any minute. But I have to be strong for him. Act all confident, like this is the kind of thing that he does every day.

The doctor arrives with a cheery smile. 'We ready here?'

I look to Dad. He gives me back a weak smile. Oh God, this is it. I have to say goodbye to him. I try to commit his features to memory. His cute wrinkled brown eyes. His rosy chubby cheeks. God, what the hell would I do if I lost him? A heavy ache hits me in the chest sending fear shooting through my body. I swallow the lump in my throat and force a smile, trying to be optimistic, when my eyes are stinging with unshed tears.

'Yep, we're good to go, right, Dad?' My voice doesn't even sound like it belongs to me.

He suddenly grabs my hand and squeezes it. 'Love you, Poppy Pocket.' Oh God, he looks like he might burst into tears himself. I try to memorise the warmth of his words.

'Love you too,' I smile. 'Now stop being all soppy and go, get your ball cut off.'

He smiles as he's wheeled away. This is fine. He's going to be fine. But then why do I feel like an orphan?

My phone rings and Jazz's name flashes up. I'm not supposed to pick up the phone in here, so I decide to let it ring off while I get the lift downstairs and step outside. I take a deep breath of the fresh air before returning her call.

'Thank God!' she shrieks down the line panting heavily. 'I'm locked in Jemima's room.'

'What do you mean you're locked in Jemima's room?' I ask down the phone.

'I mean that your Mother has gone fucking crazy. I'm half expecting her to put an axe through the door like in The Shining.' She's whispering as if she's scared for her safety.

'Don't be ridiculous,' I snort. Although anything, really is possible with my mother.

'I mean it, Pops. I've never seen her *this* bad.'

'That's because you've only been living with her a few years. Try a lifetime and you soon see the mega crazy.'

God, I need a wee.

'Maybe. Anyway, Ollie's on his way home to sort it out. I just wanted you on the phone in case she murdered me.' I hear Jemima shuffle close to the phone. 'Mummy, what does murder mean?'

Oh, Jesus.

'Err...it means...cuddle,' I shout down the phone. 'Anyway, Jazz, I've really gotta pee.'

'Ok babe, I'm out.'

She hangs up the phone, and I can finally run back into the hospital and go to the toilet. I'm sat there when I realise I can smell something fishy. What the hell is that? Has some gross woman been in here with her smelly vagina stinking out the place? Ugh, how utterly gross. I sniff a bit more and realise, to my horror that the smell is coming from my vagina. Crap. I must have an infection or something.

I quickly run up to Dad's ward and ask the nurses to call me when he's out, and then I drive home.

I'm just waiting for the doctor's surgery to call me back when I start thinking. I only came on a few nights ago. And since then I haven't had any blood. That's weird. Could it be some sort of period-related infection?

A sinking feeling creeps into my stomach. Wait...I *did* take out that tampon I put in that night...right? Please fucking god say that I took it out. I try desperately to trace my mind back. That was before the wedding, the night of such a whirlwind of emotions. Dealing with Grace's racist parents, the police, not to mention being starving. Crap, I just passed out on the bed when I got back.

I rush to the bathroom and grab my pocket mirror. I position it down there, but all I can see is my vagina. Ewe, vaginas are *not* pretty. Plus mine could really do with a groom. I try, while gagging, to spread myself open so I can see inside. It still doesn't help. Fuck.

I put down the mirror and instead feel around with my fingers. This is so *beyond* gross. Why does stuff like this have to happen to me? I can't feel any string. But wait. Yes, I think it is in there. As I pat myself, I can feel my fingers on the inside until I get to the very top. Then I don't feel my prodding. I gulp. That must be it.

What the fuck am I going to do? Should I go to the doctors and ask for help? I'd rather die than live through that shame. Nope, I'm gonna have to pull up my big girl knickers and sort myself out. Or in my case, pull my big girl knickers down further. I take a deep breath and bend over, determined.

I grab around in there until I start to wonder if I am just mutilating myself for no reason. Then suddenly I feel something move. It dislodges and I'm finally able to remove it. Blood comes gushing out along with it. I'm nearly sick from how gross this is. Thank God I'll never have to tell a soul.

I run myself a quick bath and submerge myself in it. Thank God Jazz bought me some of that fanny wash for a joke at Christmas. Who knew I'd actually need it! Not that I think I'll ever feel clean again after this.

I get out and dry myself off, but even after going into the bedroom I can't shake feeling hot, almost boiling. I just assume it's the steam of the bath, but now I'm worried. I lie down on the bed completely naked, glad for my blinds. Why am I so bloody hot? I feel a headache coming on, so I take two paracetamol and decide to have a sleep. Who wouldn't need a sleep after all that drama?

I wake up, feeling like I'm on fire. Fuck, why the hell am I still so hot?

I look at my phone. I slept for a whole hour, but if anything I feel worse. I've got a sore throat now, and I ache all over. What the hell? Am I getting the flu? I don't have time to question it as I feel vomit threatening to rise from my stomach. I rush into the bathroom, just in time to vomit into the sink. Ugh. I have to call Ryan. I make it back into the room, grab my phone and call him while I collapse back onto the bed.

'Hey, babe,' he answers. 'You okay?' he asks when I don't answer right away.

'I need you, babe. I think I'm sick.'

'Oh, babe, you don't sound well. Don't worry, I'll leave now.'

'Okay, love you,' I croak, my throat like razor blades.

'Love you too.'

He hangs up and for some reason, I'm suddenly praying to God that's not the last time I ever speak to him. I feel rough as hell. Now I'm starting to feel dizzy.

Suddenly Ryan's waking me up. I realise I must have dozed off again, and he's found me butt-naked and spread eagle on the bed. Under normal circumstances, he might have been a bit turned on, but he looks nothing but worried.

'Pops? You look awful. We need to get you to a hospital. Come on.' He takes my hand and guides me up to standing. 'I just have to get you a dressing gown or something.'

'Too hot,' I manage to breathe out, the room spinning around me.

Before I have time to steady myself I'm falling to the floor. Ryan catches me before I bash my head on the bedside cabinet.

'Fuck! Pops!'

I arrive at the hospital, carried in by Ryan, having barely remembered the journey. There's lots of shouting, and then I'm placed onto a bed. A doctor comes over to assess me. Through my dizzy haze, I see Ryan's face change with recognition.

'David?' he asks with a smile.

'Ryan! How are you mate?' he smiles back. 'It's been bloody years.'

'Too long,' Ryan agrees, back-smacking him.

Err, hello? Have they just forgotten about the patient here? I discreetly cough, which seems to make them remember I'm here. He assesses his clipboard.

'Right, Mrs Davis, your husband here tells me you have flu-like symptoms and passed out just before arriving here.'

'Yeah,' I nod weakly, my voice a croak.

'Okay. And can you think of anything specific right before the symptoms came on that you think could be related?'

Oh fuck. Could this really be related to the tampon? Am I that dumb that I didn't put them both together? Shit. And it's not like I can just tell him. He's Ryan's old friend. He'd be mortified.

'Um...'

'Yes?' he asks hopefully.

'Well...it's a little embarrassing.' A little? More like rather kill yourself than admit it embarrassing.

'Absolutely anything,' he presses. 'It could help us massively.'

I look to Ryan for support. He smiles encouragingly. 'Just say it, babe. Anything to make you better.' He looks worried sick.

Oh God. Kill me now. This would be easier if I didn't feel so lousy.

'Well...I kind of...' I lower my voice to a whisper. 'Had a...tampon stuck in me.'

Silence greets me. I can't look at Ryan, but I can feel his eyes burning into my skull.

Oh God. Just when I thought it couldn't get any worse.

'Okay,' David nods. 'And was the tampon stuck for long?'

I take a deep breath. Just get this over and done with quickly. Rip it off like a plaster.

'For three days.'

His mouth drops, but ever the professional he quickly recovers himself. I have a feeling Ryan's face is anything but recovered.

'Okay. I'm pretty sure you have what is called Toxic Shock Syndrome. You did the right thing in telling us. Right now we can just give you some antibiotics and send you home, but if you'd have delayed even by a day your life could have been threatened.'

I nod. All from a bloody tampon? I'm never bloody using them again. Not with the memory I've got.

'We'll give you something now; I'll write you a prescription. Then you can be on your way.' He smiles quickly at Ryan before walking off.

A cold, creepy silence descends upon us. I don't look at him for fear of the humiliation. That's the worst thing about being a wife. You don't just embarrass yourself; you embarrass them too. It's not my fault there's something wrong with me.

'Pops,' he sighs.

'Don't,' I snap. 'Just don't.'

# Chapter 13
## Jazz

*Wednesday 10<sup>th</sup> February*

Today I'm at Mum's, in the country. She and Edward still insist on living their life here, raising hens or whatever it is they do. I needed to get out of that house. The bad vibes with Meryl are slowly killing me, crawling underneath my skin and setting up camp. I wish she'd shout more, but this whole awkward 'I'm fine,' shit is awful. It makes my stomach churn.

Plus, it's a good excuse for Jemima to see her other Nana, although my mum insists on being called Mutti. How ridiculous. Everyone knows at her age she's not Jemima's mother. It's just embarrassing. And why a German form of Mum? We're not German. She's originally from Scandinavia for God's sakes.

Jemima's chasing ducks around the garden while Mum brings me out a cup of tea. I have to say she has become a lot more normal since moving here. I mean, when I was growing up she'd never make tea. She had staff to do all of that. Poppy still rips the piss out of me because we used to have a butler.

I'm shocked she agreed to sit out here in the cold, but like me, she's all bundled up with a scarf, hat and gloves. Sometimes there's nothing better than being outside on a cold day when the sun is shining on your face.

'So, darling,' she smiles, her Botox-filled face hardly moving. 'Tell me, how are you finding your new-found money?'

'It's fabulous, obviously,' I laugh. 'Jesus, what did you expect me to say? That I'm not enjoying it? Whoever said money doesn't buy happiness has clearly never had as much as me.'

She frowns. 'This is what I'm worried about, darling.'

I sigh. Trust my mother to bring me down. I've just escaped Meryl's madness. I was hoping for a drama free day today.

'What?' I snap, practically snarling at her. 'What are you worried about, mum?'

I imagine her forehead would wrinkle now if she could move it.

'That you'll get carried away, darling. I know you have an awful lot of money, but remember that it can still be spent and diminish.'

I roll my eyes. 'Mum, I have twenty million. I'm pretty sure I'm not going to run out anytime soon.'

'I'm just saying that you should treasure the friends you had beforehand. The people that were there for you before the money came along. As soon as I married your father I inherited a lot of fake friends.'

Oh god. Why does she feel like she can lecture me on the way I live my life? I have no idea. We're hardly close, and she was never even really present when I was growing up. How she can think she can just move to a farm and then start preaching to me is beyond ridiculous.

'Thanks, Mother, but I can run my own life.' I throw the blankets off myself and stand up wanting to get away from her.

'I'm just proud of the woman you've become.' This shocks me so much I freeze in place. It always shocks me when she says she's proud of me. It's so rare to hear. 'I don't want you to throw that all away for some new frivolous lifestyle with plastic friends.'

I can't help but roll my eyes. What a hypocrite.

'Thanks for your concern, mother. But I can run my own life. And in case you're forgetting, you're one of the most plastic people on the earth.'

Her eyes widen in shock. 'Just because I've had three boob jobs does *not* mean I'm plastic.'

I wave Jemima over. 'Yeah, well that's where we differ on opinion.'

On the way home I make a decision to ignore my batty mother and carry on living my life exactly the way I want to. Hell, I have the money now. Why the fuck would I listen to her?

## Poppy

### *Wednesday 10th February*

To: Poppyisawesome@hotmail.com
From: Lindadavis4321@gmail.com


*Oh, you poor girl! Sending all of my love to your father and your family. Have they found out if it's treatable yet?*

*Thank you so much for the photos. I have them all printed off and stuck on my notice board. I'm so grateful you let me see my baby boy growing into such an amazing man. I had a quiet Christmas, just went down the centre for a dinner.*

*Are you two thinking of having a baby anytime soon?*


*All my love*
*Linda xxx*

## Poppy

### *Wednesday 10th February*

Great, now I'm getting pressure from Linda too. That's the last thing I need right now. Despite this, today things seem a bit better. My Dad's surgery went well. They think they've got all of the cancer, but it'll be confirmed soon. He's coming home today, and I'll feel so much better when he is. I must remember to pick him up.

Plus my antibiotics have started to work their magic, and I'm feeling a hell of a lot better. Not that I think Ryan will ever look at me the same way again. I mean why does this stuff keep happening to me? Do I have dementia? Who forgets a tampon? Am I going to have to set myself reminders on my phone every time I put one in?

Today's also the day we've scheduled in to do Ryan's sperm test. I'm glad the attention is off me as Ryan hasn't stopped winding me up since the whole tampon toxic shock incident. Only, it's not something you can just do the night before and drop off. No, it needs to be fresh apparently. Done within two hours of the drop off window. Who knew?! So at 8 am we're awkwardly sat over breakfast, knowing that he has to go and wank into a cup soon.

'Another cup of tea?' I offer, skirting around the elephant in the room. Or penis.

He looks ahead as if he hasn't heard me, staring into space. Oh God, he's nervous.

'Ryan?'

He looks up as if just realising I'm trying to speak to him. 'Sorry, what?'

I swallow down the lump of panic. 'Look, babe, I know you're nervous. I would be too. But we just need to get it over and done with, you know.'

He fidgets on his chair, biting his lip. 'Yeah. I just...I've a lot on my mind. Anyway,' he shakes his head, clearly trying to pull himself together, 'I'm gonna go upstairs. Maybe...don't come up for a while, okay?'

Oh god. 'Err...okay.' This is *so* bloody awkward.

He walks away, leaving me knowing he's going to choke the chicken. It makes me wonder how many times he's done this before. I could be down here minding my own business, oblivious that he's upstairs whacking one off. I suppose I've assumed he doesn't have the time, but maybe he squeezes it in.

I bet he's so nervous. How on earth will he be able to get a hard on if he's freaking out this much? Does he have dirty magazines up there? I clean the house, and I've never found one. Mind you, I suppose magazines are pretty old school these days. There're so many porn sites you can access from your phone. Maybe I'll just go to the door and listen in; see if he's found something to watch.

I creep upstairs, cringing every time a step creaks. This feels so wrong, like I'm invading his privacy, but I want to check he's okay. I place my ear against our bedroom door, but I can't hear a thing. Silence. Definitely no slapping of skin or grunting. And definitely, no horny woman screaming to do me harder. My poor baby. I have to help him. But how can I help without coming across as condescending?

I know! I can turn him on. Of course, that's the solution, I need to give him something to wank over. I'll seduce him.

I rush to the bathroom to look at myself in the mirror. I'll admit, I don't look my best, but I'm not repulsive either. I've got slightly greasy hair, but the dry shampoo helps. My makeup is okay. I add some lip gloss and unbutton three buttons on my blouse, adjusting my cleavage, so it looks half decent.

I walk slowly to the door psyching myself up. You can do this. You can do sexy. The guy married you didn't he?

I take a deep breath and open the door slightly. Think sexy seductress. I point my leg through while singing *'I'm sexy, and you know it.'*

Then I smash the door wide open, a determined look on my face. Ryan's sat on the bed with his limp dick out, frozen, staring at me. He seems stunned. Good. He must need me to go on.

I dance on over to him, continuing the song in my head. I should have thought ahead and brought a CD player up with me.

*'When I walk in a room, everyone's looking like damn she's hot.'*

I kick my leg up onto the dresser knocking over my hair spray and moisturiser. Oops. I run my hand over it slowly, as seductively as I can. Imagine you're Dita Von Teese.

*'I dance to the beat, thrusting my hips like I'm a sexy freak.'*

I grab hold of the waistband of my jeggings and pull them down before I can wimp out. I'm getting into it now. Ryan looks totally gobsmacked. I *knew* he'd love this surprise.

I lean down to try and remove my legs from them. Damn these jeggings are tight at the ankle. Again, if I'd have been a good wife and thought ahead, I could have bought those stripper trousers with the Velcro. Would have made it so much easier.

*'This is how I creep, seducing everyone with my eyebrows, so fleek.'* I get one leg out but then trip on the other one. I crash down onto my bum but

quickly try to make it look like it's planned, thrusting my pelvis up in the air. I sprawl my hands out on the carpet and lift myself up to standing as elegantly as I can.

I pull my jumper over my head, messing my hair up and shimmy over to him, flexing my hips forward and back.

*'I really want you now and I'm not afraid to say it, say it, say it.'*

This is hard work. I'm bloody sweating. Time for my finale.

*'I'm sexy, and you know it.'* I flail my arms around, circling my hips to the imaginary music. Then I turn around and back into his lap, arse first. I sit down, expecting to feel a raging hard on through my cotton knickers. Only...I can't feel anything.

I turn round to face him. He lifts an eyebrow, a playful smile on his face.

'Babe, you're the cutest.'

He thinks I'm *cute?* Fucking *cute?*

I frown, confused. 'You mean...I haven't turned you on?'

'Oh, babe...' his smile turns into concern. 'You didn't seriously think that would work, did you?'

'Err, yeah!' I can't help but feel offended. 'At least I'm trying! You're just sitting there like having a wank is the hardest thing in the world. Just bloody get on with it.' Wow, I sounded far more pissed off than I feel.

But maybe I am pissed off. Maybe I'm a little angry at the world for having to go through this at all. I mean; I'm a young healthy woman dammit. I shouldn't have to go through this shit. Bloody Heroin addicts get pregnant and give birth to babies. They don't make it look that bloody hard. And here we are, a responsible married couple, desperate for a baby of our own, and for whatever reason we can't seem to do it.

'Pops, it's harder than you think.'

I look down at his limp dick. 'Nope, nothing's hard right now.' I can't help but be mean. He dissed my dancing. 'You know some men would pay good money to see me dance like that.'

He laughs, an adorable smile on his face. 'I suppose the world is full of strange people.'

I crack a smile, digging him in the ribs. I hate how he can make me laugh even when he's taking the piss out of me.

'It's not funny. I was trying to be sexy!'

The corners of his mouth lift like I'm adorable and tucks a bit of hair behind my ear.

'Pops, what you don't realise is that I think you're the sexiest woman in the world. That's why I put a ring on your finger and married you. But you're sexiest when you don't even realise. Not....' he points at my half-dressed state, 'like this.'

I look down at my boring mismatched underwear. I *Really* should have thought ahead.

I turn to face him, placing my hand on his chest. 'Be honest with me, Ryan. Are you scared? What is it?'

'Of course I'm scared,' he admits on a sigh. 'What if it *is* me? What if I have a low or non-existent sperm count, and it's all my fault we can't have a baby.'

How can he even think that?

'Woah! It wouldn't be your fault, babe. Whatever we have to face we'll do it together. It's not going to be anyone's fault. If we have a problem, we'll sort it out together.' I mean it too.

His sad eyes meet mine. 'Okay, I know you're saying that now. But a few years down the line you might resent the fuck out of me.'

I can't pretend I haven't thought of this myself; only fearing it's *my* fault.

I shake my head. 'I don't even know why we're having this conversation. You haven't even wanked in the cup yet. Let alone had any scary results.'

He smiles weakly, pulling my hips into him. 'You're right, I suppose.'

'Exactly,' I smile. 'Aren't I always?' I add with a chuckle. 'Now do you need me to rub my small boobies in your face for you to come or do you think you can handle this by yourself?'

He grins. 'I think I've got this, babe. But thanks. Strangely enough, it means a lot.'

We have to deliver it to the hospital within two hours of it being...err, evacuated, for want of a better word. The car journey is tense. He wanted to go alone, but I insisted I come with him. He needs my support, even if he's too stubborn to admit it.

We get caught in traffic, but make it into the car park with twenty minutes to spare. Only...then we have to find a parking space. By the time we're rushing into the reception, there are only five minutes to spare, and I'm worrying we'll have gone through all of this for nothing.

'Where the fuck do I go?' he asks, grabbing the back of his neck in panic.

I grab his arm and walk up to the main reception dragging him along with me. A lady with red hair and ridiculously long nails sits behind it chewing gum. I hate her already.

'Excuse me,' I say loudly, gaining her attention. 'But we're...um...' Shit, how do I put it? I look around at the nosey people in the waiting area. 'We're delivering...something.' I look to Ryan for help, but he's staring down at the floor, his cheeks bright red. I've never seen him so embarrassed. 'Sort of...baby related?' I try desperately to communicate with my eyes what I mean.

She stares at me blankly. Great.

'Sperm,' I whisper. 'My husband needs to drop off a sperm sample.'

Her lips fall open as she stares at Ryan in shock. Judgmental fucking bitch. She must be wondering how someone as gorgeous and manly as him can have a problem knocking a girl up. Mind your own business.

'So, the department?' I snap loudly. My hands start to shake. I could take this bitch. Visions of me reaching across and shoving her face down repeatedly onto the desk flash through my head.

'Oh,' she shakes her head as if knocking some sense into herself. 'Down the hall to the right.'

'Thank you,' Ryan murmurs, clasping my arm and pulling me towards where she indicated.

'That bitch is lucky I didn't smack her one,' I hiss, trying to channel my inner ghetto bitch. I try to think how Lily would have handled it. The girl would probably have had her face smashed into the desk by now. And her extensions pulled out.

'Yeah, right,' Ryan smiles, his skin colour slowly going back to normal. 'You hate confrontation. You'd probably just write her a stern letter.' He grins down affectionately at me.

I was actually thinking about it. Not that I'd admit that now.

'Whatever,' I snort pushing him forward.

We turn the corner and walk straight into a man with familiar blue eyes. I lean back to apologise, recognition hitting me. Crap, it's Stuart. Stuart; my ex-fucking-boyfriend Stuart. Of all the bloody people, why did we have to bump into him today? Right now?

His face lights up in realisation. 'Oh my god. Poppy! Ryan!' Damn it he sounds chipper. 'How are you?'

Oh, you know, just late to drop off some semen.

Ryan looks to me, absolute horror showing clear on his face, his eyes looking at me for guidance. Poor thing. Shame I'm just as useless.

'Um…just…I hurt my leg,' I mumble, reaching down to it dramatically.

Ryan looks anxiously at his watch. Shit, I totally forgot that we're against the clock. I need to wrap this up quick.

'Trust you, eh, Pops,' he laughs, his arrogant smirk making me want to pummel him to death.

Ryan tenses beside me. Stuart's being too familiar with me. It's pissing him off.

'Anyway, we should probably go,' Ryan says, attempting to step around him.

'Aren't you going to ask me why I'm here?' Stuart says, a ridiculously happy smile on his face.

Oh God. He's such an annoying twat. How did I ever go out with him? I must have been drunk the *entire* time.

Ryan sighs heavily, raking his hand through his hair. I suppose we can't scream for him to get out of our way as we have two minutes left to deliver a very important sperm sample.

'Why are you here?' Ryan asks, bad tempered.

There's that grin on Stuart's lips again. God, I could knock him out.

'I've just had a baby.'

Ryan and I freeze, our mouths falling open in surprise.

'Wha...what?' I manage, my tongue shaking so hard I fear I might swallow it.

Is *everyone* having babies?

'Well, obviously not me. My girlfriend Daisy.'

Daisy? I hate her already. I bet she's all cheery all the time. I bet she fell pregnant by accident; life's just that easy for her.

Ryan clears his throat, obviously trying to compose himself. 'Congratulations,' he says with as much enthusiasm as he can muster. It's still pretty poor. I squeeze his hand in an act of solidarity.

'Yeah,' I nod, unable to say anything else.

'Thanks, guys,' he gushes, his smile brighter than the sun. 'We've just brought her in today for a check-up. Only three days old. Eight pounds two. Esme Rose. As you can tell, I'm over the moon. The champ did it with no pain medication. Was just coming down here to get her a snack.'

Ugh, isn't she bloody great.

'Happy for you,' I force out, using every last drop of self-control not to grit my teeth.

'Thanks,' he gushes. 'When are you guys going to have kids then?'

Ugh. The question I dread the most. And no-one worse for it to come from than my ex-boyfriend in his smug 'just had a baby' haze.

'We're waiting, thanks,' I snap. 'Want to enjoy ourselves for a while first.' I stroke Ryan's bicep as seductively as I can.

Ryan nods his agreement.

'Well, don't wait too long,' he says, suddenly looking terribly concerned. 'You're thirty soon, Pops. No spring chicken. Daisy's only twenty-four.'

Of *course* she is. And what the fuck does he mean by that? I'm still in my bloody twenties for God's sakes!

'You wanna pop one out soon before your eggs all dry up.' He grins as if this is a hilarious joke.

'Oh, thanks,' I snarl. I look to Ryan, who looks like he might lose it. I need to diffuse this before he kills him. 'Anyway, we must go.' I hurry away with Ryan.

'I thought you hurt your leg?' he shouts after me with a chuckle.

'Oh, just fuck off Stuart!'

# Chapter 14

*Wednesday 10th February*

*From: Poppyisawesome@hotmail.com*

*To: Lindadavis4321@gmail.com*

*Hi Linda,*

*They think they got all of Dad's cancer in the operation. Fingers crossed it stays away. Really shook me, but obviously, please keep it quiet. My Dad is keeping it a secret for now. I know it's not like you'll bump into anyone living that far away from us but still.*

*No, Ryan and I are just enjoying each other for now. Plenty of time for babies. Do you have any news?*

*Poppy xxx*

Jazz

*Friday 12th February*

Poppy shouldn't be stressing me out about her Mother. I mean, Jesus, I probably know the woman more than she does. I'm the one who's endured living with her for the last couple of years. Can't she see that now I just want to have fun for a while? Go back to being the old me?

Talking of being back to the old me, Lilly and I wait in the beautifully presented waiting room in Harley Street. It's painted a pale pink and has water features in every corner, obviously designed to try and relax us. Not that it's working. Okay, I admit it. I'm nervous. I somehow talked Lilly into us getting Botox together. I'm not really sure how it happened. One minute we were having coffee gossiping about her wedding and then I just mentioned how I was sick of frown lines on my forehead and was considering Botox. I was half joking but the way Lilly nodded along made me re-consider. I mean does everyone discuss my wrinkly forehead behind my back or something? How cruel.

Anyway, she said she'd like to get rid of her laughter lines around her eyes before the wedding and then suddenly we'd booked it. And now here we are about to have our consultation.

'He's ready for you now,' the busty blonde behind the desk tells us with what I think is a smile. She's probably had so much Botox most of her face is numb. She probably needs to drink with a straw everywhere she goes. It makes me giggle. I wonder if she gets a staff discount. Those boobs can't be real either.

'How exciting!' Lilly beams. 'Just think, next time we walk into this reception we'll have younger faces.'

'Yeah,' I smile nervously. I don't know why, but I can't get Poppy out of my head. I know if she were here she'd be shouting at me about what a stupid idea this is. And how I was terrible to involve Lilly in it. But I had to get someone who was interested. Poppy's idea of looking after her skin is cleansing, toning and moisturising instead of a face wipe at the end of the day.

We walk up the white winding staircase and into the door of Doctor Isaksson. He looks up with a big reassuring smile. He's a good-looking guy in his sixties with salt and pepper hair. It reassures me that he hasn't overdone it himself like the receptionist. He looks normal.

'Good morning, ladies. If you'd like to take a seat.' He gestures at the brown leather chairs across from him.

This is why I love going private. I've never had a doctor be this friendly to me on the NHS. Mind you, most appointment rooms don't have enormous gold chandeliers, sash windows and plush carpet either.

He picks up a pen. 'I understand you ladies are interested in Botox. If you could please tell me a bit more.'

'I want my eyes done,' Lilly shouts quickly. Jesus, must she always be first with *everything?*

He stands up and walks round to look at them, pulling at the skin around it. 'Yes. A few minor crow's feet.'

'Crow's feet?' she baulks, jutting her jaw out in temper. 'I prefer to call them laughter lines. I'm too young for crow's feet.'

'Oh, you'd be surprised,' he chuckles pulling at the skin underneath her eye.

'Oh...right.' She looks to me for reassurance. I just grimace at her awkwardly. A lot of help I am. 'Well, that's why I'm here isn't it.'

He nods. 'And you, Miss Green?'

I fidget with my hands in my lap, suddenly feeling shy. Poppy will kill me when she finds out. Like she might actually slap me to death.

'My forehead.' I point as if he wouldn't know where it was. 'I've got a few frown lines I'd like to see gone.'

He pulls on the skin, his spectacles so close to my face they start steaming up. 'Frown for me?'

Does he honestly want me to pull faces right now?

I force my face into a frown, but he doesn't look impressed. 'Really try,' he encourages. 'Imagine someone you hate.'

I try to think. Truth is, that I don't think I hate anyone. Even Meryl only irritates me.

Hate's such a strong word that people just throw around willy nilly. Haha, I can't even think willy nilly without giggling. I'm so immature. 'Come on, Jazz,' Lilly encourages. Something tells me she'd have no trouble listing people she hated.

'But I don't hate anyone?' I feel ridiculously self-conscious with them both gawking at me expectantly.

'Really?' Lilly frowns, obviously trying to rack her brains for some inspiration. 'Oooh, remember the other day when you told me you wanted the last pair of Louboutin shoes on sale, but some skinny bitch snatched them off the rail before you?'

*Do I!* Little bitch is walking around London wearing my shoes right now. They were the most adorable purple and pink shoes with a crocodile skin strap.

'That's it!' Lilly shouts pointing at my head excitedly. 'There's the frown!'

I didn't even realise I was frowning. No wonder I have lines all over the place.

'Perfect,' he smiles, inspecting me further. 'Have you ever considered having some of this excess skin removed?' He pulls at the skin on my eyelids.

Now I know I'm frowning. 'Sorry? What excess skin?' I can't help but sound offended.

He hands me a mirror and then points to my eyelids. 'You have small eyes and quite a lot of excess skin on top of it. If we were to remove that and fuse the muscles, your eyes would appear bigger and brighter.'

'You think I need eye surgery?' I blurt out in disbelief.

How bloody dare he? I'm just here for some regular Botox. Not a bloody facelift!

'Of course not,' he smiles. 'But I just thought I'd mention it.'

Of *course* he did. Bastard. He sits back down and starts rattling on about the Botox procedure and possible side effects, but I can't help but feel pissed off by the rudeness of this money grabbing bastard. My eyes are absolutely fine!

I discreetly look in the mirror again. I mean, yeah they've always been small, but nothing a fake pair of lashes and some eyeshadow can't improve. But...well, now I look I suppose my eyelids *do* look heavy. I mean, hell, I *have* had a daughter who hasn't stopped in the last three years. Maybe I should look into it.

Lilly is led over to the special chair for her injections. I go with her, even though I don't particularly want to watch it. Don't get me wrong, I have no major fear of needles, but it's still not the nicest thing to watch. The doctor leans his gloved hands towards her, one of them holding the injection. Lilly puts her hand up to stop him.

'Is there a problem?' he asks concerned.

She laughs awkwardly. 'No. Sorry, it's just a defence mechanism. If I see someone coming towards me with a weapon, my instant reaction is to bat them away.'

Anyone would think she grew up in the ghetto, not Essex.

He raises his eyebrows up in amusement. 'Right. Well, you know I'm coming now.' He leans in again. She smacks his arm this time. His eyes bulge with the disbelief.

'Sorry,' she grimaces again. She takes a deep breath. 'I'm good now. Honest.'

He sighs and leans in again. This time, she hits his arm so hard the injection flings out of his hand and tumbles to the floor.

'Maybe I should go first?' I offer.

He picks up the injection; his face flushed with frustration. 'I think that's wise.'

# Chapter 15
## Poppy

*Friday 12th February*

Mum hasn't stopped calling me today, which is making me nervous. I managed to avoid her when I dropped Dad home the other day and have been avoiding her ever since. I accidentally answer while I'm on my lunch break. Luckily it was just to talk about Jazz. The woman still seems oblivious to her husband having his ball chopped off.

Anyway, apparently she's so upset by how Jazz is reacting. I did tell her that going mental and smashing all of her plates and cups around probably didn't help matters. But my mother's never been one to reason with.

I'm just driving home from work when I get hit by loads of traffic. Someone must have crashed ahead or something because it's basically at a standstill. Luckily, I remember if I come off here I can go through some country lanes. I indicate and turn in, travelling down the bumpy road. It's so thin here you have to go slow in case another car comes along. I hope to God it doesn't.

I pass a farm with a sign outside stating 'Fresh Eggs.' I slow down before I can stop myself. What was it I read in that conceiving book? It said that I should eat organic and locally if I can. Izzy's always going on at me to eat better, and she eats loads of eggs. They're full of protein aren't they? Yes, it's decided. I can be a few minutes late home.

I pull into the drive and follow it down the long twisty mud track towards what looks like the farmhouse; an old thatched roof property with ancient crumbling bricks. I can see crates of eggs to the right of the front door. I get out and go to look. They do look slightly bigger than the ones in the shops. I wonder how much they are.

'Want some eggs, do you?' a loud voice bellows from behind me.

I turn to find an enormous man of at least six foot four towering over me. He's wearing a green duffel coat with a ridiculous purple beanie hat that says 'Christmas is coming' on it.

'Err...yes?' I stammer. I try to pull myself together and look confident. 'How much are they?'

He stands closer, towering over me, so the sun is blocked. Wow, he's intimidating. Especially the way he keeps chewing his lip like that. What the hell have I done? I've just strolled into this danger zone thinking I can buy eggs. It's obviously a trap. He's clearly a nutcase or some kind of murderer. Putting that sign up to lure in innocent idiots like me. I deserve to die a horrible death.

'Depends on how many you want to buy.' He leans in further, totally invading my personal space.

I back up; desperate to get away, but feel my thighs touch the crate behind me. I lose my footing, and before I can even register what's happening, I'm tumbling backwards. I close my eyes as my back thuds against the ground. I open my eyes to find I'm sprawled out like an eagle on the floor with crates of eggs around me. Actually, they don't have any eggs in them. They're all on the floor, smashed open. Shit.

I try to sit up, but my hand slips on another egg.

'What have you done?' he shouts, leaning down over me, his face pressed into a hard line.

He bends down. Thank God, he's going to help me up. Wait, no, he's just looking at his broken eggs, distraught. What a gent. I have egg in my hair, and I've lost a shoe. I scramble (no pun intended) to get up, wiping as much egg off me as possible. This is *so* humiliating.

'You'll have to pay for this!' he demands gruffly.

Does he mean he's going to punish me? Oh wait, no, he means money.

'Err...I assume you take credit card?'

My phone rings. I take it out of my eggy jean pockets and look down at the screen. Speak of the credit card devil.

'Hey, hun. I'm just on my way to see you,' I answer.

'Thank God,' she says, her voice high and panicky.

'What's wrong?'

'It's my face,' she sobs. 'Oh, just get here quick and you can see for yourself.'

I use my key and rush in to find Jazz in the sitting room with a wet face cloth over her face. Jemima's got Cinderella on. Again. So she's quiet for now. She barely even lifts her head to register me.

'I'm here,' I say, dumping my bag on the floor. 'What's up?'

Jazz sits up and removes the face cloth. A gasp leaves my mouth before I can even consider being thoughtful. Jesus! All of the skin around her eyes is swollen, red and blotchy. What the hell happened to her? They look like they're starting to bruise.

'Did...' I look to Jemima before lowering my voice so as not to alarm her, 'someone punch you in the face?'

My first thought is it was Mum, which is worrying.

'No!' she yells. Jemima turns around before quickly turning back to Cinderella. 'As if I'd ever let anyone punch me.'

Let them? She's so ridiculous. One class of Jiu jitsu and she thinks she's a ninja.

'What the hell happened to you first!?' she demands, taking in my eggy appearance. 'You look like you had a fight with an omelette.' She explodes into giggles.

'Yeah, yeah, *very* funny,' I deadpan. 'So what the hell happened to your face? Why are you so bruised and blotchy?'

She looks down at the face cloth, twiddling it in her hands like she's nervous. 'Promise not to yell?' Puppy dog eyes look up at me with pouted lip.

Well, as close to puppy dog eyes as you can with those shiners.

I sigh, knowing immediately she's done something ridiculous. But I can't be angry. That will just prove to her that I'm an obnoxious, judgey bitch.

'I promise.' I cross my fingers behind my back.

'Okay, well...' She takes a deep breath before confessing. 'I had Botox.'

'You WHAT?' I jump off the sofa in horror. She paid someone to inject poison into her face? How insane do you have to be? The phrase more money than sense comes to mind.

'You just promised you wouldn't yell!' she shouts back, pouting up a storm.

'Mumma, I can't hear Cinderella,' Jemima moans, looking at us in disgust for having disturbed her film.

'Sorry, baby,' she says in mollifying tones, her face twitching. Is she trying to smile?

'Jazz why the,' I lower my voice to a whisper 'fuck would you mess around with Botox? You haven't got one wrinkle on your bloody face.'

Here I am worried about creating life, and she's busy messing with her face.

'I have! I have a frowny forehead. Apparently Lilly's noticed them before.'

I roll my eyes. She's unbelievable.

'Anyway, I think I've had some sort of reaction or something. It burns and itches like a motherfucker.'

I look over to Jemima, but she's so engrossed in the film she doesn't notice the bad language. I'm surprised she doesn't swear yet. I look closer at the swelling. It's almost like her skin has blistered like she's spent two days on a sun bed.'

'Well, it definitely doesn't look normal. Not that I know what normal Botox looks like.' Maybe it's normal. 'Are you sure it's not supposed to go like this before going back down?'

'No,' she shakes her head, her eyes full of despair. 'Lilly's had no reaction.'

'Lilly?' I shriek. She involved Lilly in this? I take a deep breath and massage my temples. 'You got Lilly in on your stupid idea? She could have been deformed for her own wedding.' And I don't doubt would have somehow blamed me.

She rolls her eyes. 'Pops, we didn't get it done down a back street in Soho. This was a proper clinic in Harley Street.'

I snort. 'Well if this is a good one, I'd like to see a bad one.'

Her chin wobbles, and it's then I realise she's close to tears. And I'm being horrible. Shit, I'm a bitch sometimes. I always forget that she can get upset. It's so rare for her to cry.

'Sorry, babe.' I hate to see her upset. 'What can I do?'

'That's just it,' she sobs, her voice breaking as tears streak down her cheeks. 'I have no idea.'

Jemima wraps her arms around her without taking her eyes off Cinderella. That girl's committed to her film.

I take charge and get her an antihistamine immediately from the kitchen cupboard and then ring the clinic. The doctor eventually calls me back and insists on doing face time so that he can assess it properly. How modern! Afterwards, he tells us that he's going to ring her local chemist and arrange for some Prednisone to be ready for her to collect tomorrow. Apparently she's only to take it if it's still not gone down by then. I make her a cup of tea, and we settle down to watch Tangled, Jemima's second favourite.

Thank God everyone else is out. Mum's apparently trying some new anti-gravity yoga. I dread to think how much she'll disturb the Zen in there. There's bound to be a lot of angry women demanding their money back.

'Do you think it will go down before Jem's birthday party?'

'Who knows,' she sighs. 'So what's up with you then?' she asks as she sips on her tea. Damn it, she knows me too well.

I open my mouth, unsure of what I plan to say.

The front door goes, and Ollie and Dad walk in, their work boots pounding on the tiles.

'Hiya,' they call going straight in the kitchen. 'Tea time!'

Jemima rushes out to see them. They've even got her drinking a little cup of tea now, although it's mostly milk. I'm strangely proud that she's going to be a tea-aholic like her Auntie Poppy.

'They're gonna have a field day with this,' Jazz grimaces, jumping up to check her reflection in the mirror.

They really are; poor cow.

'You did tell Ollie you were getting it done, right?' She shrugs. 'Dammit Jazz, he's going to go crazy!'

'Oh, shush your dramatics,' she dismisses jumping up and going into the kitchen.

I sit there for a second sighing, wondering if I can show my eggy self. I'll never live this down.

'Bloody hell, Jazz!' Ollie shouts from the kitchen. 'What have you done to your face?'

I smile to myself and go into them. Ollie's still staring at Jazz in horror. He notices me and his forehead frowns.

'Poppy, did you do this?'

'What?' I blurt out, my jaw dropping to the floor.

He thinks I punched her in the face? God, I know I've punched him a few times, but he's my brother. That's totally different.

'And why the hell are you covered in egg?'

I've tried to clean myself up, but it turns out egg doesn't come off so easily. I'm going to definitely need a shower.

'Calm down, Olls,' Jazz says rolling her eyes. 'I had Botox. I'm just allergic to it.'

'Jesus, is this permanent?' Dad asks staring at her in shock. He doesn't seem too concerned about the eggs drying in my hair.

Jazz puts her hands on her hips defiantly, turning to Ollie. 'And what if it is? Will you leave me because I have a puffy face?'

He rolls his eyes. 'Of course not, but I'd have to prepare myself every time I saw you. I mean, how has Jemima reacted?' He scoops her up into his arms. 'What do you think of mummy's face?'

'She looks pwetty,' she says with an adorable smile. 'She had a doctor make her more pwetty.'

Ollie looks warningly at Jazz, a vein popping in his neck. 'So now we're letting our child know about Botox?"

'I want Botox!' she sings, clapping her hands together like an excitable cheerleader. 'Me! Me! I want Botox.'

'You don't need Botox,' Jazz says, tickling under her arms. 'You're beautiful enough already.'

'But I WANT it,' she shrieks crossing her arms over her chest.

Jesus, little people are such psychopaths. Their moods change like the wind.

Dad clearly realises this could go catastrophic in a matter of seconds and steps in. 'How about Granddad makes you a cup of tea in your favourite mug?'

'Yay!' she sings, struggling to get out of Ollie's arms so that she can hug Grandad's legs.

See what I mean? Like the wind, I tell you.

He turns to flick the kettle on. It's only then that I notice Dad's ear. There's a gold ring in it. What the hell is that?

'Your ear!' I point at it wincing from the sight. 'Why is there a ring in your ear?'

Dad smiles proudly, puffing out his chest. 'I got it pierced.'

'You WHAT?' He got his ear pierced like a bloody teenager? Who does he think he is? Justin Bieber?

Jazz laughs, her face still not moving much. 'Can someone say midlife crisis?'

Dad turns scarlet, his eyes falling to the floor. 'Do you not like it, Jazz?'

I know he values her opinion. He once wore purple cords because she insisted they looked cool. Mum went mad and said he looked like a Starburst sweet.

'I just think you look like a bit of a pirate that's all,' she quickly says, not wanting to offend him. 'Maybe if we get a nice diamond stud.'

'That's what I said,' Ollie joins in with a smirk. 'Maybe even a ruby or something.'

A *ruby?* Who are these people?

'Ugh, are you all insane? It looks bloody awful! You look ridiculous. You need to take it out. Everyone is going to rip the piss out of you.'

He crosses his arms over his chest in defiance. 'I'll have you know, Poppy Pocket, that a lot of men these days have their ears pierced. Look at Beckham.'

He can't seriously be comparing himself to the sex God David Beckham, can he?

'He also once wore a dress. If you start doing that, I'm sending you to a nursing home!'

'You'll forgive me if I'm not taking tips on my appearance from a scrambled egg and burn victim over there!'

'Dad!' I can't believe he'd be so rude to us. This isn't like him at all. I'm just trying to stop him from being the subject of ridicule.

'Oh come on, Pops,' Jazz smiles, seeming completely un-offended. She bumps me on the shoulder. 'It's not *that* bad.'

'What brought this on anyway?' I ask him seriously.

I know before he even speaks that it's because of his cancer, but I wish I'd catch him off guard, so he is forced to tell them. I hate not being able to talk about it.

He looks knowingly at me. 'Let's just say I'm living life for the moment now. I don't want to waste any time. We never know how long we'll get do we?'

'Shut up Dad,' Ollie laughs. 'Don't be one of those people over fifty that constantly talks about dying. It's so depressing.'

'Oh, I won't,' he grins. 'From now on you're going to see a new and improved Dad around here.'

That's what I'm worried about.

### *Sunday 14th February*

We're all round Mum's today for Jemima's birthday party. I can't believe she's three already. Time really does seem to be flying. I wonder how old she'll be by the time we get a baby. Probably old enough to babysit. That's a depressing thought.

By the time we arrive most people are already here. It's just all of our family and a few kids from Jemima's nursery. I find Mum in the kitchen finishing off making the sandwiches as some of the kids bounce up and down to 'Happy' by *Pharrell*. I find Jazz chatting to one of the Mums. She spots me and makes a beeline for us.

'Thank God you guys are here,' she says, taking our present out of our hands. 'I hate making polite small talk to the mums. It's so boring.'

We laugh. Ryan spots Ollie and walks away leaving us to our bitching.

'I'm surprised that Mum's even dressed today. She normally turns up to the school gates in her pyjamas.'

'Jazz, you've gone to drop her off in your pyjamas!'

'God, only a few times! And I'm not just talking the top and trousers; I'm talking dressing gown and novelty bunny slippers. She looked ridiculous.'

One rule for her and another for everyone else.

'Anyway, when is Jemima going to notice we're even here?'

She's on Grandad's hip as they sway along to the music. God, to think we might have come close to losing him. It would have broken all of our hearts, but little Jem would be ruined. He's her hero.

She spots Ryan and leaps out of Dad's arms. 'Uncle Wyan! Uncle Wyan!' He picks her up and swings her around before snuggling into her neck. I just know he's inhaling her lovely scent.

'Would you look at her,' Mum says from behind me, a large glass of wine in her hands. 'So young and innocent. No idea about the cruel realities of life.'

'Alright,' I laugh. 'I doubt you'd ever make a career as a motivational speaker.'

She smiles, but I notice the sad eyes above it. What is up with her? She's normally like a Duracell bunny on speed at family events. Maybe it's because Beryl isn't here. Simon surprised her with tickets for the theatre. It seems they're getting along well. I'm just glad I don't have to listen to him sneezing. Some people are going to get seriously disturbed during that musical. Mum and Beryl always bicker, but they'd be lost without each other. It must be that.

I help Jazz organise a few games of musical statues. The parents seem personally offended when their child is out. I blame the society of everyone winning. I mean Jazz said they had a sports day at Jem's pre-school, and everyone got a participation medal. When she asked if Jem won anything they informed her that no one ever wins, everyone's a winner. How ridiculous.

I decide to go and find Ryan. We'll be singing happy birthday soon, and I don't want him to miss it. Its magical moments like these you can never get back.

I find him in the hallway on his phone. His face lights up when he sees me.

'Alright, sexy,' he says with a devilish grin.

I move into his arms and push him against the wall. He pinches my bum causing me to laugh and blush like a nun in a whore house.

'Ever had a fantasy about having it off at a family occasion?' he asks with a grin.

I can't help but raise my eyebrows. 'Are you serious?'

'Why not? The doctor said to have lots of sex. We really shouldn't ignore medical advice.'

'You ignored it when you drank on antibiotics,' I remind him cheekily.

'Can I really not tempt you?' He leans in and kisses behind my ear. My weak spot.

'Maybe.' I smile shyly, making him work for it.

He places a soft kiss on my lips and then places my bottom lip between his teeth, pulling me in even closer to him. He wraps his arms around my waist.

'Oh go on then!' I squeal, taking his hand and leading him upstairs. I'm sure someone will video the happy birthday singing anyway.

We run giggling into the first bedroom we find. We fall through the door as he nips on my ear. I jump when I find my Mum sat on the bottom of the bed crying. Ryan looks up and notices.

'Meryl,' he says clearly embarrassed. God, we're like horny teenagers.

'Mum what's wrong?'

I rush over to her, but she's already wiping away her tears.

'I'm fine.'

'Mum, it's pretty obvious you're not. Just tell us.'

'I think your father is having an affair.'

'What? Why?'

'It started with that secret trip. Some excuse about seeing a friend. As soon as he came back he was acting funny. Flinching every time I go near him. And then with the ear piercing and all this live-for-the-moment rubbish. It's obvious he's got another woman. And it's all my own fault.'

'Why would it be your fault?'

She sighs. 'I haven't kept myself up to date with all these new sexual trends.'

We both gawk at her. 'Huh?'

'Well everyone's into this bottom plaything now aren't they? I should be offering him a finger up there or something.'

'Eww Mum! Gross!'

'He's obviously found some whore that takes it up the back doors. Perhaps if I'd have taken more initiative, I wouldn't be in this mess.'

'Mum, there is no way Dad is having an affair.'

'Why? Do you know something?'

'Of course I don't. I just...he's not, okay?'

She wipes her face and pulls out a lipstick. 'Nothing's going to be saved today though so I just need to get on with it. Come on, aren't they cutting the cake soon?'

'We might miss it,' Ryan says clearly still nursing a hard on.

'Don't be ridiculous,' she snaps. 'You can't miss moments like this. You'll never get them back.'

He looks at me pained. 'I had a feeling you were going to say that.'

## 14th February

From: Poppyisawesome@hotmail.com

To Lindadavis4321@gmail.com

*Hi Linda,*

*Haven't heard from you. Just checking you're okay?*

*Poppy xxx*

## Poppy

## Wednesday 17th February

Ryan and I are back at the doctors. Again. I already feel like we're here all the time. We sit in front of our doctor, eagerly awaiting our news. Today we find out the blood and sperm test results. He fiddles around with his pen, tapping absentmindedly on his keyboard. Arsehole. Doesn't he realise we're desperate to find out?

I chew on my nails while Ryan taps his foot impatiently.

'So...' Ryan says, clapping his hands together. 'What's the verdict doc?'

He turns to face us with a fresh smile on his face. 'We've got your results back.' He consults some papers. 'Mrs Davis, our results show that you have enough FSH levels in your blood, so that's good.'

'Riiiiight? And that means...?' Doesn't he realise we don't have a degree in doctor talk?

'That's good news,' he nods encouragingly. 'Now I need you to have a blood test two weeks before you're due to menstruate. This will check that you're ovulating correctly.'

More bloody tests! My arm is going to be like a pincushion. And he doesn't realise my problem with periods.

'Well, the only problem is that my periods are all over the place.' I feel embarrassed talking about it in front of Ryan so choose not to look at him. 'So I don't know when I'm *supposed* to be ovulating.'

'Just a guestimate then,' he nods.

A guestimate? How bloody unhelpful is he? I could do a bloody 'guestimate' at home!

He turns to Ryan, already dismissing me. 'Mr Davis, we've had your sperm results back, and they show that ninety-five per cent of your sperm are abnormal.'

I cough out a splutter. What the hell is he talking about? Abnormal? That doesn't sound good.

'Sorry?' Ryan says, exasperated. 'Abnormal? What do you mean by abnormal?'

The doctor looks at him seriously. 'Normal sperm have an oval head with a long tail. Abnormal sperm have head or tail defects. These defects can affect the success of them reaching and penetrating an egg.'

Wow. Who knew this would turn into some weird science class.

I turn to look at Ryan. His face is blank, showing no emotion whatsoever, but he must be devastated. Especially after putting so much pressure on himself.

'So what you're saying is I can't get Poppy pregnant?' he clarifies, his voice shaky and void of any real emotion.

'Not at all,' the doctor says shaking his head. 'Even though you only have five per cent normal sperm that's still millions of sperm that know exactly what they're doing.'

'Millions?' I gasp. And just one of my little eggs. How is this not more straightforward?

'So why am I not getting pregnant?' I ask bluntly.

Depressing thoughts start whirling through my head. Is this *my* fault? Are my eggs crap or something? Scrambled from years of drinking too much?

'Is it...did I drink too much alcohol in the past? Or...one time I bashed my vagina on the side of the desk. Could I have damaged it, so it doesn't work properly anymore?'

I look up into the doctor's face to find amused eyes. Does he find this *funny?* Does he find me not being able to give Ryan a baby, fucking funny?

'No,' he sighs, 'this is nothing to do with past drinking or...' his face crumples as if he's about to burst out laughing. 'Or...*bashing* your vagina.' He smiles to Ryan like they're in on some inside joke. Ryan smiles back, the traitorous bastard.

'We'll need to do both sets of tests again in ninety days. That's how long it takes for a fresh sperm cycle from Ryan.'

Ryan cringes slightly. I hope he's embarrassed. I'm still angry with him not sticking up for me.

'And then what?' I demand. Waiting around for all of these tests is wasting precious time. 'What happens if the tests come back exactly the same?'

'Then, and only then,' he warns sternly, as if we're over-reacting, 'I'll refer you for further tests.'

MORE tests? God, if I hear the word tests one more time, I'll openly scream. This is ridiculous and all the more so because I know Jazz could pay for us to go private. If it wasn't for Ryan and his ridiculous feelings about keeping it a secret we could fasten this all up and get our baby. And if you think about it, Ryan's making me feel even more stressed because I'm not able to confide in anyone.

I mean, normally I tell Jazz everything. And the one time I have the biggest secret in the world and the one time she could truly help and I'm not allowed. It's so unfair. Could I go behind his back? Well, when you think of it I'd be doing this for his own good.

Could I? Fuck it. Decision made. As soon as we kiss each other goodbye I head straight to Mum's house. I need to tell Jazz.

I take a deep breath, my stomach quaking with nerves. This is it. If I tell her, I can never take this back. It's betraying Ryan. Can I really do that? Hell, can I not? If we can't have a baby, our relationship might break down anyway.

I take a deep calming breath. 'I have a secret.'

Her eyes light up like a kid at Christmas. 'Oooh, gossip! Spill.' She claps her hands together in glee. She leans in, dunking a biscuit into her tea.

'It's not gossip, and you have to *promise* you'll never tell anyone else.'

She rolls her eyes. 'Okay, okay. Spill.'

'I mean it Jazz,' I warn sternly. 'Swear on Jemima's life?'

She gasps, licking her lips, her eyes alight with excitement. 'This is some serious shit. Okay, I swear. Now, what the fuck is it? You better not be building this up only to reveal some shit-assed secret.'

'Okay.' I take another deep breath, my heart hammering in my chest. This is it. Now or never. 'Me and Ryan are trying to get pregnant.'

'Oh my god!' she shrieks jumping up and going to hug me.

The hot tea spills all over my arm burning my skin.

'Aaah! Jazz! Hot...burn...'

'Oh shit, sorry, babes. My bad.' She grabs me and takes me to the kitchen where she runs it under a cold tap. 'Anyway, congratulations! Kiss goodbye to your life,' she adds sarcastically.

I wish. She clearly doesn't understand.

'No, Jazz, you don't get it. We've been trying for a year and no baby.'

'Oh.' She frowns as if this is incomprehensible. Well, I think it's a frown. With all of the Botox, it's hard to tell. 'So what's the problem?'

'This is it,' I sigh, feeling the weight of the world on my shoulders. 'We don't know yet. Our doctor is shit and saying he might refer us, and I just can't wait any longer. It's driving me crazy.'

I never realised how impatient I was until this whole thing began. But telling Jazz is already making me feel better. It's true what they say; a problem shared is a problem halved.

She nods. 'So you want me to pay for private treatment.'

Thank God she's clicking on straight away, and I don't have to actually ask.

I stare at her discomforted. 'Would you mind?' I feel bad after accusing her of throwing money at me.

'Would I mind?' she asks flabbergasted. 'Of course I wouldn't fucking mind, you nutcase! I paid money for my face to look like *this*. Of course I'd want to spend it on something important. I need you to join the kid crew. It's lonely as fuck.'

'Okay,' I nod, finally able to smile and allow myself the glimmer of hope that it might work. 'Only Ryan doesn't want anyone to know. So it's not like you can just be seen to give us the money. We have to come up with some plan.'

'You could win on a scratch card!' she sings excitedly.

I shake my head. 'Too obvious.'

'I've got it. We'll fake up a letter. Say some great uncle left you money in a will. He'll be forced to believe it.'

'You think?' I allow myself another flutter of excitement. Could this be it? Could this be our chance?

'I *know,*' she grins adamantly. 'Start shopping for prams, because soon you're gonna be pregnant and fat.'

I can't help but let the sprout of excitement dance around in my stomach. I quickly squash it down, telling myself not to get ahead of myself.

## Poppy

## Friday 19th February

So it turns out Ryan's dumber than I thought. He totally believed our faked up letter and so by Friday we're waiting in the reception of some posh private clinic I found in Harpenden. Everything here is obviously designed to make you feel calm. The walls are painted a mellow green, annoying chiming music coming out of the speakers, glossy magazines spread out on the coffee table. We even got a world-class cup of tea in a china teacup. I do approve.

'Mr and Mrs Davis?' A glossy-haired blonde in a tight mint green pencil skirt and crisp white shirt asks.

We smile up at her as we stand.

'This way please.'

Ryan clasps my hand, giving it a small reassuring squeeze. I love when he does that. Just knows when I need him.

We're led by her to another door, down an LED lit hallway. She knocks on the door of a Doctor Amsi.

'Come in,' a loud authoritative voice calls.

We push the door open and smile at the man standing behind the desk. He looks Egyptian maybe, with a thinning dark hairline. When he walks around to shake our hands, I see he's easily six-foot-five, if not more. Wow, I wouldn't have pegged a huge doctor like this dealing with something as sensitive as infertility.

'Welcome, Mr and Mrs Davis,' he says, smiling, his eyes warm.

I sit down, already liking him. He's giving me eye contact, which is already more than my GP.

'So if you could tell me the background.'

I explain everything and hand over copies of the tests I got from my doctors. He studies them for a long time. I wait anxiously hoping he's going to whip out some magic solution.

'So...As previously told to you by your GP, Ryan has ninety-five per cent irregular sperm. That means that only five per cent of each ejaculation is actually worth anything.'

'Right,' I nod, smiling reassuringly at Ryan. I mean, our GP made out that wasn't a problem, but this guy's tone tells me something different.

'Tell me, doctor,' Ryan says clearing his throat, 'could that be because my mum was a drug user while she was pregnant with me?'

Woah. Where the hell did that come from? He hasn't voiced that fear to me before. Now that I think about it I suppose it does kind of make sense. It also reminds me that she hasn't replied to my email yet. That's not like her. She's normally far too over eager, exchanging meaningless email after meaningless email. I'll have to check it sent.

'It could be that or a list of other factors. The environment we live in these days is very high stress. I'm going to book you in for another sperm test in just under ninety days.'

'Yeah, that's what our GP said,' Ryan says looking at me as if to say *he's not telling us anything different to what we already know.*

'And, Mrs Davis.'

Oh god, it's me.

'Tell me the truth, doc,' I plead. 'Is it me? Did I damage my vagina when I tried to use that horrible huge vibrator all those years ago? Because Ann Summers said it wouldn't do me any damage.'

He looks back at me confused. Maybe I shouldn't have mentioned the vibrator.

'Or is it because I used to drink a lot? Can I drink now? I mean, not a lot obviously, but you know, an odd wine here and there?' God knows I'm desperate for a drink.

Ryan places his hands on mine as if to physically calm me down.

The doctor clears his throat. 'Damaging your vagina would have nothing to do with you being unable to conceive. And as for drinking, yes consuming copious amounts of alcohol can have an effect on your chances of conceiving. That being said, stress is also a major factor. If the odd glass of wine, when you're sure you're not pregnant, is what you want, go ahead.'

I nod, trying to steady my breathing. How did I get so hysterical in such a short space of time?

'Anyway, as I was saying, with your irregular periods it's very hard for you to know when you're ovulating. An average woman would have twelve chances a year to conceive. If as you say your natural periods are spaced apart more you could be looking at only eight or nine chances a year.'

Eight or nine chance A YEAR?

'Put that together with only five per cent good sperm production and you can see why it's taken longer to fall pregnant.'

I feel my eyes start to well up with tears. Why am I getting upset? I knew this. I was prepared for this. But...well just to hear it out loud from a proper doctor, it feels different somehow. More final.

'So are we looking at IVF?'

'I'd prefer to do ICSI with you. It's the same as IVF except we inject the sperm right into the embryo to improve the chances. However, I do want to do a few more tests first. Despite what I've said, you still do have a chance of falling pregnant naturally.'

'How?' Ryan asks in disbelief.

'If you were referred through the NHS they would class you as unexplained infertility with no problem found. Anyway, as I said I'd like to send you for a scan to see if there's any evidence you're ovulating correctly. It will give me more information than a blood test. And I'd also like to do a test to see if there are any blockages in your tubes.'

'Okay,' I mumble, more confused than ever.

On the car ride home, an unknown tension fills the air.

'What if it's me, Pops?' Ryan asks, catching me off guard. 'What if they do this test again, and it's still ninety-five per cent useless swimmers?' He seems so worried.

'I don't care Ryan. It could just as easily be me. We just have to realise that whatever happens we're here for each other. Right?'

He nods, his mind clearly already elsewhere. Will he be so easy to dismiss if it's found I'm the problem?

How can it be we're sitting in the same car, but I've never felt so distant from him?

## Chapter 17
### Jazz

*Monday 22<sup>nd</sup> February*

Ollie and I picked up the keys this morning. The *actual* key to our dream home. Can you believe it? I really can't.

I'm bursting to get out of Meryl's house. You'd think she'd have wanted to make our last bit of time together pleasant, but she's made my last few weeks a bloody nightmare.

We drive over there with Jemima in my brand spanking new white BMW X5M. It's so beautiful I may have given it a little kiss before driving her today. I totally feel like a pimp driving it. Only Jemima spoiled our fun and made us turn down the blaring NWA. In hindsight Fuck the Police isn't suitable for her anyway. Okay, I admit, it is hard to park around here. I should have bought a smaller car. Especially with a furniture delivery truck outside.

Ollie's electric blue eyes grow suspicious. 'Jazz, why is there a furniture truck bringing stuff into our house? I thought the previous owners had gone?'

I smile knowingly. 'They have silly. That's *our* furniture.'

He stares back at me like I just kicked his kitten. 'What?'

'You picked our furniture without me?' Why does he look so devastated about this? Who cut his balls off and turned him into a PMT'ing woman.

I shrug, avoiding his glare. 'Of course I did. You men are always whining that you hate all of that interior design shit. I thought I'd just take the hassle out of it.' He was supposed to be thankful.

'But I thought that's what we were going to do today. Plan out the house and start to get excited about moving in.' Sadness clouds his features. God, he's cute.

'We're moving in *today* silly,' I snort rolling my eyes. What the hell is he thinking?

His eyes widen to twice the size. 'What? There's no way it'll be ready on time.'

Oh, ye of little faith.

'Yes, it will. Come on, I'll show you.'

We get out of the car and carry Jemima to the door. 'Welcome home, baby. This is your new house.' I place her down on the floor, and she walks into the sitting room.

It's already painted a neutral palate; so three workmen I hired are placing down the new grey velvet sofas I bought. The sheepskin rug is rolled out, and the glass tables placed around the room. Next will be the huge TV mounted onto the wall, a few pictures up and it's done.

'So wait.' I turn to face him. His jaw is tense, his nostrils flaring. 'You ordered all of this without me, and you expect us to move in *today?*'

'Yes,' I answer slowly so as not to confuse him again. 'I assumed you knew this.'

What the hell is he so angry about?

His nose crinkles in confusion. 'But, we're not even packed up at home.'

'There are professional packers there right now.' *Honestly,* he must think I'm so unorganised.

'Touching all of our stuff?' he asks, his pupils flared. I nod. 'I bet Mum's loving that,' he scoffs.

Like I care what *she* thinks. I just want to get out of the witch's house.

'Look, I really don't see what the damn problem is. I'm just getting shit done. Why are you pissed about this?'

'It's just...' He rakes his hair through his silky blonde locks.

'Just what?'

'This doesn't feel like my house,' he admits on a sigh. 'Nothing in it was picked by me. It doesn't feel right. And anyway, what about Jemima? Her room will never be done by the end of the day.'

'*Yes,* it will. That's their top priority. They're on it right now.'

He sinks down onto the sofa.

'At least admit it's comfy,' I say my mouth twisting with a smile.

He swallows hard. God, his Adam's apple is so bloody hot.

'Okay, it's comfortable,' he admits on a sigh. 'But I'm still not happy.'

Jemima walks up to him slapping her hands on either side of his pouty face. 'Ah, Daddy, don't be sad.'

He plasters on a fake smile for her benefit. 'I'm not, princess.'

She smiles, her nose wrinkling up. 'I know what you need. Do you want me to murder you?'

His mouth drops open in horror. Murder? Oh shit. I remember the phone call with Poppy. She thinks murder means cuddle. Damn Poppy confusing things.

'Cuddle! She means cuddle,' I quickly add, trying to soothe over it.

A streak of disappointment runs across his face.

He sighs again. 'I'm going for a walk.'

## Poppy

Ryan's been a bit distant since the doctors and annoyingly healthy. Normally we'll have a cup of tea and a few biscuits in the evening, but he's not so discreetly changed it to warm lemon water and kiwi slices. I mean, like I'm not stressed enough, now the guy wants to take biscuits away from me.

Today's the day of my scan. So as instructed, I've drunk two litres of water. I normally drink that throughout a day, so I thought it would be no problem, but not being allowed to pee is torturous. Ryan guides me into the waiting room filled with lots of women, like me, hopping from foot to foot trying not to pee themselves. The pressure on my bladder is unlike nothing I've ever felt before.

'I wonder if I just had a small wee would it really matter?'

'Yes, Pops,' Ryan snaps. 'We have to do this properly. Especially with all of the money it's costing.'

Oh yeah, I forget he doesn't realise this is Jazz. He thinks I inherited it, so it's our money. Probably thinks there are lots of other things we could be doing with it. Like re-plastering our spare room and getting the garden landscaped. But of course, this is more important. All of that stuff can be done another day. Whereas we're both not getting any younger. The ticking down to me turning thirty is scaring me. I guess I just always assumed I'd have a baby before I turned thirty. But then my younger self also saw me marrying Gary Barlow from *Take That*, so I think it's safe to say I had high expectations for myself.

I look around the waiting room at the all women. None of them look like they're just about to piss their pants. A woman reading a magazine catches my eye before she quickly pulls it up, entirely covering her face. What the hell is that all about?

I stare until she risks a peek again. Oh my God, I know those big blue eyes. I grasp onto Ryan's forearm to steady myself. I suddenly feel dizzy.

'What?' he asks, concern marring his face.

'I think...' I swallow so I can talk properly. 'I think that's Nicole over there. Your...your ex-girlfriend Nicole.'

His eyes nearly bulge out of his head, and I feel the goose pimples rise on his arms. He follows my eye line. We wait until she peeks from behind the magazine again. This time, I'm sure it's her.

'Nicole?' I call over, unable to help myself.

She jumps in her seat and finally lowers the magazine fully. Enough so that I can see her small bump through her wrap dress. Oh my God. She's pregnant. She's here for a normal pregnancy scan.

She clears her throat awkwardly. 'Err...hi!' She stands up and walks over to us. 'How are you?'

I actually feel sorry for her. This must be mortifying for her. Whatever happened between us, happened a long time ago.

None the less, I still wish I wasn't make up free with sagging jogging bottoms on. She looks so well put together.

'We're good thanks,' Ryan says grabbing me by my waist and pulling me protectively into his side. I look up to him, glad for the gesture.

She nods slowly, forcing a smile. This is beyond awkward. You can tell she's considering whether it would be rude to sit down already.

'Congratulations,' I say pointing to her bump.

Ryan's hold gets tighter on me.

'Thanks,' she smiles shyly her cheeks reddening. 'And congratulations to you too.'

'Congratulations?' I look to Ryan confused. Oh crap. She thinks I'm pregnant too.

'Err...I'm not actually pregnant,' I admit begrudgingly. It's hard to think up a convincing lie while your bladder is trying to burst out of your body.

'Oh.' Her forehead creases and you can tell she's wondering why on earth I'm here if not for a pregnancy scan.

'Is your husband here?' I ask to try to break the focus on me.

'Oh,' she smiles sadly, quickly looking down at the floor. 'No. I don't have a husband.'

Probably tried to steal someone else's again. Home wrecking whore. Oops, maybe I'm still a bit bitter.

'That's okay!' I smile, trying to make her feel better despite my own discomfort. 'Loads of people have a baby before they get married these days. It's really no big deal.'

She nods, squirming visibly. 'The father isn't involved. At all.'

Oh my God. She's all on her own. I know the history we've had, but I can't help but feel sorry for her. Imagine being all alone and pregnant. Although being here shows she must be loaded. I can't feel too sorry for her.

My phone starts buzzing in my pocket. I pick it up quickly before it starts blaring out Beyoncé, so as not to disturb anyone.

'Hello?' I whisper, not having given myself the chance to see who it was.

'It's me,' Ollie says on a sigh.

'Sorry,' I quickly apologise to Nicole and Ryan, turning around for a private conversation. 'Alright? You sound down. I thought you were getting the keys today.' He should sound excited.

'Yeah. We got them.' Another sigh. Jesus, what the hell is wrong with him?

'And?' I hiss. I need the toilet too fucking bad right now to pussy foot around this idiot.

'And it's nothing like I imagined. Jazz has picked the house, the area and even the furniture.'

'Oh'. I can see how that could make him feel emasculated. I mean look at the fuss Ryan made about picking the curtains. I really thought he wouldn't give a crap. But give a man his own house and he wants to make it his kingdom.

'Anyway, we ended up arguing, so I went for a walk. I've tried to find the positives of the place. But I can't even find a place for a pint.'

'It *is* eleven in the morning, Ollie.'

'That's not the point,' he moans. There are only poncy wine bars and the people here seem stuck up. Most of the women carry these dogs the size of rats. If Jazz thinks she's getting one of those she has another think coming.'

I look around at Nicole, giving her and Ryan a polite smile. God, just to think of Ryan's ex, pregnant with a baby. He must be thinking he should have stayed with her. Someone with fabulous fertility.

'Anyway, Ols, I've really gotta go.' I hang up before he gets a chance to reply and grimace apologetically at Ryan.

'What was that all about?' Ryan asks with a fake smile. I can already tell he's not really interested but is feeling uncomfortable with Nicole. Why is he so nervous? It's me having the scan.

'You might have to take Ollie out for a pint later. Trouble in paradise.'

'When isn't there?' he laughs, breaking the previous atmosphere.

'Anyway,' Nicole nods. 'It was really great to see you guys. Good luck with...' she looks down at my stomach 'err...everything.' Then she goes back to her seat.

We nod and walk away. I can't help but feel sorry for her. Yeah, she might have tried to steal Ryan, but now she's looking at a future as a single mum. I know from Jazz and Jemima's first year how hard that can be, regardless of how much money you have.

'That's sad isn't it?' I say to him quietly. 'Being all alone like that.'

'I'm sure she's fine,' he says dismissively. He turns to me, an excited grin on his face. 'Anyway, imagine,' he whispers into my ear. 'She could do the scan and say 'oh look, there's already a baby in there.'

I turn to look up at him. He has a playful smile on his face, but I know him too well. He's hopeful. Still hopeful that this will all work itself out naturally.

'Don't get your hopes up.' I smile weakly. 'This is just to find out if I'm ovulating. One step at a time.'

The worst thing is that I might have to do this ten times before we find out. The doctor explained that because of my irregular cycles we don't have a clear indicator of when I might ovulate, so if not today I'll have to come back once a week until I come on my period.

'Mr and Mrs Davis,' an African nurse with the coolest P Diddy braids calls.

We follow her into a room with a reclined chair, almost like that of a dentist chair. I wobble over to sit on it. If I make any fast movements, I'm going to piss myself for sure. It's actually taking all of my mental and physical strength not to let it happen. Come on, Pops, do those pelvic floors.

'Hi.' Another nurse smiles, gesturing for me to move down the bed slightly. 'So you know what this scan is for today?'

Ryan nods. She suddenly clocks how stunning he is, her eyes roaming over him appreciatively. Yeah, yeah, get in line.

'I'm about three seconds away from pissing myself!' I blurt out with zero class.

She looks back at me; her jaw slack with alarm.

'I'm sorry, but I really, really need to go. So...if we could hurry this up it'd be appreciated.'

My god, my forehead is actually sweating. Don't they realise how desperate I am?

'Of course,' she smiles, lifting a sort of wand and putting that weird jelly stuff on it. 'If you could just lower your joggers for me.'

I push them down slightly. I don't know why. Surely the woman is scanning my stomach, not my vagina?

'Just a little bit more.' She grabs them and yanks them down even more so now you can see the top of my pubic hair.

Mortifying. This is actually *mortifying*.

'Now forgive me if the gel is a bit cold.'

She places it on my lower stomach, and I grimace. Cold's not the fucking word. Get a polar bear, lock him in a freezer for three weeks and that's what it feels like. Oh my god. Did a tiny bit of wee just come out from me flinching? Hold those pelvic floors, Poppy!

'Right,' she says, as laid back as ever while pushing down on my stomach so hard it feels like it's going to come out the other side. And why is she deliberately pressing on my bladder when she knows I'm about to explode? 'I've got good news.'

I look at the grainy black and white screen. Don't tell me Ryan's right and there's a bloody baby in there. Surely I would have noticed?

'It looks like you're ovulating at the moment.'

'Yes, Pops!' Ryan says with joy. 'Your ovaries are fine.'

God, the relief is coursing through my body. I can ovulate. I'm not totally broken. I can finally relax. My body is working just as it should be.

Uh-oh. I relaxed too much. Pee starts spilling onto my knickers.

'Oh my god.'

I try to sit up and wince, desperately trying to pull my pelvic floors to stop the flow. But it's no good. It's like the floodgates have opened, and even Moses himself couldn't control them. I look to Ryan in panic. He stares back at me confused. Maybe they won't notice.

'Oh my goodness,' the nurse exclaims as my wee drips onto the tiled floor. 'Are you okay dear? You need to get to the toilet.'

'I...know,' I gasp, trying to move off the chair, but I can't move. Instead, I stay very still, curled up into a ball. I just have to let this pass.

'Jesus, Pops!' Ryan yells.

I stop, *finally,* after what feels like minutes of shrieks from all of them. I look up to find them staring at me in disbelief. The nurse is collecting tissue and attempting to mop it up from the floor. Shit, it's like a little river.

I can't even look at Ryan right now.

'I'm so sorry,' I exclaim, crouching down to try and get the tissue from her. 'Let me clean it up.'

'No, it's fine,' she snaps, carrying on like a pro. I suppose she's seen worse.

'No, really. It's the least I can do. I'm just so sorry.' I grab the tissue out of her hand a bit more forcibly than first intended. She wobbles and then falls back.

Into. The. Stream. Of. Piss.

She freezes in disgust, curling her legs up into her stomach.

'Oh, my goodness!' she screeches.

I stare on in horror.

'Oh my god! I'm so sorry!' I grab her and pull her up, attempting to dab at her wet clothes.

I look up to Ryan. He has his head in his hands, clearly distraught by what a fucking disaster I am.

'Um...babe...' No reply. 'Are you...ready to go?'

I want to get the hell out of here. There's just no recovering from this. Ever.

He looks up, his eyes pained. I've let him down again. Jesus, why can't I stop myself being such a dick? It's like an illness.

'Yeah,' he says quietly, raking his hand through his hair. 'Let's go.'

I walk towards the door, my head hung in shame.

'Oh and I almost forgot,' the nurse calls from the floor. 'Remember to have lots of sex as we know you're ovulating.'

I look up at Ryan. I'm guessing the last thing he wants me to do right now is sleep with him.

## Chapter 18
### Poppy

*Monday 22nd February*

I still can't believe I wet myself. And in front of Ryan of all people. He got a carrier bag from his boot for me to sit on during the way home. Anything to protect his precious car. We travelled in silence, and I headed straight for the bath when we got in, attempting to wash away the shame. Then we did a good job of pretending it never happened.

Luckily Izzy called and persuaded me to do a yoga class tonight to try to take my mind off it. Not that I told her the real reason I'm down. Normally I'd totally talk myself out of it, but that baby-making book says it's good for you. And I could totally do with some zen in my life right now. So I'm forcing myself to go.

Lilly calls as I'm leaving the house.

'Hey, Lil,'

'Hey, babydoll,' she sings. 'How's my favourite old married wench?'

'Less of the old,' I laugh.

'Okay.' I really want to tell her about bumping into Nicole, but then I'd have to tell her about the scan. And there's no way I can mention that without a barrage of questions.

'Anyway, I was just calling to see if you guys needed anyone at work?' She sounds a bit edgy. I can imagine her chewing her lip.

'Err...I don't think so. Who for anyway?'

She sighs heavily. 'Ugh, for me. This PA business is dwindling. Ever since Cheryl forgot to pick up that Olympian's dry cleaning we're not getting many new clients. He must have badmouthed us to everyone. Total diva. It's like yeah, what's your talent? Oh, you run? Well, that's impressive. That's something every three-year-old can do.'

I burst out laughing. I love when she goes on a hilarious rant.

'I'm pretty sure the speed is the talent.'

'Whatever. He's clearly a prick if he's slagging us off. I'm tempted to key his Porsche.'

'No, Lilly! Remember the anger management course. Deep breaths.'

Lilly lost her temper on a bus about a year ago and ended up punching the driver in the face. She says that the driver was baiting her, but I guess I'll never know. The police were called, but luckily they let her off with a fine and an anger management course. I can't say I've noticed a difference. I personally think that could more likely be the reason business is drying up.

'Anyway, I could ask Jazz if you need some help with cash flow?'

'Don't you fucking dare!' she barks. 'I am *not* going begging to Jazz, thank you very much. It's all completely manageable,' she groans. 'For now.'

'Okay, but keep it in mind. Anyway, I've got to go. Meeting Izzy.'

'Ugh, what exercise class has she roped you into now?'

I smile. At least she understands the hardship.

'Yoga tonight.'

She chuckles. 'If it's anything like that retreat you went on, run for the bloody hills!'

I can't help but smile at the memory. Not at the crazy bastards that ran it, but at Ryan when he rescued us. Being stuck in that cupboard with him. It makes me hot just thinking about it.

'I will. Bye.'

'Laters!'

I start the engine of the car wondering if I can really be arsed with this. Yes, yes I can. I force myself to drive there and then bend and stretch like no human ever should. And it hurts. I ache like a bitch as I'm walking out, every muscle in my body screaming in protest.

'I don't think I'm going to do it again,' I whinge, struggling to walk.

She chuckles darkly. 'I keep telling you; the more you do it, the better your body adjusts to it. And it's *so* good for you.'

I roll my eyes. 'Yeah, yeah, so is water but you don't see me swapping it for wine, do you?' I snap dryly.

She snorts. 'Whatever. Maybe we should try Qigong next then?'

'What the hell is that?'

It sounds like a dish on a Chinese takeaway menu.

She starts flinging her arms about like a fairy. 'It's all about releasing your body's energy. So good for you.' She takes in my appalled face. 'Or maybe we'll just go for a regular run?'

Oh crap, I don't want to get into running again. It's just so horrific feeling all of your fat bouncing up and down like that. Izzy doesn't understand that because she's all lean muscle.

'Well maybe we *should* look into this Qigong first,' I say, quickly playing for time.

I've been thinking about it the whole yoga class, and I'm pretty sure I want to talk to Izzy about Linda. I'm worried about her. She still hasn't replied to any of my emails. Plus, I'll admit it, I want to offload my secret on someone and who better than nicer-than-nice Izzy? Surely she won't shout at me...right?

'Izzy...'

'Yes,' she says her eye scrunched up in suspicious.

'If I tell you something, do you promise not to tell anyone?'

'Of course,' she nods. 'Why? What's happened?'

'Oh, nothing,' I shrug, desperately trying to ignore the churning in my stomach and just come out with it. 'Okay, I'm just going to come right out and say it.'

'Go on then!' she laughs.

'I've kept in contact with Ryan's Mum.'

She stops walking and turns to look at me; her face dropped in shock. 'You're joking?'

'Do I look like I'm joking?' She shakes her head as if it wasn't rhetorical.

'So remember how I told you she turned up at the wedding and asked me to send on a photo to her?'

'Yeah...'

'Well...she posted a letter to me a few weeks later with her email address. I emailed over some photos of the wedding and...It's kind of gone from there. Now we message fairly regularly.'

'I can't believe this.'

'I know, I'm a terrible person!' I hang my head in shame. 'But it's not like I'm telling her anything personal about Ryan. Plus she knows he doesn't want anything to do with her ever again. In the whole time since the wedding, she's never once asked me to have a word with him to see if he'll come round.'

'Yeah, because she knows what a terrible mother she is.'

'I know, I know, but you didn't see her at the wedding. She's still his mother, and she's not asking for anything in return. Come on Izzy, I thought if anyone would understand it'd be you.'

'Why, because you think I'm a pushover?' she asks, her hands on her hips.

'No!' God, why is she getting so defensive? 'Anyway, the only reason I'm telling you is because I'm worried about her. She hasn't replied to any of my emails lately.'

She goes to open her mouth.

'And,' I interrupt, 'I don't think it's because she's back on drugs. I just...I don't know; I don't like not knowing.'

She sighs. 'Then track her down.'

'Well, that's what I was thinking too. Only...she lives in quite a rough area and I was wondering...'

'If I'd come with you,' she nods, quickly catching on to my plan. 'Okay, fine. But just for the record, I'm not happy with you lying to Ryan.'

'God, you're a goody two shoes sometimes.'

I spot her car in the over-crowded badly-lit car park. Michael treated her to a gorgeous black Audi TT, which she fondly refers to as Trevor Tate. It looks like someone has scraped some of the ice off her front windscreen.

That's sweet of them. That'll save us some time. It's only when we get closer that I realise something is written on it.

I frown, fastening my pace to try and get a better look.

'Izzy. Has someone...'

'I've seen it,' she nods, not seeming surprised. As we get closer, we see that someone's scraped in the word slut. Wow, that's brutal and so untrue.

'Who the hell would have done this?' I ask in disbelief, looking around the dark car park. It suddenly feels creepy, the shadows possibly hiding the culprit. I pull my coat up around myself, and motion for Izzy to let us into the car quickly. We dash in and hurriedly shut the doors behind us.

'Lock the doors!' I scream, a tad dramatically.

She clicks them and then stares back at me, terror taking hold of her face. Her puppy brown eyes are wide and vulnerable.

'Shall we call the police?' I ask.

Do we even call the police over something so trivial?

'No!' she shouts quickly. 'It's fine. I can handle it.'

'Handle it?'

She looks away guiltily, starting the engine. I put my hand over the handbrake

'Wait...are you telling me this isn't the first time?' She looks out of the window. 'Izzy?'

'Well...'

'Well, what?' I demand, losing my patience with her.

She sighs heavily. 'I have been getting some prank calls lately,' she admits begrudgingly, still not looking at me.

'What?' I fold my arms over my chest, glaring at her.

She turns as if the heat from my stare has somehow penetrated her. 'And...'

'*And?* There's more?' I hiss in disbelief. I cannot *believe* she hasn't told me before now.

'Well, at first, I thought it was just teenagers or something messing around. You know, got hold of my personal training card. But lately, I mean,

I'm probably just being paranoid, but I kind of feel like I'm being followed.' She visibly shivers as she anxiously scans the car park.

I audibly growl. *'What?* And this is the first time I hear of this?'

She shrugs and turns the heating on. 'I didn't want to worry anyone.'

This bitch is unbelievable!

'Please, *please* tell me Michael knows?' I ask already knowing the disastrous answer.

'Like I said, I haven't wanted anyone to know.' This bitch is crazy! 'He already treats me like I'm breakable in public.'

It's true that he's ridiculously protective over her, but rightly so. When they first got together, the press followed them everywhere they went and made a big thing about the age gap. Now, it just seems to be at special events, but he still does everything he can so she can have as normal a life as possible.

'But you should have still told him. If anyone can find out who it is, it's him.'

I wonder who it could be. Maybe one of his deranged, jealous fans? God knows he has enough of them.

'Could it be a Sworsky whore?' That's actually what they call *themselves.*

'That's what I thought too.'

It would make sense. They've been known to try and get past security just so that they can breathe the same air.

I grab her by her shoulders. 'You *have* to go to the police. This could be more serious than you think. Your life could be in danger.'

'No, honestly, Pops,' she smirks as if I'm over-reacting. 'If I felt in danger, I would, but this is the first time they've actually done anything in person.'

'Which means they're escalating!'

'They'll get bored eventually, and besides, I don't want to worry Michael at the moment. He's really stressed out with his new film.'

When isn't he stressed? He's always bloody stressed out, but I know the pressure is on with this one. People are talking about Oscar nominations, and yet he's still not happy with the way the film is turning out. Weird, creative genius.

'Poppy, promise me you won't say anything,' she begs, taking my hand in hers.

I consider it for a second. I'd be putting her in danger. What if something happened to her?

'I honestly don't think I can. I'm worried about you.'

'Please, Pops,' she whines, 'if you love me at all you'll let this die down,' she says sternly. 'I promise to tell you if anything else happens. Okay?' She smiles so hopefully at me I actually feel bad.

'Okay,' I finally relent, 'but you better promise your perfect arse you tell me. Otherwise, I swear to God, Izzy, I *will* sit on you.'

## Jazz

### *Tuesday 23rd February*

Ollie finally came back last night, wobbling after a few pints. He grunted at me, made himself some toast and then went to bed. Real charmer, I've got there.

He hasn't stopped sulking since. He claimed he didn't like the memory foam bed this morning, even though it took him two seconds to start snoring last night. I'm really sick of him acting like such a little child. I already have one of those, and I really don't want another.

So I decided late last night to invite Meryl over. It seemed to appease him this morning for a while at least. There's no point in me keeping her an enemy. I know deep down that she's just upset because she thinks she's losing us.

Besides, if I can show her the fabulous life we can have down here she might start seeing things my way. If it helps with Ollie all the better.

Anyway, so far it's going well. She loves the house and is impressed with how I've kept Jemima's room as homely as possible. I brought the same bed covers from home and made sure her night-light was plugged in.

But...well, I hate to admit it, but she was really unsettled last night. I mean; it's to be expected. A new house to get used to. She had me up fifteen times while Ollie snored, loudly and obnoxiously, next to me. I could have punched him in the head. In the end, I brought her into bed with us, which I never normally do. But I was just so bloody tired. I hope she doesn't expect that every night.

Anyway, Meryl seems happy enough when I suggest we go for a fancy lunch down the road. I know this gorgeous little French restaurant, which does the best tuna steaks ever. The three of us settle down into a purple velvet booth scanning the extensive menu. Meryl and I both order tuna steaks while Jemima just has French fries. The kid is the fussiest eater in the world. Maybe now I can hire some child therapist who will snap that out of her. Hmm, that's worth a thought.

I know I need to apologise to Meryl for how weird things have been between us. I just hate it hanging over us in the air; unresolved issues. But I also hate apologising and admitting I'm wrong.

I take a deep breath and a large gulp of my white wine. 'I'm sorry things have got shit between us.'

She nods and takes a large swig herself. 'I'm sorry I went so...well.' She looks down at the table tracing the side of the menu with her index finger. 'I'm sorry that I over-reacted. I just...I hate the thought of losing you three. You're my favourites you know.' She winks devilishly.

'Meryl! You can't admit to picking favourites,' I giggle. 'What about Poppy?'

She laughs evilly. 'You know I love her too, but, well, I can't help it if I'm more emotionally attached to you lot.'

I suppose she's right. We have been living together for the past three years.

'Anyway, I need to confide in someone about Douglas.'

'Douggie? What about Douggie?' The poor man deserves a medal for putting up with her.

'You mean Poppy hasn't told you?'

'No!' I'll bloody kill her for holding something back from me.

She takes a deep breath and braces herself against the table. 'I think he's having an affair.'

My mouth drops open. Did I hear her right?

'WHAT? An affair? No way!'

She nods her head, circling her finger around her wine glass. 'I'm almost sure. He went away for a few days to visit a friend. That's what he said anyway. But...well, since he's come back he's acting ever so strangely.'

'Like how?' I just don't see it. Douggie doesn't seem the type. But then maybe all men have it in them. What a depressing thought.

'Flinching every time I go to touch him. And whenever I ask him even a simple question he's acting all scared and defensive like I'm a big bad wolf or something.'

I place my hand over hers in solidarity. 'I honestly think it's a misunderstanding. He's not the sort.'

She sniffs. 'I know I'm not easy to live with, but the truth is, without Douglas I'd be nothing. He's my first and only love.'

'*Jasmine!*' someone squeals from behind me, interrupting us.

I turn my head to see Lettuce Rosemont bounding towards me, laden down with designer shopping bags. *Great.*

She air kisses me on both sides of my cheeks. 'How the devil are you? I heard you were moving back to the area.' She's so ridiculously posh it's as if speaking hurts her voice box.

I nod. 'Moved in yesterday. I'm just down the road.'

'Fab!' She turns towards Meryl. 'And is this your nanny?' She leans right into her face totally invading her personal space. 'VERY NICE TO MEET YOU,' she shouts loudly.

Meryl nearly jumps out of her skin. What the hell? She looks back to me with alarmed eyes.

'I'm not deaf!' Meryl snaps, clutching at her ears. 'Although I might be *now.*'

Lettuce seems taken aback. 'Oh, sorry. I just assumed you'd be foreign.'

She giggles like this is hilarious.

'And what?' Meryl challenges her. 'Foreigners can only understand English if you *shout* the words?' She sips her wine calmly.

I clear my throat, trying to break the atmosphere. If Lettuce badmouths you around here, you might as well be dead. 'Lettuce, this is my mother in law, Meryl.'

Lettuce looks her up and down disapprovingly. I know it's really wrong, but I can't help but see Meryl through her eyes. Yes, she's wearing a zebra print suit, and her hair is up in a pineapple style clip. But she's still my Meryl.

'Nice to meet you,' she says disingenuously before turning back to me. 'I didn't know you got married!'

'Oh, I haven't. Just a figure of speech.'

Her brows meet in the middle before obviously deciding she doesn't care enough to ask.

'Anyway, when are you going to get yourself a nanny? Then we can go shopping together.'

'Jemima can come with me?' I offer, confused. She hasn't heard about the John Lewis fiasco has she?

Meryl widens her eyes as if in warning of our last shopping trip.

'Actually, on second thought maybe not the best idea. Yeah, I'll let you know when I've got childcare sorted.'

She hands me her silver business card. 'Fab. Call me darling. I've missed you *so* much.' She air kisses me again before she sashays away.

'Not enough to contact you before now,' Meryl says under her breath.

I roll my eyes. She doesn't realise how once you're off the scene you're easily forgotten.

It really gets me thinking about how she dresses. If she's going to be with me a lot, maybe I should insist on her wearing designer.

'Have you ever considered a personal stylist?' I ask tentatively, twirling a napkin in my hands.

She gasps dramatically. 'Are you insinuating that I have no dress sense?'

Oh god, she's got me there.

'No. It's just...'

'Because you're not too old for a tanned arse, Jasmine!' Her cheeks are practically puce with fury.

My mouth drops open. 'Meryl! You're not even my mother. You can't say things like that to me.'

'Like hell I can't,' she snorts. 'I'm your mother in law. Well, as good as. I can say whatever I want.'

I roll my eyes. 'I suppose no-one's stopped you before,' I comment under my breath, but loud enough for her to hear.

'And I won't be taking fashion advice from someone who wears a leopard print fur coat thank you very much.'

Now she's trying to insult me?

'This is Versace!'

'Pat Butcher more like!' she scoffs. 'Anyway, you need to be concentrating on Jemima right now. Have you enrolled her into nursery here? And have you met any local mums?'

Err...that's all totally on my list.

'Of course,' I smile confidently hoping she can't tell I'm lying. ''Now can we have lunch in peace?' I snap.

She's got me thinking though. Of course I need to enrol her in nursery. And I really should make some local friends. Not that I even like *mum* friends, but I did chat to a few mums at her old nursery. It made time pass quicker when waiting for her at the gates. Yes. First thing tomorrow I'm finding her a nursery.

# Chapter 19
## Poppy

*Friday 26<sup>th</sup> February*

I still can't believe Izzy. What is she like, not telling me? Hopefully, she's right and whoever it is will get bored soon, but I'm not so sure. Anyone that scrapes 'slut' is clearly mentally unstable.

But I must try to concentrate on myself. Today I'm getting this weird dye-stuff injected into my tubes. Not your normal Tuesday morning. I'm here alone. After pissing myself in front of Ryan at the scan, I'm terrified something will go wrong today that will totally tip him over the edge. Make him see that he's married to an absolute dickhead. It helped that he said he had a meeting he couldn't get out of.

I'm taken into a changing room by a nurse and change into a hospital gown. I hate these things. They always feel so papery. You would have thought that with it being private they'd be a bit lusher. Maybe cute, furry dressing gowns with those plush slippers or something. I take off all my jewellery, realising only now how when I'm nervous I normally twiddle my wedding band.

I'm then taken to wait outside a room, which I assume is where it's going to happen. There are signs warning that it's an x-ray. That's weird. I didn't think I was having an x-ray.

A tall, thin lady doctor comes out and smiles at me. Please say it's her doing this procedure. If I get a man, I might die of shame.

'Mrs Davis?'

Oh, thank God.

'That's me.'

I stand up, conscious that people can see my arse from the back of the gown.

'Follow me.'

I walk into the room warning of an x-ray and sit on the bed when she gestures towards it. I twiddle my fingers in my lap self-consciously. This is already so embarrassing. I mean; I'm going to be showing this woman my vagina in a few minutes. I feel like we should be better acquainted. I still hide myself away when I wee in front of Jazz.

But I shouldn't be embarrassed. I keep myself pretty trim down there. I have a special lady shaver for you know...down there. Only...well, it might look a bit strange. I put it on charge all last night, only when I went to do it this morning I realised that Ryan had unplugged it to charge his phone. Selfish bastard. But I mean, I hadn't told him the importance so how would he have known? Anyway, I reasoned that it had probably charged enough to use.

So I positioned myself over the toilet and began shearing away, like a farmer shearing a sheep. Don't get me wrong, it wasn't exactly a jungle down there, but I hadn't maintained in a few weeks. Anyway, I'd just done one side perfectly when the bugger ran out, leaving me looking ridiculous. I grabbed some house scissors and began hacking away at the other side, but it still didn't match.

Then I realised that I'd need to, at least, shave a bit of that side, so my bikini line wasn't horrendous. Only...well, I was in a rush, and I thought I could do a dry shave. Big mistake. I came up in an irritated rash, which I hope to god has gone down by now, and I ended up nicking myself quite badly. So badly that I had to put a plaster over it. Except the only plasters we had in the house were princess plasters for Jemima. So my vagina is currently half perfect, half spotty rash, hacked hair with a princess sticker that says 'princesses don't cry.' It basically couldn't have gone worse.

'Right,' the lady says looking at her clipboard. 'Do you have any questions before we proceed?'

'Err...'

'Anything at all,' she smiles warmly. 'Don't be embarrassed to ask.'

I'm embarrassed about this whole bloody scenario.

'Well...' I start twiddling my fingers around the bottom of the gown. 'Why does it say x-ray? Are you going to x-ray my vagina?'

She laughs, but quickly covers it with a cough, trying to remain professional. 'Sorry, I still have a bit of a cold.' Yeah right. 'No, we'll inject dye into your tubes and then watch through an x-ray screen to see if the dye gets around all of your tubes. It will show any blockages you might have.'

'Oh. Okay,' I nod. That makes more sense. Dumbass.

Another woman, well she could almost be described as a girl she's so young, walks into the room. Is there no bloody lock on that door? What if someone comes in while my legs are spread and they see me, vagina first? God, the idea is mortifying. And that's if it's another doctor. What if it's just a lost patient, thinking it's the toilet. God, they'd be in for a nasty surprise. Especially with the current state of my vagina.

'This is Cassandra. She'll be assisting me today.

I clear my throat, which is suddenly dry. 'Okay.'

Don't be nervous, Poppy. Man up. If you can't get through this how do you ever expect to give birth to a baby? I remember Jazz's tortured face too much. I'm doing all of this so that I can one day go through that torture myself. God, why do I want this again? That's right, for a little bundle of joy. A mini Ryan or mini me. This will all be worth it if I get that at the end. Just breathe.

'Now if you can lie down on the bed and part your legs so that the soles of your feet are touching, a bit like a star shape.'

I do it, hoping to god I've not already embarrassed myself.

'Perfect,' she reassures with a smile. 'Now, Poppy, I'm going to remove your paper knickers and then we'll begin.'

'Okay.' I smile as confidently as I can.

I force myself to look up at the ceiling. This might be a private hospital, but it still looks like they have a damp problem.

I take a deep breath and blow it out as slowly as I can. That's it, in through the nose and out through the mouth. You've got this, Poppy. It's fine.

I feel her untying the knickers and then a little laugh escapes from her. She quickly covers it with a cough again. She's seen the disastrous vagina.

'Sorry,' she apologises, leaning up so I can see her face. 'This cough can sound like a laugh.'

You've got to hand it to her. She's, at least, *trying* to remain professional.

'What is it?' Cassandra asks, moving round to openly stare at my vagina. 'My God!' she gasps when she sees it. 'What happened?'

Oh God. This is *so* humiliating.

'Um...I had a...bit of an..incident,' I admit reluctantly. 'It's a little embarrassing.'

Cassandra laughs at the same time as the doctor says, 'we're professionals.' She glares at Cassandra. 'Please don't be embarrassed. She shoots more daggers at Cassandra in warning for her to shut up. She stifles her giggles, but not enough for me to have already burned up with mortification.

This couldn't be going worse right now.

'Cassandra,' the doctor says sternly, 'if you could please set up the x-ray.'

She nods, having finally pulled herself together. She pulls a large mechanical thing over my stomach. I can see that she's still smirking. She'll probably tell all of her friends about this later. Have a real laugh. What a heartless bitch. She shouldn't be working here at all.

'Right, Poppy. I need you to take a deep breath and try to relax as much as possible.'

Relax? Is she fucking insane? I'm hardly at a spa right now.

I ignore my own negativity and take a deep breath, imagining calm, loose vaginas. That's it Poppy, calm, loose vaginas.

She inserts what feels like a speculum tube, a bit like when you have a smear. Okay, so far so bearable.

'You'll feel a slight pressure now as we insert the dye.'

I nod, praying to God it's not too bad.

Period-like pains start erupting in my lower stomach. Wow. This is weird. Just slightly cramping; nothing really to worry about. I take another deep breath, relieved at how easy this is. Totally better than I thought.

I turn towards the small screen they've pulled next to me. Apparently what I'm seeing are my tubes. I'm almost getting into it, working out where things are; when the pressure increases. Holy fuck, does it increase. Down in my vagina, it suddenly feels like someone is blowing up a balloon. No scratch that, is blowing up a balloon and trying to turn it into a balloon animal. Why is there so much bloody pressure?

'Ah,' I say, in a desperate attempt to get their attention.

The British in me doesn't want to complain. But shit, it's getting worse. Any minute now I'm expecting my vagina to burst and fly around the room, smacking both the women on the forehead before making a horrific deflating noise, much like a fanny fart, and falling limply to the floor.

I can't help it. I need to say something. Or shout or scream or smack this bitch in the face.

'My vagina feels like it's going to explode!' I scream at the top of my lungs.

Silence fills the room. Uh-oh. I have a feeling I was a tiny bit loud. I should have probably built up to it more.

The doctor clears her throat. 'Not long now.'

She moves and points to the screen where there's a weird shape formed on the screen. 'As you can see the dye has gone all the way around, so I can tell you there are no blockages.'

'Yeah, so when will it be over?' I snap, starting to sweat. I just want this done now. I suddenly wish I had brought someone with me. It would be nice to have someone's hand to hold.

The pressure is suddenly released, and the machine over my stomach moved out of my way. Thank God. I take a few deep breaths to centre myself. The relief is overwhelming. I feel like I've run a marathon, totally wiped out.

Now that I sit up I do kind of feel a bit embarrassed. I mean, screaming out like that. What the hell am I going to be like in labour? I'll defo have to have an epidural.

'Err, thanks,' I nod to the main doctor, not knowing what else to do. Why the hell am I saying thanks for torturing my vagina? I really need to stop myself from talking sometimes.

'No problem. I'll write up this report and have it to your doctor by the morning.' She smiles reassuringly at me again. They must include that on the course she did. Clearly Cassandra never attended. She's still trying to hold herself together.

'Now you can go back to the cubicle, get changed and go home. You may experience period like cramps for another twenty-four hours, but it's nothing to worry about.'

'Thanks,' I say again with a nod. I just want to get the hell out of here and pretend this never happened. Maybe put on a rom-com and have a good cry.

I rush towards the door and close it behind me, breathing a huge sigh of relief. I hear them both burst into hysterical laughter. Bloody bitches. Don't they know I'm vulnerable right now!

I rush back to the cubicle, throw my clothes back on and rush out to my car. I shut the door behind me and try to relax. You're back in your car now Poppy. There's nothing to worry about.

Only, well my stomach does feel really crampy now. And I feel ridiculous. And more than anything, lonely. I've never felt so lonely in all of my life. And then I realise that in my pitiful state of despair I never took the time to actually take in the prognosis.

My tubes are fine. The scan came back fine. His sperm is officially classed as fine, considering five per cent still means millions of swimmers. What the hell is causing us to be infertile if everything works properly?

Jazz

*Monday 29<sup>th</sup> February*

I've found the perfect nursery for Jemima. It's absolutely beautiful and only down the road from me. It not only does all of the normal nursery crap but they also have classes from the Chelsea Ballet School! How amazing is that? My little Jemima could be the next Nutcracker. Although, if she's anything like me she'll be a nutcracker, with or without being a ballerina if you know what I mean. There are also drama classes, sports and the best bit, animals! They have their own class rabbit, and they even hatch ducklings and goslings throughout the year. How cool is that!

Although, you should have seen the parade of yummy mummies at the gates this morning. I rocked up with half brushed hair, no make-up and a thrown on poncho with my boots, but my god, these women must have got up at the crack of dawn to look that good! Impeccable makeup, and I'm talking contoured cheeks and smoky eyes. They wear dresses and skyscraper-high boots.

Plus they all have their nannies with them. I actually heard one Mum refuse to kiss her child goodbye because it would smudge her lipstick. I'm gonna have to start setting my alarm. At the old nursery in St Albans, they all thought *I* was glamorous. Now I'm like a gremlin in comparison. Any excuse for a shopping trip.

I met one Mum, who introduced herself as Catherine Harringate the third and invited me to an afternoon round at her house today. I'm nervous as hell as I wait outside her house with Jemima. I have her dressed in a little navy flowery dress with sparkly converse. She looks beyond adorable. And this time, I brushed my hair and put makeup on.

I lean down to her. 'Remember what Mummy said?'

'Be a good girl,' she smiles.

'Exactly. Good girl.' I wink, and she winks back. She really is beyond cute sometimes.

I clasp her hand a bit tighter. I can't believe how nervous I am. Why do I even care about getting in with this clique? Oh, that's right. I need some local mummy friends. I'm doing this for Jemima. She needs to fit in. At least I know I look fabulous in my mustard skater dress, purple knee high boots and green faux fur coat.

The door swings open and Catherine Harringate the third smiles broadly showing sparkling veneers. Maybe I should get my teeth done too. Okay, now I know I'm nervous. My teeth are perfect. What is it about having a kid that zaps your confidence?

'Jasmine! How lovely of you to have come. Come in. We're just in the kitchen.'

I follow her downstairs to a huge open plan kitchen. Its layout is a lot like mine, but next to her table and chairs is a sofa with a few wooden kids toys thrown around. The other kids seem to be here too. Hugo, Floris, Ottilie, Montague, Epiphany, Arlo, Finnian and Randolph. Bunch of ridiculous names if you ask me. Next to them on the sofa are the nannies. God, they really do take them everywhere.

'Everyone, this is Jasmine Green. She's just moved back to the area.'

'Darling, why did you ever leave?' a blonde with far too much fake tan asks me.

'I met my partner,' I answer briefly, smiling with fake confidence. I don't want to tell them he knocked me up, and I moved in with him and his mother. Somehow, I don't think these are the kind of understanding friends I was hoping to meet.

'Welcome,' a beautiful brunette smiles. 'I'm Ottilie's mum. Where's your nanny?'

I take my coat off, faking the confidence I don't feel. 'Oh, I don't have one.'

A huge gasp fills the room. Wait, they can't be gasping at my dress. I deliberately chose something sensible. I look up to see them all horrified, eyeing each other back and forth as if I'm mentally unstable. Wow. This is about me not having a nanny. Overreact much?

'No nanny?' another one repeats slowly. 'But then who...who helps look after her?'

'Her Dad and her Nana. Plus I've got a lot of friends who help. My bestie's great with her.'

Times like this I really miss Poppy being just around the corner.

'But...but...' another one mutters. 'Why would you do that to yourself?'

'Yes, and what about when you go skiing?' Another one chimes in.

'Skiing?' I ask, totally confused at what these nitwits are talking about.

'Yes. In the Alps. We go every year. We assumed you would too?' Catherine Harringate the third chimes in.

Why the hell would they assume that? We went a few times when I was a teenager, but I never took to it. I preferred to sleep in all day and party at night.

'I think Jemima's too young for a skiing holiday,' I laugh. Unless I get her a cute pink sleigh. Now there's a thought.

'Of course she is,' another one splutters, almost spilling her tea. 'Which is why you leave her at home with the nanny. My God, you poor thing, how have you been coping?'

I roll my eyes. Dramatic much?

'I did have one when she was a baby, and I'm considering getting another, but I just don't really think I need one.'

Plus, as I look around at the nannies interacting with the children I feel nothing but pity for them. These mothers obviously don't work. Why don't they want to spend time with them? Jemima is already growing up far too quickly for my own liking. I notice she's bossing around Randolph, getting him to make a bed for her dolly. That's my girl.

'Well,' Catherine says, trying to cut the tension. 'Each to their own I suppose.' She picks up a plate of biscuits and offers them to me. 'Lemon biscuit?'

I smile, take one and stuff it into my mouth. Ugh, it tastes like stale cardboard.

'Gluten, lactose, wheat, and sugar-free. I'll give you the recipe if you like.' She smiles like she's Suzy homemaker. I bet she didn't even bake them.

'Mmmm,' I manage. God, could I possibly spit this out? It's vile. Why on earth would you bother making a biscuit if you leave out all of the good stuff?

'Mummy, look I built a man,' Hugo says to his Mum, tugging on her sleeve, obviously desperate for her attention.

'Yes, lovely, darling,' she says dismissively not even looking at it as she files her nails.

Poor Hugo. He looks crushed.

'Mummy.' I look down to see Jemima looking guilty. 'I wet myself.'

Oh crap. I jump down to find her tights soaked through all the way down to her sneakers.

'Baby, why didn't you tell me?' Normally she's so good.

She shrugs, jutting her bottom lip out like she might start crying. Probably nervous at being surrounded by these weirdos.

'Oh my god!' Catherine shrieks. 'She weed on my rug! That cost ten thousand pounds!'

She *must* be bloody joking. Ten thousand on a rug? Even I'm not that ridiculous. I ignore her and start stripping Jemima.

'Don't do that here,' she insists, her mouth gaping open. 'There's a bathroom upstairs.'

Honestly, this bitch is beyond ridiculous.

'It'll be done in a second,' I say through gritted teeth, pulling down her knickers.

Two balls of poo fall from her knickers onto the floor. *Eww!!*

'She's pooed herself!' Catherine screams jumping up onto her chair like the poo was going to run over and touch her.

'Sorry, mumma,' Jemima says, her eyes welling up, looking like she might burst into tears. My poor bambino.

'Don't worry, baby.'

I don't bloody blame her when she's surrounded by nutty women like this.

I quickly pick up the poo with baby wipes, clean her up and change her into new knickers and tights. Thank God I remembered them.

'I'm sorry, but I'm going to have to ask you to leave,' Catherine says, still on her chair like a scared kitten.

'What?' She can't be serious. She must be joking. *Right?*

'I'm sorry, but I can't have Arlo regressing. He's been potty trained six months now, and I'm not having him going back to that because of a bad influence.'

'Bad influence?' I repeat, a shocked smile on my face. This woman is actually fucking crazy. 'Are you fucking serious?'

'I am,' she nods sternly. The others stare on disapprovingly. Like I'm stood over a dead lion with a shotgun in my hands.

Jemima holds onto my leg. 'Sorry, mumma.'

'Don't worry, baby. We're leaving this horrible place.' I start leading her towards the stairs to the front door when an idea pops into my head.

I tell Jemima to stay there and march back into the room. The women look up horrified. I walk straight over to the rug and squash the poo from the baby wipe onto her precious rug. She screams in horror like I've stabbed her.

'There,' I smile evilly. *'Now* it's worth nothing.'

# Chapter 20
## Poppy

### *Thursday 3<sup>rd</sup> March*

We sit across from the doctor, in his brightly decorated office, holding hands. This is it. This is when we're going to find out what is wrong with us. The doctor studies our test results, his expressions changing every few seconds. I can't read him at all. My thumping heart is desperate to know if it's about to be broken.

'So...?' I ask, desperately, unable to curb the intensity in my voice. Haven't we already waited long enough? I feel like he's dragging it out like they do on the X Factor when they have to eliminate someone.

He clicks his pen and leans back on his leather chair. 'Well, you have what the NHS would call unexplained infertility.'

'Which means?' Ryan asks, the frustration clear in his tone.

'They'd look at these results and tell you that as there are no problems you'd have to wait three years for a free round of IVF.'

Three years!

'Riiiiight...' I have a feeling he's going to have a different opinion. I'm hoping. 'But what would you say?'

'As I said before, I'd suggest ICSI.'

'So wait,' I try to clarify, my head spinning. 'You're saying that we *could* have a baby? Just by this ICSI thing?'

'Yes,' he nods. 'With your age and the fact that you don't smoke and are healthy, the chances of success are quite high.'

A glimmer of hope swims through. 'Well, we'll have that then,' I say, new wonder in my voice. There is hope after all!

'Wait, how much are we talking?' Ryan asks, his forehead creased with worry.

The doctor places his fingers together on the desk. 'A round of ICSI, including all injections and aftercare, is five thousand pound.'

My jaw drops onto the floor. 'I thought IVF was only three grand.' Or is that a boob job?

'Like I said. ICSI is a more complicated procedure, but I would recommend it for you.'

Shit the bed. Five grand. That's a lot of dosh, but luckily I have Jazz.

'Okay. Well, we'll book it in now then please.' There's no point wasting time. My eggs are wasting away as we speak.

Ryan turns to me as if I'm mad, his probing stare causing me to squirm. 'Poppy, where the hell are we going to find five grand?'

I have to mention Jazz, but I know he's going to say no. I need to be brave. This is the chance for us to have a baby.

'I'm sure Jazz would lend it to us,' I whisper back.

His face turns to fury, his breathing erratic before he tries to contain himself. He turns back to the doctor. 'Thanks for everything, doctor, but we're going to go away now and think about it.'

What the hell is he doing? I want to book it now. Enough with the time wasting!

'In the meantime I assume we can have a copy of the test results for our NHS specialist?' he asks as he stands up.

NHS specialist?

'Oh, of course,' the doctor nods back. 'I can email them over to you.'

I'm still sitting here flabbergasted. What the hell is he talking about? Didn't he hear the doctor? Three years. It would take three bloody years before they'd even think about treating us. When we can just borrow the money from Jazz and book it in immediately. What the hell is his problem?

He walks out of the door and practically sprints down the hall. I follow him blindly, slowly filling with rage. What the hell is his problem? Does he not even want this baby? Because I wish he would have told me that before I went through these awful tests.

As soon as we're in the car I face him, arms folded over my chest, ready for a fight.

'What the hell is wrong with you?' I shout far too loudly. 'Why won't you just let me borrow the money from Jazz?'

He stares back at me, seeming just as furious. 'Because I don't want her to know about this.'

'Why not, when she can help?' My voice erupts into an angry growl.

He runs his hands through his hair making it look just fucked.

'Because I don't want everyone knowing that I'm not man enough to get my wife knocked up.'

I can't believe him. I know I should feel bad for him, but I don't. The selfish bastard. Thinking of himself again.

'So wait, let me get this straight. Because you're embarrassed; I can't confide in my *best friend?*'

The fact that I already have shouldn't be relevant here.

'Yes,' he nods, looking out the window, his forehead creased in turmoil.

'You don't think it was *embarrassing* for me to have my vagina on parade while they pumped me with dye and watched my uterus on the screen like it was a fucking mini movie!' I scream, my hands trembling with rage. I still feel slighted that he didn't come with me, and I'm sure it comes across in my tone.

He looks at me like I'm overreacting. It only makes me madder.

'I'm sorry if that was embarrassing, but it had to be done so we could get to here.'

'How convenient,' I snort. 'I have to go through all of that, and you just have to wank in a cup.'

He sighs, suddenly looking tired. 'I did offer to come with you,' he tries to reason, attempting to calm me down. He fails.

'No, you didn't. You gave me a half arsed 'I could try to re-arrange it'. That's not the same, Ryan.' My voice breaks; fucking traitorous emotions. 'Do

163

you know how lonely I felt going in there? Everyone else had someone with them. Either their partners, or their mum, or a friend. But oh no, because you're insecure, I'm not allowed any support.'

His lips press into a hard line. 'I could have re-arranged it! You should have just said.'

'Well, maybe I was too embarrassed to beg you to love me. Maybe I assumed after all these years together you'd be able to read me and see that I wanted support.' I'm aware I'm losing it, but it's too late to reign myself back in.

'So now you want me to read your mind and work out whether what you're saying is actually the truth?' He runs his hand through his hair, ruffling it up again. It annoys me that it makes him look sexy.

'Most husbands would just know.'

He sighs loudly and exaggerated. 'Look, we're getting off subject here. The point is that I don't want to borrow the money from Jazz. Or anyone for that matter. Call me old-fashioned, but I'd like to pay for my own baby.'

'She wouldn't be buying us a baby! She'd just be helping us create one.'

He raises his eyebrows at me. 'Which is weird. Admit it; if we were conceiving a baby naturally would you want Jazz involved? In the room watching every detail?'

Eww. Why did he go there?

I roll my eyes. 'You know that's fucked up.'

'Whatever. We'll start saving. And either we'll be able to save the money, or we'll wait the three years and get a free round on the NHS.'

I can't believe my ears. He's actually considering waiting *three years*. Three fucking *years*. Three sets of three hundred and sixty-five days. That makes...well, it makes a long fucking time.

'I can't believe you're considering waiting that long. I'll be thirty-three then! Only two years away from my fertility plummeting to half. And let's be honest, it's clearly not the best to start with.'

He grabs my hand and squeezes it reassuringly with a sad smile marring his lips.

'Pops, this is how I feel. Please support that.'

'Don't you realise that I'm going to need support while I'm going through all of this? And that's before the actual IVF. How do you think *I'm* going to cope?'

He squeezes my hand again before bringing it up to his lips and placing a gentle kiss.

'You have me.'

I shake my head. He'll never understand what it's like for me. I begrudgingly nod, giving in. I don't have the energy for a fight right now, especially when it doesn't look like he's giving in. I can't believe he's not more considerate of my feelings.

Maybe I can come up with another scheme with Jazz about coming into more money. I stare out of the window as he starts the engine, wondering if I'll ever be truly happy again. Can we really come back from this?

'And I trust that you won't be getting any more random inheritance, right?'

Oh shit. He's onto me. He's not as dumb as I thought. I begrudgingly nod as a lone tear falls from my eye.

We go round Mum and Dad's afterwards. I think it's because we don't want to talk to each other right now, and our house will just be too awkward. Plus, it was nice having Mum so pleased to see us. Bless her, but she's so lonely since Jazz, Ollie and Jem moved out.

I refused the wine and went for tea, even though Ryan quite happily took a beer. It shouldn't have pissed me off as much as it did, but the man's just been told he's got abnormal sperm. Surely the natural reaction would be him wanting to be healthier? Not slugging down his sorrows in a beer. Maybe I'm over-reacting. This whole baby-making thing is turning me into a right psycho.

I'm stopped from my thoughts by a loud sound. It sounds like a ridiculously big motorbike.

'That'll be your father,' Mum sighs grabbing my arm. 'Come on.'

Ryan and I look at each other in confusion before being dragged out of the front door. Dad is sitting on top of what looks like a brand new black shiny motorbike, decked out in leathers. He's holding a helmet with fire flames down the side of it.

'What the hell is this?' I shriek my mouth open in disgust.

It's official. Dad's having a breakdown.

'It's my new motorbike,' he grins, looking like a child on Christmas morning. 'Don't you love it?'

'I do!' Ryan beams, going up and stroking it like you would a cat. 'How much?'

'Just under 8k,' he replies.

'What? How the hell did you afford that?' Mum shrieks. 'I thought you said you were getting a good deal.'

He grins excitedly. 'Jazz bought it for me.'

I'm going to kick Jazz's arse.

'You let Jazz buy you a death machine!' Mum shrieks.

'How do you even know how to ride it? You could have killed yourself already!' I hate these things. They just scream death and danger.

'I've been taking lessons. Bit of a natural according to my instructor.'

Taking lessons? Since when? Who is this person standing in front of me? This isn't my pyjama-loving father.

'What on earth possessed you?' I look to Mum. 'I can't believe you allowed this!'

She takes a slug of her wine. 'I tried to talk him out of it, darling, but it turns out when your dad wants something bad enough he can be a very stubborn man.'

'I don't have to ask your mother permission for everything, you know,' he says, crossing his arms over his chest like a spoilt brat.

We all laugh, which I suppose doesn't help.

He does look cute; bless him. Like a chubby child on his new toy.

'Just...just don't kill yourself okay.'

'Promise,' he grins.

# Chapter 21

Jazz

*Friday 4th March*

I finally called an agency and asked them to send over some potential housekeepers.

'Do you have any references?' I ask the Armenian lady in my lounge.

She's really cute. On the plump side with big goldfish eyes that bulge out every time she speaks as if everything shocks her. Frizzy black greying curls surround her round face, concealing some of her double chins.

'Yes. I have numbers,' she says in her broken English. She rummages around in her bag and gets out a list of names and numbers.

I smile gratefully and take it from her, scanning speedily down the names. Shit, Catherine Harringate the third is on this list.

'You cleaned for Catherine Harringate?' I ask in surprise.

She nods eagerly.

'And why did you stop working for her?'

Her face falls. 'She not like the way I clean floor. She say I damage expensive rug.'

'Her rug?' I laugh. 'You mean, the ten thousand pound one?'

She nods sadly. 'I think a lot of money for stupid rug.'

I laugh loudly, throwing my head back, so it turns into a real witch's cackle. 'I think you and I are going to get on just fine. Can you start right away?'

'Oh! Yes,' she grins clapping her hands in glee. 'Thank you so much, Miss Jasmine. You not regret this.'

'Make sure I don't,' I wink, walking up the stairs. 'Tell the agency to send the paperwork and cancel the other applicants.'

Well, that's one job down. Thank God. Everything seems to be such hard work here in Chelsea. Jemima's not settled here at all. Although her nursery teacher says she doesn't cry when I leave, she's clingy as hell on the walk. I hope to God the kids aren't dicks to her just because I ruined that rug. But I'm still glad I did. Probably gave the sad bitches something to talk about for days. Good, at least they're leaving someone else alone while they're wasting their breath slagging me off.

Plus Jemima is still wetting and pooing herself. I'm sure it's some kind of anxiety over being uprooted. It seems I was so excited to have my old life back I forgot to really think about it. That's always been my problem; act first, think later. She's been living with Nana and Grandad for as long as she can remember and I've just dragged her away from them. Them and the nursery she loved and was settled at. I'm such a bad mother.

Plus, I'm sure it doesn't help that Ollie is still sulking. Every night when he comes in he whinges about not being able to get a parking space anywhere near the house. He's still working for his Dad and hasn't mentioned giving it up yet. I think it's just an excuse to get away from me at the minute. Then he eats his dinner and is off to bed. His commute is a lot longer now, so he's shattered. And it doesn't help that I'm so shattered from Jemima by the time he gets in that I basically clock out for half an hour, going through my Facebook. I just need some me time. Now I realise how much easier it was when Meryl was always around. Who knew my child could be so demanding? I don't know where she gets it from.

The thing is, that even though I'm sure I've made a mistake, I don't want to admit it. I know I'm a stubborn bitch, but I just can't bear for everyone to tell me I told you so. Instead, I've been going out with my old crowd a few nights a week. Poppy's always busy, helping Lilly with the wedding. It's the only release I get. If I didn't have that, I would literally have nothing.

I'm just getting ready in my dressing room when Ollie comes in. He leans against my wardrobe with his hands crossed over his chest.

'Who is the lady hovering downstairs?' he asks, outraged.

Ah, he's met Lucine then.

'That's Lucine. She's our new housekeeper.'

'Another decision made without me,' he says under his breath with a sigh. I decide to ignore it. 'Out again then, are we?' he asks with raised eyebrow, zero humour in his voice.

'Yep,' I nod, not meeting his eyes. I can't. He'll see how miserable I am.

'This is bullshit,' he says curtly, his tone livid.

I start and turn round to stare at him. 'What the hell are you talking about?'

'This.' He points around at the clothes like they're offending him. 'This, going out every night. Leaving me alone with Jemima, who by the way now wakes up, at least, three times a night, crying. She hates it here.'

I turn my head sharply away from him, clenching my jaw to stop me shouting random swear words at him. He's calling me a bad mother, the bastard.

'Well, she never wakes up when I'm here.' He could be making it up for all I know.

'Doesn't that tell you something?' he snorts, a note of petulance in his voice. 'She wants her mummy.'

My chest aches at the idea. Damn, wretched guilt growing inside my heart. Could that be it? But I can't let a three-year-old dictate my life.

'Well, I'm very sorry,' I snort, 'but if she thinks I'm going to stay in every night while she sleeps she has another thing coming.'

A streak of disappointment flashes through his face.

'I thought we were going to settle down together. I'm serious about wanting another baby.'

I scrunch my face up in disgust. How can he even be serious? Especially when we're bickering like this.

'I told you, Ollie, I don't want any more children. I've just got my life back. And you're already pissed that you have to *babysit* the daughter you have.'

He looks away; hurt pouring from his face. He takes a few moments to gather himself.

'I'm just pissed I have to do it in this house,' he snaps, throwing his arms about dramatically like I'm forcing him to live in a garden shed.

'*Our* house,' I correct him.

Sadness clouds his baby-blue eyes. '*This* has never been my house. It might be yours, but it's never going to be mine. I feel like I'm staying in a hotel.'

How much of an ungrateful fucker can he be? People would *die* to live here.

I purse my lips, anger seeping from my pores. 'Well, if you don't like it you know what you can do. Move back in with your mother.'

Shit, why did I just say that? His face drops before he covers it with indifference. Crap. What have I done? I've gone too far.

'Fine,' he nods, visibly wounded. 'I'm going to stay with Mum. You can stay in and look after Jemima yourself.'

He storms out of the room slamming every door behind him. The front door finally slams waking up a crying Jemima.

Ugh, fuck my life.

## Poppy

Jazz called me, hysterically crying, so here I am. It's such a pain in the arse having to come all this way, but I know she'd do it for me if it weren't for Jemima. I've been a good friend and brought wine. I took a quick pregnancy test before I left, so I know I'm not pregnant. And fuck me, do I want a large drink right now.

When I find Jazz in her sitting room with a bottle of white wine and a straw, I know it must be bad. I present my two bottles to her. She nods gratefully in understanding.

'Explain,' I demand, getting her bottle opener and opening another one.

I make myself comfortable on her sofa, which is hard considering it's all about the style and nothing about the comfort. She's on the comfy one. Then I grab another straw from the opened pack on the coffee table and join her.

'I've fucked everything up,' she whines, pushing her curls back off her forehead.

I roll my eyes. She can be so dramatic.

'That could mean anything. You're going to have to be specific.'

Her eyes glisten with unshed tears. 'Ugh, your brother hates me. I've done everything wrong ever since I got this money. It's like a curse or something.'

I can't help but laugh. 'Oh yeah, I feel really bad for you,' I mock. 'It must suck so hard to be rich, counting your gold and diamonds every night.'

'Money doesn't buy happiness,' she reminds me with a sad smile.

'All I'm saying is I'd rather be crying into fifty-pound notes,' I deadpan.

She laughs, but it's forced, clearly only for my benefit. 'Why am I such a dickhead, Pops? I had a great thing going with that sex rod of a brother of yours.'

I nearly vomit in my mouth. Sex rod? Eww. Now I have images invading my head of Ollie with a massive fishing rod as a penis, catching Carp from it.

'Eww, too much information!' I screech, going to cover my ears. They can't stop the images though.

More tears fill her eyes and begin to overspill. 'And then I just push him away because I'm too busy wanting to get my old life back.' She rubs her face wearily.

She really doesn't understand that she can't rewind time.

'Babe, you have Jemima now. Your life will never be the same again.'

'I know,' she nods, resigned. 'I just...I guess I didn't realise how good I had it, until I didn't. Does that make sense?'

'Kind of,' I shrug. I'm drinking this wine far too quickly, and it's going straight to my head. I really should have eaten dinner. But a pack of Pringles kind of counts, right?

'Why are *you* upset anyway?' she asks, noticing my drooped shoulders and generally defeated demeanour. I thought she'd be too upset to notice me.

'You mean *apart* from the fact that I can't get pregnant?'

She rolls her eyes. 'I keep telling you, babe, you just need to have a mind blowing orgasm. It's not a myth. Is Ryan really satisfying you?'

I heave myself off the sofa and throw myself onto her on the other sofa, grabbing her for a cuddle. It's also another way to shut her up.

'Yes, he satisfies me, thank you very much! And don't worry about Ollie. Despite everything, he loves you and so do I. Come on, let's watch *While You Were Sleeping*.'

She rolls her eyes. 'You really think a stupid rom-com is going to make me feel better?'

She doesn't? Sometimes I seriously question our friendship.

I slap her hand. 'Not a stupid one. I said *While You Were Sleeping*. And need I remind you that poor Sandra Bullock has had her fair share of relationship strife?'

She rolls her eyes again but moves so that I'm spooning her.

'Fine, wife; just shut up and download it.'

## Chapter 22
### Poppy

*Saturday 5th March*

I wake up; bleary eyed, to find Jazz's face squashed right up against mine and Jemima jumping on the opposite sofa singing, 'Auntie Pwoppy is here! Auntie Pwoppy is here!'

Shit, what time is it? I find my phone half under the sofa and look at the time. Shit the bed, it's ten to nine!! I promised I'd go and watch Dad play his first rugby match with Ryan's team.

I jump up, my head pounding, reminding me that things should be very slow and gentle today. I leave Jazz to it while I call a cab and pour Jemima out some cereal.

I throw some water over Jazz's face when my cab beeps from out front. She startles, spluttering the water from her mouth.

'Wake up and look after your daughter, whore,' I say before kissing her on the cheek.

She looks up at me with puppy dog eyes. I almost feel bad for the water. *Almost.*

I don't get to the pitch until ten am, just before kick off. Nobody's happy with me, but they're lucky I'm here at all. I did also grab Ollie and reason that I wouldn't ask him about Jazz if he brought me a large cup of tea with six sugars and a huge iced doughnut. That seems to have helped.

Dad has insisted on joining the guys this weekend; playing rugby. We've all tried to talk him out of it. I mean; playing amongst young twenty and thirty-year-olds is such a stupid idea. I told him that if he wanted to do some exercise, there's a group for men over fifty who work out in the park at lunchtime every Saturday, but the cocky bastard just laughed in my face.

Even now, walking onto the pitch with his beer belly protruding out of his rugby shirt he looks arrogant as anything. He has no idea he's about to get the pounding of his life. I try to make it to Ryan's matches as often as I can. Actually, that's a lie, as often as I can get away with. If I can come up with an excuse and lay in my cosy bed instead, then I'm doing it.

'Your Dad really isn't afraid, is he?' Izzy laughs, watching him chatting away to the rest of the team.

I chuckle. 'Ryan had to beg their coach to let him play with them. They're only humouring him.'

With that in mind, I call Ryan over. He jogs over to me, those hairy legs so bloody muscular. I'm so lucky he keeps in shape. Maybe I shouldn't eat the rest of this doughnut. Ah, who am I kidding?

'You alright, babe?'

'Apart from freezing my tits off,' I laugh. 'Yeah, I'm good. Anyway, listen; please spread the word to go gentle on Dad. He still thinks he's twenty.'

He grins. 'You've got to love his enthusiasm. If I'm that eager at his age, I'll have done well.'

I bet he's going to be one hell of a good-looking older man. I'd say he'd pull off grey hair well.

I look at him sternly. 'I mean it though, babe, I don't want him seriously hurt.'

'You have so little faith,' he laughs, sporting a comical face. 'I've already told the guys to go easy on him. Today's not a real match anyway.'

'Thank God.'

He smiles at me. It's the smile I love the most. The one where he gazes down at me adoringly, like he thinks I'm the sweetest thing in the world. Not that I don't love *all* of his smiles.

'Give me a good luck kiss before I go on?' he jokes, pouting his lips.

I lean in and press my lips against his cold ones. His chilly hand strokes down my cheek, making me tingle down to my toes. How is it he can still do this to me after all these years? He leans back and smiles down at me with a sexy glint in his eye, promising it will be continued later. I shiver, and it's not just from the cold. He's *so* hot.

He jogs back onto the pitch, helping my dad with his mouth guard. This is what we need more of. Me and him just connecting; just fancying each other again. Having sex for the pure joy of having sex. Lately, it's so regimented. Knowing we have to, so our chances are increased. Sometimes I just want to sleep, but I think he'd be upset if I said 'just try not to wake me up.'

I'm watching nervously, biting my lip and practically holding my breath, when I hear a lady telling another that she's having acupuncture tonight. There's an idea. I read in one of the online forums that acupuncture can help with problems conceiving. Maybe it can work for me too.

When she's not looking I Google the place she was talking about and book an appointment. I mean it's worth a try, right? What could go wrong?

'Fancy a walk?' Izzy asks, pulling me out of my daydream.

Bless her, always wanting to exercise. But it makes sense, especially since we've brought Toffee with us for some fresh air. Grams can't give her the long walks she needs anymore.

We start walking towards the woods where the mud is more slippery. Thank God I thought to wear wellies.

'So, how are you?' I ask, us both knowing I'm really asking about her crazy stalker.

'Yeah, I'm good.' She shrugs like it's no big deal.

'Any more weird calls?' I press.

She starts teasing Toffee with a stick, obviously playing for time. 'I've had one or two.'

I can't stand her indifference towards her safety.

'Oh for God's sakes, stop underplaying this! I think you need to call the police.'

'I have, okay!' she admits reluctantly. 'They said there's nothing much they can do until they actually cause harm to me.'

'You *are* shitting me right?' I shriek. 'This nutcase has to hurt you before they'll protect you?

What kind of crazy-arsed logic is that?'

She shrugs as if it's no big deal. 'That's just how it is.'

I can tell she's more scared than she's making out. For her to actually take action and call the police proves to me that she's more concerned than she's making out.

'Well then let's hire a private detective if the police won't get involved.'

'A private detective?' she repeats, her eyes wide. 'That's a bit dramatic isn't it?'

'Izzy you have a stalker!' What part of that does she not understand?

An old lady walking her dog looks at me with raised eyebrows. Obviously a *bit* loud.

'Quieten down,' she hisses. 'I don't want the whole world knowing. Okay, if it's that bloody important to you, I'll hire a private detective.'

I take a deep breath to try and calm myself down. 'I just think you should know who's doing this,' I try to reason.

'I am kind of interested, if I'm honest,' she admits begrudgingly. 'I've started thinking that it could be his ex-wife.'

I've secretly had those fears too. From what I know about her from Michael, she's a nutcase.

'Then it's decided. First thing Monday morning I'm calling one.'

'Fine,' she shrugs nonchalantly. 'Anyway, what about Ryan's Mum? Have you heard from her?'

'Ssshh!' I look around nervously; checking that no one we know is in earshot.

'No. I was actually thinking we could sneak off and go to her place now if you fancy?'

I must still be drunk, but I can't help but worry about her.

She rolls her eyes. 'Why not. Get it over and done with.'

We make our way back to the match to see that it's half time already. Dad runs over to me with a massive grin on his face.

'I told you, Poppy, I'm doing great out there!' he says, out of breath.

'These young-uns have nothing on me!'

Is he serious? Can he not see they're going easy on him?

'Well, maybe now that you've got it out of your system you can stop playing,' I say hopefully.

'Don't be silly, Poppy!' he chuckles. 'I'm having so much fun; I'm going to make this a regular thing.'

Is he insane? He'll kill himself.

'But Dad, you need to rest!' I lower my voice to a whisper and pull him away from Izzy. 'You've barely recovered from cancer.'

'I'll rest when I'm dead,' he chuckles, completely unconcerned about himself. 'It wouldn't hurt if you got yourself involved in some exercise too.'

My face drops. That cocky bastard. He smiles before jogging off.

And picking on my weight? He's been hanging around with Mum too long.

I call Ryan over. 'You okay, babe?' he asks, his forehead furrowed.

'Yeah,' I nod, squashing down the feelings of hurt. 'Me and Izzy are gonna go into town for some shopping.'

I hate lying to him, but it's not like I can be honest right now.

'No worries,' he nods, pecking a quick kiss on my lips.

'And remember how I said to go easy on Dad? Well, I take it back. Tell the boys to go to town.'

Sometimes you have to be cruel to be kind

## Poppy

Thank god I brought Izzy with me. This area is rough as fuck. The address Ryan's mum had previously given me is for a tower block of flats that belong in a gangster movie. I stare up at it in horror. I just hope to god there's a lift. She's number one hundred and seven and something tells me that's not on the ground floor.

I buzz her number and wait, checking over my shoulder every two seconds. Thank god we came in daylight hours. I dread to think how scary it is at night. I buzz again, but there's no answer.

A teenager in a hoodie comes bursting out of the door. I grab it before it slams. I suppose this is our only way in.

'Come on,' I motion to Izzy.

Fear crosses her face. 'I have a bad feeling about this.'

'Oh, shut up your whining,' I snap.

She's supposed to be here to calm me, not build on my anxiety.

We walk through the dark corridor, a light flickering on and off above our heads. Did I say like a gangster movie? I meant a horror film. I'm actually glad I was nice enough to continue emailing her. Coming home to this every day is enough to turn anyone suicidal. At least, she had my emails to perk her up. I'm surprised this place gets Internet at all.

We follow the signs telling us that flat one hundred and seven is on the twelfth floor. Thankfully there's a working lift. Izzy tries to talk me out of it, insisting the fitness of the stairs would do us good. She never fails to amaze me.

We trudge down the hallway and towards her door. I knock as loudly as I can. No answer. I bang with my fist. Still no answer. I look at Izzy with raised eyebrows.

She smiles before joining me banging heavily on the door.

'Hey!' someone shouts from behind us.

We both jump and turn to see an overweight man hanging out of his flat dressed only in a wife-beater vest and boxer shorts.

'What you want?' he snarls. Crap he's scary.

'Err...we're looking for Linda Davis. She's my mother in law,' I explain hurriedly.

He rolls his eyes, apparently totally inconvenienced from being interrupted watching Jeremy Kyle.

'She's gone.'

'Gone?' Izzy gasps, eyes bulging out. 'As in *dead?*'

I roll my eyes. God, she can be dumb sometimes.

'Not dead. Just left,' he explains on a sigh. 'Got sacked from her job so she couldn't pay her rent. They evicted her.'

'Evicted her?' I repeat totally confused. 'Where did she go?'

'No idea,' he says gruffly, completely uninterested.

'Well, when did you last see her?' I press, desperate for any kind of information. This can't be a dead end.

'Few weeks maybe. Dunno,' he shrugs.

God, he's helpful. Not.

'Okay, thanks.'

I take Izzy's arm and drag her back towards the lift.

'Wait,' she says, struggling from my grasp. She runs back to his door and knocks. He answers immediately; obviously knowing it's us again. 'If you ever want to get fit and lose some weight here's my card.'

My mouth falls open. That's it Izzy; anger the scary man further.

I drag her away just before he slams the door in her face.

'Jesus, Izzy, if you go around insulting people like that no wonder you have someone prank calling you.' I pull her into the lift.

'I'm just trying to help,' she retorts, clearly hurt.

'I doubt he'd be able to afford you anyway.'

'Oh, I'd make an exception for someone like him. I'm sick of training already thin actresses.'

'My heart bleeds,' I mock.

At that minute, the lift goes up back and then stops completely. I start stabbing at the buttons, but it's no use, we're stuck. Great. Just great.

I slump down onto the floor. Only me.

'So, where are we going now anyway?' she asks. I stare at her. '*Obviously* once we're out of this lift. I mean, she must have someone she'd have gone to.'

I shake my head. 'No. That's the thing, Izzy. She has no-one.'

# Chapter 23
## Jazz

*Saturday 5<sup>th</sup> March*

What the hell was I thinking moving away from my family and friends? I must have been high at the time. High on money, and memories of my childhood, clearly. I hate how I can't just walk to Poppy's and demand she pour the wine.

So when Lettuce Facebooked me and asked if I fancied going out with her, I said yes. Like I said, she might not be my favourite person in the entire world, but she's always been nice to me. Plus, I don't really want to turn away any friends here, and if Lettuce doesn't like you, your social life might as well be dead.

So here I find myself in JuJu in Chelsea while Lucine babysits Jemima. We're in the VIP area, which is slotted away in a completely private corner. I'm sure lots of people like that, but not me. I prefer to be where the action is. Somewhere I can throw my moves on the dance floor. Not that Lettuce isn't a laugh. She's actually got one of the loudest laughs I've ever heard, making people's heads turn wherever she goes. I am enjoying myself, especially with every Porn Star Martini I drink here. It's the most gorgeous drink; martini mixed with vanilla vodka, passion fruit liqueur and a splash of pineapple. Plus it's served with a shot of champagne on the side, which doesn't hurt.

The DJ is playing some good tunes, but I can't help but think it would be more fun if Poppy were here. We could go to any shit club and have a hilarious time. Lettuce is just so Chelsea. Stereotypical rich girl who has no idea about the real world. It's made me realise that I used to be just like her. Only real life hit me hard in the face when I had Jemima.

Lettuce comes stumbling over to me. 'Babe, we're all going back to mine.'

'Oh okay,' I nod. 'I might just head home.'

'Don't be ridiculous!' she snorts. 'You're coming with us whether you like it or not. It's *so* lame here.'

I actually like it, but it's not worth saying to her. Especially when she's so trashed. I follow the crowd out as we all get cabs back to her mansion. Mummy and Daddy bought it for her when she turned twenty-one. It's basically only a bit smaller than mine, and ultra-modern, all black and white chrome with clean lines.

I'm glad to be back to a house setting though. I kick off my shoes and settle in her bar. That's right, she has a bar on the top level. It's got every drink you can ever imagine with huge corner sofas covering most of the walls. We all slouch down and begin to relax, chatting about aimless stuff.

'Right, who's got it then?' Lettuce grins, getting a chopping board out.

Are we eating cheese? Well, that's bloody random. Not that I don't love a bit of cheese.

'Me!' says SJ, one of her friends with inflated lips and enormous tits. She takes a small bag out of her bra and starts pouring it on to the chopping board.

Shit, it's coke. They're all doing cocaine? I haven't done coke since I was twenty-two, and I have no intention of doing it again. The scary thing was that it felt far too good like I could literally take on the world. It was such an amazing high that the next day I wanted to do it again. I was smart enough to find that scary. I must have an addictive personality or something, but I knew that I could never do it again without turning into a total cokehead. And that is *never* a good look. It helped that I told Poppy, and she went fucking ballistic at me. That girl is such a goody two shoes.

The board is passed to Elisia; the girl SJ sometimes becomes a lesbian with. Basically, every time they've been drunk since I've known them. Elisia snorts it up her nose like a pro and passes it around to the others, each of them greedily snorting their line and then rubbing the remaining into their gums.

Their mate Elisia seems quite greedy with it, continuously snatching it back. The board is getting closer and closer to me. I really don't want to do it, but I also don't want to have to come up with a lame excuse. I don't want to be the boring mummy they all assume I am.

Instead, I stand up. Lettuce and a few of the others look at me with raised eyebrows.

'Just going for a cigarette,' I smile, grabbing my bag.

'You can smoke in here,' Lettuce says with a confused wrinkled forehead.

Shit.

'Thanks, but I want some fresh air anyway.'

I pad down the two sets of stairs in my bare feet wondering what I'm even doing here. I could be home right now with my darling daughter asleep next door to me. I've never been a gushing mother, but I suddenly want nothing but to be a boring mummy. There's so much more honesty with a child. No bullshit. If she doesn't like something, she just tells me. She's like having a mini best friend with me the entire time. I suppose it's been easy since we moved her to see her as a hindrance first, but I don't have the time to just enjoy her lately. I've always been competing with Meryl for her attention, but without Meryl around it's hard to just kick back and have a giggle with her.

I look out at the modern garden. Footsteps are suddenly behind me.

'You okay?'

I turn to find one of Lettuce's male friends. He's actually the one I scoped out earlier. He doesn't seem as loud and obnoxious as the others and is pretty gorgeous. But then who isn't in Chelsea?

'Yep,' I nod quickly. 'Just a bit drunk,' I lie.

He smiles knowingly. 'I'm not into that shit either.'

I turn back to him completely shocked that he's sussed me out. He's not into drugs?

'Really?' I ask in disbelief. I thought everyone did it nowadays?

'Really,' he nods. 'I'm too sensible for my own good. My mates are always taking the piss out of me and calling me Grandpa.'

I laugh and allow my shoulders to relax for a second. He's actually a nice guy. He reminds me of my Ollie in his demeanour. I miss him so bad. He hasn't been back since he left and I'm too stubborn to contact him.

Now that I can look at him up close I can see that he's actually an incredibly good-looking bloke. I suppose I didn't notice before because he just has short brown hair and is of average build. But up close I can see how blue his sparkling eyes are. Blue and sincere-seeming, somehow.

'What's your name again?'

'Rupert.'

I can't help but giggle. 'Like Rupert the bear?'

He smiles, well naturedly. 'Yep, just like Rupert the bear. Don't think I haven't heard every joke already.'

'Really?' I snort. 'I bet you haven't heard this one. How do you apologise to a koala?'

He looks back at me funny. 'Err. Don't know.'

'BEAR your heart and soul!' I double over laughing. Maybe I'm more drunk than I thought.

'Most people call me Rupe.'

'Well, I might call you Ert,' I joke.

His face remains impassive before he bursts out laughing.

'It's true what they say about you; you're one of a kind.'

I smile sadly. People are still talking about me then. Nosy bastards.

'I think I'm just going to call a cab,' I admit on a sigh.

'I can drop you home if you like?' he offers with a sincere smile.

I assess him. He doesn't seem creepy or to even seem to be trying it on with me. But wait, has he been drinking?

'Aren't you drunk?'

He chuckles. 'Didn't you just hear me? I'm a Grandpa. I've been on slimline tonics all night.'

'Oooh, slimline!' I giggle. 'Watching your figure too are we?' I laugh loudly, realising I haven't laughed properly with Ollie since before we got the money.

'You don't look this good from guzzling beer all day,' he says with a wicked grin.

Yeah, now that I look he does seem pretty trim. Not that my Ollie isn't. Oh God, I just want to go home, cuddle under my duvet and question every stupid thing I've ever done.

'Okay,' I nod. 'I'll take that lift as long as we go now.'

'That's fine,' he smiles, humour curving his lips. He looks down at my bare feet. 'But don't you want to go and get your shoes first?'

'Ah,' I wave dismissively. 'You wear one Louboutin you've worn them all.'

He looks at me strangely, the edges of his lips creeping into an almost awed smile.

'I think it's safe to say that I've never met a girl like you before.'

I chuckle as I follow him towards the door. 'Oh, you have no idea.'

We drive in a comfortable kind of silence. I keep looking out of the window to check he is actually driving me home; you know, just in case he's a psychopath. Clearly I've been hanging around with Poppy too much. But he seems normal enough.

I turn towards him; sitting cross-legged on the chair. 'So how come you're so normal then?' I ask in all seriousness.

He smiles, amused eyes twinkling as streetlights hit them. 'My parents. They insisted on sending me to a normal school.'

'You mean...not private?' I shriek, sounding very Chelsea myself. That's so cruel. He must have been so bullied.

'Yep, just normal. You have no idea how hard it was being the posh boy. I got the shit beaten out of me most days.' He laughs as if this is a fond memory. Weirdo.

I direct him where to pull in.

'Well, thanks for the lift.' I smile at him gratefully, hoping he doesn't try to kiss me or anything.

'Would you be up for going out for a quiet drink one night?' he asks shyly. 'Something a lot different to tonight.'

I fiddle with my handbag. 'Erm, well the thing is that I have a kind of boyfriend.'

He chuckles darkly. 'A kind of boyfriend?'

'Yeah. It's...well, it's complicated right now. But I'm not exactly available. And, well, I have a daughter too.' That normally has them running for the hills screaming 'she has a baggy pussy!'

'I know,' he nods. 'Lettuce said.'

'What?' This has my attention. 'You asked about me?'

'Of course.' He smiles with a wink. His smile is so kind and genuine seeming.

'You're kind of sexy.' My eyes widen. Did I really just say that out loud? Oh my God, I'm mortified. 'I mean...that's what a single person would say.'

'Well, thanks,' he says, his voice showing he's suppressing laughter.

'Err...yeah. Anyway,' I point towards the house. 'I better, you know...'

'Go in?' he asks, his lips twitching.

'Yeah, go in,' I nod like a fool. 'Thanks again.'

I get out of the car and practically run up the stairs and thrust the key in the door. I open it and rush in and am just about to close it when I realise he's still there, checking I got in okay. He waves to me before driving off. Do nice men like that still really exist?

## Poppy

### Monday 7$^{th}$ March

So after work on Monday, me and Izzy tell Ryan we're going to get our nails done. In reality, we head to the private detective agency I've found online. Apparently they're really good and professional. To be honest, I'm still expecting a sweaty, overweight man in a shitty office in the back of an alleyway. But when we arrive it's all glass and chrome. It just looks like a normal solicitors.

The receptionist is extra cheery and offers us a drink while we wait. We both refuse politely. Izzy looks at me, biting her lip. She's nervous. I don't blame her. I'm nervous. Not that I can show Izzy that. I need to act like a strong independent woman so that she can feel supported.

'It's going to be fine,' I whisper, smiling encouragingly. 'Just remember we're here to put a stop to this stalker.'

'I know,' she nods, biting her lip even harder. She's really not good under pressure. At least I'd like to think I could hide it better.

'Miss Bianchi?'

We both look up to see a red headed lady with a sharp pointed bob. She's wearing skyscraper heels and a well-tailored black suit. She looks like she means business. I wish I could be tough like that.

'Follow me please,' she smiles tightly.

We follow her down a long corridor and into a room with a large wooden table. I hope she doesn't expect us to sit at opposite ends. We'd have to shout to each other.

'Please take a seat and tell me what you'd like from me.'

Izzy sits down, twiddling her hands in her lap, a long silence hanging around us. Luckily the woman sits across from us.

'I'll start then, shall I?' I say sarcastically to her before turning back to the woman. 'We have two people we'd like you to look into. The first is my mother in law, Linda Davis. She was evicted from her flat a couple of weeks ago, and I have no idea where she could be. Here is her last address and email address.'

'Thank you. That should be easy enough. And the other?'

I point to Izzy. 'She's got a stalker. The police won't help, and she refuses to stress out her boyfriend, but this person is getting worse.'

'What exactly are we talking about here?' she asks, already taking notes.

'Phone calls,' Izzy admits. 'And...' she fidgets in her seat. 'Well, I kind of feel like I'm being followed, but that could just be me being paranoid.'

'And the other night they scraped *slut* into her car,' I add, wanting her to get the full story and not think Izzy's imagining things. God knows she's playing it down enough.

'Okay,' she nods, scribbling on her notepad. 'And do you have any idea who the culprit could be?'

I look to Izzy, but she just seems shy again. 'We think it's a fan of her boyfriend. You see she's going out with Michael Sworksy.'

The woman gasps. 'I thought I recognised you!' she says to Izzy in delight. 'I must have seen you in the papers. I love his films!'

Izzy nods awkwardly.

'Sorry,' she says, quickly recovering herself. 'That was very unprofessional of me. Yes, I am aware of his career. That could be a possible reason.'

'It could also be his ex-wife,' I add.

'Of course, I'll look into everyone,' she nods seriously.

'What exactly do you need?' Izzy asks tentatively.

An hour, yes an hour later, we leave completely drained. We had to give full names for everyone in Izzy's life, which is a lot harder than you'd think. Especially when she has such a big client list. Which makes me think it really could be a disgruntled client. She's always refused to date anyone she coaches and maybe there was a psycho in there somewhere. I know I wanted to kill her when she tried to restrict my sugar. I mean Michael's been divorced for years. Why would she suddenly turn crazy?

I drop her off at Michael's house, happy that she's safe for now. He bought a house, or should I say mansion, not too far from us. He's so paranoid that his house has more locks than a prison. He even had a safe room built in, which at the time I totally teased him about. Now it doesn't seem that stupid. I just hope to God this detective figures it all out quickly before something actually serious happens.

# Chapter 24
Jazz

## *Thursday 10th March*

Okay, so the Botox didn't go as planned, but I still can't stop looking at my face in the mirror. That doctor commenting on my eyes keeps playing on my mind. I have always had tiny eyes, but I've never had a second thought about it. Only...well since Jemima's been born I do seem to have developed a lazy eye on one side. When I'm really tired, it's quite noticeable. So...okay I kind of snuck off to a consultation with him and he's said it's a really quick operation, and he'd make my eyes appear much bigger. Plus he'll even them out, so they match, and I don't look like one of my eyes is giving up.

So today I'm going in to get it done. Only, well I haven't exactly told anyone. I've asked Meryl to look after Jemima, claiming I'm going on a spa break. She was just so over the moon to have her she didn't even ask any questions. Ollie's still living at his Mum's, so things between us are fraught. I'm hoping my little makeover will impress him. I mean how are you supposed to gaze into your love one's eyes and confess your undying love when they have such tiny eyes?

Except I am a *little* scared. Apparently I'm going to be awake when it's done. I mean; can you imagine the horror on my face when he told me that? I actually ran straight out of the building. But I'm manning up and doing this. It will be worth it in the end. I hope.

Poppy

Needles. I've always hated them, but if I'm going to have to go through IVF, I better get used to them quick. I'll be like a pincushion soon. Whenever I've Googled things to improve my chances of falling pregnant acupuncture always seems to pop up. Plus, I read that if you do it while the eggs are implanting there are higher success rates. So it's definitely worth a shot.

Only now I'm lying in just my knickers and a towel on some sort of rickety massage table while a man with grey nostril hair comes at me with a needle. What the hell was I thinking? This is torture. I'm putting myself through torment, and I'm not even having IVF yet. What the hell is wrong with me?

'If you just try to stay calm,' he warns, seeming very annoyed by my anxiety.

You'd think he'd be well used to this kind of thing. I mean do people enjoy this? Freaks, the lot of them.

He's coming for me again. Shit. Think calming thoughts Poppy. God knows if you can't do this, how will you ever give birth? But I can't stop shaking and if I'm shaking the needle might go in wrong and hit a vein. I could bleed out before the ambulance even arrives.

'I'm just going to place this one between your eyes to help with reducing stress.'

Reducing stress? How is sticking a needle in between my eyes going to calm me down right now? The man is mental. He edges closer with the needle squeezing the skin at the top of my nose. Ugh and he smells like mustard.

'Stop!' I shriek when he's just about to do it. 'I changed my mind. I can't do it.'

He leans back with a sigh. 'Mrs Davis, there's really nothing to worry about. This won't hurt a bit.

'Really?' I whimper, wanting a hell of a lot more reassurance than that. 'Not even a *bit?*'

He frowns. 'Well, maybe a little bit. But nothing to write home about.'

Okay, now I'm concerned. What if his pain threshold is higher than mine? Of course it would be; he's a man. And he's got greying hair. For all I know he fought for our country. That could be a fake leg right there. Blown off, to smithereens, and he'd just say 'ah nothing to write home about.'

He's clearly a crazy bastard.

'I'm sorry, but I can't.' I sit up and clutch the towel to my chest.

'Let me just place this one.' He's coming for me again. The bloody lunatic!

I jump off the bed and edge into a corner. The man's still coming for me. He's fucking crazy.

He tries to smile reassuringly, but he just looks more like a psychopath. 'There's really no need to be scared.' Says the man stalking me around the room with a needle.

'Leave me alone!' I cry finding the door handle and escaping through it.

I slam the door shut and hold the handle on the other side so that he can't get back out to me. It's only then that I feel a chill on my back. I realise I am in fact back in the reception area with only a towel covering my modesty. Why did I have to choose today to wear a thong? Now everyone can see my arse cheeks and judge my orange peel. Everyone waiting to be seen watches me with amusement. The judgmental bastards.

I hold the towel even closer to myself and attempt a dignified walk to the reception desk. I can put in a complaint and tell them I won't be paying. Only the towel doesn't seem to want to go with me. I tug harder, looking down to see what the problem is. Oh, the towel is stuck in the door. Crap.

'Err...if I could have my towel back please,' I shout through the door, unable to open it myself.

There are a few seconds of unsettling silence.

'You've somehow managed to wedge the door shut,' he shouts back. 'I can't open it.'

He *has* to be friggin kidding me.

'Um...' I look back to the reception. The receptionist is just staring at me open mouthed making no attempt to help me. 'Do you have any spare towels? Or even better...clothes?'

Two hours. That's how long it took them to get that door open. All they could find was one clean towel, so I had to sit there in the reception shivering like a homeless person every time someone came in from the cold high street. They'd all stare at me in bemusement. Yes, ha de ha, very bloody funny. I'm in a towel; laugh it up. I've had to listen to the receptionist whisper what happened to each and every person. It was beyond humiliating.

In the end, they had to call in a local handyman to take the door off the hinges. Only I could fuck up a door that much. It got worse when that handyman was Ryan's friend from rugby. Kill me now. I wanted the place to swallow me up. I'm sure it's all over St Albans by now. All because I couldn't handle one bloody tiny needle. How on earth am I ever going to go through IVF?

I'm nearly at my car when my phone starts vibrating in my handbag. I begrudgingly answer it recognising a local number.

'Hello, is that Mrs Davis?' a cheery voice asks.

Is it sad that I still get a thrill when people use my married name? Reminds me how lucky I am.

'Yes. Who's this?' I'm still too frazzled from the acupuncture nightmare to sound polite.

'This is Nurse Dackerie from Spire hospital in Bushey. We have your friend Jasmine Green ready for collection.'

Jazz? Why the hell is she in the hospital?

'Huh? Collection? What are you talking about?' Maybe it's just a wind-up.

'Um...She's out of her eye surgery,' she explains. 'She said that you were to collect her? Are you...not aware of this?'

Jazz has had eye surgery? Oh my God, is she okay? Did she get hit by a car or something? Or pecked in the eye by an angry bird? I keep telling her not to feed the pigeons.

'Don't worry. I'll be there right away.'

I rush to the hospital, my mind running with frantic thoughts. The whole way over here I've been contemplating calling and telling Ollie, but I've reasoned that if she wanted him she'd have given the nurse his number. Things are still weird between them, and I don't want to get involved.

When I'm finally directed to her room, I burst the door open and freeze in place. She's sat in bed, but her eyes are bandaged up completely, her blonde curls bursting out from underneath. Oh my God, what the hell happened to her? Is she blind?

'Hello? Who's there?' she asks, an edge of vulnerability in her voice.

Oh my God. My poor little Jazz!

'It's me.' I shake my head realising she might not recognise my voice. 'It's Poppy.'

She releases a breath in relief and slumps back down onto the bed. 'Thank God. Sorry you had to come collect me. I just assumed I could take myself home, but I didn't realise I was still going to be blind.'

How can she be so calm right now? She must still be in shock.

I place my bag on the floor and move to the green chair next to her. 'Of course I'd collect you, hun. I mean, it was a shock obviously, but I'm just glad you're okay. I mean...you are okay, right?'

'I'm honestly fine,' she nods, talking to the window rather than me. It would be comical if it weren't so serious.

'You're saying that with bandages over your eyes right now. I mean, what happened? Are you...' my throat tightens at the possibility, '*blind* or something?' My voice breaks, just thinking about how she'd cope.

She'd never see Jemima again. Oh my God, how would she look after her? How would we even begin to tell her Mummy can't see anymore? It's just heartbreaking.

I can already imagine someone buying the rights to it and turning it into a film.

'Of course I'm not blind,' she snaps, looking at the wall instead of me.

I'm so confused right now. 'But...why the bandages? They said you had eye surgery?'

193

'I have,' she nods. 'I had the skin over my eyes tightened.'

Wait...did she have...cosmetic surgery?

'Wait, did you *need* this?' I ask anger rising in my chest. I've just raced here living out every possible scenario in my head, and she's had bloody cosmetic surgery.

'Well...' she fidgets with the end of her gown, clearly sensing my tone. 'I kind of did, as I could barely see.'

I see right through her, no pun intended. She had no problem with her vision.

'But you didn't need it. It's cosmetic isn't it?'

Of course it is. She's in a private hospital. This is just like the Botox. I'm such a dumb bitch sometimes.

'Maybe,' she says vaguely, lying back down, crossing her arms over her chest.

I can't believe her. 'Jazz how could you have been so stupid? Especially after how you reacted with the Botox?'

'Oh chill out, Grandma,' she snaps sounding more rattled than she has the right to be. 'I really wish you'd just support me.'

Uh, she's always on about this support thing. She watches too much Oprah.

'I can't support you in this.'

'Hidey hi!' a cheery nurse with flushed cheeks says, peeking her head around the doors. 'I think we're ready to take the bandages off now.'

'Thank God,' Jazz says with a sigh.

I roll my eyes. She sounds like such a spoilt brat.

The nurse fusses round with the bandages while I consider what she might look like. I hope it's not scary. I haven't had the chance to prepare myself. She finally steps aside so I can see her fully.

Jesus, fucking Christ.

My mouth drops to the floor. She looks awful. Her eyes look like they've been pinned up, they're so open she actually looks permanently stunned. Plus she has red, angry blotches around them, quickly starting to bruise. She's going to have two black eyes. You can see the line of the stitches on her eyelid. I flinch, imagining the pain. She looks like a bloody monster!

'How does it look?' she asks, seeing the concern on my face.

'Err...' I look down to avoid having to look at her. It's making me feel queasy. 'I'm sure it will look better once the swelling goes down?' I don't even *sound* confident.

'Exactly that,' the nurse nods. 'Would you like to see it for yourself?' She takes a mirror out of a cupboard and hands it over to her.

She glances into it, her shocked, wide eyes almost popping out of her head. 'What the hell? I look like I've just had a fight with someone! Tell me this is going to go down quick!'

'Of course,' the nurse nods. 'In about two weeks, as the consultant told you.'

Knowing Jazz, I bet she barely listened.

'It's...really not that bad,' I say attempting to smile. I know it comes out more as a grimace. 'Just...maybe we should have Jemima overnight?'

She nods sadly and listens while the nurse instructs her of the eye drops and cream she needs to apply four times a day. How the hell is she going to manage to look after herself?

'Yeah...maybe you're right,' she admits. 'Looking like this, I might scare the shit out of her.'

## Jazz

Well, that was fucking horrific. Never again will I be having any surgery awake. I don't care if they refuse to give me anything; I'm running into a wall and knocking myself out. I just...I can't even talk about what they did to me. Not yet.

I hated having the bandages over my eyes, making me effectively blind. Every time someone opened the door, and I heard footsteps my whole body went on high alert. I'd ask if anyone was there. Some nurses reassured me;

some just pretended they didn't hear me. Bloody bitches.

And they left it until after the surgery to ask who was collecting me. I thought I could just leave myself, but they said I needed someone to come in and discharge me. The only person I could ask was Poppy. Not that I asked her. I just gave them her name and number hoping she wouldn't be too angry.

Poppy was totally over-reacting though. I mean, my eyes aren't *that* bad. Especially now, as I prepare to give myself the last set of drops for the night. Bless her, she stayed and made sure I had everything I needed. I secretly love the fuss. Well, not even secretly really. I wanted her to stay and look after me, but she said she had to get back to Ryan. Like he can't look after himself. It's not like he's had eye surgery, but whatever.

I look into the mirror and just about manage to put the drops in myself. My eyes have swelled a lot more in the last few hours, so it's hard to actually get the drops in, but I do the best I can. According to the nurse, I need to put this cream on just before I go to bed.

I squeeze it in my left eye, the cold sensation making me wince. Ugh, it's like squirting glue in my eye! And now I can't see out of that one, the gunge quickly clouding my vision. Great. I quickly look around the bedroom to see if I've got everything I need before I do the other one. Yeah, good enough. I squirt it in the other eye, immediately blind.

I feel my way into bed, squishing my face against the 100% Egyptian cotton pillowcase. God, I'm glad I'm rich again. Meryl used to wash with something that smelt of oranges and didn't use fabric softener at all. The pillows would feel like I was trying to squish my face into sandpaper. I once made the mistake of mentioning it to her, but she was so horrified she ended up going off on a rant and telling me that if I was that specific I could do my own washing. And that was never going to happen.

I feel myself just drifting off to dreamland when a sudden thirst hits me. Damn it, I didn't bring up a drink for myself. Ugh, and the kitchen is two floors down. I'd just get something from the tap in my en-suite, but it tastes like crap. I really want an Evian.

I try to open my eyes, but it's still all blurry as hell. Oh God. I can feel my way down there, right? I use my hands against the walls to find the way down, taking each step carefully. One step at a time; just like I teach Jemima. I know I've made it into the kitchen when I hear the buzzing of the fridge freezer. Thank God, my tongue feels like Gandhi's flip-flop.

I place my hands out in front of me and attempt to walk towards the noise, groaning at the effort. All of a sudden a dark, intense pain takes over the side of my face, the pain so consuming that I stumble and crash down onto the floor.

'Ow! What the fuck?' I shriek, still unable to see anything. It doesn't help that the light isn't on.

'Oh. I so sorry, Miss Jasmine.' Is that the voice of Lucine?

'Lucine?'

'Yes. It me, Miss Jasmine. I, so sorry. I thought you were walker.'

What the hell is she talking about?

'Walker?' I shriek, clutching at my throbbing hand.

'Like Walking Dead? You know...how you say...zombie.'

'Zombie? You thought I was a fucking zombie?' I'm only now realising that she must have smashed me over the head with something.

Jesus, I could have this woman for assault.

'I so sorry; but your eyes. They open, but they look just like walker. You had hands out in front. Just like walker. You groan. Just like walker.'

'Yes, but walkers aren't real!' I yell, clutching the side of my head in agony.

Am I the only person not obsessed with that show? Ryan and Poppy won't leave the house or even answer the phone when it's on.

'Not yet. But I thought it had started. You lucky I not stick knife in your head.'

'Are you *honestly* saying I'm lucky that you didn't stab me in the head?' I shout, my head ringing. Why am I paying this woman?

'I sorry, Miss Jasmine. It not happen again. Would you like some tea?'

'No. I just...I wanted some water.' My voice breaks from sudden emotion brewing in my chest. I should have just stayed in bed.

'I get it for you. And some ice for your head.'

I nod, unable to speak. This could only happen to me. Right now I really just want to go to bed and forget the whole awful day.

She gets me a bottle of water and helps me drink it with a straw. After she helps me back up the stairs, checks my head and then tucks me into bed. She kind of reminds me of my nanny growing up. The last thought I have before I drift off to sleep is that the person looking after me is my maid. It should be Ollie. But it's not and it's probably all my own fault.

# Chapter 25
## Poppy

### Friday 11th March

I still can't believe Jazz has ruined her face like that. I've been calling her four times a day to remind her to put the drops in, but she insists she's fine. Times like this I really miss her being around the corner. She'd never admit it, but she needs looking after. And with Ollie still being at Mum's, she's there all on her own with Jemima. I have no idea how she's coping. She must be scaring the crap out of all the kids at that new nursery.

She's still insisting she's coming to Lilly's hen night on Saturday even though I heard the nurse tell her she'd need two weeks to fully recover. She shouldn't be coming out clubbing and getting drunk, but it's like talking to a brick wall.

Not that I don't have enough to worry about. Grams hasn't called me back today. She always picks up her phone, and if she ever misses it, she calls me right back. It's not like her at all. So when Ryan calls and says he's going to be late home, I think it's a perfect opportunity to drive up and check on her.

She's another stubborn one like Jazz. She likes to pretend that getting older isn't affecting her, but I know it is. It's impossible not to. Hell, I'm not even thirty yet, but I'm already falling apart. I squatted down to collect some dropped scripts today, and I couldn't get back up without pushing off from the floor. It was *beyond* embarrassing. Especially when a runner had to come and help me up. Jessica joked that I had a big birthday coming up. I was mortified when the runner said 'no way! I didn't think you were forty yet.' I mean, was he serious? He looked serious, but I'm sure he was taking the piss.

*Right?*

I get out of the car and knock on the door, noticing the dead flowers in her hanging baskets. Normally Grams would rather die than see her flowers like that. I hop impatiently from foot to foot, expecting to hear movement inside. No answer. No movement.

I knock on the door again, louder this time. Now I'm really starting to worry. I breathe a sigh of relief as I hear footsteps. I smile as the door begins to open. She's fine, of course she is. The thoughts of finding her dead in the bath are just bloody dramatic. I really need to stop watching CSI.

The door opens to reveal Teddy, Grams' elderly next door neighbour and long time friend.

'Hello sweetheart,' he smiles, rubbing what seem like tired eyes. 'I thought she said she didn't call you.'

I frown. What does he mean?

'Come on in,' he sighs, leading me towards the back of the house and the kitchen.

I follow, wondering what the hell is going on. Grams is sitting on a chair around her rustic farm table, but her face is contorted in discomfort.

I find my legs rushing over to her, immediately wanting to take her pain as my own.

'Grams? What's wrong?'

'Oh, nothing,' she dismisses, shooing me away with her hands.

'Nothing my arse,' Teddy says from behind me, arms crossed over his chest.

'What happened?' I ask him, rather than her. I already know she'll try to lie to me.

'Had to use my key,' he says shaking my head. 'I knew something was wrong when she didn't answer the door for Deal or No Deal. We normally watch it together. So I used my key and found her on the kitchen floor.'

I swing my head around accusingly to Grams. 'What happened? And tell me the *truth*,' I warn with my eyes.

'I just lost my footing,' she shrugs. 'When you get to my age sometimes you just lose your balance.' She smiles like it's no big deal at all.

'Did you hurt yourself?' I find myself physically checking her over to see if she's got a bump on the head. Anything that will require hospital.

'Just some bruising.'

'She couldn't get up!' Teddy exclaims gruffly. 'I had to help her. God only knows how long she was lying there.'

I raise my eyebrows at Grams in question.

'I'd only just fallen!' she pouts, crossing her arms like a stubborn child.

I decide to change tact. Maybe seem a bit calmer, rather than accusing.

'I know what it's like Grams,' I say softly, smiling kindly. 'I bent down today, and I couldn't get back up.'

She smiles sadly. 'It's a sad state of affairs when your body starts going.'

'Grams you need to see the doctor. Let him check you out. I mean, you might have low blood pressure or something.'

She shakes her head adamantly. 'I only saw the doctor last week for a check-up. I'm absolutely fine. Just old.'

This is awful. What if she starts having falls like this regularly? We're too far away to be checking in on her twice a day. Which if I'm honest with myself is what I know she needs now. She's the most important person in Ryan's life. God forbid if she was to fall and we didn't find her in time. I know Teddy checks in on her, but he's old himself. I can't put that kind of pressure on him.

'I can see you worrying,' Grams smiles. 'You're so easy to read,' she chuckles. 'I'm fine! And you mustn't be worrying Ryan with this. That poor man already works too hard. Land this on his shoulders and you'll both be calling me six times a day. I couldn't bear that.'

I roll my eyes. Who is she kidding? She loves when we call. You can hear her voice brightening up as she realises it's you. The truth is that we didn't even think of Grams when we moved to St Albans. I suppose we just assumed everything would carry on as normal. It's easy to forget people get old and need more care. But it's hard to visit when you have to cheat busy traffic each time. She should really move closer to us.

'Maybe you should consider...'

'I'm not moving,' she interrupts, putting her hand up to halt me. 'Forget that idea straight away. And I mean it Poppy, if this gets back to Ryan I'll be *very* disappointed in you.'

Great. Just what I need. Another secret.

When I get back to St Albans, I head straight to Mum's house. It's already eight pm, and I haven't eaten anything. Plus, I know the fridge at home is empty. I really need to do an online shop. Mum's always got food in the fridge that I can binge on.

'Hi darling,' she sings from the kitchen as soon as I let myself in with my key. 'Come through, I've made you a dinner.'

God, sometimes she can really be the best. I called her on the way home and may have mentioned that I was hungry. A few times.

I walk into the kitchen to find a chicken dinner with mash, broccoli and gravy. I love that woman. I practically run to the breakfast bar; hop up on the stool and start shovelling it in my mouth.

'Thank you so much,' I say through a full mouth.

'Honestly, Poppy,' she says with distaste. 'Anyone would think you hadn't eaten in days!'

'Sorry,' I cringe for her benefit. I'm not really embarrassed at all. Just glad I can finally fill my stomach.

Loud rumbling noises vibrate through the house. That'll be Dad on his new motorbike, the absolute tool. The whole neighbourhood must be talking about how he's clearly having some sort of breakdown.

'That'll be the men,' Mum sighs, getting up.

'Men?' I echo. 'What, not just Dad?' Now I ask I realise the noise is very loud, and there must be at least three engines out there.

I get up and follow Mum out to the front of the house. I grab my coat and walk out to see what all the fuss is about. I stop in my tracks when I see them. Dad, Ollie, Richard, Henry, and Ryan. All on motorbikes of their own.

What. The. Hell?

'What the hell is going on?' I shout over the engines.

'We all bought motorbikes!' Ollie shouts back with an excited grin on his face.

'You bought them?' I stammer, completely thrown.

'Well...Jazz did,' Ollie smiles. 'She wanted to treat us.'

I will fucking *kill* Jazz. It's not enough putting my Dad's life in danger, but now she wants to risk my whole family's life on these death traps.

'Made up then have we?' I tease.

'We're getting there,' he shrugs, clearly not wanting to go into it in front of the others.

I sigh, exasperated from his stubbornness. 'You two really need to sort it out. She needs you right now.'

'Right now?' he repeats, his eyebrows narrowing on me. 'Why?'

Oh crap. He doesn't know about her eyes?

'Didn't you see her today?' I know if he did she couldn't hide those shiners around her eyes.

'No,' he frowns. 'She paid before we got there. Why, what's wrong with her?'

'Oh...nothing,' I shrug. 'Just bloody call her yourself.'

He stomps off in a mood. Mature, real mature.

I stare at Ryan. He seems beyond ecstatic, grinning from ear to ear.

'What do you think, babe?' he asks.

I can't even begin to answer him right now. I'm likely to boil over with rage. How the hell could he have done this? He refuses to borrow money off Jazz for IVF, something we actually need, in order to have the family we so desperately desire. Yet he'll gladly take her money so he can buy a stupid motorbike. A stupid and very dangerous machine, which he has no experience of driving.

'You can't even drive this thing!' I shout, the last engine dying down.

'We've been taking lessons,' Richard says. 'Jazz paid for us to do an intensive course.'

My lip curls up. I could literally growl I'm so furious. Oh did she. Ryan's avoiding my eye line now, obviously realising my reaction. How could he have been doing lessons and not told me? The lying bastard. I'm so mad I'm sure I'm radiating hatred. I can feel my cheeks heating with rage.

'Now we're like Sons of Anarchy!' Henry says. 'We're going to get leather jackets printed and everything!'

He is far too excited for a grown ass man.

'Jesus,' Mum says under her breath next to me. 'Bunch of Spanners more like.'

Despite my rage, I can't help but burst out laughing. At least someone is on my side here.

That's when I realise that Ryan not only went behind my back to do this and the course, but he actively lied to me. He told me he was working late tonight when really they were out getting these bloody bikes! I glare at him before turning on my heel and stomping into the sitting room.

Ryan eventually follows me in, helmet in his hands and shuts the door behind him.

'You alright, babe?' he asks as if he'd seriously have no idea why I'd be mad.

'Do I look alright?' I snarl, glaring at him. I feel like I could burn him with my penetrating gaze right now.

'Err...no?' he answers, eyes wide in fear.

'I can't fucking believe you!' I explode. 'You won't take money for IVF, but you'll take it for a motorbike. You're a selfish bastard, Ryan! And didn't you think I'd care about you buying a death machine? Jesus, I've been busy looking after Grams while you're playing with motorbikes!'

'Look after Grams?' He frowns in concern. 'Why, what's wrong with her?'

Oh shit. I'm not supposed to say. I promised.

'Nothing! I just meant visiting her is all.'

'Oh,' he nods. 'Please don't be mad, babe.' He puts on his best puppy dog eyes. God, he's good at it. 'I could hardly tell the boys no because Poppy won't let me. They'd all say I was whipped. Plus, if I were to refuse they'd try to find out why and I don't want them all to know I can't knock you up.'

Why is he still feeling such guilt over this?

'Ryan, stop blaming yourself! God, it's exhausting enough carrying around this secret without worrying about you too.'

He huffs out a big sigh, his body slumping, defeated. 'I'm sorry, Pops. Come here.' He grabs me into a hug and crushes me so tightly into his chest that I struggle to breathe. 'You're right. You need to tell Jazz.'

I lean away and look into his face to see if he's really okay with it. 'Really?'

'Yeah,' he nods solemnly. 'I'm sorry. You're right; I have been selfish. It's a big burden for you to carry and you share everything with her. Do it.'

He has no idea how much of a burden off my shoulders that is.

I kiss him sweetly on the lips. 'Thank you, babe.'

He crushes me back into another hug as if I might disappear. 'You're very welcome. But I'm keeping the motorbike.'

*Saturday 12<sup>th</sup> March - Lilly's Hen Night*

After much deliberation, and by deliberation, I mean arguing with Jazz, Izzy and Lilly's cousin Annie on Facetime for three hours, we've decided to go on a wild night out to London for Lilly's hen night. We wanted something a bit different and decided on The Blitz Party in Shoreditch. I'm shocked as we walk in, how different the vibe is from any other club. First of all, everyone, including us, is dressed up in 1940's get up. Everywhere you turn, are victory curls, tea dresses and men in military outfits. Yum. This is the kind of place to come if you have a uniform fetish. Not that I do. *Obviously.* But damn, some of them are fitties.

It's set into a railway arch and inside is decorated like a secret air raid shelter. A swing band is playing on stage, everyone already bopping along as they hold their ales or gin cocktails. Professional dancers are doing the lindy-hop around us as if to show how boring our modern day dancing is. There are sandbags, oil lamps, blackout curtains and ration books for bar tabs. There's a strange sense of camaraderie in the air as if we're all in this together. There are announcements to say that war is coming, and we must fight for our country. It's strangely intoxicating.

We get ourselves a drink and then hit the dance floor. Lilly's invited another five close friends; Annie, Danielle, Alex, Kirsty-Anne and Kellie. We've all spent hours at Lilly's battling over one mirror to get our victory curls perfect. My hair's already basically flat. Damn thick hair.

It's so cool here that I can't help but feel very trendy for once. We are *so* cool to be doing a hen night here. My idea of a night out in Brighton seem lame now.

Jazz signals for me to go to the toilet with her. She shouldn't be out at all with those eyes. They're still completely swollen, but she's packed on loads of eye shadow to try and hide it. She looks like a bloody drag queen.

I don't need a wee, so I get chatting to two randoms at the sinks; out for their mates 30th. They're dressed in matching navy blue polka-dot tea dresses and have drawn a line at the back of their legs with eyeliner. They've really bothered. Next to them my brown and cream tea dress from the charity shop doesn't look that cool.

'Here's our mate now,' they say looking behind me as a toilet flushes.

Out walks Nicole. Ryan's ex-girlfriend, Nicole.

Jesus, is this woman following me around or something? Her face tells me no. She seems just as mortified to see me.

'Take your time preggo,' one of them says sarcastically to her chuckling. 'You're pissing like a bloody racehorse!'

'Well, I *am* pregnant,' she snaps, trying to hide the hurt from her face.

'Hi, Nicole,' I say smiling sweetly.

She's wearing a red polka-dot dress, her bump so neat and compact that from the back you'd never know she was pregnant at all.

'Hi, Poppy,' she nods shyly, tucking a bit of hair self-consciously behind her ear. Her victory curls are bloody perfect. She starts making her way over to the sink.

'No way!' her other mate shouts. 'You guys know each other! What are the odds?'

'Wait,' the blonde says, her eyebrows knitted together. 'You're not *the* Poppy. Are you?'

Nicole shoots warning daggers at her.

'You are!' she starts laughing. 'What are the odds?'

Their other mate looks really confused.

'She's Ryan's wife,' Blondie explains.

'Her ex,' she nods, figuring it out. 'Wow. I totally saw you differently.'

Another loo flushes and Jazz comes stumbling out. Oh god, please be calm Jazz. Please don't over-react.

'I thought I heard you,' she says staring daggers at Nicole. 'What did I tell you when I last saw you at the wedding?'

She looks to the floor, her face reddening.

'I told you to start running, that's right,' she says, her eyes alight with fire. And I'm gonna say the same thing to you right now.'

'Jazz,' I say, attempting to calm her down. 'It's fine. That was years ago.'

'No-one ever forgets the bitch that tried to ruin their best mates wedding.'

Nicole's two friends are immediately beside her. Now that they're not sat on the sink they actually seem quite tall and intimidating.

'Jazz, stop.' I put my hand up to stop her approaching them. 'She's pregnant for god's sakes.'

Jazz looks down and takes in the very discreet bump. Her face falls. 'No way,' she whispers in disbelief. 'I am going to fucking *kill* Ryan!'

She starts for the door, but I grab her arm and swing her round to us again. 'Ryan is not the father,' I shout, apologizing to Nicole with my eyes.

'Oh.' Now she looks a little embarrassed. 'Well then, I suppose that's fine.'

'Sorry,' I say to the three of them starting to back away. Back away before we get our arses kicked.

'It's fine,' Nicole waves dismissively. 'I did try and ruin your wedding. I never got the chance to say sorry. I am, you know...sorry.'

'That's all in the past now,' I shrug. 'Don't worry about it.'

Jazz is still glaring at her, so I take her hand and all but drag her out, not letting go until we're in the foyer area. It's relatively quieter than the main rooms, but still loud enough that we have to shout in each other's ears.

'I can't believe you're so calm with her,' she shouts at me.

'I actually saw her the other day,' I admit into her ear. 'When I was having a scan she was there too.'

'And this is the first I hear of it?' she gasps in disbelief.

I shrug; exhausted at the inquisition. 'I just knew you'd make a big deal out of it is all. Plus, at the time Ryan was still getting me to keep everything secret.'

'It *is* a big deal!' she screams. 'That bitch tried to steal your man!'

'Yeah and now she's pregnant by another.'

She crosses her arms over her chest. 'I suppose,' she admits reluctantly. 'But you still should have told me.'

'Look, enough about her. When are you going to sort this shit out with my brother?'

She rolls her eyes. 'There's nothing to sort out. He's the one that left. He hasn't even thanked me properly for the motorbikes, just a lame text.'

'Ugh, Jazz cut the crap. This is the one time where it's not okay to be stubborn. I mean; you have Jemima to think about.'

'Yeah, I do,' she shouts. 'But he didn't think about that when he walked out on us.' She scratches her eye removing some eye shadow so you can see the angry stitches behind it.

'I just think you need to talk to him about why he left. There must be a reason. Something you can work through?'

'Well, I'm just where he left me. If he wants to talk, he knows where I am.' She scratches at her eye again.

'What the hell is wrong with your eye?'

'Nothing,' she shrugs, one of them starting to water.

'I told you it was too soon for you to be wearing make-up over it. The stitches haven't even healed yet.'

'Yes, which is why I had to cover them up,' she retorts snarkily. 'I didn't want people thinking I'd come as Frankenstein tonight.'

'Yeah, but did you really need the glitter eye shadow?'

Hurt radiates from her eyes. 'Sometimes I really wish you weren't such a know it all.' She flounces off into the main room like the drama queen she is.

I sigh, forced to follow her.

When we find Lilly and her mates they're all doing shots at the bar.

Danielle, who insists on us calling her D, is flirting outrageously with a guy. They keep whispering things into each other's ears and then giggling. Izzy seems uncomfortable and glad to see us.

'Woooo!' Lilly shouts at us when she's done another shot. 'Come on, let's dance!'

'You okay?' I ask Izzy over the swing music.

'Yeah,' she nods. 'They made me do a shot, but I'm okay.'

That's weird. She normally loves shots. I wonder why she's not doing them, but it's so loud in here it's easier to just ignore for now. My throat is already feeling gravelly from having to scream everything.

We move into the centre of the dance floor where plenty of hot men in uniform are scouting the talent around them. Times like this I'm so glad I'm married. It's such a meat market. God knows I was always terrible at meeting new people and as for dating? Ugh, I'd rather eat my own foot.

The band on stage consists of a short lead singer in a suit, vintage looking black and white brogues, and a white beret. There's a guitar player, a man tooting the hell out of a trumpet, some dude thinking he's really cool with his clarinet, and some man who is actually shit hot at double bass.

We dance as well as we can, but it's hard to dance to this stuff. There's no running baseline. I don't know any of the songs, so I'm just bopping my head along in the sea of people. After what feels like a lifetime of dancing, explosions of red, white and blue confetti release above us. I look at the others screaming in happiness. It's actually kind of magical.

I glance at my watch. Thank God, it's midnight. This Cinderella needs to get home. How that bitch ever wore shoes out of actual glass, I'll never know.

Thankfully Jazz told me earlier that she'd planned for a tacky pink party bus to pick us up at quarter past. From the looks of it, she'd be too drunk to remind me right now. I signal to them that I'll be back, but Izzy comes with me. We walk into the foyer area, and I'm shocked to see Nicole sitting all by herself.

Izzy looks at me as if to question whether we should ignore her.

'You go and check if it's here yet,' I tell her.

I walk over to Nicole. I can't help but feel sorry for her. I mean where are her mates? They shouldn't be leaving pregnant women like this.

'You okay, Nicole?' I ask with a friendly smile sitting down next to her.

She forces a smile, but it doesn't meet her eyes. 'Yeah, fine. Just working out how to get home.'

'Where are your friends? Surely you'd go with them?'

She looks down at her lap. 'They left for another club. I'm not up for it.' She glances down at her bump. 'I shouldn't have even come really, but I didn't want to let my mate down.'

Jesus; what a bunch of bastards.

'That's understandable. They still shouldn't have left you. Especially in your condition.'

'I suppose I just kind of feel like I'm in between friends right now. My regular mates aren't interested in carrying around a frumpy pregnant person, and all of the pregnant mums I meet are all married, or they, at least, have someone.'

'And you don't?' I know she said that the dad wasn't involved, but I kind of assumed she'd have someone.

'Nope. It didn't last long,' she admits, her eyes darting from side to side as if ashamed.

There's an awkward pause where I can't think of what to say.

'Anyway, let's work on getting you a taxi, shall we?'

She looks down beaten. 'I've tried. The guy said there's been some big crash. Minimum, hour wait for a cab. He told me to sit back here, and he'd come and get me when one gets here.'

'That was nice of him, but you're local to us now, right?'

She nods. 'I'm in Watford now.'

I do find it odd that she decided to move so close to St Albans, but whatever. I hope it wasn't deliberate.

'You can come in our party bus. I'm sure Lilly won't mind.' Actually, I'm sure she *will* mind, but I'll just have to calm her down.

Izzy runs back in. 'Disaster Pops! Apparently there's been some big crash so they have no idea how long it will take to get to us.'

Shit. And we've missed the last train. How are we going to get home? Well, this is a bloody disaster.

'I'm too tired for this,' Izzy snaps, suddenly looking exhausted. 'I just want my bed.'

This isn't like Izzy at all. Normally she's the life and soul of the party.

'Me too.'

'We should get the others.'

Izzy nods and goes back into the main room leaving me with Nicole.

'Don't worry, we'll look after you.'

A couple of minutes later our crowd come spilling out. Lilly and Jazz's faces turn murderous when they spot Nicole.

'What the fuck is she doing here?' Lilly growls; towering over her with threatening eyes.

'Leave her alone Lilly, she's pregnant!'

'That's not *my* fault!' she barks back. 'This is *my* hen night, and if she thinks *she's* going to ruin it by trying to claim back Ryan she's mistaken!'

'Lilly, stop being ridiculous,' I snap too tired for her aggressive shit. 'She needs a lift home, and we're going to be decent human beings and help her.'

'What's wrong with her own taxi?' Jazz asks arms folded defensively over her chest.

'There are no taxis. Apparently there's been some accident.'

'Oh no,' Danielle says pouting at the man next to her. It's the guy she was flirting with at the bar.

'Luckily for you lot I brought my van,' he says, his eyes alight with mischief.

His mate looks worried, frowning heavily at him. 'Yeah, but haven't you had a bit to drink?'

'I'm fine,' he dismisses.

We don't have many options here. We either get a lift home with him or wait for minimum an hour. And my feet are killing me. Everyone looks to me for an answer. I've clearly been nominated as the responsible one. Again.

'Well, let's, at least, *see* your van,' I say, deciding to compromise.

He grins like a wolf. 'Follow me, ladies.'

I help Nicole up and follow the crowd outside. Don't ask me what makes me look back at the seat, but I do. And there, where Nicole was sitting is a little puddle of dark liquid.

'Wait,' I say, stopping her. I pull her back so we can get a closer look. Is it...blood? Then I look at the back of Nicole's dress. She has a blood patch. Oh my God. She's bleeding.

Nicole seems to realise at the same time, her face losing all colour.

'Don't worry,' I say, immediately springing into panic mode.

I pull her outside to the others who are already halfway out of the driveway.

'Guys, I need help!' I shout at them, not stopping for a second. I'm basically dragging Nicole along after me. 'We need to get to a hospital!'

Jazz hears me and spins around. 'What?' she yells back. Her eyes fall down. I follow her eye line to see blood trickling down Nicole's leg.

Oh my God. Shit just got real.

'Stop!' Jazz screams running in front of the others. I can just about make out her trying to explain to them. Within an instant they're all running back, offering words of encouragement and helping Nicole walk towards the van.

'We need to get her to the hospital,' Izzy says. 'She could be losing the baby.'

'Shut up, Izzy!' I hiss, glaring at her in warning. 'Don't worry her.'

'I'm already kind of worried,' Nicole admits, her eyes filling up with liquid.

'Okay, where is the nearest hospital?' I ask them.

'The Royal,' Annie says having already Googled it on her phone. 'It's definitely the Royal.'

'Okay, can we get there without hitting the crash traffic?'

'Just get her in quick.'

We find the van and are immediately bundled into the back by the men.

'Shouldn't she be in the front?' Annie asks looking at Nicole.

But before any of us have time to reply we're thrown back as he speeds off.

'Jesus, this guy's a nutter!' Lilly squeals. 'Where's D?'

'She's in the front with him,' Kirsty-Anne replies.

'Probably blowing him,' Annie laughs.

We turn a corner and get thrown over each other.

'Fuck! Is this guy sober?'

Jazz looks at me as if this is the wrong thing to say. 'How are you feeling, Nicole?'

'Why do you ever care about her?' Lilly shrieks. 'The bitch tried to steal Poppy's man!'

'Lilly, now is so not the time!' I shout back as we tumble around another corner.

'I don't want Ryan,' Nicole says desperately. 'I just want to get to the hospital.'

'Are you having any labour pains?' Jazz asks. 'You know, like tightening's?'

'I don't think so,' she shrugs.

'Oh trust me,' she grins wickedly. 'You'd *so* know.'

'Whatever,' Lilly snorts. 'Still a bitch if you ask me.'

The van comes to an abrupt halt throwing us all against the front.

'We're here,' he shouts through.

'Thank fuck we're even alive,' I scream, hitting the panel between the driver and us aggressively.

We help her out and hurry her into the main reception of the hospital. They immediately put her in a wheelchair and begin to whisk her away.

'Wait!' I shout running after them. 'Nicole, who should I call for you?'

Her eyes well up with fresh tears. 'No. There's no one,' she admits sadly.

'What?' She has no-one? How can that be? What about the baby's father at least?

The nurse starts to wheel her away again. I look back to the others wondering if I should leave her here.

'I'm going with her,' I call back. I turn to Nicole. 'I'm coming with you.' I clasp her hand in mine. 'Don't worry, I'm here.'

Forty minutes later we know a lot more. They immediately wired her belly up to some machine to check the baby's heart rate, which seems to have been fine. Then she had her blood pressure checked and after chatting with the doctor, she had to spread her legs and be checked down there. They said she has an ectropion on her cervix, but that it shouldn't have caused that much bleeding. Either way, they're happy for her to go home as long as she's closely monitored.

They leave us alone so she can get cleaned up and ready to leave. I help her put her shoes on.

'So...I mean, I don't want to pry, but when you said you had no-one to call, do you really mean *no-one?*'

'Yep,' she nods. 'Tragic isn't it?'

'But what about your family?'

'Both my parents are dead. I'm an only child.' She shrugs as if it's no big deal when I can see that it's hurting her to have to admit this to me.

Imagine feeling that alone in the world. Not having anyone you can truly be yourself around. It must be exhausting.

'Well, don't worry. At least you have a successful business to fall back on,' I say trying to make her feel better.

She laughs, although I can tell it's anything but funny. 'Nope. Not anymore.'

'What do you mean?'

'We had a big celebrity wedding. The bride wasn't happy with the flowers and blamed me. The whole reputation of the company was at stake, so Cathy bought me out. It was the only way the business would survive.'

Shit. 'I had no idea.' She really has nothing.

'That's why I moved to Watford. I couldn't afford London rent anymore, and my parents had left me a flat in their will. I moved out the tenants and moved straight in.'

Shit. It's all making sense now.

How the hell can I drop her off home now knowing she's all alone in some little lonely flat in Watford? The doctor says she needs to be monitored. What if she falls down and bashes her head or something? Her and the baby could die. No matter what's happened in the past, I could never forgive myself if that happened and I hadn't done absolutely everything in my power to stop in.

I make a rash decision, knowing it's going to not only shock her, but also shock the shit out of the girls.

'You're staying with us tonight.'

Her eyes nearly bulge out of their sockets. 'No. Thanks, but no.'

'It's not a discussion,' I growl. 'You're not going home to your flat all by yourself when the nurse says you need looking after. It's not happening.'

She stares back at me completely bewildered. I'm starting to feel offended she's not bowing down to how nice I'm being.

'No honestly, but thank you.'

I pull up my hand, silencing her. 'Please don't argue with me. It's been a long arse night and I really just want to be able to sleep tonight knowing you're safe. Come on, you're coming home with us.'

She smiles sadly; her eyes glistening with what I hope are grateful tears. I mean; I'm not abducting the bitch. I hope she doesn't think that.

We go down in the lift and out into the reception where everyone is waiting for us. It's easy to spot our crowd as we're all spread out on the plastic chairs giggling like schoolgirls.

'How are you?' Izzy asks rushing over. 'Is the baby okay?'

'I'm fine,' she nods. 'The baby is fine. Nothing to worry about.'

'Thank God,' Jazz says quietly.

'And...' I take a deep breath and try to quash down the panic of their reactions, 'She's coming back with us and staying at mine.'

'The *fuck* she is!' Lilly howls. She pulls me by the elbow away from their earshot. 'Are you fucking crazy? That bitch is a home wrecker, and you're willingly inviting her into *your* home? You're crazy!'

'Would you calm down,' I hiss. People in the waiting area are looking over at us. They might as well crack open the popcorn; they're being so nosy. 'I hardly think I'm going to wake up in the middle of the night to find her straddling Ryan.'

She narrows her eyes at me like I'm stupid. 'How do you know that? This is the same cunt that tried to steal him only a few years ago.' Does she really need to use the C word? It's so unnecessary. 'I mean, where is her baby daddy?'

'He's not involved apparently.'

'Shit! And she hasn't even got a man.' Her brows snap together. 'You're a crazy bitch if you think I'm going to let you do this.'

'Let me?' I snort. I hate when she tries to tell me what to do. 'Lilly, no offence, but I can do whatever the fuck I want.'

She stares back at me in disbelief, an eerie silence descending upon us.

'Fine!' she says quietly before turning on her heel and storming back to the group.

Her being quiet and not shouting is almost more terrifying. What the hell have I done?

I follow her back catching a sympathetic smile from Jazz. 'Where's our ride anyway?' I ask them all, looking around for that guy. He can't have just abandoned us, right?

'Him and D went outside a while ago,' Kellie explains on a yawn.

'Yep,' Jazz cackles, 'I think she's *pretty* busy at the moment.' She's mimicking a blowjob by pressing her tongue against her cheek.

'Here she is now,' Alex calls.

We follow her eye line to see D walking in. The guy's not with her and with each step I can see she's distressed, her hair ruffled and her eyes red-rimmed.

'Ho-bag what's wrong?' Annie asks her.

She sniffs, still attempting to look brave. 'That guy's a prick; that's what.

He wanted me to have sex with him in the back of the van and when I said no he chucked me out and drove off. He's left us here.' She falls into Annie's arms sobbing rather unattractively.

What a bloody creep, but I suppose we did just meet him a few hours ago. He could have been an axe murderer for all we knew.

'Don't worry,' Izzy coos, still seeming a bit on edge. 'We'll get a taxi.'

We have to wait two and a half hours to get a taxi. Apparently with the backlog of the traffic accident and the time of night that's just how it is. We wait so long Lilly and Kirsty-Anne actually walk to the local shop and buy a bottle of vodka which we've all been sipping on just to pass the time. By the time it arrives, we're all a bit pissed again. Well, apart from Nicole, who's been napping on the uncomfortable chair. Thankfully when it finally arrives, we find it's a small minibus rather than three separate taxis.

'Shame we don't know where that fucker lives,' Jazz laughs as we board the bus. 'I'd love to key his car.'

Lilly cackles like a true, evil witch.

'Actually...' D says with a funny look on her face.

'What?' Lilly shouts with excited eyes.

'He did tell me where he lived.'

'What? Why?' Izzy asks in horror.

'He said he was from Borehamwood, so I asked where about. My Nan lives in Borehamwood, and he said he's the house right next to The Albert pub.'

'Driver!' Lilly shouts. 'We need to take a detour to The Albert pub in Borehamwood.'

'Lilly,' I try to warn. 'Don't you think we're all too tired to be traipsing to Borehamwood?'

'Yeah, Lill,' D agrees, thankfully seeing sense. 'It's not worth it.'

'Is it or is it not my party?' she screeches like a diva.

'Err, yeah,' Jazz giggles.

'Exactly,' she chuckles. 'So it's my party and if I want to go to a random arseholes house in Borehamwood; I will.'

Oh God, there is just no reasoning with this woman. Nicole leans her head back. God, if I'm tired, she must be beyond exhausted. We all make ourselves comfortable, trying to relax on the awkward seats. After hours on hard plastic ones, they're still heaven. I just hope Lilly changes her mind before we get there.

I must have dozed off when I hear the commotion.

'Hey, lady, get back in the car! I didn't sign up for this!' the mini cab driver shouts.

I look out of the window and what greets me will never be erased from my memory, no matter how hard I try. Lilly is stood on top of a car and is squatted, shitting on it.

What. The. Fuck?

Jazz is trying to drag her off the thing, with the others split between trying to help her and trying calm down the taxi driver.

'I'm not getting arrested for this,' the taxi driver shouts.

'Lilly!' I whisper-hiss. 'Think of the anger management course! The judge would throw the book at you if he found out.'

The girls manage to eventually drag her back onto the bus, but not before she's keyed *cunt* into the side of his car. I just really hope it's the right house.

Lilly plonks herself down in the seat across from me looking very pleased with herself. 'Now that, that is what you call the perfect end to a hen do. Let's go.'

You couldn't make this shit up.

When we get back to mine, I set Nicole up in the spare bedroom and get her some tea and biscuits. Ryan doesn't wake up as I creep under the covers. I really don't want to think about what he's going to say in the morning.

## Chapter 27
### Poppy

*Sunday 13th March*

My phone, buzzing on my bedside table wakes me up. God, what time is it? It barely feels like I've gone to sleep at all. Grams' number flashes on my phone screen. What the hell is she doing calling so early? It must be...I look at the clock...okay it's nearly nine in the morning.

'Hello?' I groggily answer, sounding like I stayed up til 5 am at an underground rave.

'Poppy.' It's Teddy's voice on the other end, and he sounds tense.

'Teddy?'

'Listen, there's not much time to explain, but Grams has had another fall. I'm with her waiting for the ambulance.'

A swoop of fear takes hold of me. My stomach curdles at the thought, immediately feeling ill with panic.

'Oh my god.' I sit up and remove the sleep from my eyes, him now having my full attention.

Ryan stirs and looks up at me, his eyes half closed. 'Who is it?' he whispers, throwing his arm over his eyes.

I open my mouth to tell him but I'm interrupted.

'She's given me strict instructions that we're not to tell Ryan.'

'What?'

How can she be so ridiculous? How can she be serious enough for an ambulance but her not think Ryan has the right to know?

'Who is it?' Ryan asks again, now having concern etched into his forehead. 'Is something wrong?'

Shit, I can't lie. It's too soon after waking up to do any of this. I turn away from him.

'We're headed to Northwich Park Hospital. I'll meet you there and remember not to tell Ryan.'

I hang up as slowly as I can and try to get my brain to work. I can't believe she's told me not to tell Ryan. She's so infuriating. But can I really refuse an old lady's wish?

'Pops, you're worrying me now,' he says, his eyebrows knitted together in concern.

'Err, sorry.' I shake my head, desperately trying to think up an excuse. 'That was Izzy. She needs me to go over straight away.' I jump out of bed and start looking for a clean pair of jeans.

'Why? What's happened?' He sits up and watches me with suspicious eyes

'She...' God, think of something dramatic enough to cause this reaction in me. 'She...fell down the stairs.'

'WHAT?

Okay, I possibly went *too* dramatic.

Shit, I should come with you.' He jumps out of bed, ready to come with me, reaching into his drawer for some boxers.

'No!' He narrows his eyes at me, obviously suspicious why I wouldn't want him to help. 'I mean, but that's not the reason she wants me round. She got up and was fine after that. But then...' think of something way less serious, 'she...had an argument with Michael.'

I pull my jeans on so I don't have to watch his reaction.

'Really?' he asks with brows knitted together. 'What about?'

God, he's a nosey bastard. I need to get to Grams.

'About...her inability to walk down stairs. They really went at it apparently. She's upset and just wants to talk to a girlfriend. You understand, right?'

He smiles, already lowering himself back down onto his pillow, clearly deciding to get another hour in. 'Okay, send my love.' He's basically snoring before he even finishes his sentence.

I grab a t-shirt from the fresh washing I haven't put away yet and throw it on. I rush out of the house towards our car and race towards the hospital as quickly as possible, my head banging from sleep deprivation. Okay and maybe a bit of vodka. It's only then that it dawns on me. Nicole is in the spare bedroom. I've left Ryan home alone with his ex-fiancé. His pregnant ex-fiancé, who is, in fact, single. What the hell have I done?

When I finally find Grams, she's on a ward. It was harder than I thought trying to find her, as I couldn't remember her actual name. I went through all of the typical Nan type names: Mary, Beatrice, Susan. Then I suddenly remembered seeing a letter in her place addressed to Bridget Davis.

I pull back the curtain to find her asleep in the bed, her forehead cut and stitched up. My poor Grams. Teddy's sat next to her.

He smiles kindly. 'I'll get us both a cup of tea.'

I sit down on the chair next to her and sigh, noticing the previous bruise on the other side. Like this, she seems so vulnerable. So alone. Her words aren't here to shush my worrying. I can take in her injuries for myself.

I realise with filling dread this is it. This is the time I have to make a decision. We can't keep going on like this; she needs help. Someone to constantly check in on her. But she doesn't want to move. How the hell can I change her mind?

She stirs slightly and slowly her eyes open. The relief I feel when I see the same brown eyes as Ryan look back at me is beyond anything I've previously experienced.

'Poppy,' she whispers with a smile. 'It's not as bad as it looks.'

'Yeah, right,' I snort, suddenly welling up with tears. 'You've had stitches. The doctor says if you hadn't had been with Teddy when you fell you could have bled to dead with you being on Warfarin.'

She laughs lightly. 'You young ones are so dramatic.'

'I'm not being dramatic, Grams!' I snap, losing my patience with her. When is she going to get this? 'And I am *not* happy with you getting me to lie to Ryan about this. He deserves to know.'

'He'll just worry himself into an early grave, and I am *not* having that on my conscience. God knows that boy's been through more than most.' I know she means because of his mum, who's still currently MIA.

'Whatever. I'm taking you home with me. There is no way you can be left to recover on your own.'

She sighs, her eyes heavy with resignation. 'Normally I'd argue with you, but, to be honest, Poppy, that's a bit of a relief. I just don't want to be a bother to you.'

I snort so hard I almost hit her with some snot. Is she crazy?

'Grams, when are you going to realise that we love you? You're not a bother to us, and you never will be.'

'Even if that is the truth, I don't want this getting back to Ryan.'

'But, -'

'I mean it, Poppy,' she says sternly, making me sit up straight and take her seriously. 'You tell Ryan, and I'll be straight out of that door as soon as your back is turned.'

How can she be so feisty at eighty-three?

'But, you're making me lie to my husband. It's not right.'

She smiles condescendingly like she finds me adorable.

'Poppy, stop worrying. We'll come up with some reason why I'm staying. He'll be none the wiser.'

I shake my head in disbelief. She's crazy if she thinks we can get away with this.

'How the hell are we going to hide that big cut on your head?'

She shrugs as if she's way ahead of me. 'A hat sweetheart. You young things have no imagination.'

I roll my eyes on a sigh. 'Whatever.'

My phone beeps loudly in my bag.

'You'll get told off for having that thing on in here,' she reprimands. Still well enough to be bossy I see.

I ignore her and check it; already knowing it will be Ryan. I wonder how he's found Nicole this morning. Maybe he walked down naked to get some cereal, and she was sat at the table eating his coco pops. He'll kill me.

*'What time are you going to be home? Does Izzy want to come round for a roast dinner?'*

Huh? How can he not have noticed her? Unless she's still asleep in the bedroom. Oh god, just thinking about them bumping into each other is filling me with stomach-churning anxiety. I can feel heartburn lurking, ready to attack.

I decide to text back and get it over and done with.

*Don't be mad but Nicole is in the spare room.*

No, actually I could be a bit smarter than that. What if she's already gone? I delete it and type again.

*A friend stayed in the spare room. Could you check on them?*

Then I worry he'll do it in just his boxers. That's enough to tempt even a hardcore lesbian.

*And make sure you're dressed.*

There, that makes me feel a bit better.

'So,' I turn back to Grams, 'what excuse are we thinking up?'

Her grin takes up almost all of her face. 'That's the spirit, girl.'

I just hope she doesn't make me live to regret it.

I help Grams into ours later that afternoon, Toffee dragging on her lead the minute she senses Ryan. I've got Grams wearing the biggest hat of hers; we could find in her house. That just happened to be a ridiculous navy wedding hat. I tried to argue that it looked too obvious, but it was the only one that covered her head, so I've just had to go with it.

'We're back,' I call to Ryan, struggling in with her on one arm and her bag and Toffee's lead in the other.

'Good timing,' he shouts back from the kitchen. 'The roast potatoes are nearly done.' He walks out wiping his hands with a tea towel. His expression changes when he sees Grams. 'Oh, Grams, that's a big hat.' He smiles at me in amused questioning.

I decide to release Toffee to distract him. She runs straight up to him jumping straight up and onto his balls. He doubles over in agony, shrieking obscenities.

'Thank you, Ryan,' she smiles, ignoring his clear pain. 'I've always liked it. People have often told me I suit hats.'

'Err...yeah,' he says bemused. 'Didn't you wear that to Teddy's grandson's wedding?'

'Civil partnership actually, Ryan,' she says as if Ryan is ignorant. 'And yes, this was the hat.'

'So a burst pipe then?' he sighs. 'That's bloody unlucky.'

'Yep,' she smiles sadly. 'Should be sorted out in a few weeks.' She looks at me as if to warn that she doesn't intend to stay any longer.

'Yeah, anyway, did you err...find anyone in the spare room?'

He never texted back, and I haven't stopped panicking since.

He shakes his head. 'No. But they left you this note, which sounds a bit like you had a dirty night with them.' He grins and hands over a crumpled piece of paper.

*Thanks for a great night x*

'Ha ha! That's random!' I shrill, laughing loud and unnaturally.

He looks at me a bit strangely. Perhaps I laughed a bit too hard.

We sit down to a delicious dinner, and then I settle Grams on the sofa with her feet up. She looks so funny still in her enormous hat. Every time I look at her, I giggle.

I decide to take Toffee out for a walk. The poor thing is getting a bit long in the tooth herself. She's no puppy anymore, not that it's stopped her from whining at the door all afternoon. Plus, after that mammoth dinner, I could do with the exercise. I swear Ryan's a feeder.

'Alright,' I say, clipping the lead on her. 'We'll go for a walk. There's a nice little park just down the road.'

We walk leisurely down the road, well leisurely apart from Toffee pulling terribly on the lead. I have no idea how Grams does this. My back and arm are already aching. Unless she's perfect for her and she knows she can take the piss out of me. We've still come so far considering the first time I met her I jumped onto a table in fear. Don't get me wrong, I still don't like other dogs, but Toffee's different. She's just like a little hairy human. She even has expressions like a person. I swear I've never seen anything like it.

I let her off the lead when we get to the park and throw the ball for her a few times. She spins around, far too excited for this pitiful display of exercise. That is until she starts circling in the middle of the football pitch. What is she doing? Oh crap. I forgot about this part. She's doing a poo.

I look away, trying to give her some privacy. I mean I'd totally hate having to do my business in front of everyone. In fact, she looks a bit nervous. She's straining, but no poo is actually coming out. Poor love. Maybe I should sing to her. Try to take her mind off it.

Hmm, what should I sing to a dog?

'What's up pussycat, woooah, wooo-oooah.'

She stares at me with a bemused expression, her head leaning to one side. Why am I singing about pussycats? No, I need to think. I know!

'How much is that doggy in the window? The one with the waggily tail!'

Again, she's not amused. Maybe she wants something more current. Maybe some Taylor Swift?

'We are never, ever, ever getting back together. Oh weeeee, are never, ever, ever getting back together. You go talk to your friends, talk to my friends, talk to me.' I'm getting really into it now, swaying my hips to the music in my head.

It seems to be working as it's starting to come out like whipped ice cream. Eww.

'Because weeeeee are never, ever, ever getting back together.'

She stops pooing just as I finish singing. A round of applause makes me jump out of my skin. Two teenagers swigging from cans of beer are laughing at me, clearly revolted at how old and ridiculous I am. I should come up with something really witty as a retort. Only...well, I have nothing.

I turn to run away instead.

'Don't forget to pick up your dog's shit,' one of them says with a cruel smirk. Jesus, when did kids get so cruel? Can't they see when a girl is down?

'Of course not,' I snap.

I march over to it, faking confidence and riffle through my pockets. Why didn't I think of a poo bag? Oh crap. I must have something in my pocket that will do. I rifle through, finding gum, a hairband, and an old tissue. Aha! I have a scrunched up carrier bag in here – alleluia! I had visions of me trying to pick it up with just the tissue. Eww, gag.

I put my hand in the carrier bag and also use the tissue. I place my plastic covered hand around the poo. Oh God, it's still warm. I heave so badly I almost vomit all over it. That won't help anyone. I grasp it and quickly turn the carrier bag inside out and tie it into a tight knot. Phew, thank God that's over. I've broken a sweat and everything!

I put Toffee back on the lead and walk out of the park, avoiding the arsey teenagers as much as I can. I press for the Pelican pedestrian traffic lights as the cars can really zoom down here. With my luck, I'm not taking any chances.

A car booming down the road slows when the lights change to red. I start walking across happily when I notice the guy leaning out of the window shouting at me.

'Did you really need to use the lights, you health and safety dog-owning pillock!'

I stop in my tracks. I don't think I've *ever* been called a pillock. It's weird, but it does something to me. It's not even a swear word, but I feel anger rising up from my gut. How dare this guy think that his time is more important than my potential life. Who died and made him the King of England? Nobody. Who does he think he is with his swish BMW? I'd like to teach that rude arse a lesson. I look down at the bag of pooh in my hands. No. I couldn't.

'Hurry the fuck up!' he screams again, his face red with fury. Jesus, living on the edge of life much? 'You women have too much time on your hands!'

That's it. The moment I see red. Every frustration that I've ever felt surfaces in me, directed at this one man. This one waste of oxygen.

I raise the bag in my hand, swing it back and launch it at him. It goes straight in his car, his windows luckily being down. I see the shit almost explode out of the bag and all around the car. The man's face is a picture. Complete and utter disbelief.

'Eat my shit!' I scream, so loud I myself jump. I pull on Toffee's lead as I run down the road and down an alleyway shortcut so he can't follow me.

Well, that was a new level of angry, Poppy.

## Monday 14th March

I can't stop thinking about Nicole. Is she at work? I don't have a number for her so it's not like I can send her a quick text to check on her. Plus, I don't know where she lives in Watford. I've already had Jazz, Izzy and Lilly text me to ask how it went down Sunday morning. Nosy bastards.

Grams seems better today. I realise that I feel a lot calmer with her being here so I can check on her whenever I want.

Dad's at mine, looking at one of my leaky taps. Not that he's a plumber, but he generally has more idea than me. After about fifteen minutes I think he's fixed it. Well, he went into this long arsed speech about what he reckoned was wrong. I zoned out, to be honest. Only now he's still hanging around.

'Tea?' I offer, boiling the kettle. 'Tea?' I shout to Grams in the sitting room.

'Please, my love,' she calls back.

'How are you feeling then?' I ask. Maybe he wants me to talk to him about the whole thing.

'Better than ever, love,' he grins checking to see that Grams isn't within earshot. 'Never felt better in my life. I'm living each day to the fullest now.'

I raise my eyebrows and stare at him sceptically. 'Just be careful you don't wear yourself out too much. I mean, you did have cancer. You should be resting.'

'Ugh, resting,' he snorts rolling his eyes. 'I hate when people say that. Like I'm going to waste the rest of my life, no matter how short, *resting*.'

I roll my eyes. 'Look, I'm not telling you to never leave the house again, but I do think you're going a bit crazy lately.'

'I think you're over-reacting,' he smirks, accepting the made cup of tea.

The front door slams and I turn to see Jazz rushing in. I hate how she just lets herself in all the time, albeit less frequently since she's moved.

'Jazz! What have I told you? That key is only for emergencies.'

She rolls her eyes. 'This *was* an emergency. I was late.'

'I mean it, Jazz.' I do my best to look authoritative, but I can't help but let a giggle escape. 'Me and Ryan could be having sex on the sofa one day.'

She bursts out laughing at the same time that Dad looks away, horrified.

'Oh *please*,' Jazz laughs. 'I bet you two hardly ever make it out of the bed. Missionary, Saturday morning after a cup of tea, right?'

'No actually!' I shriek, going bright red. If only she knew how much bloody sex I *was* having.

'Anyway,' she rolls her eyes as if I'm ridiculous. 'Douggie, you ready to go?'

He raises his eyebrows excitedly. 'You bet.' He puts down the tea and reaches for his jacket. His new ridiculous leather jacket.

Jazz and Dad being together when he's vulnerable like this worries me.

'Err, sorry, but where are you going?'

'Nowhere,' they both say at the same time. Their eyes dart guiltily at each other.

Okay, now I'm worried

'Cut the crap. What are you two up to?'

Jazz purses her lips together in a tight smile. 'I'm not a grass.'

She can be so absurd.

'It's okay, Jazz,' he nods. He faces me faking bravery.

I brace myself. Oh my God, what if he's found another lump and he's too afraid to tell me? What if the cancer has spread and it's too late? What if he couldn't bear to break my heart and so he's confided in Jazz instead.

He takes a deep breath. 'I'm getting my first tattoo.'

I stare open mouthed at him. What? Here I am worrying myself to death over him and the guys getting himself a tattoo, like a sailor. Sixty-year-old family men don't get themselves tattoos. What is he thinking?

'WHAT?'

'He knew you'd react like this,' Jazz snorts, leaning on one hip. 'Which is why I offered to take him. I want to get another one anyway.'

'Since when?' I snap. She's *such* a bad influence.

'Since last week,' she retorts, sticking her tongue out at me.

'Mature. *Real* mature.' I turn back to Dad. 'What the hell will Mum say?'

He smiles warmly like a lovesick puppy. 'She'll be overjoyed love. I'm getting her name.'

'You're...' I place my hands over my temples, trying to make sure this isn't a nightmare. 'You're getting Meryl tattooed on you? In *ink?* Forever?'

He laughs like I'm hilarious. 'We've survived a lot, love. I hardly think we're going to break up now.'

'That's not what I meant.' I cross my arms over my chest. 'Just...why? Why now?'

'I told you – '

'Yeah, yeah,' I interrupt. I finger quote 'live for the day.' I snort. 'Mid-life crisis more like. You're going to look like an idiot.'

'What makes you think it will be anywhere people can see?' he asks with a cheeky wink.

I almost vomit.

'Please, *please* God, tell me you're not getting it tattooed on your arse. Because I *cannot* condone that!'

They both fall about laughing. Yeah, *I'm* the ridiculous ones. Not these two idiots.

'On my chest,' he laughs.

His chest? God, does he think he's going to look like Tom Hardy or something?

'Well I'm sorry, but I cannot give you my blessing.'

They both double over again laughing. 'I'm not looking for your blessing, love,' he says with a sad smile like he pity's me or something.

'Yeah,' Jazz agrees. 'Like you said, he's a man in his sixties. I'm pretty sure he's old enough to get it done without mummy's permission.'

God knows where she's taking him.

'Fine!' I shout. 'But I'm coming with you.' I grab my coat. 'Grams, I'm popping out,' I say to her popping my head into the sitting room.

'Thank God for that,' she laughs. 'I can't stand all the fussing over me.'

Jazz sighs dramatically. 'She's going to be such a buzz kill.'

Buzz kill my bloody arse. I'm fun. They can't even handle my fun. Just because I don't want to sharpie a flower into my skin with a protractor.

Okay, so it's not really what I was expecting. Call me a stereotypical judging bastard but I totally expected some brick warehouse type building with a huge muscled guy named Butch leering at us with a needle. Not this place. It's all marble floors, hot pink walls, and black leather lounge chairs. It looks more like a hairdressers than a tattoo studio. I don't think Dad liked it either. I think the new found rebel in him wanted to go to some grungy place and have the possibility of getting an infection. But this all looks very clean; it even smells of disinfectant.

'So, Jazz, what are you getting?' I ask, trying to take my mind off all of the needles about to penetrate their skin. If I think about it too much I'm woozy.

'Oh, I'm having Jemima's name,' she smiles, tapping away on her phone.

'What, in case you forget it?' I laugh.

'No!' she snaps. 'Because she's special to me.' Her brow line frowns. So much for that Botox. 'Well, either that or my star sign. I haven't decided yet.'

God, she's fickle.

'Well tick tock,' the tattoo artist says to her with a smile. It's a woman, not a big burly man. She's totally fabulous and I kind of wish I was her. She's tall and lean, her milky skin covered in the brightest and most vibrant tattoos I've ever seen. Now, someone like that was born to have tattoos.

'We'll start with you then shall we?' she says to Dad. He suddenly looks a bit pale.

This could be my chance to change his mind.

'Dad, remember you don't have to do this,' I say offering a sympathetic smile.

'God, stop whinging, Pops,' Jazz exclaims throwing her head back in despair. 'I told you Douggie, *total* buzz kill. We should have just dropped her off somewhere and said we were getting petrol.'

'You *wouldn't* have!' I shout horrified at the thought of being abandoned somewhere scary.

'I would have,' she grins, winking. She's so evil sometimes.

'I'm sure anyway,' he says, sticking his tongue out at me as he sinks himself into the leather seat.

Like I said, such a bad influence. The girl talks through with him what he wants and then draws it onto a transfer piece of paper. Once agreed with Dad she shaves an area on Dad's chest and then cleans it with a wipe. He's going to look so ridiculous. She transfers the design onto his chest, a bit like those fake tattoo transfers I used when I thought I was a cool teenager. She cleans then puts on some plastic gloves. She gets out needles and plugs them into her machine.

God, is it me or is it hot in here? They need to open a window. Let some fresh air in or something. God, just looking at those needles is making me feel a bit queasy, my stomach churning. Jazz is next to me rattling on about her tattoo, but all I can think about are the needles about to puncture into Dad's skin. This is why I could never do this myself.

I try to look up at the ceiling to distract myself, my stomach heaving, but it's freshly painted white. There's no stains or anything to concentrate on. God, I can hear that buzzing sound now, only it's becoming quieter as the ringing in my ears invades. Gross. I make the mistake of looking back down.

Dad is grimacing while she's already etching on his chest. Oh God. It's too much.

'I feel a little...' I barely get my words out before my head swings back, and I'm greeted again with a quick view of the ceiling before everything turns black.

When I come to, I'm lying down in one of those chairs. Jesus, did I really just pass out at the idea of a needle? How am I ever going to be able to give birth?

'Oi oi, sleepyhead,' Jazz laughs leaning in over my head. 'Thought we'd lost you there for a moment.' She throws her head back cackling like a witch.

How mortifying. I missed the whole thing. Wait, my Dad. Did he get the tattoo?

'What do you think Pops?' Dad asks appearing in front of me. He opens his shirt and shows me...well, it can only be described as the worst tattoo in history.

Meryl is written in swirly black writing with a rose being the 'L' at the end. It's garish and bold and...just wrong. It's also wrapped in cling film, which only makes it look worse.

'She loves it!' Jazz exclaims jumping up and down on the spot. 'I told you she would. And check out mine.'

She pulls her hair over one side. Just below her ear is a small J. J for Jemima. Or Jazz I suppose. I actually like it. It's gorgeous. Totally her and discreet enough for it to still be classy. I admit that part of me expected her to get a sleeve done with a collage of Cinderella and the lion king.

'It's actually nice,' I admit begrudgingly.

'Don't sound *too* impressed,' she snorts. 'Anyway, it was a hell of a lot easier once you'd passed out. You do like to bring drama wherever you go.'

'Pot calling kettle,' I say under my breath.

'Are you going to tell her, Jazz?' My dad asks her, seeming nervous.

'Tell me what?' God, they have *more* secrets? What could it be this time?

He already has a pierced ear and a tattoo. If he tells me he's off to join a band, I'm having him committed.

Instead, Jazz's eyes light up devilishly. 'We got you a little surprise.' She looks down at my tummy. Oh my god. What?

I pull my t-shirt up on one side, and I myself have been wrapped in cling film. No. No, she wouldn't. She seriously wouldn't have got me tattooed while I was unconscious would she? Hell, what am I talking about? This is Jazz; of course she'd get me tattooed while I'm unconscious! But then surely the tattoo artists take some kind of moral oath to avoid this kind of thing getting them sued. But then I suppose if Jazz threw enough money at her she'd soon forget that. Fuck!

'Jazz! I scream. 'What the fuck have you done?' I sit up too quickly, the blood rushing to my head. 'What the hell is tattooed onto me? FOREVER might I add!'

This is horrendous. I want to rip it off.

'Oh chill. You got Ryan's name.'

*'Please* tell me you didn't.' It's so stereotypical. And if it's half as ugly as Dad's I'm going straight to have it lasered off.

'Of course I didn't,' she laughs, before turning serious again. 'Yours says Jazz and I have Poppy.'

'What?' She *cannot* be serious.

'I told her not to love,' Dad shrugs. 'But she paid the woman a lot of money to agree to it.'

'Where's your Poppy then?' I demand. 'I hope it's ugly as fuck, and somewhere everyone will see.'

She folds her arms across her chest.

'No, you silly bitch. It's on my arse. That way only *special* people see it.'

She got a tattoo on her arse? Why the hell would she do that?

'And meanwhile, mine's on my stomach! How is that fair?'

She rolls her eyes. 'Come on, Pops, you hardly wear crop tops anymore. We're not in the nineties, and you haven't got the flattest stomach.'

Now she's calling me fat. Worst day ever.

I decide to hit her where it hurts. 'Why is it, Jazz, that you're sounding more like my mother each day?'

She inhales a sharp breath, her eyes wide. 'You take that back.'

'I will not.'

I have to see this thing. Face up to what I'm going to have to see every day for the rest of my life. I grasp onto the side of my t-shirt and carefully peel it back. I try to brace myself, inhaling a deep breath. It won't be that bad. It can't be that bad.

I pull it back to reveal...nothing. There's nothing there. I check all over my stomach. Huh? I rip the cling film off fully searching for something.

'Got ya!' they both shout. I look up to see them rolling around in hysterics. These guys are dead.

## Chapter 28

### Poppy

*Tuesday 15th March*

Izzy's on me, the minute she comes into work.

'How's Nicole? What happened the other night?'

I may have been ignoring her questioning texts, but everyone's been hounding me, and with looking after Grams and Dad insisting on tattooing himself, I'm frankly exhausted at the end of each night.

'I'll tell you later,' I mumble vaguely running away from her.

She finds me at lunchtime. Of course she does. She's nothing if not tenacious.

She quickly got herself a reputation around here. As soon as she walks into a room everyone immediately hides their cupcakes and tries to duck out of the room. Only today, when I really look at her, she seems skinnier than normal. I realise her arms look weak and brittle, rather than their usual strong and muscular. I know it's the stress of her stalker, and I want so badly to reassure her that she's safe. Only I know she isn't.

'Come on,' she pesters. 'It's your lunch break. We can squeeze in a quick walk.'

'Around here?' I force a laugh. 'There are hardly any scenic routes.'

She smiles knowingly at me. 'It doesn't matter. Now get off that butt of yours. You're never going to get the butt you want by sitting on the one you have. We're going.'

God, she can be a bitch sometimes. That's what depriving yourself of sugar does to you.

I step out into the cold, crisp weather, wrapping my scarf securely around my neck. I changed into my trainers I keep here, knowing that my converse won't do it. The last time she suggested a quick walk I ended up with three blisters.

'So where are we going then?' I ask, already irritated as the cold wind assaults my face. I was really not made for the outside.

'Let's just see where the moment takes us, shall we?' she says, her eyes alight with mischief.

I sigh and follow her down the road. She can be so annoying. 'So how are you anyway?' I ask.

She throws her arms in the air. 'Ugh, you're not going to start lecturing me are you?'

Jesus, overreact much?

'Why would you say that?' Whatever I said has affected her. She's slowed down her pace. I'm already puffing, my face on fire, so I'm kind of glad.

'Ugh, Michael is on at me, saying I seem stressed. I'm not even that stressed!'

'Yeah...you *really* seem calm,' I say sarcastically, letting out a small chuckle.

She sighs, slumping her shoulders in defeat. 'Sorry. I just...I suppose it's safe to say that this whole stalker thing is affecting me a bit. Anyway, why don't we walk down here?'

Hmm, she's a bit quick to change the subject. She points to a country lane I've never noticed before. There's a sign advertising dog kennels, a luxurious stay for your pet.

'I'm not sure this is a public road,' I query, trying to encourage her back.

'Don't be silly,' she laughs. 'I could be enquiring about putting my dog into kennels.'

'You don't even have a dog!' I stomp after her.

'They don't know that,' she giggles.

It's the first time in ages I've seen her look carefree and mischievous. I can't let her down, so I follow her.

I have to ask her about her weight. I wouldn't be a good friend if I didn't, but it doesn't stop me not wanting to.

'So...' how do I put it? 'Is the worrying affecting your eating habits?'

She stops in her tracks, narrowing her eyes on me. 'Has Michael spoken to you?'

'No!' So he's asked about it too. Interesting. 'Why?'

'Ugh, I'm sick of everyone sticking their nose in.' She picks up her pace, racing away from me.

'I'm sorry, okay!' I say hands up in defeat.

'Yes I'm stressed,' she admits, her face twisted in clear distaste at having to talk about it. 'And yes, I find it hard to eat big meals when I'm stressed, but I'm very capable of feeding myself thank you.'

Now I feel bad. I don't want to be adding to her stress.

'Okay, sorry.'

'How are *you* anyway?' she asks, clearly trying to turn the attention back to me.

'I'm fine,' I shrug between laboured breaths.

'Yeah, right,' she grins stopping to pet a horse. I think she needs the distraction to calm herself down. 'I know you. You're probably stressing over at least three things right now. I don't think I've ever known you not to be. You're a natural worrier.'

'No, I'm not!' I carry on walking, hoping she doesn't press further.

She laughs, openly enjoying my discomfort. 'You so are!'

Well, it's not like I can tell her the real reasons why I'm stressed. Trying and failing to get pregnant, Grams' failing health, my Dad having a mid-life crisis after a cancer scare.

'So how is Nicole now anyway?'

I shrug. 'I don't know. It's not like we're besties.'

'Alright!' she laughs. 'Sorry I asked. But she did stay the night, right?'

She's so bloody nosey.

'Yeah, but she was gone in the morning. I don't have her number or anything, so I guess that's the last I'll hear of her.'

Dogs barking ferociously pull me back to our surroundings. Wow, we've walked quite far now. There are two beefy men to our left in the distance, staring at us from under a crappy car bonnet. An unsettling feeling creeps over me.

'Yeah....Izzy, I really don't think we're supposed to be here.'

She follows my eye line. They widen when she sees how unfriendly they seem.

'I think you're right. Let's head back.'

We both turn and start power walking away from them. Is it me, or has the dog barking got louder? Tell me they haven't released the dogs on us. I look to Izzy, and she seems just as freaked as me. Before I know it, our power walking has turned into a jog. Rain starts pouring, heavy droplets caressing my cheeks. It's like a black cloud has surrounded us making the one pm hour seem more like ten o'clock at night. It's like we've walked into a horror movie.

We sprint towards the exit, but there's now a gate closed over it.

'Did you see that gate on the way in?' I shout over the noisy rain.

'Of course not!' she shouts back over the rain pounding on the ground. She looks for a way to open it, but there doesn't seem to be a latch.

'Oh shit.'

I look back to see the men walking towards us. They seem *really* pissed now, their faces like angry Rottweilers.

'Shit, we're going to die here.'

'Quick, we need to jump it!' she yells, her brown eyes frantic. 'Give me a leg up.'

My pulse leaps as I help Izzy scale the gate. I push her over, and it's only then I notice a red sign attached to it.

PRIVATE PROPERTY. NO TRESPASSERS.

Motherfucker. Why couldn't we have seen that on the bloody way in?

'Now help me,' I cry, clambering up onto the gate. God, this is harder than I thought it would be. My legs have turned to quivering jelly.

'Hey, you two!' a burly voice shouts behind me.

Izzy looks me square in the eye as unfiltered terror runs through them.

'I'm sorry.'

Then she turns and runs. Runs away from me and off into freedom.

That. Little. Bitch.

# Chapter 29
## Poppy

### *Thursday 17th March - St Patrick's Day*

It's Paddy's Day today, which you'd think would cheer me up. Everyone even remotely Irish, up and down England, is due to be shit faced by midday. Except me. I'm the only miserable bastard that's stuck at work contemplating my fertility.

I hurry home and slip into a green jumper which says, 'What's the craic?' to try and get myself in the mood.

'Ready?' I ask Ryan as I apply some lipstick in the hallway mirror.

'I don't think I'm going to go.'

I swivel round to him in shock. Him not attend our family's annual St Patrick's Day? Why the hell not?

'I don't really think I should be drinking,' he reasons with a shrug. 'You know, if I'm going to have my sperm tested again.'

I smile sadly at him. My poor Ryan. He wants his sperm to be perfect. Shame I'm not feeling so sensible. I really, *really* want a drink. No, fuck it, I want to get shitfaced. All this not drinking is driving me insane. Of course, I'm no alcoholic, but when you can't have it, you soon miss it. I just need something to force me to relax. To stop all of these baby thoughts from invading my brain for one evening.

'Are you sure, babe? I mean, one night won't make that much difference, right?' I know that he needs a break from it too and what better way than us letting loose together. It could be just what we need.

'I'm sure,' he nods determinedly. 'With your family around it'll be impossible not to drink loads.'

I'd be offended if he wasn't right.

'Besides, this way someone gets to stay in with Grams.' He puts his hands in his jean pockets and leans against the wall. He looks beyond sexy. If Grams weren't next door, I'd attempt to ravish him, right here right now.

He does make sense though. I'm not going to lie and say I wasn't worried about leaving her. Not that I could voice that fear to him, without him getting suspicious. She's still wearing stupidly large wedding hats, so he's none the wiser.

My phone starts ringing with an unknown local number. I put my finger up to motion to Ryan I'll be one second.

'Hello?'

'Hi, am I speaking with Mrs Davis?' an authoritative female voice asks.

'Yes.'

'Good. It's Carrie Marsh here from the detective agency. I have some information for you and Miss Bianchi and I wondered if I could organize to come round to your's to go through it?'

Oh, okay. I wonder what she's found. Hopefully, something to put this nutcase behind bars.

'Yeah, sure.' I grab my diary and flick through it. 'I can do the 21st in the evening.'

'That's perfect. I'll be there at seven.' She hangs up without a goodbye.

She must have found something serious if she wants to tell us in person.

I turn back to Ryan. It's weird, but I kind of feel like I have to ask permission for me to go out and get a bit crazy tonight. I'm supposed to be staying healthy too and don't want to feel like I'm letting him down.

'You don't mind if I go though, right?' I ask tentatively, grimacing as I wait for him to respond.

'Course not, babe. You need to let off some steam.' He stands behind me massaging my shoulders. God, that feels good. 'You're so bloody tense lately.'

He's telling me! 'Yeah. I...' I turn to face him. God, he's gloriously handsome. It still shocks me sometimes. 'Do you think it would be really bad if I had a drink tonight?'

'Of course not,' he smiles, cradling my head in his palms. My stomach instantly settles. 'Pops, the doctor never told you to give up alcohol. Just to not binge drink. So have a couple of glasses of wine and relax.' He kisses me on the end of my nose, leaving me feeling cherished.

I hug him so tight; letting his warm muscles relax my tight ones. He's going to be the best dad in the world someday. I just hope it's with me.

Four hours later I'm...well, I think it's fair to say I've had those few glasses of wine to relax *and* some. But it's not my fault. Wine relaxes me and relaxed Poppy wants to party. Jazz keeps telling me it's a good idea too, which should be a big warning bell sounding in my head. Reckons I need to let go of some steam and anxiety.

Plus my entire family is here egging me on. They don't know we're trying. The minute I'd try and say I wasn't drinking they'd instantly jump to conclusions, and I just can't bear for anyone to mistake me as pregnant right now. It would break my already fragile heart.

So yeah, I had a *little* whiskey with my Dad. I had a *few* beers with Ollie. And okay, maybe I did some green looking shots with Jazz and Abbey. She normally stays in to look after Hazel but tonight her and Jazz shared a babysitter. You can tell too as she's a *bit* drunk, to say the least. The last time I saw her, she had glasses in her hair. She doesn't wear glasses.

Mum's just got the spoons out and is on the small stage area, playing along with an Irish band. My God, spoons must be the most ridiculous instrument ever thought of. No wonder people call the Irish backwards. You have to salute us really, finding a dual purpose for cutlery.

Jazz drags me onto the rug in front of the fire, which seems to be the makeshift dance floor. She swings me around, the whole time begging I do some Irish dancing. Things seem a bit less awkward between her and Ollie. Before I know it, I'm flinging my legs in the air and shouting for people to get out of my way. Like a *real* diva. I do a turn and stop when I see Abbey in the corner. Not just in the corner, but face down on a table surrounded by people. They're carrying on like nothing's the matter.

I grab Jazz, and we go over to her. I smile politely at the people around her while smacking her cheeks.

'Come on, Abs. Up you get,' I sing loudly into her ear.

No answer. Jazz looks at me with furrowed eyes.

'Abbey? Wake up!' I slap her hard on the back. 'Shit,' I say more to Jazz than anyone.

The pub manager walks over, his beer belly falling out from under his t-shirt. 'I've called an ambulance,' he says calmly. 'The poor cow's unconscious.'

Really? I thought she was just asleep.

Shit. Henry will kill us. I have to tell him.

Jazz stays with her while I weave through the people searching for him. I find him having Jaeger bombs with Ollie at the bar.

'Henwy,' I slur. Oops, maybe I *am* drunker than I thought. The room does seem to be spinning a bit. 'Abbey. She's passed out. They've called an ambulance.'

'What?' he gasps, his face tense. Obviously wants to blame someone. 'Take me to her.'

God, he's a bossy pants.

By the time we make our way through to the corner a paramedic is already with her. They're trying to lift her into a wheelchair thing. Shit. This doesn't look good.

'Abbey,' he cries, lifting her face up off the table. She's really out of it; bless her. It just flops back down afterwards.

'Ugh, leave me alone,' she moans from under all that hair.

He rolls his eyes at me and lifts her into the wheelchair. As soon as she's seated she starts vomiting. *Everywhere.*

'Oh my God!' People shriek, ducking and diving to get out of her way.

'What da hell's wrong with da girl?' Irish people ask each other.

Obviously not used to people that can't handle their drink. Now I come to think of it I don't think I've ever seen Abbey trashed. Maybe that's why.

Mum's still obliviously playing spoons on stage and Jazz is now up there trying to take the Bodhran from a man with Claddagh rings on nearly every finger. He's not having any of it.

'I'll help you out,' I volunteer, trying to duck every time vomit comes my way. Eww, it stinks. I walk out in front of them to the main entrance of the pub. The fresh air hits me like a brick to the skull. Shit. I *am* drunk.

There are two ambulances driving away. Where are they going? The patient is here you arseholes!

'Wait!' I shriek, running after them. 'Where are you going?!'

I sprint as fast as I can until my face feels like it gets smashed in with bricks, my jaw screaming in agony. I fall back, dazed and smash the back of my head on the ground. My entire head throbs so much with screaming agony that I close my eyes. Anything to try and stop the pain. Only I can't seem to open them up again.

## Jazz

What the fuck is wrong with her? Running into an ambulance. That's a new form of stupidity even for her. Way to totally kill my alcohol buzz.

Once she's loaded into the ambulance along with Abbey, I get my phone out to book a taxi. I have to follow her there. She'll be so confused when she comes round. I'll let Henry tell Meryl and Douggie, although I really should be the one to break it to Ryan.

'Hey.'

I turn around to find Ollie with his hands in his pockets. 'You wanna share a taxi to the hospital?'

I smile sadly at him. The urge to run and throw myself into his arms is overwhelming, but things are still weird between us. I mean; he left me for God's sakes. I decide to nod instead.

He goes inside to get our coats. Where did it all go wrong? It doesn't help that I'm drunk right now and could really demolish a kebab. He comes back, handing over my faux fur yellow coat. I throw it on, shivering from the cold night air. Spring my arse. It still feels like winter.

We stand in an awkward silence until the cab finally arrives.

I get in and stare out of the window. It's starting to rain, to match my mood.

'I hope she's okay,' I say, just to say something

'Of course she will be. She's Poppy. She always bounces back.' I turn round to see him smile in the night, the passing streetlights illuminating his clear blue eyes.

I long to get those eyes sparkling again. They used to alight with excitement and enthusiasm every time I looked at him. Now I can see the stress behind them. I hate to think I'm the reason for that stress.

I turn in my seat, so I'm facing him more. I will his eyes to find mine again, but they're busy looking at my lips. I bite my bottom lip in an attempt to excite him. His pupils dilate in seconds. It gives me a thrill knowing I can still have that kind of effect on him.

I raise an eyebrow in challenge, a smirk playing on my lips. His eyes finally find mine, and now they're radiating with hunger. I squeeze my thighs together, desperate for some kind of contact from him. Some kind of touch.

A glimmer of a smile graces his lips. He's teasing me, and he knows it. The bastard.

I take a deep breath to try and focus, but it only forces the smell of his favourite aftershave down my nostrils. God, I ache to taste those lips again. They always taste of mint. But I'm too stubborn to be the one to lean in first.

His breathing accelerates, his chest heaving up and down in heavy rasps. He wants me too. I know he does. He leans in ever so slowly. I lean in a little too. He moves so he's only mere centimeters from my lips, his eyes taunt me, daring me to make the next move.

Oh, fuck it. I crush my lips against his, reveling in the feel of those soft lips. He groans, causing my pulse to leap. God, I miss making him groan. My trembling hands travel down his back, pressing him further against me as his tongue explores my mouth, as if for the very first time.

His warm lips pull away from mine, leaving me feeling bereft. I look around us to see that we're here, at the hospital. I stare back at him, waiting for an explanation.

'Ollie, can we go back to how it was before now?'

He looks down and sighs heavily as if the weight of the world is on his shoulders.

'Jazz, it's going to take a lot more than just a kiss to solve all of our problems.'

## Poppy

### Friday 18$^{th}$ March

When I wake up in the hospital, I'm told off by Ryan, then Mum. Jazz can't stop laughing every time she looks at me. I now have a broken nose and two black eyes. Apparently they took me to hospital in the same ambulance I deliberately smashed my face into. Turns out there weren't two ambulances at all, and the one there was, was at a standstill, not trying to drive away. Yeah, a *bit* drunker than I thought.

They confirmed a broken nose, had to re-click it back (gross) and sent me home. Luckily I was still drunk when it happened, and I can only thank God that I can't remember it properly. Whenever Ollie talks about it, he actually gags and says he'll have nightmares for a week. Great. Just great.

This is all I need a few weeks before Lilly's wedding. But despite it all, my day is made when Jazz says she ended up getting off with Ollie last night.

### Monday 21$^{st}$ March

Four days later and I'm back seeing my regular NHS GP. I don't exactly look like an eligible person to be asking to give birth to a child. More like a crack whore. Lilly's been making me Facetime her every morning so she can see how bad it'll be for the wedding.

I'm told by the receptionist that my normal GP is ill, so they have a locum replacing him. That's fine by me. I shouldn't have even bothered coming. It's not like they're going to tell me anything I haven't already been told. We need IVF, actually ICSI to be exact, and we'll need to wait three bloody years to get it on the NHS. This appointment is just for me to share our results and put us on the waiting list.

My name flashes up on the screen, alerting everyone in the surgery that I'm here. I hate that. I drag myself through the hallway, pausing to knock on the door. I always do. I know they're expecting you, but I still feel it's only polite. Imagine if they were picking their nose or had their hands down their trousers or something. It would be embarrassing for everyone involved.

'Come in,' a stern, male voice calls. Oh great, another man. I was really hoping for a sympathetic woman I could cry all over.

I take a deep breath and open the door, sitting down on the uncomfortable plastic chair next to the doctor who's turned away typing into a computer. Bit rude.

He finally turns around to face me, and it's like a brick is dropped in my stomach. No. It can't be. Please, please, *please* not him! It's the guy I threw dog poo at.

'You,' he gasps, his eyes shadowing over with evil intent.

How the hell am I going to play this?

I go for confused. 'Hmm?' I mean I must look different with a broken nose and two black eyes, right?

He shakes his head as if throwing out his thoughts. 'And what is the problem today, Mrs Davis?' Thank God he's going to be professional.

'Run out of dog poo bags?' he smiles sarcastically.

Or maybe not. Okay, so he totally recognizes me. Crap.

'No.' I look down in a flush of embarrassment. I sigh, one blush blending into another. 'I was...' What am I thinking? I can't talk about my fertility with this arsehole! 'In fact, I think I'm probably better waiting until my own doctor is back.'

'Please, Mrs Davis,' he says forcibly as I stand up. 'I didn't mean to be unprofessional. Now, is this to do with the fertility results that were faxed over?'

I fiddle with the buttons on my jacket. 'Err...yeah. But I mean, they already told us there's no hope and that we just have to wait the three years or pay to go private.'

He looks over the results paper in front of him; his glasses pushed tightly into his forehead.

'Well, I don't know what you've been told, but of course there's still hope for you both.'

'Huh?' I can't help but sound like an idiot.

Then I remember the private doctor explaining that the NHS wouldn't find a problem. So confusing.

'Even if you do wait until your three years are up, that's only less than two years now. Plus with you being so healthy you're bound to get pregnant from it.'

'Really?' I hope he's not making promises he can't keep.

'Oh yes,' he nods, adamant. 'This is really nothing to worry about.'

Says the man. I can't stop worrying about it.

'Okay...well, great! So we just...'

'Carry on having lots of sex,' he nods, saving me from my embarrassment. 'The more the better, to cover every possibility. In the meantime, I'll write a letter with these results to your NHS referral so you can be put on the waiting list.'

Who knew? He's actually an alright guy. I smile appreciatively.

'Oh, and I have something for you.'

He reaches into his bag on the floor, rifling through it. Is he going to give me some kind of reproduction leaflet or personal book he's read on it? This man is beyond sweet. I totally misjudged him. He must have just been having a bad day that time.

'Ah, here it is.' He scribbles on a bit of paper and hands it over to me.

I stare at it, confused. This is a car-valeting bill for eighty pounds.

'I've put my bank account details on there for you to transfer at your earliest convenience. Now that I have your name and address I'm sure you'd rather handle it this way then have me go straight to the police.'

My mouth falls open. Nope, still a bastard.

I nod sheepishly before getting up and walking out, my cheeks flaming.

Carrie Marsh, the private detective, walks into the house as business-like as ever. Izzy's still not here yet, but I kind of want to hear what she has to say before she arrives. Especially if she has any info on Linda.

'So, you didn't say much on the phone, but I assume this visit means you have something?' I ask as we settle down at the kitchen table.

'Yes,' she nods, ever the professional. 'Is Miss Bianchi here?' She looks around her as if she's going to jump out and shout 'got ya'.

'She hasn't arrived yet,' I nod. 'Probably stuck in traffic. But feel free to tell me while you wait. Only my Grandma is upstairs.'

I told Grams I was having someone round to write a will, so she's upstairs in her room. I gave her my iPad so she won't miss out on her shows.

She opens her briefcase and rustles some papers, avoiding eye contact. 'I'm glad actually. I have some things I'd rather discuss with you confidentially.'

'Oh...?'

Should I offer her some tea or something first? The English in me feels like I should, but I'm too curious. Has she found Linda?

'I'm afraid that I haven't had any luck finding your mother in law. Every lead was a dead end. It's like she's disappeared, but I'll keep looking.'

That's upsetting. She led me to believe her case would be easy.

'Thank you.'

'Now,' she crosses her legs, 'I realise the main assignment was investigating on behalf of Miss Bianchi, but while she was under my observation, I noticed a few things.'

'Riiiigght,' I frown suspiciously. 'What kind of things?'

She hands over a collection of A4 printed photos. I narrow my eyes at her, confused, before scanning over them. It's Izzy with a guy. Just the back of his head. I turn to the next photo and see Ryan. Oh, the poor cow thinks she's involved with Ryan.

I actually laugh. 'You must be confused. See, this is just my husband, Ryan. She's not cheating on Michael or anything weird like that.'

'Oh, I'm aware of who he is, which is why I wanted to bring this to your attention.'

I'm expecting her to laugh and say silly me, but she's still deadly serious. Is she thick?

'But like I said, don't worry. They're just friends.'

I mean, I get how some people don't understand how a guy and a girl can legitimately be friends. Especially Ryan and Izzy, who did once sleep together many years before we got together, but they're honestly besties.

She purses her lips. 'I don't think you're aware that they met up on three separate occasions.'

This is getting ridiculous now. She's clearly no Columbo.

'They meet up all the time! This is seriously not news to me.' I lean back in my chair, amused.

'Mrs Davis. You need to hear this,' she insists, grave-faced. 'They met up at a hotel. I checked the records. They checked into the same room each time. Each stay was for a few hours.'

Huh? Hotel room? Few hours?

My head is whirling, the same thoughts going round and round. Ryan and Izzy? What could they have been doing for a few hours? Why do I not know about this?

'I'm sorry to be the one to break this to you, but it appears that your husband is having an affair with Miss Bianchi.'

And just like that, my world falls apart around me.

# Poppy

## *Friday 25th March – Good Friday*

I couldn't concentrate for the rest of the meeting. Izzy arrived soon after, so I didn't get a chance to answer Carrie's questions. She was asking me if I wanted him under surveillance, but I couldn't think straight. I mean, my Ryan having an affair. While we're trying to get pregnant? It just seems too far-fetched. Plus, this is Izzy. She's one of my best mates. They wouldn't do this to me, right?

When she arrived, she was all kisses, sweetness and light. Not a harlot hussy that's been sleeping with my husband. I'm sure she wouldn't do that to me. To Michael. Plus she wouldn't have put herself under surveillance knowing that they'd see her and Ryan together, right?

She was understandably scared shitless when we found out it was Michael's ex-wife Verity that's been stalking her. We kind of half expected it, but to get confirmation that it's her, was scary. Except I couldn't comfort her. Instead, I felt numb, like I was out of my body or something.

The main thing is that she can now take the pictures and information she's collected to the police and get her arse arrested, although Carrie said there's not much they can do anyway. Izzy promised she'd do it first thing this morning, but I haven't heard from her. Normally I'd chase her up to make sure she hadn't chickened out, but instead, I just want to stick my head in the sand.

Tonight is Grace's birthday party. Her actual birthday was Tuesday, but she wisely decided to make the most of the long bank holiday weekend. As usual, I'm dreading it, all the more for doubting my marriage. It's always just an excuse for her mates to point and stare at me, whispering horrible things. I really don't get it anyway. She's supposed to have moved on. She's married my brother for God sakes, so who knows? Maybe they'll be nice to me for once.

'We ready to hit it?' Jazz asks, an excited grin on her face. Ollie rolls his eyes behind her. I'm glad to see them getting on, even if they aren't back together yet.

She's wearing a gold sequined boob tube and matching floor length skirt. A bit dressed up for Grace's living room but whatever.

I sigh heavily, but pull my shoulders back, determined. 'As I'll ever be.'

'Good enough,' she smiles, knocking at their door.

I take a discreet deep breath. It's only one night, but my God, I already feel a huge headache beginning to throb at my temples.

Richard answers the door with a huge smile. 'Hi everyone! So glad you came.'

I raise my eyebrows at him. Maybe he can't stand her mates either.

The guys do a weird kind of man hug thing while Jazz kisses him on both cheeks and slaps his arse. He just chuckles, well used to her by now.

This house always smells of too much strong perfume, almost like a tart's boudoir. Whenever I mention it to the others, they all say they can't smell it, but they must be being polite. It invades your nostrils as soon as the door is open.

The others start to head towards the small kitchen at the back of the house, but Richard pulls me back and inadvertently into one of their huge fake twig plant things they insist on dotting around the place. I've never liked this house. As soon as Grace moved in she insisted on redecorating the entire house, so there was no trace of his ex-wife Annabel in sight. Now it's all black and white and over the top. A bit like how I imagine Dracula's house would be. If he was gay and married a drag queen.

'Not you, Poppy,' he smiles. 'I just want a quick chat.'

Quick chat? Jesus, what the hell does he want to talk about? We never have a 'quick chat.'

'How are things?' he asks, crossing his arms and attempting to be natural.

'Err...fine,' I nod, finding it hard not to crease my forehead at him.

'Good, good.' He leans back against the wall. 'I don't want to sound insensitive, but I have a few colleagues from work here tonight. I'd appreciate it if you didn't get really drunk and cause an incident.'

My mouth drops open so low I think it's going to touch their £200 per square metre white tiles.

'Incident? What the hell do you mean by incident?'

He huffs and stands up straight. 'I mean you're here sporting a broken nose and two black eyes. If you could reign it in it would be much appreciated.'

I'm stunned. I mean, not how he's talking to me like he's still at the office. That, I'm used to. But reign it in? If I could reign it in, doesn't he think that I'd have already done it by now? But you know what? Instead of having a full-blown row with him right now I decide I can't be bothered. It's already going to be a long night. I have to keep hold of my energy.

'Don't worry, I'm not drinking tonight.' Is all I answer instead.

He smiles wide like I've just promised nothing will happen. As if. This is me we're talking about. Alcohol or not there's always the possibility of me falling down a set of stairs.

I go to join the others in the box-like kitchen. You'd think they'd have had it extended, but apparently that's their plan for the future. Grace doesn't cook anyway, so they much prefer their through-lounge.

'Everything okay?' Ryan asks with concerned eyes, wrapping his arm around my waist. *See,* do husbands still do this stuff when they're fucking around? I don't think so.

I lean into him. 'Yep, just being told off and warned to behave tonight.'

Jazz turns from pouring out her drink.

'You're fucking joking?' she snorts, outraged on my behalf.

'It's fine,' I say quickly, hoping she won't march straight over to him and cause a scene. I'm sure somehow that would still be my fault. 'But does anyone have any paracetamol? I already have a headache.'

God, I sound like a whiner, but it's true.

'Me too,' Ryan smiles. 'I've had a look in their cupboards and can't find any.'

'Don't worry,' Jazz smiles handing me over a lemonade. 'Jazz to the rescue! I'll go and get some.' She disappears off into the crowd with Ollie following on behind her. He's like her lapdog.

'Don't worry,' Ryan says pulling me into his chest, his voice like melting honey over my doubts of him. 'We don't have to stay all night.'

I nod, so grateful that he knows me. And I *know* him; he's no cheater.

'But...' I look up into his chocolate eyes. 'We should go and see the birthday girl.'

He smirks knowing this is torture for me. We walk into the living room to find the party already in full swing. Jesus, who would have known it would already be this crazy by 9 pm? There are two women in bikinis dancing on top of the sofa and the patio doors open into a setup marquee with a fully functioning bar, laden with pink cocktails already mixed up. Damn it, they look yummy. But no. Sensible Poppy tonight.

We find Grace, dressed in a skin-tight black dress, which although it has a collar is then cut out to reveal as much of her breasts as possible, almost all the way down to her belly button. Far too revealing for a mother-to-be in my opinion, but I suppose my opinion means nothing around here.

'Happy birthday,' I say as chirpily as I can. It's hard when you want to knock that person unconscious. 'Here.' I hand over her present. A present bought from an assigned list she gave us all. I told Mum she was being ridiculous, but she just praised her for being so organized. I may or may not have ended up screaming, 'why don't you just bloody adopt her then!'

'Thanks, Poppy,' she says, eyeing my outfit sceptically. I don't know why; I look fine. I'm wearing my best jeans and a purple camisole. Even Jazz said I looked pretty. If only I could be that rude. 'Please put it on the gift table.'

I look to where she's pointing, and the coffee table is overflowing with different coloured gift bags. Jesus, someone's popular. Or just scared of her. I bet it's the latter.

'Found them!' Jazz sings in my ear. I swing round as she places two paracetamol in mine and Ryan's hands.

At least I can last this night without a headache. I gulp them down with my lemonade and then hand my drink over to Ryan. So he can do the same.

'Let's just pray to God the night isn't too long,' I shout into Jazz's ear.

'And that you behave yourself,' she says back mimicking Richard with a cheeky wink.

I can't help but smile back. I'm counting down until the acceptable time of eleven to say we have a headache and are going. Not long now.

Izzy and Michael turn up about fifteen minutes later with two huge bulky bodyguards. I run up to them laughing; now sure Izzy would never cheat with Ryan.

'You guys are joking right?' I point towards the scary looking men. 'You think Izzy is going to get attacked here or something?'

Michael's face is anything but joking. He looks seriously pissed off actually. I'm just glad she's finally told him.

'Poppy, please don't remind me that you knew all of this and failed to tell me. Frankly, you put Isabella's life in danger, and I find that hard to forgive.'

'Life in danger,' I splutter, looking to Izzy for help. She sheepishly looks down at the ground. 'I think that's a little dramatic.'

'Well I don't,' he snaps, avoiding my gaze as he scans the room.

'It was me that got her to tell you at all,' I retort. How can he be mad at me? 'If she had her way it would still be a secret.'

I realise too late that by saving myself, I have effectively thrown Izzy under the bus. Whoops.

His eyes flare with anger as he turns them on Izzy.

'Let's just all get along and have a good time, okay?' she says smiling hopefully.

She's right. In fact, I feel a great big whoosh of sudden enthusiasm. Damn it, we're here to celebrate the birth of Grace. Yeah, I hate the bitch, but she's carrying my niece or nephew, and that's important.

I turn around and bump straight into Nicole. What the hell is she doing here?

'Nicole?'

Her eyes widen. 'Poppy! Hi! I thought I might bump into you tonight.'

What is she talking about? 'Really?'

'Yeah, I met Grace at a pregnancy class. We've become friends.'

Of course they have. Grace knew this would upset me. She's totally done this deliberately. What a spiteful bitch.

'Nicole!' comes a voice from behind me. I know it's Grace. I turn to find her smiling smugly. 'I see you've met Poppy. Oh no, wait. You guys already know each other.'

If there weren't a stupid law about laying out pregnant women, I'd be all up in her face right now. But instead, I have to act like an adult. Behave civil tonight and then go home and bitch about her later.

I look to Nicole, and she has the decency to look embarrassed.

'Sorry. I shouldn't have come. I knew it would be weird, but Grace insisted and well...the truth is that I don't know anyone here.'

I can't help but feel sorry for her. Pregnant and alone in a new area.

I pull her away from Grace. 'How have you been feeling? Anymore bleeding?'

She shakes her head as if trying to pull herself together. 'No. I'm fine. Honestly, I'm fine.'

That's a bit too many fine's. She's clearly not fine at all.

The track changes to 'Blurred Lines' by Robin Thicke and the sudden excitement that courses through my veins is like nothing else. It's been bloody forever since I've heard this song! And I want to dance. I want to dance away all of my worries, and it seems like the best song in the world to do that to.

'Come on, Izzy!' I shout, grabbing her by the arm. 'Let's dance! I bloody love this song!'

## Jazz

Ugh, I feel so rough tonight. I've got some kind of a virus, so I'm not drinking as much as normal. Parties are really lame without alcohol. Actually, most things. I woke up this morning with a raging temperature so called my private doctor out straight away, sure that my tattoo must have been infected. I'm never bloody ill. She assured me that the tattoo is fine, and it just sounds like a normal virus doing the rounds. She insisted on taking a blood test anyway. You'd think with all this money I could refuse them sticking me with needles but apparently not. She also advised staying in to rest but fuck that.

I look around the room and notice Poppy. Something's definitely up with her. She's been acting really weird since we got here. Normally she'd be shy without any drinks in her, but I know she's only had lemonade, yet she's been on the dance floor screaming 'I love this song!' every time a new beat drops. She's dancing so hard she's got visible sweat on her upper lip glistening in the disco light, the tops of her hair stuck to her head. What the hell is up with her?

I should ask her. Maybe she's taking some new weird fertility drug, which makes you act mental. I put down my drink, but when I turn around, I find she's gone.

'Ollie, where did Pops go?' I ask as he walks back over to me with a drink I have no intention of drinking.

He scrunches his face up in regret. 'Last thing I saw she was telling everyone, she was a mouse. Then she disappeared. Did she take something?'

Take something? Does he mean drugs?

'No! Don't be stupid!' I shout. 'Poppy would never take anything like that.' Especially with her trying for a baby, but it's not like I can tell him that.

'I'm telling you, babe, she's on something.' His eyes are narrowed in worry.

'She hasn't – ' Oh shit. Those paracetamol pills. I glare at him. They *were* paracetamol, right? 'Where's Ryan?'

'He disappeared long ago,' Ollie laughs. 'I just assumed he was embarrassed by Pops.'

Uh-oh. I need to see if he's affected too.

'We have to find him. Plus I need to go and find the guy that gave me those paracetamols.'

We both separate, with me scouring the crowd for the guy. Let me think. I asked Grace's friend Sasha if she had any. She told me to speak to her friend

Alice. When I found Alice she told me I needed Rick. But he was super friendly and just handed them over as soon as I asked. Surely he wouldn't have done that if it were drugs. And I didn't even pay him.

I see him in the corner, laughing maniacally. Jesus, is he on something too?

I walk up to him; my shoulders pushed back in what I hope is a confident manner.

'Yo, Rick, I wanna speak to you!' I shout aggressively.

He excuses himself from his lady friend, who looks like she could actually be a man friend in disguise, and guides me away from people.

'Something wrong with the merchandise?' he asks, crossing his arms over his chest.

Merchandise? My stomach plummets. Oh God, I'm right.

I shake him by the shoulders. 'What the hell did you give me?'

He frowns thoughtfully. 'MDMA. Like you asked.'

Is this guy deaf or just dumb? I've given Poppy and Ryan MDMA. Jesus, what if she's already pregnant? This could kill the baby or, at least, give it brain damage. Even if she's not, it's not any good for her.

'I asked for paracetamol! Not bloody ecstasy!'

He looks towards Alice. 'You told me Alice sent you and that you wanted paracetamol. That's our code. That's what people ask me for when they want a tab.'

'And the fact that I didn't pay you didn't raise any alarm bells?' I'm screaming now, hysterical.

He shrugs. 'Grace told me about your money. I knew you were good for it.'

'Shit.'

This is a fucking disaster. I put my hand up to my forehead as if I can slap away the oncoming headache.

'I actually thought you were testing it out yourself, and you might get me some big time contacts.'

Is this guy for real?

'Are you STILL seriously talking about business right now? My friends have unwillingly taken MDMA, you bonehead!'

He grimaces. 'Yeah...sorry about that mix-up.' Then he turns around, not a care in the world.

Shit. How the hell am I going to sort this out?

## Poppy

People aren't understanding me when I tell them I've become a mouse. I mean, what the hell is their problem? It's not like I can explain it to them properly either. I don't bloody know what happened myself. I was just dancing with everyone, minding my own business when I suddenly felt these whiskers growing and then I couldn't speak. I can only squeak and say; I'm assuming, 'I'm a mouse.'

Well, fuck those non-believers. I know what I am. That reminds me of that song. 'I am what I am! And I am what I am!' Or something. God, I really need some cheese right now.

But first I need to climb up these walls. I'm pretty sure there's a cat somewhere around here. I can't tell you why, but I just *feel* it. I run towards the wall and clamber up it, but I fall back down on my arse. Damn my part-human body letting me down. I back up again, ready to launch myself towards it when I hear someone shouting.

I turn, my whiskers twitching, to see Jazz shouting at me.

'No! Do *not* launch yourself at that wall again!'

I can't really make out what she's saying right now, so I just stare at her. Man, she's pretty. Obviously, why my brother wanted to bone her. Eww, that's gross. I wonder if she really does all of that karma sutra shit. She *is* really bendy.

'Are you even listening to me?' she demands, hand on her hip.

'Err...yeah?'

Would you look at that! My voice is back.

## Jazz

Jesus, she's far worse than I thought. Her eyes are like saucers, and she keeps doing weird things with her mouth and twirling what I'm guessing are imaginary whiskers. Jesus. I need to get her out of here. I grab her by her arm and drag her behind me, looking for Ollie.

I find him outside leaning against a wall.

'Hey, any luck finding Ryan?' I ask him.

He gives me a bemused smile before pointing to a small crowd. I frown; completely confused. I shove Poppy into Ollie.

'Watch her.'

'There's a cat here! Eep!' she shrieks, trying to climb Ollie, real fear appearing on her face. Jesus Christ. A three-year-old is easier.

I push through the small crowd so I can see what they're all staring at. Lying chest down on the floor is Ryan. He appears to be swimming the breaststroke. Everyone is laughing at him, but he seems oblivious, desperately swimming to some imaginary goal.

I lean down, getting as close to his face as possible.

'Ryan!' I clap my hands in front of his face, his glazed over eyes slowly coming into focus.

'Jazz?' he asks in disbelief. 'What are you doing here? Can't you see I'm trying to swim the channel?'

Oh, dear God.

I signal to Ollie to bring Poppy over.

'We need to swap,' I tell him, as he bats off Poppy's climbing attempts again.

'Poppy!' Ryan sings when he sees her.

'Ssh!' she snaps. 'I'm a mouse. And there's a cat in the house. A cat I tell you!'

'No way!' he gushes in awe. 'I'm swimming the channel!'

'Good for you!' she claps.

I roll my eyes at Ollie.

'Ryan's too big for me to move. You're gonna have to take him back to his. I'll get Poppy to Izzy's. I have a feeling they're going to be extra hard work together.'

He sighs heavily. 'You're the boss.'

# Chapter 30
## Poppy

### Saturday 26<sup>th</sup> March

When I wake up, my head feels heavy. Like a weight is attached to the back of it, meaning there's no way it's coming off the pillow. I attempt to stretch, but my body feels so tender, like I've danced for hours or something. What the hell happened last night? I try to trace back through my memory. Did I...think I was a mouse? No, I must have dreamt that, crazy bitch that I am. I mean, I didn't even drink alcohol last night. I don't think?

'Morning, sleeping beauty.'

I turn around in the bed to see that I'm sharing it with Jazz. And wait...I look around...this isn't my room either. This isn't even my house or Jazz's for that matter.

'What the hell happened last night?' I croak. God, I feel like crap. I'm beyond tired; my eyelids screaming in protest at being open and my throat feels like gravel.

'It's kind of a long...sort of my fault kind of story,' she says smiling regretfully.

When she's finished filling me in, I sit there and try to process it all. Here I am, supposed to be keeping my body in tiptop condition so I can conceive and instead it's processing MDMA! This has probably knocked my body back by what...like a year or something?

Apparently Jazz already filled me in last night, well this morning, at three am and I went into a full on panic attack screaming that I was a good girl who didn't do drugs.

'I just don't get how you could be so stupid,' I snap at her. 'I mean getting paracetamol from a total stranger! What the hell is wrong with you?'

'I didn't see you asking any questions about where I got them from before you shoved it down your throat.'

'That's because I foolishly trusted you!'

'Oh, whatever bitch. I think I got my comeuppance by staying up all night with you checking you weren't choking on your own vomit.'

Ugh. I can't even be bothered to argue. I'm so tired and depressed right now.

'I can't even move,' I moan. 'I'm sorry or whatever. I'm just going to go back to sleep for a few hours.'

She smiles sadly, pushing some hair off my face. 'Okay, muffin. Oh, and don't worry, Ryan's fine too.'

Shit. I didn't even consider Ryan. I'm the world's worst wife ever.

I turn away from her and pull the covers over my face. Hopefully, when I wake up everything will seem better.

When I open my eyes again, I'm on my own, and it's dark. I fumble around on the nightstand to find a lamp, illuminating the strange room. I never noticed before, but there's a weird painting of Jesus getting some goats drunk. It must be some weird expensive art that everyone hates, but is too chicken to go against.

I wander downstairs and find Izzy and Michael in the huge all-white sitting room. Izzy's doing yoga and Michael looks to be working on some sort of script. He notices me first. I suppose because he's not doing a headstand.

'Hi, sleepy head,' he says, lowering his glasses from his nose.

I smile, my cheeks reddening. I can't believe my boss saw me like that. 'What time is it?'

'Gone two,' he smiles, looking out of the window. 'Not that you'd know it was daytime at all with this weather.'

I sheepishly look down at my feet. 'Sorry I ruined the night.'

'Don't be silly,' Izzy says in her side warrior two pose. 'I mean, apart from us all worrying about you, it was kind of hilarious. You thought you were a mouse for goodness sakes.'

I grimace. God, how long is it going to take to live this down?

'Anyway. I'm feeling better now. I'm assuming Jazz has gone?'

She nods. 'Yep. She had to get back to Jemima.'

'Cool. I'll call an Uber.'

'Take my car,' Izzy offers. 'Michael won't let me drive it at the moment; he's insisting on getting the limo to take me everywhere.'

I laugh, the sound rattling around my head. 'You're joking.'

She glares at Michael. 'Do you know how ridiculous I look rolling up to personal training sessions in a limo?'

I burst out laughing.

'Exactly.' She raises her eyebrows at him.

He throws me the keys, which I of course drop. 'Take it and grab a jumper too. It's freezing out.'

I smile gratefully and pull on Izzy's pink hoodie she hands over. I look outside. It's heavily raining, the sound almost deafening everything else out. I pull the hood up and use all of my remaining energy to jog to the car. Now I just need to get home, check Ryan's okay and collapse into bed again. Thank God for the long weekend.

I drive as carefully as I can, the ground slippery in the heavy rain. It matches my mood, so I don't really mind it. At least my neighbours can't see me drag my sorry self into my house. They're all perfect, my neighbours. All married couples with kids. It's like they're placed there deliberately to show Ryan and me what we could have won.

Anyway, I mustn't depress myself with thoughts like this today. I'm guessing I'm already on a massive come down. No need to add fuel to the fire and all that.

Ryan's parked like an absolute plank, meaning I can't pull onto the drive. It takes me ages to park across it even though it's hardly a parallel park. Maybe I should sneak in some more driving lessons. I mean, it's not the worst idea, right? Well...unless they realise how bad I am and end up taking my licence off me for good. That would be awful. Okay, terrible idea.

I pull the hood back over my head and open the door, ready to sprint to the front door as fast as I can. I've barely set one foot out when my shin screams with agony. What the fuck was that? Agh!

I look up to see a masked figure holding a baseball bat. Oh my God. It's not Halloween. What the fuck? I can't breathe; fear gripping my insides.

I barely have time to panic before a black pillowcase is thrust over my head, and everything goes dark.

I'm hauled over someone's shoulder and thrown down into somewhere dry before I even consider screaming. An engine starts up while someone ties my hands behind my back. Okay, now would be the time to scream. Except nothing comes out. I'm paralyzed with fear. And why aren't they saying anything? That seems almost more terrifying.

I'm thrown onto my front, the material over my head pushing into my mouth. Oh my God, treating me like this they'll end up suffocating me before they get what they want. Oh God, and what the hell *do* they want? Are they going to rape me? I freeze, my complete body going rigid.

Why the hell would I have been taken? Was this just an opportunist? But then it does seem highly unlikely that two men would be driving around in the leafy suburbs of London Wood looking to kidnap the first female they set eyes on. Unless they're completely insane. I'm probably giving these people too much credit. Of course, they have to be in some way crazy.

But why me? And why as soon as I got out of the car? Shit, my shin is still throbbing. The shock of everything must have taken away some of the pain. Could Ryan have a secret gambling habit that means he owes a fortune, and I'm the leverage? God, you really do never know someone. You're married to them and then bam! You wake up, and they're fucking Izzy and having you kidnapped.

Wait, what if *they've* had me kidnapped? What if *they're* going to weigh me down with bricks and put me in the Thames? I might never be found. They'd be free to live happily ever after without me around. Would my Mother even care?  Or would she be pleased with the new and improved (and very skinny) Izzy?

I have to stop second-guessing why they've taken me and start thinking of every thriller movie I've ever seen.  Okay, let's think.  What does he tell her to do in Taken?  Shout out what they look like?  But I'm not on the phone to my Dad.  And even if I was, I have something over my head so I can't see a thing.  Okay, think.  Didn't I once read that if you're ever kidnapped you should kick out their brake lights?  Oh, no, that was so that you could stick your arm out if they put you in the boot.  I'm assuming I'm in some kind of van.  I stay still and try to make an extra effort in listening to what's around me.

It must be a guy that has me in the van.  He smells like a mix of body odour masked by some very cheap Lynx aftershave and he's chewing gum loudly.  No woman would chew that loud.  I'm also guessing from the noises that it *is* some kind of a van.  Not that either of these tell me anything!  Oh God, I'm done for.

The van starts to slow down slightly, meaning I'm not twisted every which way, and then the engine is turned off.  Oh God.  Whatever is going to happen, it's about to happen right now.  Shit's about to get real.

I'm silently pulled up and over someone's shoulder.  I could struggle but at this point, I don't think there's much point.  They obviously have me somewhere secret, or they wouldn't risk me being seen at all.  God, what a bad hostage I am.  I'm too much of a people pleaser.  If I make it out of here alive, I'm going to do more of what I want and less of what others expect from me.  It's bloody exhausting.

I'm placed into a hard chair, and then the pillowcase is finally pulled off my head.  I blink rapidly, my eyes trying to get used to the bright florescent lighting.  Where the hell am I?  An old warehouse?  I internally roll my eyes.  How bloody cliché.

I focus on the woman in front of me, frowning.  She's got short blonde hair and a rocking body.  Her eyes though, they have that crazy look in them.

'It's not her.  It's not her, you idiot!' she screams.

I force myself to take her in fully and realise she's Richard's ex-wife Verity! Shit. She must have thought I was Izzy. I suppose I was coming from Izzy's, in her car and wearing her pink hoodie. God, I actually feel dumb for not realising sooner. Worst hostage ever.

'Are you...his ex-wife?' I stammer.

She glares back at me. Maybe I shouldn't have spoken at all. She looks crazy. Don't get me wrong, she's all glossy bob and perfectly winged eyeliner with a face like a porcelain doll, but underneath that you can see. Her eyes are bloodshot and distant. Her lipstick smudged. Yep, this bitch is crazy.

'Yes. I'm Mrs Schorsky. And you are?'

'Oh sorry,' I blush. Why the hell am I blushing? 'I'm Poppy Davis. I'm Izzy's friend. I'm guessing you got the wrong girl?'

She ignores me and talks to the guy behind me. 'I thought her arse was too big to be Izzy. She's like a little stick insect. Something that just crawls into your house in the summer and needs to be *squashed*.'

*Squashed?* I swallow down the lump in my throat. She wants to squash Izzy? I knew she was obsessed with her and even hated her, but I didn't think she wanted to squash her. I'm assuming that means kill. But I mean...how on earth do you go from disliking someone to wanting to watch their life leave their eyes.

'You don't mean that,' I say with a forced smile, trying desperately to add some much-needed light onto the situation.

'You have no idea what I mean,' she snaps back. 'That little bitch has exactly what's mine.'

I frown but quickly cover it with indifference. Not exactly true though.

'Didn't you leave him?'

Her eyes are aflame with fury. 'Only because he pushed me to the brink! Do you know how much that man's anxiety can affect him? He used to wake me up at three am to ask if I thought he should cut his hair!'

Whereas, you seem completely sane.

'Okay,' I nod carefully. 'So surely you're better off without him?'

'Don't get me wrong, that's what I thought at first too,' she nods pacing in front of me.

'But...?'

'Yeah, but what?' the guy interrupts. 'You said this was all about the money?'

'Oh shut up, Graham! You really think I'd go to these lengths just for money? I have plenty of money.'

'I thought you loved me,' he whimpers back, his face twisted in hurt.

'I never told you anything like that!' she shouts back. 'I offered you the money, and that's it. Anything else you've imagined up is purely that; your *wild* imagination.'

'You bitch,' he cries dramatically before running from the room.

Wow. This is getting weirder every second.

Now, it's just her and me. I don't actually know whether I'm any better off now. She could probably still take me. Especially with my hands tied behind my back. Damn, I really wish I'd done those body combat classes with Lilly. She could kill a Russian spy now, and I can't even hurt a flea.

'Anyway,' she says rolling her crazy eyes. 'Where was I? Oh, that's right. I assumed I was better off, and I obviously kept an eye on him over the years. But now he's with this Izzy girl. Well, should I say CHILD that he's robbed from the cradle, he...well, he seems to have changed.'

'Changed?' I echo.

'Yes, changed,' she nods. 'I've seen them out together. He seems...relaxed. Even...happy.'

'But that's because he's with Izzy,' I try to reason. 'She's just a calming influence.'

'Oh, is she?' she barks harshly, her eyes alight with pure hatred. 'What I really don't want to hear right now is how bloody wonderful this Izzy is! Whatever's happened, I want him back and she needs to hand him over to me, or there'll be consequences.'

I gulp. 'What were you going to do to her?'

'Kill her,' she shrugs as if it's of no consequence.

Oh God. I'm starting to panic now. My legs are shaking uncontrollably, and my left eye keeps twitching. She probably thinks I'm winking at her. She must think I'm a right weirdo. Actually, maybe not. For her to think I'm a psychopath would be too much.

'So...now that you've found me instead...' I gulp loudly. 'What are you going to do to me?'

'Hmm...'

I shouldn't give her much time to consider this.

'I suggest you just let me go. Call this a day and all that. Maybe you could even see a doctor for those murderous thoughts of yours.'

She laughs loudly, smacking her thighs as if it's the funniest thing she's ever heard.

'Those doctors don't know a thing!' she screams. 'I took myself off those pills months ago, and I feel much better. Bloody load of pill-prescribing junkies! That's all they are. They're a disgrace to the medical profession. Instead, I've been healing myself with crystals.'

Oh Jesus.

'And how is that working out for you?'

'Great, actually,' she says, obviously not noticing my sarcasm. 'You're not dead yet, are you?' She smiles before edging closer towards me and producing a small knife from her back pocket.

Shit the bed. She's actually going to do this; kill me. I'm terrified of the pain I'll feel. Of how I won't get a chance to say goodbye to Ryan. How I'll never be able to give him a baby. And Jazz. And oh God, Jemima. I'll never get to squeeze those chubby cheeks again or listen to that adorable lisp. I'll never get to Lilly's wedding. If I weren't already dead, she'd come and kill me herself.

Even Izzy; cheating, backstabbing, reason I'm here in the first place, Izzy. Through all of it, I still want to believe the good in her, and I know it exists. She's just been...shall we say confused lately? If I ever see any of them again, I'll make sure to hug them extra tight. Not that I'm going to get a chance.

I open my eyes to see hers lit up with excitement. She's actually genuinely thrilled at the idea of slitting my throat. What a total psychopath.

Surely Michael had an inkling of this before he married her? I refuse to believe that she wasn't born this evil.

Suddenly a crash comes from the other side of the warehouse. Both our heads spin round to face it.

'What was that?' she hisses.

'As if I'd know,' I snarl sarcastically. 'I was too busy thinking of my loved ones before you tried to kill me.'

She leaves me on the chair and walks over to investigate. Just before she's at the door it bursts open and two policemen jump forwards; an overweight one carrying a baton, waving it as fiercely as his chubby arms will let him. Another, skinnier, black one holds a stun gun. Thank God!

'Put the weapon down and get on the floor!' the chubby one shouts as they both edge closer.

'Why should I? She snarls, a hand on her hip.

The black guy doesn't even hesitate. He shoots that stun gun right at her. She vibrates, her whole body shaking violently before crashing down to the floor.

'Poppy!' I look away from her still trembling body to see Ryan running towards me.

Oh my God, what is he doing here?

He's with me in a second, wrapping me up in his strong arms. I really want to hug him back, but my arms are still tied. Instead, I bury my head into his neck, inhaling his beautiful scent that I never thought I'd be able to smell again.

'How did you find me?' I mumble into his neck.

He pulls back; his forehead creased with the most adorable wrinkles. 'I saw you get snatched outside our house. I couldn't believe it. I jumped straight in the car and followed you guys while phoning the police. I'd have come in sooner, but that guy was here too, and they told me to wait for them. I'm so sorry.' He leans over my shoulder to untie my arms.

'Don't be sorry. Shit, she was about to...' I gulp, sudden terror rising through my veins. 'She was about to....' My chest shakes uncontrollably, and before I realise what's happening, I've broken into a hysterical sob, the tears clouding my vision. I'm vaguely aware of being carried by his strong arms back to the car. But I still don't feel safe. Maybe I'll never feel safe again.

'Ryan...' I suddenly have to know if he's shagging Izzy. 'You, and Izzy. You're cheating on me aren't you?'

He frowns before bursting out laughing.

'Of course not, you nutter.'

'Well someone saw you going into a hotel room with her.'

He smiles like I'm adorable. 'Yep, she's been giving me yoga lessons. I read online that they're good for stress, and I'm too embarrassed to take a class with women.'

The relief flowing through my body is immense.

'Why didn't you just tell me?'

'I didn't want you laughing at me,' he admits.

'I'd never laugh at you.' I crush myself into his chest again. 'Take me home.'

'With pleasure.'

# Chapter 31
### Jazz

*Friday 1st April*

I still can't believe Poppy got kidnapped. I mean there's bad luck and then there's Poppy. At least that nutcase got locked up. I can't believe they've been keeping it from me. The huge bodyguards at Grace's party make sense now. I just thought Michael was paranoid.

I'm round at Poppy's house by midday. First I had to convince her to come to the charity event tonight that Ryan's sister is putting on. You'd think the woman was actually a hermit; sometimes she just detests leaving the house. But I suppose she is still traumatized. Anyway, now that's out of the way I'm trying to convince her to prank call, Lilly. It is April fool's day! I mean, has everyone lost their sense of humour?

Jemima didn't laugh when I covered the toilet seat in cling film either. She just got really distressed, and then I had to shower her. Should have really thought that through. I've already called Ollie pretending to be a debt collector claiming he owes fifty thousand. He nearly shit himself the poor thing. I should really call him and tell him it was a joke. Don't want him having an actual heart attack or anything.

'Jazz, it won't be funny. She'll just freak out.'

'That's why it'll be so funny!' I insist giggling. I can't help but feel mischievous on a day like today. It was created so we could be silly.

'Yes, auntie Pwoppy!' Jemima sings. 'Let's call her!'

Bless her. She loves Lilly. She always calls her the lady with red hair.

Poppy, at least, looks like she might be relenting slightly. 'Maybe one call,' she says, trying to hide her smile. I remember that smile. It's the one she used to have in Uni before we'd do something stupid. I miss that smile.

'Okay, so what shall we say? That the wedding's been double booked? That the hotel has fallen down?'

She rolls her eyes. 'No. We'll have to go with something more discreet. Like I said I don't want her to shit herself completely.

I try to think of something that wouldn't be the total end of the world. I know. Our bridesmaid dresses. I've got it. I find her in my contacts and press dial.

'Hey, Jazz,' she sings cheerily down the phone. 'How are you doing?'

'Yeah, I'm okay,' I say almost failing and giggling at hearing her on loudspeaker. 'Only...'

'What?' She already sounds worried. This is going to be hilarious.

'Well, the shop called and said that our bridesmaid's dresses have been discontinued from the supplier.'

There's a long pause. I'm about to ask if she heard me when she speaks. 'You. Are. Joking.'

Poppy starts pissing herself but forces her own hand over her mouth to muffle the sound.

'Why the FUCK does this stuff have to keep happening to me? Huh? WHY!'

Wow. She lost it pretty quick. We both look at Jemima, but she's playing with her dolly, apparently oblivious.

'It's okay, Lilly,' Poppy says, winking at me like she has an idea. 'Mum says we can borrow her bridesmaid dresses from the loft.'

'Your...mum's? As in from the *eighties*?' She sounds horrified.

'Yeah, don't worry,' I add, smiling so wide it hurts my mouth. 'We've tried them on, and they fit like a glove.'

'No! No, no, no, no, NO! I am not having you wearing ridiculous eighties bridesmaid dresses. This is a fucking disaster! Talk about the last thing I need right now.'

Poppy grimaces and looks at me, her eyes wide with panic. She's wimping out already.

'Don't worry, Lilly,' she starts.

'It's not the end of the world,' I interrupt knowing Pops is losing her nerve too early.

'Yes, *actually* Jazz, it is the end of the world,' Lilly responds dramatically. 'I don't even know if there's going to be a wedding with how Alex and I are arguing. This wedding stress is killing me, and I just had another client let us go because of cutbacks. So, yes Jazz, it *is* the end of the fucking world as I know it.'

Oops. I look at Poppy mirroring my panic.

'We're sorry, Lilly,' Poppy cries down the phone. 'It was just a stupid joke for April fool's day. We didn't mean any harm!' I knew she'd bottle it

'Yeah, we're sorry,' I add grimacing.

There's a pregnant pause. Pops and I look between the phone and each other. Shit. We may have just pushed her to a breakdown.

'Err...I was only joking too,' she says unconvincingly. 'April fools!'

Oh God, this is awful. The poor thing.

'Are you still coming tonight, yeah?' I ask, trying to change the subject.

'Yep. I'll be there,' she sniffs. 'I've got to go anyway. Bye!'

She hangs up. Poppy glares at me.

'It'll be funny will it?'

'Alright!' I admit. 'It was a stupid idea, but how did I know she'd go absolutely ballistic like that?'

She puts her hand on her hip. 'Have you even met Lilly?'

'Okay! Chill bitch. I'll make it better tonight.'

Maybe I'll buy her a handbag. My phone starts ringing, and we both look at it expecting it to be Lilly. But no, it's a London number.

I sigh and answer it. 'Hello?'

'Hi Jasmine, it's doctor Wilcox.'

That name always makes me giggle. 'Oh, hi.' What is she ringing me about? Oh yeah, it must be my blood test results. Probably going to tell me I'm anaemic or something. They always pick on the vegetarians.

'I'm calling about your blood test results.'

Knew it. I stand up and walk away from Poppy and Jemima.

'Yep, what about them?'

'Well, you tested very low in your iron levels.'

Maybe I'm telepathic.

'I always am,' I nod, wishing she'd just get on with prescribing me some iron tablets.

'Well because of that I decided to test your hCG levels and...'

HCG? What the hell is she talking about?

'I'm calling to let you know that you're pregnant.'

I freeze, my heart deciding to stop and exit my body. Pregnant? I blink a few times and wipe away the stray tears falling down my cheeks. I can't be.

'Are you...are you sure?' I ask quietly, not wanting to alert Poppy and Jemima.

'Quite positive.'

'Wait, is this an April fool's joke? Because I really don't find that kind of shit professional.'

There's a pause. 'I'm assuming this wasn't a planned pregnancy?'

'No. No, it bloody wasn't,' I snap looking down at my flat stomach.

'Look, why don't you come down to the clinic tomorrow morning. We're open for a few appointments and that way we can give you a scan and see how far along you are.'

I have to gulp back the bile. How far along. Oh my God, how the hell can this be happening?

## Poppy

### *Friday 1st April*

I still can't believe it even happened. I was kidnapped. It's like something that happens in the movies, not real life. Apparently she's been arrested, and I know she wasn't even after me, but I still can't shake feeling unsafe. When I think about how close I was to my life being over, it just feels like someone is strangling me with fear.

The only bit I'm thankful for is that it happened during Easter weekend, so I've been able to just gorge on chocolate and eat my feelings. Plus Jazz coming round and prank calling Lilly cheered me up for a little bit. Well, until we upset her. I've texted her sorry fifteen times with no reply. That must mean she's really pissed.

Jazz is acting a bit weird ever since she took that phone call. When I tried to grill her about it, she tried to claim it was a wrong number. Err, I've never heard anyone chat like that to a wrong number. Something's up; I just don't know what yet.

We arrive just after eight. I can't believe we promised we'd come here, but I want to keep Julie happy. Plus it's given all of us a night out. It can't be that bad. It's set in a dark, dingy social club with a small stage.

'I'll get the drinks in,' Ryan says, disappearing to the bar. Sometimes he reads my mind. I really think I'll need a lot of wine to get through this evening. Julie spots us and comes running over.

'You guys came!' she gushes. 'I'm so pleased you made it.'

'It's for such a good cause,' Jazz shrugs, like she's a real charity goer.

'It is!' she says, lighting up at the obvious idea of Jazz donating. 'We have a silent auction going on all night. You should take a look, Jazz.'

'Yeah, yeah,' she waves dismissively. 'If you want me to donate just ask.'

Lilly snorts. 'Don't be looking at me. We're skint with the wedding coming up.'

'Oh yes,' Julie nods. 'Poppy mentioned it. Have you ever thought of asking guests to donate to charity rather than give gifts?'

Lilly glares at her as if she's mental.

'Are you insane? Why the hell would I do that? This bitch needs a new toaster and kettle set.' She flounces off, finding a table at the front. Alex follows after her.

'Anyway,' she smiles at me. 'You should come and meet my parents.'

Parents? I immediately think of her Mum. Her still, very much missing, Mum. But of course, she means her adoptive parents. Ryan's met them a few times, but I never have. Due to her Mum's drug problem she ended up being taken into care and was luckily adopted to a loving couple in Wheathampstead. I only found her a few years back. Ryan was raised from being a baby by his Grams, so neither of them had any idea she even existed. I've always tried to let him spend time with her on his own. They've had a lifetime of catching up after all.

'I'd love to,' I force out with an unconvincing smile.

I follow her into a corner to find a couple in their early seventies. She's wearing a long skirt and top with beads around her neck. They look like those anal beads you see in sex shops. I wonder if the old man bought them for her hoping for some fun, only for her to put it round her neck and thank him. He looks respectful too, in cream chords and a checked flannel shirt. They look cute. Homely.

'Mum, Dad,' Julie smiles. 'This is Poppy.' She presents me with her hands.

'Err, hi.' I awkwardly wave.

Her mum stands up and before I know what's happening she's engulfing me in a hug. Oh. She's friendly. She smells of rose petals and is so warm I could curl up beside her and happily take a nap. But then I suppose when wouldn't I take a nap?

'So lovely to meet you,' she praises. 'I've heard so much about you from both Julie and Ryan. He thinks so much of you.'

'Really?' I'm always desperate to find out what he says about me.

'Of course,' she says, releasing me back a little. 'I feel like I know you already.'

Her Dad is already standing up, and her Mum basically transfers me from her arms into his. He pulls me into a bear hug. Wow, this family are affectionate. Julie must have found it strange coming from such a tumultuous life to belonging to this loving family.

'We're so glad you made the effort to come,' he says with a crooked smile. 'Any and every exposure for this great charity is so appreciated.'

I nod, not even knowing what charity it is. I search around for Ryan.

He's just bringing the drinks over to the table. A Boy George tribute band is setting up. Jazz and Lilly are laughing hysterically already. I really need to keep them in check tonight.

Ryan spots me watching and hurries over, slipping his arm around my shoulders. 'Daniel, Clare, I see you've met my Poppy.' He squeezes my shoulders affectionately.

'She's as lovely as you described,' Clare says. 'We must have you over for dinner one day.'

Oh God. I don't know if I have the patience right now to sit through a boring dinner. Not when there's so much to do, and I have so much on my mind. Not that I can say that.

'Sounds lovely,' I nod.

We make our excuses and go back to our seats.

'The only good thing about this place being a shit hole is that the drinks are dirt cheap,' Ryan says.

Jazz sips on her drink. 'Ugh, the glasses are dirty though.' She stands up and walks to the bar.

The Boy George tribute band, start singing and are truly awful. We end up chatting over it most of the night. Then an entertainer comes onto the stage.

'Hello ladies and gentlemen!' he smiles with a big cheesy grin. 'I'm here to do some hypnotizing. Do I have any volunteers?'

I burst out laughing. You'd have to be mad to volunteer to do that.

'Poppy will do it!' Lilly shouts, giggling.

My mouth drops open, and my shoulders start to envelop my head. Swallow me up, please. There is no way I want to do this.

'Yeah go, Poppy!' Jazz giggles.

'Shut up!' I hiss back at them.

The guy notices them, of course he does; they're practically stood on the table hollering him over.

'We have a volunteer,' he grins, walking towards me.

'Oh my God, oh my God, oh my God.' I look to Ryan in desperation.

'Help me! I can't do it. I'll die of embarrassment.'

'What is your name, young lady?' he asks pushing his microphone under my chin.

Oh God. I can already feel myself hyperventilating. He just wants your name, Poppy. Just your name.

I open my mouth to speak but make the mistake of looking around me. Everyone is staring. Already laughing at me. Laughing at what a loser I am. I can't do it. This is before he has me barking like a dog.

'No,' is all I can stammer out.

'I'll do it.' I turn to see that it's Ryan who's spoken. He's going to do it for me. He's volunteering as a tribute, just like in the *Hunger Games*. Well, although this isn't as serious. Maybe half as serious.

'You'd really do that for me?' I ask over the mayhem.

'Of course,' he grins. 'It's only a laugh, right?'

He walks up to the stage amid cheers from everyone.

'Hello!' the cheery guy on stage says to him. 'What's your name?'

Ryan leans into the microphone. 'Ryan,' he smiles shyly.

I can practically hear every woman in the room swoon. Yeah, yeah, bitches he's mine.

'Let's start with a simple one. Sit down here for me will you, Ryan?' He pulls up a chair from him. Ryan catches my eye and grimaces. He's so cute.

'Ryan, I need you to look at this clock.' He dangles a pocket watch on a string in front of his head. His eyes follow it. '*And* you're asleep,' he says, clicking his fingers in front of his eyes. Ryan's head drops down at exactly the same time. What the fuck?

Ryan wouldn't play along with this. He hates fakes. This guy must be doing this for real, although I find that very hard to believe.

'Ryan when you awake you will only tell me the complete truth. Three, two, one...you're awake.'

Ryan's head snaps back up. He looks around a bit dazed. Everyone laughs.

'Right, Ryan. Let's find out a few things about you. What's your wife's name?'

'Poppy.' His response is almost automated, like he's in no control of it. It's weird.

'Who is your best friend?'

'Ollie,' he answers automatically.

Ollie stands up and takes a bow as we all cheer.

'Great. We're all getting to know Ryan aren't we?' the guy encourages the crowd. 'What's your favourite sexual position?'

Oh my god.

'Doggy style,' he answers without a pause.

The crowd erupts in laughter. I hang my head in shame while Jazz and Lilly whoop and Ollie pretends to vomit.

'Now, who is the love of your life?'

'Nicole.'

And just like that, my heart drops out into my knickers.

He looks up as if just realising what he's said. 'She *was* the first love of my life. Poppy is the second. I love her more than anything.' His eyes finally start to find me. 'She's my world.'

'Thank God for that, right?' Jazz whispers into my ears.

'Yeah,' I agree, clapping along with everyone.

I hope I'm convincing because right now my heart is breaking. Why don't I feel better now he's explained it? Why?

## Jazz

### *Saturday 2nd April*

I still think she's wrong. She has to be. I mean; I can't be pregnant. Jesus, I can't even remember the last time I had sex. I definitely don't want a baby. I've made that clear to Ollie several times. But now that it's in there, it's a hell of a harder decision to make. I'm just going to shut up and have this scan for now. See what I'm dealing with.

'If you just lie down for me, Jasmine,' Doctor Wilcox says.

She smears the jelly on my belly and then presses on my stomach. A blurry image appears on the screen in front of me. I'm still praying to a God I don't believe in that she's wrong. That she's going to look at the screen and be like, 'Oh, I made a mistake! No baby there.'

'Here's your baby,' Doctor Wilcox says with a wide smile.

I take a deep breath before looking closely at the image. Shit, that's very clearly a baby there. I can make out its arms, legs and head. Holy fuck. This is really happening. How could this have even happened? I'm on the pill for God's sakes. Can I sue them?

'I'd say you're about thirteen weeks.'

'Shit,' I mutter more to myself. That's too late for me to have an abortion.

'How did this even happen? I take my pill at the same time every day religiously.'

'Well obviously stop taking it now,' she smiles as if this is funny. Crazy bitch. 'You could have been sick or had diarrhoea, been on antibiotics, or simply sometimes it doesn't work. That's what that one per cent is there for.'

'This is a fucking disaster!' I can't even cry right now. I just feel numb by it all. I must still be in shock.

She takes a few pictures and then turns the screen off. 'You do have options, Jasmine. You're still well within the twenty-four week period. You could choose to terminate.'

Terminate. That sounds so final. I suppose it is. That's why I can't rush this decision.

'But...it's a proper baby now, right?'

'It depends on your definition. Some people believe that a child only has life once they're born.'

'Cut the crap. I can see it's a baby. That means I wouldn't be able to just take that pill, right?'

'Right,' she nods. 'It would be a surgical procedure.'

I grimace. 'Would it be...' I almost can't say it. 'Vacuumed out?'

She smiles sympathetically; her eyes drooped. 'It would be vacuum aspiration, yes. As long as you had it done before fifteen weeks, so we'd have to move quickly.'

'God, or there's *worse* procedures?' I can't imagine anything worse.

'Yes. I can talk you through all of it if you like, but I don't want to overwhelm you.'

'Oh God.' I clasp my head in my hands spreading the jelly on my stomach all over my top. 'This is a disaster. I don't want a baby, but I don't want an abortion.'

'Take some time,' she nods. 'Go away and think about it. But…if there is a possibility of you keeping it you must start taking folic acid immediately.'

I nod as I collect myself. I can't even think about this here. I need to hole myself up at home and have a serious think. But as I walk home I can't stop from thinking. It's impossible to block it all out. Could I do it again? Go through that whole baby thing? Ugh, first there's the pregnancy. Getting massive again. Feeling ill most of the time. Random strangers touching your belly.

Then the birth. I shudder just remembering the pain. The only thing that got me through it was knowing that I only had to do it once. How the hell would I go through it again? And this time, knowing that it does hurt like a motherfucker.

But the worst thing of all is the thought of having a baby again. The late nights, the crying; just the whole, being responsible for keeping something alive. I feel like I've just got my life back with Jemima turning three. How the hell can I go back to doing all of that with a three-year-old running about?

And the thought of Jemima getting less attention from me hurts like a knife twisting in my heart. If she got ignored because I was too busy, well, it would break my heart. But how the hell can I tell Ollie that I'm pregnant but don't want it? He's told me numerous times that he wants another kid.

Even if I do decide to keep it how the hell can I look Poppy in the eye and tell her I'm pregnant? Her heart will break into a million pieces. I can just imagine her pretending to be pleased for me. I can't do that to her. Why is life so unfair? She's desperate for a baby and can't get pregnant and then there's me who seems to fall pregnant at the drop of a hat. It's fucking ridiculous.

I let myself in at home, glad that Jemima is with Ollie. I run up to my bedroom; kick off my shoes and dive under my warm duvet. The tears start rolling down my cheeks, and I let them fall unwiped. What the fuck am I going to do?

## Chapter 32
### Poppy

*Monday 4th April*

This past week has been tense. Edgy. Awkward. Unusual. Just a few words to describe our house at the moment. I didn't tell Grams about what happened on our night out, but she's noticed that something's happened. She keeps asking if we're alright, and I have to just shrug her off. Ryan must have apologised a thousand times, but...you just can't take that back stuff like that.

She was the love of his life. No matter what he does or says from here, there's just no escaping that. To add to the shitty atmosphere we've had to continue having sex every second day. You have no idea how hard sex is when you're heartbroken and thinking of your partners ex.

My phone starts buzzing on my nightstand. Richard flashes up. What the hell is he calling me about? He never calls me. Probably telling me off again, but for what I don't know.

'Hello?' I answer begrudgingly.

'Hi, Poppy, I wondered if you could do me a favour?' he asks in high, sharp tones.

Wow, straight in there. No, how are you? Just straight for the favour, the little bastard.

'What?' I blurt out impatiently.

'Go and check on Grace?' He must hear me sigh because he continues. 'She's off work today because she was feeling sick and now I can't get hold of her on the phone.' He sounds panicked.

'She's probably just asleep or something,' I offer flicking through

Facebook on my iPad.

'Probably,' he hesitates, 'but I wouldn't be able to live with myself if she's seriously ill and I didn't send you to check on her.'

God, way to totally overreact.

'Ugh, guilt trip me why don't you?' The idea of leaving the safety of my warm duvet fills me with dread. It's *so* cold outside.

'Is it working?' I can hear the smile in his voice, which is so rarely directed at me I can't help but relent.

'Fine. I'll go and check on her, but you owe me. Big time.' Not that he'd ever help me without moaning about it for years after.

I throw on some shitty clothes; tracksuit bottoms and a baggy jumper and drive round there. I'm just pulling up on the drive when I spot someone huddled over next to the front door. Shit, has Grace fallen?

I rush out of my car, leaving the door open and run over to her. Now that I'm closer I can see that her hair is shorter. Has she cut her hair?

'Grace?'

Scared blue eyes look up at me. I see that it's actually Nicole. Love of Ryan's life, Nicole. What the heck is she doing here? And why is she huddled over crying?

'Nicole?'

She sniffs, wiping her nose with the back of her hand. Her eyes are glassy and red-rimmed, and there's not one scrap of makeup on her face. She must have been crying for hours.

'What's happened?'

'Nothing,' she cries, her eyes swimming with more tears. 'I'm just so lonely,' she chokes, her voice breaking. 'Grace isn't in, and that's, that's when I realised I have no one. No one!'

She collapses onto me, sobbing heavily. Wowza, this was not what I was expecting. I wrap my arms around her; my jumper already damp from her tears. I can't leave her here like this.

'Why don't you come back to mine for a cup of tea, hmm?'

Once I've got her settled down with a cup of tea and tin of biscuits, she's a lot calmer. The tears have dried and in their place are desolate eyes.

'I don't know why you brought her here,' Grams hisses at me in the kitchen. 'You're too nice for your own good sometimes.'

'I can't just ignore a crying pregnant woman.'

'Better you than me,' she scoffs. 'I don't trust that woman.'

I walk back into the sitting room and sit down opposite her. I have to find out what this is about.

'So...are you ready to talk about what upset you so much?' I ask, with what I hope is a kind smile.

She stares down at the table. 'You wouldn't understand. It sounds stupid.' She looks past me, her breathing becoming erratic with what I can only assume is panic.

'Don't be silly. Just tell me. I'm here to listen.' God, I sound like an agony aunt.

'I'm just so lonely, Poppy,' she finally admits. 'You have no idea how alone I feel holed up in that flat. Within a couple of months, I've kissed goodbye to my business, my boyfriend, my trendy flat. Now I'm living in a shitty flat my parents left me in their will, and I have no-one.'

'What about your friends? They seemed nice that night.'

Now I think about it, she didn't actually call them when we took her to hospital. I'd have been straight on the blower dramatically screaming that I was dying.

She shrugs, her shoulders slumped. 'They've been as good as they can, but they're party girls. The idea of settling down and having a child is so far into the future for them. They don't want a big pregnant woman bringing them down.'

Poor woman. They do say you find out who your friends are when you have a baby.

'So has Grace been a good friend?' I can't imagine her being anything but bitchy, but then I suppose Izzy and Jazz keep her around.

'Yes,' she smiles kindly. 'I know she said you don't really get on, but she's been good to me. She even offered for me to stay a few nights at hers, but the decorators are re-doing her bedrooms.'

I'm sure that's a lie. That would have definitely got back to me via Mum.

'I just want some company. Being pregnant makes me feel so alone, and I dread to think how I'm going to manage all on my own.'

I can't imagine it myself. The idea of packing the hospital bag knowing you'll be doing it all yourself is enough to break my heart. I have to think up a solution for her.

'I mean....you could always...'

'Stay here?' she asks, her eyes lighting up in relief.

Woah, where did that come from? I was going to say stay at Grace's and sleep on the sofa.

'Err...' How do I get out of this?

She grabs me into a crushing hug. 'Thank you so much, Poppy. You have *no idea* how much this means to me! Just to have someone to talk to, that I know I can lean on.'

Oh god. This got out of hand pretty quickly. How the hell can I break it to her now that she's misunderstood me? She looks so happy and relieved.

'The thing is..,' I say scrunching my face up in regret, 'Grams is staying here at the moment.'

'No way! I just thought she was visiting. I love Grams!' she coos jumping up and down in her seat. 'Oh, it just gets better and better.'

Jesus. Thank God she's upstairs hiding right now.

'Nicole?' Shit; spoke too soon. I turn to find Grams looking at her; the colour washed from her face. 'Did I just hear you're staying here?' She looks at me, eyebrows raised, waiting for an explanation.

'Grams!' she jumps up and throws herself into her arms. Grams shakes her head at me from over her shoulder. She pulls back. 'Or should I say *roomie!*'

'Can someone please tell me what is going on?' she demands, hands on her hips.

'Err...it's a bit of a long story.'

Grams wasn't best pleased, to say the least. Don't get me wrong, she acted polite enough in front of Nicole, but she was giving me those looks. You know the looks your mum used to give you when you were messing around in a supermarket. That kind of *you wait till we get home* death stare. I somehow managed to get to her flat and help her pack a bag. That 'bag' ended up being two suitcases. I mean how long is she expecting to stay? I just assumed a few days until she was feeling better.

I'd be more pissed off if it didn't actually solve a problem for me. At least this way I have someone to look after Grams while we go away for Lilly's wedding. It has been playing on my mind. Jazz offered to pay for a carer to move in, but I know she won't go for a stranger helping her. Old people can be so proud. If someone told me they'd move someone in to cook and clean for me, I'd have died and gone to heaven.

Nicole is upstairs unpacking in our box bedroom, which must be hard considering we use it as a junk room most of the time. I'm downstairs anxiously waiting for Ryan to get home. I have no idea how I'm going to tell him. No idea. His car pulls onto the drive. Okay, this is it. Deep breaths.

'Hi, babe,' he calls as soon as he's walked into the front door. 'Put the kettle on, will you?'

'Already done.' I smile as he walks into the kitchen, throwing his wallet and phone onto the kitchen table.

'Thank God. It's been a bitch of a day.' He does look tired; his eyelids drooped, and his forehead wrinkled. He grabs my head and kisses me on my forehead. 'Its times like this I miss it being just us two living here,' he whispers. 'I could just walk around in my boxers and chill.'

Oh God, this already isn't going well. How do I tell him that now his ex-fiancé has also joined us?

'Well, actually, I have something to tell you.' My voice sounds wobbly and high pitched. He must know something is wrong.

His eyes widen, lit up like a fat kid at an ice cream van. 'No,' he whispers. 'Are you...pregnant?'

My stomach plummets. Oh god. Just when I thought it couldn't get worse.

'No, babe,' I sigh, stroking his bicep reassuringly. 'I'm sorry. I'm not.'

He quickly re-arranges his face, trying to hide the disappointment I see so clearly in his eyes.

'I'm sorry, babe.' He stands up and grabs me into an embrace. 'I don't know why I jumped to conclusions. I just...I had a shit day, you know. I suppose I was hoping for some good news.'

'No, it's okay,' I mumble through his shirt currently crushed against my mouth. 'I don't blame you. Why was it such a crap day anyway?' Maybe if I change the subject, I'll make him feel better.

He sighs as if the weight of the world is on his shoulders. 'Ugh, I just had _'

'Hi, Ryan.'

Oh crap. He releases me, us both turning to see Nicole at the doorway. She's fidgeting sheepishly, but...well, I can't put my finger on why but I sense that it's an act. She no longer seems sad; more eager to talk to Ryan.

'I just want to say that I know this is going to be weird for you, but I'm so grateful.'

Ryan looks back at me; his forehead creased to within an inch of his life. 'Huh?' is all he can come out with.

I can't speak. Literally lost the skill of speech.

'Oh...you haven't told him yet?' I avoid all of their glances. This is not how I wanted to tell him. 'Ryan, your wife has been so kind to me. She's offered to let me stay for a few weeks.'

Weeks? Shit.

'She has?' He glares at me with such intensity I actually shiver.

'Now I understand that this could be awkward, but I'm so appreciative,' she gushes. 'You've no idea how depressed I've been. You know how sorry I am for everything I did before, right?'

He rakes his hand through his hair. 'Of course I do. I just...I don't know if it's a good idea,' he finally admits.

Thank god, he's said what he's been thinking.

'You'll hardly know I'm here, I promise.' She gives the best puppy eyes while crossing her fingers over her chest.

'And at least, we'll have someone to look after Grams while we're away at the wedding,' I offer weakly.

'I suppose,' he says with a tight smile. 'Just make sure to look after Grams well,' he warns her with hard eyes.

'I will.' She skips away, as happy as a pig in shit.

'Poppy...' he begins as soon as she's upstairs.

'I know!' I interrupt. 'But she basically invited herself to stay and then I couldn't...'

'You couldn't say no,' he finishes, nodding knowingly. 'Why am I not surprised?'

'You don't mind?' I ask scrunching my face up in a grimace.

He rolls his eyes skywards. 'It doesn't look like I have much choice now does it? But the question is, are you? I mean, don't pretend you haven't been weird since that whole hypnotizing thing.'

'I know,' I nod. 'I'm sorry, but the truth is that I do trust you.'

'Really?' he asks with half a smile. 'It's not that long since you were accusing me of having it off with Izzy.'

'I know. I'm an awful wife, but I do trust you with her.'

'I'm glad.'

# Chapter 33
## Poppy

### *Tuesday 5th April*

Izzy came around unexpectedly last night for a chat, like the house wasn't packed enough already. She thankfully understood my reasoning for letting Nicole stay. She's far more agreeable. Sometimes I wish I was married to her. It would be so much easier. I have a feeling she was trying to stay out and away from Michael, not that she'd ever tell me that in front of Ryan. I'd have offered for her to stay the night, but with the house now being at full capacity, it's kind of a nightmare. Anyway, she didn't leave until late, so we just went to bed exhausted and then rushed to the airport this morning having only thrown things haphazardly in the suitcase.

I tell Jazz the predicament I've got myself in as soon as we get to the airport. She laughs her arse off before telling me that I'm mad. Yeah, thanks, *real* helpful. Jazz.

The plane ride is awful. We have to endure turbulence, and that is without the eight-month-old twins behind us screaming the entire time. It's easily the worst flight of our lives.

After that flight, I definitely need a holiday. Not that I feel this will be a holiday at all. I kind of feel like I'm going to be working this whole time. Lilly can be a mean taskmaster at the best of times. The fact it's her wedding has me fearing physical violence.

I turn on my phone to check for any irate messages from her. There's only one. How weird. I open it up and get confused when I see my own name. I don't know any other Poppy, do I?

*It's Izzy. You must have accidentally taken my phone! Have a great holiday. Btw I have seventy-two messages from Lilly. Good luck xxx*

Great. That's just bloody great.

Izzy ended up staying at home. She's still quite freaked out by the whole Michael's ex thing and there's still some legal stuff to be sorted.

Ollie, Jazz, Ryan and I pile our exhausted bodies into the crowded bus outside of the terminal. From the raging heat, I'd say either the air conditioning is broken, or it never existed in the first place. We sit behind a couple having a domestic and four teenage lads who smell like they last bathed a year ago. Gross.

I lean over to Ryan. 'I don't know about you, but I'm going to need a bloody good drink when we get there.' For once I'm glad I'm on my period.

He smiles. It's that smile he pulls out of the bag every now and again, and it shocks me every time. It's the smile that says 'you're the best thing that's ever happened to me'.

'Me too, babe.' He takes my hand and kisses it. It's weird how I can still swoon.

'I am fucking gasping for a drink right now,' Jazz says from behind me. 'Remind me again why we let Lilly organise our trip? We could be in a fucking limo right now.'

I giggle. 'I really doubt they have limos just hanging around here.'

She crosses her arms, leans back and puts her headphones in. 'Whatever.'

Our coach pulls up thirty minutes later at a hotel that looks nothing like the picture Lilly sent me. This place is only half built, with sweaty builders bottoms on show everywhere. I check the sign 'Paraiso Hotel'. Shit. This is the place?

'No way!' Jazz shrieks from behind me. 'No fucking way am I staying here. Lilly must have lost the fucking plot.'

That's what I'm beginning to think. We begrudgingly get our bags and head out, walking towards what is signposted to be the reception. It's actually really nice once we're inside: all marble floors and teak wood. Shame about the drilling sounds.

We sign in, Jazz snottily requesting a suite as far away from the noise as possible, and are just about to head to our rooms when Lilly arrives.

'Thank fuck you're here!' she screams before launching herself at me.

I flinch, unsure if she plans to hug me or hit me. Luckily it's a hug. She pulls back, and I can see that she's been crying, her eyes are red-rimmed and puffy. Her hair is messy too. That might not sound like a big deal, but I have *never* seen her hair out of place. Not even one bloody hair. It's normally blow dried to perfection. *Perfection.* This is just...well; it looks like she's run her hands through it one hundred and twenty times. Which by the look of her face, she might have.

'Lilly, what the hell is going on?'

'I...She...I can't even...' she bursts into angry tears, pushing her snotty face into my chest. 'It's a fucking disaster!'

Ryan eyes me alarmed. I can't offer him any kind of reassurance in my face.

'Sit down, Lil,' Ollie says, taking her hand and guiding her to a nearby seat.

Thank God one of us is calm in situations like this.

'Excuse me!' Jazz calls to the lady behind reception. 'But we'll be needing a bottle of tequila over here.' She plonks herself down on the floor in front of her while Ryan and I stand, awaiting her news.

'Okay, come on, Lil,' I try to press. 'You have to tell us what's going on.'

'Like you don't already know,' she half laughs, half cries. 'Only half of the hotel has been fucking built!'

'We did kind of notice that,' Ryan nods with a grimace. 'We're assuming you weren't informed they were having renovations?'

'Renovations?' she screams back, causing him to jump a foot. 'More like continuing to build the thing! I had no idea, but apparently I signed away any right to sue them in the contract.'

'Shit.' Well that was helpful. Come on Poppy, now is the time to pull something out of your arse.

'I'd like to see that contract,' Ryan says, putting on his legal hat.

'But so what if we hear a few drills over the ceremony? The main thing is that you and Alex are finally going to be married.'

She stares back at me like I'm medically insane. 'Poppy, the only reason we've delayed getting married for all these years is so that we could have the perfect bloody wedding. I think you'll agree that this couldn't get any more bloody imperfect.'

I grimace.

'Where's that tequila?' Jazz screams, getting up to go and investigate.

'But I thought you were coming out here a month ago to check it out?' I'm sure she said that.

'I was! But I had a last minute meeting come up, so I just video conferenced them. I thought everything was under control. By email, they seemed quite bloody organised. Now I realise its run by a bunch of foreign fuckwits!'

'Well...you have to kind of expect the foreign,' Ryan says smiling tightly. He's amused. One of my best friends is having a nightmare right in front of him, and the sadistic bastard is amused.

'I think you should go and check us into our room, don't you.' I stuff the key card into his hands and point towards the bags. He rolls his eyes but does what I ask.

'And the worst thing,' she says, wiping her tears with a tissue Ollie's passed to her, 'is that my hair is dealing horrifically with the humidity. I mean look at it! I don't get it. We've been abroad before. There's no reason why it should act this way!'

'Maybe stress?' Ollie offers unhelpfully.

We both glare at him. He looks from my face to hers.

'What was that, Ryan?' he calls, even though he definitely didn't call him. 'You need my help with the bags? Sure thing.' He practically runs away from us.

'That's not even the worst of it, Pops,' she cries, her voice breaking.

'There's more?' I ask in undisguised horror.

'I know, and it's worse than my hair!' I stifle a giggle. 'The hotel bloody double booked. They're trying to speak to the registrar right now to see if they can stay longer and somehow marry both of us. But even if they can we can't both have the main hall for the reception.'

'Shit.' Again, totally unhelpful Poppy.

Jazz bounds back in with a bottle of Tequila and three shot glasses.

'Don't worry girls, I have the alcohol!' she sings, waving it in the air.

'I can't do Sambuca remember! It makes me spew,' I complain.

They both glare at me.

'Babe, if you want to be selfish right now, go ahead, but one of your best friends is going through a crisis.' She points to Lilly. 'And if you can't pull your whiney knickers up and get pissed with us then you're no friend at all.'

I huff out a laugh. She can be so ridiculous. I look to Lilly, and she has her pleading eyes on.

'Please, Pops. Take one for the team.'

'Oh God. Okay, but just one.'

Jazz

Thirty minutes later, we girls are in mine and Ollie's suite. It's still awfully old fashioned, ugly pine furniture everywhere, purple shag-pile carpet under our sandaled feet. I insisted that Alex and Lilly take it from us, but Lilly is still trying to argue with me. God, she's stubborn. Lilly's mobile starts ringing pulling her out of her concentration.

'Hello? Hello?' she says eagerly down the phone. 'Oh yeah, hi.'

Poppy looks hopefully at her.

'Really?' She looks crestfallen, hugging herself with one arm. 'Okay. Okay.' She slowly hangs up the phone and stares into space, running her hands through her red hair.

'And...?' I beg.

'They can't do it,' she says sadly, her neck tense, her eyes fixed ahead. 'The registrar can't fit us both in. It's over. We're not getting married.'

What? It can't just be over as quickly as that can it? For God's sakes, I have money, shit loads of it. Surely I can fix this.

'Fuck that!' I scream angrily. I take her by the shoulders and try to shake some fight into her. 'We're flying you home, and we can have an amazing wedding organised within a few days.'

Tears shimmer in her eyes. I've never seen her so vulnerable.

'You don't get it Jazz; we're skint. We spent all of our money doing this. The business hasn't been going well lately, so there's just no spare cash.'

Do people constantly forget that I'm a millionaire now?

'Fuck that!' I laugh. 'You don't need money. I have shit loads. Come on, we'll have the best wedding London has seen!' I clap my hands excitedly.

'Really?' Her eyes light up but quickly fade again. 'But the whole point of being abroad was being able to keep it really small, so I don't have to invite the arsehole end of my family. Plus, my Nan got married here.'

I can see why that would be special to her.

'And they were together until the day my Nan ran off with that business salesman.'

What the fuck? I just assumed one of them would have died or something. Hardly a beautiful love story.

I put my thinking cap on. It's easy when you're not drinking tequila like the others. Not that they realise. I might be conflicted about this baby, but I think I know deep down that I intend to keep it.

'I've got it! My mum's villa. We can get it all decorated and fly everyone out first thing tomorrow morning.'

If I'd have been a good friend I would have offered for her to use it from day one, but I know how proud Lilly can be so thought best to let her get on with it.

'Really? Are you sure we could?' Lilly laughs, not quite believing me.

'You tell me, chick,' I smile mischievously. 'You say you run a PA business. Here's my credit card. If you can organise it, you can do it.'

Her eyes widen to double the size. 'Did I just die and go to heaven?' She screams, jumping up and down on the bed like a child.

It's so nice when I can use my money to make people happy.

I pick up the phone and dial reception. 'We need champagne!'

## Poppy

I've never seen Lilly move so fast in all the time I've known her. By ten pm we've not only got most things sorted for tomorrow, but we're also on our way to a club. It's actually the only club here at all so it'll have to do. I'm a little bit squiffy already what with the champagne and tequila, but I've kept my wits about me. Ryan, on the other hand, seems to have got *very* drunk with Alex and Ollie. He was actually the driving force that brought us to the club. The normal Ryan wouldn't be arsed. But I like this side of him, and it only comes out to play occasionally.

We queue up, the line quickly decreasing with drunken revellers excitedly dancing in. They're checking women's bags, which I always think is good. Shows they actually care about whether people are going to try and do drugs in their club. The amount of times I've gone in a club toilet only to hear someone snorting coke up their nose in the next cubicle.

Ollie, Alex & Ryan get in first while our handbags are searched. Jazz and Lilly skip in, and I'm just about to join them when a hand on my shoulder stops me.

'You're not going in,' a husky Spanish accented voice says from behind me.

I turn to the Spanish bouncer with the unibrow, confused. 'Sorry, what?'

He meets me with an accusing glare. 'We found your drugs.' He produces a mint from the bottom of my bag.

I almost burst out laughing.

'What are you talking about? That's a mint.'

Maybe he's actually joking.

'Of course it is,' he grins, laughing to his other bouncer friend.

So...not a joke then? What the hell is going on here?

'I'm telling you! It's a bloody mint. Just smell it.'

'I'm not smelling your drugs,' he growls with disgust. His colleague nods at him. 'Ilevarla a la estacion de policia.'

What did he say? Policia? That's definitely police. Okay, now I'm worried.

'What? But my friends!' I point towards the club, but everyone has already gone in. Shit the bed.

I *cannot* believe that I'm in a Spanish prison cell right now. I've probably already caught a Spanish plague from being here. It's beyond ridiculous. They didn't even let me have my one phone call. The whole operation screams backstreet if you ask me. I keep imagining the guys finally realising I'm not behind them. They must be going out of their minds by now. And how long are they going to leave me here anyway? What if I'm kept overnight and they still don't know what's happened to me. I could miss the morning flight. I could miss Lilly's wedding. Jesus; all over a mint. All because I should have cleared my handbag out ages ago. All because I enjoy fresh breath. This could literally only happen to me!

'Mrs Davis,' an officer finally says appearing in front of my cell. 'My deputy is ready to see you.'

At least they speak English here otherwise, I'd be totally lost.

I nod and allow him to lead me out of the cell. In situations like this, it really doesn't help that I allowed Jazz and Lilly to dress me. I'm wearing the shortest pink dress to exist in the world. It barely covers my vagina. Even Ryan was a little concerned about the length. They probably think I'm a hooker too.

An older officer with greying hair stands in front of me with his hands on his hips.

'*This* is the drug dealer?' he asks the other officer. Thank God he's actually English.

'According to Carlo at the club,' his colleague says.

The sergeant kisses his teeth. 'Let me see this drug.'

'It's not a drug!' I wail, hands out in front of me to beg. 'It's only a mint.'

Damn, why didn't I learn Spanish before I came here? What the hell is mint in Spanish? Maybe the word for drug is actually mint, and that's where this whole problem lies.

'Let me see,' he says, snatching the plastic bag out of his colleague's hand. He pulls out the mint and brings it to his nose, sniffing it. *Finally,* someone who will smell it! Then he licks it.

He turns back to his colleague. 'It's a mint, you idiot! This is the third time this month. Carlo is an idiot. Now take her back to the hotel and apologise.'

Well, thank fuck for that.

# Chapter 34
## Poppy

*Tuesday 5<sup>th</sup> April*

When I'm dropped off at reception, Ryan is already there talking to the receptionist.  I can't make out what he's saying, but he's pulling his hands through his hair.

'Ryan?'

He turns, his face flushed.  His eyes soften when he sees me.

'Pops!'  He runs the short distance and scoops me up and into his arms, crushing me against his chest.  So hard he's restricting my breathing.

'Stop.  Can't.  Breathe,' I just about get out.

'Sorry.'  He places me on the ground, his hands now on my shoulders as he checks me over.  'I just...fuck, Pops, where have you been?  We've been going out of our minds?'

Is it wrong that I'm glad I made an impact?

'You noticed then?' I snort.

'Noticed?  Pops as soon as we were in we couldn't find you.  We've been freaking the fuck out.  We had to search the entire club.'

'Really?'  I'm strangely attracted to the concerned Ryan.  He really cares about me.

'Of course.  Then the bouncer said you'd been arrested, but wouldn't tell us where the local police station was.  That's why I came back here.  I've been trying to get a taxi to take me there.'  He turns back to the receptionist.  'Obviously, cancel it now, please.'

She looks unsure but nods anyway.  She probably doesn't even speak

English.

Ryan's phone rings and he answers it immediately. 'Yeah, I've got her....I know...don't worry, she's safe. I'm taking her to bed.' He raises his eyebrows comically at me.

*Ooh.* Am I going to get ravished because he missed me so much?

He hangs up the phone and smiles at me.

'Am I going to get punished for being such a naughty girl?' I ask him in my most sultry voice.

He sighs. 'Pops, I told you I'm not comfortable with the spanking thing. I was brought up not to hit girls. That bloody movie has ruined my life!'

I scoff. He can be so dramatic.

'Alright, calm down, Mr Magnolia. Just take me to bed.'

The next morning Lilly is organising at full force. I haven't seen her phone away from her ear the entire time. We're flying in three hours and are currently trying to herd all seventy of her friends and family onto two coaches.

'Poppy!'

I turn round to see Lilly, still with her phone by her ear, looking concerned. 'What's up?'

'I need you to keep my Mum and Dad away from each other.'

I already know that they divorced when Lilly was seven. It was really hard on her, being the only child. She's always envied the relationship I have with Ollie. Not that she comments on my non-closeness with Henry and Richard. Anyway, apparently this is the first time they've been in the same location for at least fifteen years. How awkward.

'Sure. Why, have they already clashed?'

She sighs. 'Apparently they've been arguing over who I'm closest to. The fucking idiots. They were *this close* to not getting invited.'

'Okay, I'm on it,' I nod as reassuringly as I can. I find Jazz and grab her. 'We need to take one of Lilly's parents each and keep them separate until the wedding.'

'Okay, bagsy the dad,' she grins, her eyes lit up in mischief.

'No way! I don't want her mum. Last time we met, she told me about her crochet patterns for forty-five minutes. I can't endure that again.'

She squeezes my shoulder with fake sympathy. 'Yeah, good luck with that.' She grins and runs off before I can beg her to change her mind.

When our rented coaches arrive at Jazz's Mum's villa, there are audible gasps from everyone. I've been to her old villa, which was pretty fantastic with five bedrooms and six bathrooms, but I haven't had a chance to visit this new place. And wow. Just wow.

The gold metal gates open, leading us up the cream bricked long driveway surrounded by palm trees. You can see the garden at the side from here with the lavish twenty-foot pool. I'm so hot and bothered I'm tempted to run, strip naked and dive straight into it, but I'm sure the wedding party would have something to say about that.

'And then that was the year I took up knitting,' Lilly's mum Carol continues. 'I tell you, the patterns I started with might have been simple, but my God, it took me nearly an hour to master how I even held the needles.'

Kill me now. This is torture. I bet Jazz is having a whale of a time with Lilly's Dad, doing shots of bourbon, while I listen to this boring bitch. I really can't believe Lilly came out of her vagina. Maybe she's adopted. It would totally make sense; only she shares her red hair with her Dad. Still, maybe she was a love child that this lady accepted as her own? It doesn't seem that ridiculous.

The coach stops outside the villa. Actually, villa isn't the right word. Mansion seems to fit it better. It's a grand yellow modern building with grey shutters. There's a double garage to the right, not that you couldn't fit twenty cars on this driveway. I already said wow, right?

Lilly suddenly jumps on the bus with a megaphone. Who the hell gave her a megaphone?

'Listen up, people!' she blares out.

Everyone covers their assaulted ears.

'Lilly, you don't need the megaphone,' I shout at her. It's nice to shout at someone. Her boring mother really put me in an aggressive mood.

'Really?' She begrudgingly puts it down. 'Right, listen up, people. Jazz's mum has kindly offered us her home this weekend. That means that we respect it. Uncle John, no smoking inside. Aunt Mary no cooking, at *all*. Apparently they have maids anyway. Mum, don't be boring people with your knitting stories.'

She huffs beside me. 'I've been doing no such thing! Poppy here has been enjoying my stories, haven't you, Poppy?'

Everyone turns to stare at me expectantly, amused smiles on their faces.

'Err...yeah.' I can't break the poor woman's heart.

'Anyway, back to the bride,' Lilly shouts again through her megaphone. 'Even though there are like a bazillion bedrooms, we're still going to have to squeeze in. So we're looking at roughly four people to a room. I've already organised extra blow up beds, so you should be comfortable, BUT choose wisely. If I hear *anyone* having an argument today, I'm going to murder them. Do you understand?'

They all begrudgingly nod. I remind myself they must be well used to her.

'Now, the wedding will be today at five pm in the garden. I need you all there looking fabulous ready to coo at me in my amazing dress. If you're late, you won't be allowed to witness the ceremony.' She glares deliberately at a few. 'Do you understand?'

Everyone murmurs 'yes'. God, she's bossy.

The house is even more fabulous inside. All whitewashed walls and floor-to-ceiling windows; showing off the distant mountain views at the back of the house. The infinity pool looks like it goes straight into the ocean. I imagine it would normally be a peaceful place, but right now it's full of little Spanish maids directing people to bedrooms. It's already one pm. Only four hours until the wedding. I swallow nervously.

Jazz pinches my arse behind me. 'Alright, cheeky,' she giggles.

'Hi,' Lilly and Alex say, beside us. Lilly's holding a clipboard and checking things off.

'Say goodbye to your bride, Alex,' Jazz grins, grabbing Lilly's hand and yanking her beside us.

She looks up from the clipboard. 'Huh?'

'We're going to the guest cottage to get her ready.'

'This place has a guest cottage?' I gush. 'Could it get any bigger?'

Alex grins. 'Thanks again so much for this, Jazz.'

'My pleasure,' she beams back.

We leave her chaotic family and make our way over to the guest cottage. As I guessed, it's nothing like a 'guest' cottage. It's bigger than my house. Although once inside this has a homelier feel than the main house.

'Sorry about the decoration,' Jazz says, putting down her crate of champagne on the dining room table. 'Mum's not got around to renovating this bit yet.'

'I love it,' Lilly says. She looks at me. She knows I do too.

It's all old bricks and traditional Spanish paintings with a huge fireplace dominating the room. Sure, it smells a little musty, but it's still beautiful.

'So...can we finally see the dress?' I ask eagerly. It's been in a heavily guarded dress bag the entire time, and she's the only loser bride in the world that only took her mum with her to pick it. I'm half expecting her to show me a homemade crochet dress. Ugh, I shiver at just the possibility.

'Nope,' she grins, hanging it up on a curtain rail. 'I stink. I'm going for a shower. No peeping!'

She skips off upstairs, her previous stress having vanished. Funny how money really can fix everything.

Jazz opens the champagne, popping the cork off the main light. Whoops. Alex and Lilly are going to have to live by romantic candlelight tonight. Not the worst thing I suppose. We should really try and make the place look as romantic as possible. You know, really special. Especially with all of the stress that they've gone through.

'So,' Jazz says with a mischievous glint in her eyes. 'Shall we take a peek at the dress?' She hands over a champagne glass for me to sip.

I click my tongue and cross my arms over my chest. 'You *cannot* be serious. She would kill us.'

'How the hell will she ever know?' She flicks her hair behind her shoulders and heads over to the dress bag.

'No, Jazz!' I hiss rushing after her. 'She's only in the shower. She could come in at any moment.'

Her eyes mock me. 'With that old shower I don't think so,' she giggles. 'It's a nightmare. Come on,' she whines, stamping her foot, 'I've supplied the wedding venue. The least she can do is let me see the dress.'

'But she wants it to be special,' I retort, angry on Lilly's behalf. 'She wants us to see her dressed in it and gush at how beautiful she looks.'

She rolls her eyes. 'We'll do that anyway. Duh.'

'But it won't be the same, and you know it.' The fact that my own fingers are itching to rip it open is irrelevant.

'You are *such* a goody two shoes. Well, *I'm* looking.'

She is such a spoilt brat.

'Fine!' I snap crossing my arms over my chest and turning away from her and the dress. 'But I won't take any part in it.'

I hear the zip pulled down and then a gasp escapes her mouth.

'Oh God, what is it?' Knowing our luck it's already stained. Lilly will freak the fuck out.

'It's just...it's beautiful,' she says on a whisper.

God damn it, I really want to see it now. If Jazz is near speechless I can't even imagine how overwhelmed I'll be with it. But I need to be a good friend. But then...I suppose I've proved my good friend capabilities by chatting to her mother about knitting for the last few hours. I should get some kind of medal just for that.

I slowly turn, my eyes still scrunched closed. Oh, fuck it. I really want to see. You don't just get a gasp like that from Jazz for no big deal. And she's in the shower. She'll be none the wiser.

I open my eyes tentatively ready to take in the beauty. My mouth falls open. It must be the most beautiful thing I've ever seen. It's a sweetheart neckline with lace cap sleeves. At first glance, it seems white, but on closer inspection the dress seems to be pale pink with bold lace appliques lying atop tulle, cascading to a subtly flared fishtail skirt. It's bloody stunning and will suit Lilly down to the ground.

'It's stunning.' My voice is only a squeak. I'm just...wow. *What* a dress.

'It really is,' she nods, gazing at it in awe. 'It...' she looks down, her cheeks turning pink.

'It what?'

She blushes. *Actually* blushes. I don't think I've ever seen her blush.

'What is it? I push with a nervous giggle.

'Nothing!' she laughs, avoiding my inquisitive gaze. 'It just...for a second there I was jealous.'

I narrow my eyebrows at her. Jazz jealous of someone else? I've never heard her jealous of anyone. Well, apart from Angelina getting to shag Brad every night.

'Because of the dress?'

'Yeah.' I raise my eyebrows, demanding further explanation. 'Okay,' she smiles shyly, 'for a second, and I mean like a *split* arsed second, I imagined myself wearing this dress walking down the aisle to Ollie.'

I gasp. There's nothing else for it. She's never talked about getting married and has always shut us all down whenever we've suggested it.

'You...you want to marry Ollie?'

'No!' There she goes again blushing.

'Jazz!' I jump up and down on the spot. 'You totally do!'

'No!' she shouts, crossing her arms over her chest. 'You know how I don't even believe in marriage. It's just...one hell of a dress; that's all.'

'Are you sure?' I grin, teasing, already imagining the huge hat I'll buy. I tickle her arm, and she bends her body to escape it, tripping on a rug and toppling to the floor.

I laugh and jump on top of her, messing with her hair.

'Oh, Ollie,' I joke in a sing-song voice, 'I want you to marry me and make me the happiest girl in the world.'

'Get off me, you idiot!' she shouts from underneath me.

Her getting angry only makes me laugh harder.

'I want to be a princess for the day,' I joke. 'Marry me, Ollie, marry me!'

She spits her hair out of her face. 'I mean it Poppy; get off me. I'm pregnant!'

The world stills around me, but my head still feels like its spinning. I shake my head to try and force myself to concentrate. Pregnant? Jazz pregnant? Shit, Jazz the girl I'm still straddling on the floor. I scramble off her like she's on fire.

She looks back at me, just as shocked that she's told me. I almost want to ask if she's joking, but I can see from the fear in her eyes that she's not. She's scared of how I'm going to react. I wait for the feelings of resentment and anger to overwhelm me, but...they don't. I stare back at her, waiting for them to kick in and ruin our friendship, but...they don't. Instead, I find myself smiling from ear-to-ear, an excited tingle travelling from my neck down to my arms. Jemima's going to have a baby brother or sister. I'm going to be an auntie again. My best friend and brother created another baby.

I grab her into a bone-crushing hug as tears fall from my eyes. She pushes me back.

'Wait...you're not upset?' she asks suspiciously.

'I'm totally not bullshitting you when I say I'm so happy for you. I don't feel pissed off that it's you and not me.'

'Well, that's weird,' she smiles. 'But Ollie doesn't know, and you have to promise not to tell him yet. I'm still so confused about the whole thing. I even asked about an abortion.' She looks ashamed to even admit that.

'Like you could have gone through with it,' I grin, remembering how she ran out from the abortion clinic when she was pregnant with Jemima.

She looks down at the floor with slumped shoulders. 'Why is life so unfair, Pops? You're desperate for a baby, and I don't want one.'

I can't help but agree with her.

I shrug. 'Shit happens. Maybe I'm not meant to be a mum, just an amazing Auntie.'

'No, Poppy,' she smiles sadly. 'You are one hundred per cent meant to be a mother, and I'm going to do everything in my power to help make that a reality for you.'

I crush her into another hug. 'I can't believe this. I'm so happy for you.' I pull back and smile. 'Is this why you're now thinking about marrying him?

'No,' she laughs. 'I don't need a piece of paper to feel secure in my relationship. I just liked the pretty dress.'

'The pretty dress you weren't supposed to look at!' Lilly shrieks from behind us. We turn to see her on the bottom step of the stairs in a towel. 'You bitches are fucking dead!'

# Chapter 35
## Poppy

Luckily Lilly is so overtaken with rage at us seeing her dress she doesn't seem to have overheard Jazz's confession.

'So are you sure you have everything taken care of?' I ask Lilly as she hangs up the phone.

We've just changed out of the purple satin dressing gowns Lilly got made for us with 'Lilly's Bitches' printed on the back and are now sipping champagne in our plum maxi dresses. Well, I am, Jazz is pretending to. Lilly seems ridiculously calm all of a sudden. It's quite unnerving. The phrase 'calm before the storm' comes to mind.

'Yeah. It honestly is,' she smiles as if shocked herself. 'I know they say money doesn't buy happiness, but my God, Jazz, the minute you told me I could use your card, well it was suddenly easy. With money you can get *anything* done.'

Jazz smiles sadly, looking down into her champagne glass. 'Yeah, except get your boyfriend to be happy.'

'What?' Lilly splutters. 'There's something up with you and Ollie?'

Bless her. She's been so involved with the wedding she hasn't noticed much else around her.

I've only heard bits from both of them. I know Jazz said she hasn't told him she's pregnant yet, but I didn't realise it was so serious.

She rolls her eyes. 'He just keeps saying I'm throwing my money around at everyone. And I mean, look around, I'm kind of proving his point right now.'

'No, Jazz,' Lilly says, placing her hand over hers. 'You saved the day. If it weren't for you, I'd be crying my way back to England by now. All of our money would have been completely wasted, all of our friends and family's money down the drain. You really have saved the day.'

Jazz smiles sadly. 'Thanks, skank.'

We all laugh.

'Is it really that bad between you and Ollie?' I can't help but ask. 'You've seemed fine since you've got here.'

She sighs wearily. I direct her towards a chair so she can rest.

'I just don't know if we want the same things anymore. He wants to stay in St Albans. I want to live in Chelsea. I feel like I'd resent him if I just gave in and moved to a normal house in St Albans.'

'Is St Albans really that bad though?" I ask. I can't help but sound offended. It's my hometown.

'Of course it's not,' she sighs. 'But you grew up there. It's your home. I grew up in Chelsea, so that's *my* home.'

I suppose I get that, but I really hope they don't end up splitting up over a bloody location to live. It seems so ridiculous.

'Anyway,' Lilly says adjusting her crystal headpiece. 'I hate to sound selfish, but this day is about me remember.'

We all laugh, the tension immediately broken.

'You're right,' Jazz chuckles. 'You look amazing.'

'You really do,' I nod.

The dress looks even more spectacular on her, showing off every beautiful curve of her body, her boobs hidden enough to be respectful for a wedding but on show enough to prove they're fabulous.

My phone starts ringing. No, actually, Izzy's phone starts ringing. Mum flashes up. I should answer it really. Her Mum must be worried what with everything that's happened recently.

'Hi, it's actually Poppy,' I answer awkwardly.

'Poppy?' her Mum repeats, confused. 'Why do you have Izzy's phone?'

'I took it by mistake. I'm actually away for Lilly's wedding right now.' Hopefully, that will mean she won't stay chatting for long.

'Oh, well, I don't want to keep you, only...' She sounds anxious.

'Only...what?' I can't help but enquire. I've only met her a handful of times, and she's this cute little Italian lady always trying to stuff meatballs down your throat.

'I'm worried about my Isabella.'

She must mean about the whole stalker thing. 'Honestly, don't worry about it, Mrs Bianchi. She's in prison now.'

'It's not that. It's just...' her voice turns grave, 'have you noticed Isabella eating less than normal?'

That's a random question. But yeah, I've obviously noticed how she's lost weight recently. I've even tried to talk to her about it. Yet I don't want to worry her mum unnecessarily.

'Um...not really,' I answer vaguely. 'I mean, yeah, her appetite has changed with the stress of everything, but I don't think it's anything to worry about,' I try to reason. Why is she asking though?

'That's where you're wrong, Poppy.' She takes a deep breath. 'I'm guessing Isabella never told you she suffered from an eating disorder when she was younger?'

I nearly drop the phone. I quickly turn away from Jazz and Lilly fussing over her dress, so they can't read my horrified face. Izzy? My Izzy suffered from an eating disorder? I mean; I know she's strict about her food, but she's always eaten. Just healthy stuff. She's a personal trainer for Gods sakes. She's supposed to eat all that rabbit crap.

'I'm guessing from the silence she never told you?'

'No,' I admit. I can't help but feel like a shitty friend. How has she never confided in me before? And why didn't I push further about her eating? Too busy worrying about my own problems.

She sighs down the line. 'It started when she was seventeen and stressed with her A Levels. She started controlling her food at first, but then it quickly turned into her surviving on only black coffee and a banana a day.'

Crap. This is all making sense now. I thought I was just worrying too much, but I've been right. She's gone back to her old ways.

'That's why we sent her on the nutritional course. We wanted to show to her how her body *needed* food and how it was good for her. That's why she became a personal trainer. Only now I'm worried she's throwing it all away again.'

Shit. What a fucking disaster. With the stress of Michael's ex, she's almost definitely resorted back to her old coping habits.

'I'll be honest. I think you should go round and see her. Maybe get a doctor involved. I'll text Michael and let him know. I would ring him but Lilly's going to be married in the next ten minutes, so I'm a bit strapped for time.'

'Thank you, Poppy. I'm sorry to ruin your holiday.'

'Don't be silly.' I've got a bad feeling about this in my stomach. 'I'll text him right away.'

'Thank you.'

I hang up and turn round to see Lilly and Jazz staring at me.

'What the hell is going on?' Jazz asks with a hand on her hip.

'Oh, nothing,' I say vaguely, already tapping out my message to Michael.

'Didn't sound like nothing,' Lilly says, narrowing her long lashes at me. 'It *sounded* like someone was about to steal my thunder.'

I laugh as I finish typing, ignoring her drama queen ways.

*Michael, Izzy's mum called. We think she has a problem with eating. She is going to come round with a doctor. Listen to her and look after Izzy until I get back xxx*

There's a knock on the door before Alex's friend, Ben, pokes his head round. 'We're ready for you ladies when you are.' He stops in his tracks, his mouth falling open when he takes in the vision that is Lilly.

'Shit, Lil. You look amazing!'

'Don't I know it,' she grins, doing a girly twirl.

Jazz coughs not so subtly. 'And what about us?'

We both smile sweetly and spin around for him in our long plum maxi dresses. Thank God she put us in flip-flops, or I'd be panicking about falling down.

'Right, let's do this!' Jazz shouts eagerly punching the air.

Lilly lifts her dress off the floor, showing off her stellar purple heels. We follow her out of the cottage, the sun still as bright as earlier. We cross the lawn, past the pool and round the corner to where everyone is waiting for us. I actually gasp from how amazing the place looks. Lawn chairs are placed on either side of a makeshift aisle in the grass where flower petals have been dropped. There's candles either side of it, in lanterns, and fairy lights everywhere above us as we walk down the aisle, in the trees, around the house. The whole place looks magical.

I make it up to the front of the aisle where a Spanish man that I'm assuming is the registrar is waiting alongside a beaming Alex and Ben. We're right on the edge of the cliff here, the view of the crystal blue sea in front of us. I wait for Lilly up front as she gets gasps and appreciating smiles. She deserves every single one of them.

When she reaches me she hands over her bouquet and then, only then, does she look at Alex. It's almost like she's been avoiding him until now. She catches his eye, and it's like her defences come down, and she finally relaxes, her shoulders sagging with relief. He smiles at her and gives her hand a little squeeze. Her eyes immediately fill up with tears, and it's only then that it hits me; Lilly really does love Alex. I don't know why I ever doubted that, but I suppose with her being so fierce all the time, I kind of mistook her for being slightly cold. I was always too busy listening about their arguments. I never stopped to notice the true, unconditional love there.

The service is beautiful, especially with the Spanish accent of the registrar. It makes everything sound more romantic. Then we're moved on by a toastmaster to sit down for the wedding breakfast. Two enormously long tables are laid out on the lawn, set with the grandest silver cutlery among purple and cream flowers and different height candles. With the view of the sea and the fairy lights around us, it's hard to not find it enchanting.

Ryan grabs my hand under the table. 'Remember our wedding?' His hand lightly strokes up my arm, along the back of my neck, making me shiver and finally resting his hand on my lower back. I gaze into his beautiful whiskey coloured eyes, a bit drunk on Prosecco.

'It was all a bit of a blur,' I admit shyly.

He tucks a bit of my hair behind my ear, his eyes misting over with love. 'I remember how I felt when you were walking down the aisle towards me.'

Butterflies flutter in my stomach at the memory.

'Was that before or after I fell?' I giggle.

'Before,' he laughs. 'The concentration on your face was so bloody adorable. I thought; I'm marrying a woman who even has trouble remaining upright when walking. But I didn't care. I still knew you were the best thing to have ever happened to me.'

My mouth drops open. He's never told me this before. 'Really?'

'Yeah.' He puts his hand over his heart, so I know he's serious.

'Then I fell and ruined everything.' God, just the memory of it has me cringing.

'You didn't ruin anything.' I remember how he came and helped me up. 'I helped your adorable arse up, and I knew at that moment that you would always do the same in return. You'd always pick me up when I fell.'

Oh my God, he is getting deep tonight.

'And,' he pecks a kiss on the end of my nose, 'I was right.'

'God, who knew you were so charming?' I grin comically.

'You'll know just how charming I can be later.' He wiggles his eyebrows suggestively. 'I bagsied us a room.'

'Really?' I ask narrowing my eyebrows at him. I thought everyone was sharing. 'Our own room?'

'Yep. You just wait and see.' He winks, and I'm left wondering while I tuck into the starter.

I really can't believe Lilly managed to organise all this in a day. Less than a day. I suppose money really does talk, but then it always talks louder when it's being shouted by an angry, red-headed bridezilla.

It's the most beautiful evening. We get to know Lilly's crazy family over lots and lots of wine. Then there's a small dance floor with a live local band. Everything is so relaxed with the fresh summer air; even in near pitch black,

I still only require a small shawl to cover my shoulders from the cool breeze.

It's finished with the most spectacular firework display as Ryan cuddles me from behind. Slowly, drunken people start staggering off to bed, and when there are only us left, Ryan turns to me.

'Are you ready to go to our VIP room?'

I smile sleepily. I'm so tired, but I'm still excited to see what this is all about. I've tried to work it out, and I can't see where this extra room has come from.

'Follow me.' He takes my hand and drags me along with him. We walk a little further along the grass and around the side of the house. There, under a little tree, is a little tent, lit up with fairy lights and rose petals in a path leading to the entrance.

'A tent?' I grin, raising my eyebrows. 'This is so cute.'

'I knew you'd love it,' he smiles, kissing me quickly on the lips. 'Alex said if he did that for Lilly she'd refuse to sleep there, but I know you're not like that.'

I yawn. 'As long as you cuddle me to sleep I'll be fine.'

He wiggles his eyebrows. 'Oh, I'll do more than cuddle you to sleep.'

I wink. 'Now, there's a promise.'

# Chapter 36
## Poppy

*Friday 8<sup>th</sup> April*

I haven't been able to stop worrying about Izzy all the way home. Michael hasn't returned any of my calls, and I don't know what that means. When our taxi pulls up outside our house, Izzy's car is there. Uh-oh. I have a feeling this isn't going to go down well.

Ryan grimaces at me as he pays for the taxi. I obviously filled him in as soon as I could. Izzy gets out of her car and walks straight to the front door watching as we struggle with our cases.

'Hi, Izzy,' I say tentatively.

'Hi,' she answers curtly.

We open the door and go straight into the sitting room. God, it's so nice to smell home, the comforting scents of vanilla and jasmine. I knew those candles were worth the price tag. Ryan goes into the kitchen and boils the kettle, thank God. I sit down on the sofa and wait for her to explode at me. From the look in her eyes, I know it's not going to be pretty.

'You had no right,' she declares looking me dead in the eye. I actually shiver. I've never seen her like this. 'No right, to tell Michael that. I should have been able to tell him myself; when I was ready.'

I sigh. This is not what I want to be doing after a flight.

'Look, I'm sorry, but your Mum phoned and told me everything, and you have to admit that you have a problem. Something is wrong with you.'

'Yeah, I'm stressed is all!' she shouts back. Her eyes are sallow, her cheeks gaunt. 'I mean, God, first I have a stalker, and then my best friend almost gets murdered by her. I'm pretty sure it's a normal reaction to be stressed.'

Is it weird that I got a thrill from her calling me her best friend? Not the time, Poppy.

'You have to admit you have a problem,' I stress. 'I'll come to the doctor with you.'

'It's not as easy as that,' she cries, her eyes filling with tears. 'I don't want to be locked up in a hospital again. Yeah, things might have gotten out of hand, but I'm not that bad. I promised myself I'd never be that bad again.'

'Look, why don't I go with you? We can speak to Michael and make sure you get the best care possible. I mean with all of Michael's money you can basically have whatever you want.'

She twiddles the end of her sports top through her fingers.

'I'm just so embarrassed that he knows how weak I am.' Her voice breaks with emotion, like she's truly humiliated.

I move to sit next to her, stroking her arm reassuringly.

'You're not weak, Izzy. You're just ill.'

A tear falls down her cheek. She looks so tortured. I grab her and force her into a cuddle, rubbing her back like I do with Jemima when she's upset.

I feel better now I've cleared the air with her. She promises me that she's going to take Michael up on his offer for private treatment. I walk her out to her car. I stop when I realise one of her tyres is flat. Hang on; both tyres are flat.

'Oh no!' Izzy squeals, running over to them. 'How could this have happened?'

I follow her around the car to see that the other two are flat also. I touch one of the tyres, and it's clear it's been slashed. A sickening feeling creeps up my spine.

'Izzy, get inside,' I say quietly and as calmly as I can. I don't feel it. I feel hysterical, it's rising up in my throat, trying to choke me.

'Wait, are they slashed?' she utters in disbelief, her face losing all colour.

This is literally the last thing she needs. I don't like us being outside like this. I suddenly feel exposed, like we're sitting ducks waiting for a sniper to take us out. I watch too many crime shows.

'Inside now.' I grab her shoulder and drag her back inside.

'Calm down,' she says pushing me back once we're inside and I've loosened my grip on her. 'What the hell is wrong with you?'

Is she for real?

'With *me?* You're the bitch that's just had her tires slashed, and you're acting like it's no big deal.'

'I'm just trying to stay calm about this,' she retorts, her foot tapping nervously. 'She wants me to be scared! I will not rise to it!'

'You think it's her? She's supposed to be in jail.'

'Of course it's her,' she snaps.

Jesus this is serious, she's going to attack again, only this time, she's going to get the right girl. Memories of her insane eyes when she kidnapped me invade my mind, causing my breathing to falter.

'It *could* just be kids.' She shrugs, clearly trying to talk herself out of being hysterical.

'I do *not* have that kind of thug around here. This is St Albans for God's sakes! And she's in jail.'

'You're right. We're obviously getting ahead of ourselves. Let's just call the local garage.'

An hour later we're in the garage waiting room, sat on uncomfortable purple chairs, waiting for the tyre's to be replaced.

'I'm telling you we should call the police.'

'No. Not until I talk to Michael. It's just tyres.'

'Yeah and it's just your life you're dicing with.'

'Whatever.' She stands up and walks over to the corner of the room, pretending to be looking at the adverts on the wall, when her phone beeps. She looks at her screen briefly. 'Voicemail,' she explains. 'I must have bad reception here. It's probably Michael; worried.' She presses a few buttons on the phone and then holds it to her ear.

'Yeah, with good reason,' I say sarcastically.

She turns away while she listens, obviously wanting some privacy. I suppose a good friend would give her some privacy, but I'm too scared to be alone right now.

Suddenly Izzy turns back to me, her face draining of all colour. What's happening?

'What? What?' I beg.

Her phone slips out of her hand and crashes down onto the floor. I grab it and bring it to my ear. It's music playing on the other end. It takes me a second to realise that it's by that new, weird London Indie band.

*'Did you see me standing there? Did you know, or were you unaware? Did I want you to, did I want you to notice me or is it too soon to see?*

*Did you know that you looked at me? Did you see the sparkle in the lights? Did you know that I was standing there, watching your every move?*

*Did you know, know my name at all?, Do you know that I was at your window, did you know that I was watching over you, making sure he would leave you alone? Did you know that I was always there? Watching!'*

Oh my God. The words, they're as much as a direct threat as I can imagine.

I grab my phone and speed dial, Michael. I don't even know where he is today.

'Hi, Poppy. How are you?' He sounds so carefree and breezy. That's about to change.

'Michael, where are you?'

'At the studio, why?'

'Okay, it's a bit of a long story but stay there we're coming straight to see you.'

A burly man with an awful lot of chest hair comes into the waiting room. 'All done, ladies.'

'Why? What's going on?' Michael asks down the phone. 'Are you in trouble? Is it Izzy?'

'We think the nutter is playing with us. She is still in jail, right?'

'As far as I'm aware, but I'll make some calls. I'll come and get you.'

'No, I don't want to sit still any longer. We're coming to you.'

I take the keys from the man, trying desperately to ignore Izzy chewing her nails off. We have to get out of here ASAP.

My phone starts ringing again. Ollie's name flashes up. I pick it up as we get into the car.

'Poppy? I need your advice.'

'Ugh, I do not have time for your baby-daddy dramas right now,' I snap. 'I'm dealing with something more important now.'

'Baby-daddy drama?' he repeats, a question in his voice. 'What do you mean?'

Oh shit. What have I done?

'Err...nothing.' I throw Izzy into the car and then race round to dive in myself.

'Wait...baby-daddy drama? She's not...Jazz isn't pregnant again, right?'

'Oh, for fucks sake, Ollie, I don't have time for this!'

I drive like a maniac to the studio. I'm probably endangering our life far more than Michael's ex right now, but I can't help but feel spooked right through to my soul. Like knowing something awful is about to happen. I just...well I want to be with Michael as soon as possible. I haven't even called Ryan yet, but I know he'll freak the fuck out, and I'm trying to do damage control right now.

I clear my throat as we pull into the parking lot.

'Okay.' I swing into a huge space and still manage to get the parking line in the middle of the wheel. Oh well. 'Let's just hurry.'

I jump out of the car and grab Izzy's hand like she's Jemima and sprint towards the entrance. We get waved in immediately by the security guards. Just seeing them makes me feel safer. The studio is creepy like this. Not everyone is in today, so a lot of the corridors feel like a zombie apocalypse has happened, and everyone forgot to tell us. Any minute now I'm expecting Daryl to jump out with his crossbow and tell us to come with him if we want to live.

Sigh. I *wish* that would happen. I'd even take the zombie part if I got to be protected by Daryl. But with my luck, I'm more likely to get torn apart by a zombie first.

We turn a corner and nearly jump out of our skin when we see a dark clothed figure approaching us.

'Aaaagh!!!' we both scream in unison, jumping out of our skins. I push Izzy in front of me as a shield.

'Calm down, girls.' I try to get my heart to calm down enough so I can hear what this person is trying to say. 'It's just me!'

My ear ringing lowers enough for me to be able to make out its Michael. Oh, thank God.

'Reception called and said you were coming up,' he explains, attempting to calm us.

Izzy throws herself into his arms. 'Oh, Michael,' she wails. 'When is it going to end? She sobs.

He looks at me over Izzy's shoulder. 'I just spoke to my solicitor. They've released her. Someone paid her bail money.'

'Shit.'

The ground bounces from someone else, suddenly running up behind us. We all tense up in fear. It's only one of the security guards. 'Ah, here you are. Sir, we've had sightings of someone around Miss Bianchi's car.'

'And have you checked it?' he asks with authority, cradling Izzy tighter to him.

'Yes, sir,' he nods. 'I'm afraid her tires have been slashed.'

Again? Oh dear God. She followed us.

By the time I get home its 6 pm. We called the police, but she'd disappeared by the time they got there. They said they'd look into it but, to be honest; I don't have much faith. They seemed bloody useless, with one of them looking like he was barely out of nappies.

As soon as I shut the front door behind me I breathe a sigh of relief. Safe at last. I tried to ring Ryan so he could pick me up but he said he was at Richard's house after being talked into helping him with some flat-pack furniture, so I didn't want to worry him and tell him everything that had happened. I just pretended I was calling to find out what time he'd be home. No point in him rushing back for nothing. I cannot wait to go to bed already. I might even skip dinner. That's how tired I am.

Quiet chatter comes from the living room. Has Grams got someone over? I walk tentatively into the sitting room. My mouth drops open when I see not only Grams and Teddy but Ryan's mum, Linda. What the hell? She looks awful, dirt and grime across her face, hair that hasn't been washed in weeks and eyes full of tears.

'Linda?'

Grams purses her lips. Teddy seems uncomfortable.

She clears her throat. 'Hi, Poppy.'

I look between them all. 'What's going on here?'

Grams stands up and takes my hand, guiding me to the opposite sofa.

'Love, we need to ask you a favour.' I stare back at her, my eyes like saucers. How is she so calm about Linda being in the same room as her? 'Teddy found Linda today while he was out shopping. She's been living on the streets.'

Crap. That would make sense; how she completely went off the radar.

'Poor thing,' Teddy says, placing his hand on Linda's shoulder. 'She didn't want to come with me, but I insisted. I know there's a lot of bad blood between you all, but I couldn't just leave her there.'

'You did the right thing, Teddy,' Grams nods. She turns back to me. 'Poppy, whatever's happened between Linda and me in the past, she's still my daughter, and I hate to see her like this.' I nod, still in shock. 'Besides, I've checked her arms. No track marks. She seems drug-free.'

Oh please God, let that be true.

It's only then that I realise Linda hasn't told them that we've been communicating all this time. She's kept my secret.

'So what are you asking?'

'Well, she needs looking after,' Grams says. 'So I'm going to move back to my house, with her, and care for her.'

Is she serious?

'No way, Grams! The whole reason you're here is because you need looking after. There's no way I'm letting you do that.'

'I understand,' Linda nods, looking down at the floor. She turns to Teddy. 'I told you this was a mistake.'

She goes to stand up, but I stop her.

'Wait. I'm not sending you away though. I agree with you Grams, whatever's in the past is in the past. I'd let you stay here, but there's no room for you.'

'Yes,' Gram sighs, 'Poppy's got Ryan's ex-fiancé shacked up in the other bedroom.'

'What?' Linda gasps in horror.

'It's a long story,' I reply rolling my eyes.

'You really are too sweet, Poppy,' Linda says with a fond smile. 'But more than that I know that Ryan still hates me and probably always will. I can't exactly hide in a cupboard.'

Hmm...She couldn't hide in a cupboard, but it does give me a crazy idea.

'What if...'

'What if what?' Grams asks eagerly.

'I mean...we could hide you in the loft.'

'The loft?' Teddy shrieks. 'Jesus Poppy, is that really any better than being homeless?'

I shrug. 'I think so.'

'I agree,' Linda says with a bright smile, her eyes now hopeful. 'I could stay up there no problem as long as you give me a bucket to pee in and drop in some food occasionally. Trust me, when I say that's more than I've had where I've been.'

I wonder when she last ate.

'Do you really think we could do it?' Grams asks anxiously, twisting her earring around.

I nod. 'We could.'

'But, Poppy,' Linda says, placing her hands over her face. Her nails are full of in-ground dirt. 'You have to realise that if Ryan finds out about this, he might never forgive you.'

Oh god, what bloody choice do I have? I want her to have a roof over her head, and I want her to have a chance at a future. I know she needs people who care about her to assist with this. Plus, if she's in the loft then we can hide her until we can get a flat or something sorted for her.

'I'm in.'

# Chapter 37
## Jazz

### *Saturday 9th April*

I'm desperately trying to get Jemima to eat homemade spaghetti bolognaise. She's such a fussy eater. She only eats the tray meals you can buy and refuses to eat anything home-cooked. Not that I made this. Lucine did, so it's bloody delicious. If I made it, I couldn't blame her for refusing.

The doorbell rings, and I take my chance for escape.

'Mummy's going to get the door. You stay here and eat this all up.'

Lucine winks at me.

I jog up the stairs and swing the front door open to find Lettuce's friend Rupert beaming back at me.

'Ert!' I joke. 'What are you doing here?'

He grins as if pleased I remembered his name. 'Was in the area and thought I'd pop in and check on you. Hope that's okay?'

'Yeah, of course.' I look down at myself in my jogging bottoms. 'As long as you don't mind me being this much of a state. I'm just feeding Jemima.'

He follows me down to the kitchen where Lucine is watching Jemima.

'Would you like a cup of tea?' I offer, remembering to be polite.

'Love one, please. Milk, one sugar.'

I nod at Lucine, who is already boiling the kettle. What the hell did I ever do without her?

He sits down with me at the table. 'Come on, Jem, just a few more mouthfuls,' I beg, already knowing I'm going to give up.

'No!' she screams picking up the bowl and launching it up into the air. I watch in horror as it lands on top of Rupert's head, the sauce trickling down his face.

'Oh my God!' I shriek. I jump up and grab the bowl while Lucine runs over with a tea towel. I turn to Jemima. I could kill her! 'I can't believe you just did that! Say sorry.'

Her bottom lip wobbles before bursting into angry, hysterical tears. Oh for God's sake. I pick her up to console her, even though it was her fault in the first place.

'I'm so sorry, Rupert.'

'It's okay, honestly,' he shrugs, using the tea towel to try and get the spaghetti out of his hair.

Having a child is the worst.

'No, it's not,' I insist. 'It's all in your hair. You're going to have to shower. You can't go home like that. Go upstairs and have a quick shower.'

'Are you sure?' He asks, scrunching up his forehead.

'Yes, please,' I nod. 'It will make me feel better. By the time you come down, Lucine will have your tea all ready, and I'll even get her to knock up some biscuits.'

He rolls his eyes. 'If you insist, thanks.'

He turns to leave, 'And what do you say to Rupert, Jemima?'

He turns back to hear her say a mumbled sorry. 'It's honestly fine.'

God, he's polite. If someone else's kid did that to me, I'd go spare.

He's barely up the stairs when the door knocks again. Bloody hell it's like Piccadilly Circus today! I run upstairs and answer it. Ollie stands on the doorstep looking ridiculously handsome. What is he doing here?

'Hey. I didn't know you were coming over today.' I'd have put some bloody makeup on.

He ignores me and pushes past, walking downstairs to the kitchen. God, when did I think all of these stairs were a good idea? I'm going to have an arse like Kim Kardashian.

He kisses his hello to an excited Jemima before turning back to me.

'When exactly were you going to tell me you were pregnant?' he whisper-hisses.

Oh my god. How the hell does he know that?

'Um...'

He frowns, visibly wounded. 'Was it because you were planning on getting rid of it without me even knowing!'

'No!' I take his arm and drag him away from Jemima. 'Although...if I'm honest the thought did go through my mind,' I admit with a whisper.

'How the hell could you not tell me?'

The hurt twists inside me. Oh God, he looks so betrayed.

'How the hell did you even find out?'

'Poppy let slip.'

Of *course* she did. Remind me to murder her.

'I just can't believe this. You know how gutted I was that I missed out on your pregnancy with Jemima and that I want another baby. But there you were ready to just get rid of it without even telling me.'

'I wasn't! I said I only considered it.' I sigh; the weight of the world suddenly on my shoulders. 'The truth is that I *don't* want another baby. This was a total fuck up, and I'm still totally confused.'

'Err...Jazz?' We both turn to see Rupert in just a towel, dripping wet. 'Really sorry to interrupt you, but do you know where my clothes are?'

Well, this doesn't look good.

Ollie's eyes burn with rage, his breathing accelerating so fast I think he's going to take off.

'I can't fucking believe this!' he growls, storming out of the kitchen.

Fuck. I run after him. 'It's not what it looks like! He just needed a shower!'

But he's not listening. He's too busy slamming the door in my face.

Well, I think that went well. Not.

## Poppy

I'm at home with Izzy, talking through her starting her stay at The Priory when my phone rings. Jazz. Jesus, one drama at a time.

'Hi, Jazz, can I call you back?'

'No!' she shouts before breaking into a noisy sob.

Shit, what's happened? Is someone seriously hurt?

'What's wrong?'

She cries loudly down the phone. 'Ugh, everything's fucked because you told Ollie I'm pregnant!'

'Huh? I haven't told him anything.' Wait, what did I say to him on the phone the other day? I was so panicked it's all just a blur of a memory.

'What? That makes no sense. Ugh, it doesn't matter because he saw Rupert in just a towel, and so it's ruined anyway.'

'You slept with Rupert? Oh Jazz,' I sigh. Why does she insist on letting herself down like this?

Izzy's eyes go as wide as saucers.

'I didn't sleep with him!' she screams so loud Izzy hears. 'Not that your brother believes me. Oh god, can you come round? I need someone I can cry on, and Lucine's not a great hugger.'

'Okay, but I'm with Izzy. Can I bring her?'

'Yeah, that's fine,' she sniffs. 'Fuck it, bring Grace too.'

Ugh, why must she always involve her? 'Fine,' I sigh. 'See you soon.'

An hour later we're all in her sitting room with three bottles of rose. You have no idea how sad I was when I realised I'd be the only one drinking them. Jazz and Grace are pregnant, and Izzy's still only drinking water and nibbling on cucumber sticks. She's going into the Priory tomorrow, so we've turned this into her goodbye party.

'Anyway, you just need to speak to Ollie tomorrow and sort it all out,' I try to reason for the third time.

'But there's just so much against us,' she sighs sinking herself back into the sofa.

'There's also so much going for you both,' Izzy says, still ever the positive even if her own situation couldn't be worse. 'At least you don't have a crazy stalker ex-wife out to kill you.'

'Well obviously, when you put it like that,' Jazz laughs.

'Jazz, please just sort it out with him,' Grace says, rubbing her bump. 'If you break up we won't be able to go on double dates anymore.'

Is that all she's concerned about?

She chooses to ignore her insensitivity. 'But you guys know how I hate apologising. Especially for the whole Rupert thing. For him to just assume I was shagging him is well out of order.'

I roll my eyes. 'Jazz he walked in wet from a shower in just a towel asking for his clothes. What the hell was he supposed to think?'

She glares at me. 'Ugh, trust his sister to stick up for him.'

'I'm serious though. Don't let both of your stubbornness mess up your future together. You're crazy if you don't see how perfect you are together.'

She stares into space. 'He is kind of dreamy, right?'

'Totally,' Grace grins. 'He gets that from Richard.'

Izzy's phone starts ringing. She stands up and turns away from us to answer it.

'More juice,' Jazz demands, thrusting her glass in my face as if she were Jemima.

Izzy turns back, her face drained of all colour, the phone still at her ear. She throws the phone down on the sofa and starts crying.

'No, no, no, no, no,' she cries hugging her arms around herself.

I jump up and console her. 'What's wrong? Who is it?'

'It's...her,' she stutters. 'She says she's in the garden.'

'What?' Jazz shrieks. She jumps up and runs over to the back window. She flicks a switch, and the garden light comes on. 'How the fuck did she get into my tree!'

I rush over to see. She is, she's actually climbed her tree. How the hell did she even get in there?

'That's it!' Jazz announces. 'I'm going to kill this bitch.' She goes to march downstairs.

Damn it, this woman is not stable. She almost killed me. I can't just let my pregnant bestie confront her.

I turn to Grace, who is hugging Izzy. 'Call the police.'

I run down after her and into the garden. Jazz is already at the bottom of the tree shouting at her.

'Come down, you crazy bitch!'

'Jazz, just leave her and come inside. She's unstable.'

I look up at her. It's hard to make her out in the dim light, but I can see her crazy eyes glistening back at me.

'The police are on their way,' Grace says as she walks out behind us. 'They're coming for you!'

I have to try and reason with her.

'Look, why don't you just come down from there and we can talk?'

She grins like the Cheshire cat. She looks just as crazy.

'Okay,' she says in a childlike voice.

She jumps, making us all flinch at the sound of rope tightening. I open my eyes to see her dangling from a rope in front of me. Oh, my fucking Jesus. The bitch has just hung herself! In front of us.

I vomit. All over the grass.

'Help me, Poppy!' Jazz screams, trying to lift her body weight up.

Do something, Poppy. Do something.

I force my legs to move and walk over to her, grabbing onto her leg and trying to help prop her up but she's already floppy. Oh my god, if I'm holding a dead body right now I'm going to puke again.

Grace appears with a knife from the kitchen. 'Try and keep her still,' she orders while hacking away at it.

She finally falls floppy to the floor.

'What the hell are we going to do now?' I shout. 'Do you know CPR?'

'Do I look like I do?' Jazz screams back.

Grace pushes us both away and starts pumping her chest. Jazz runs in and calls an ambulance. How can this really be happening? Grace breathes in her mouth and starts pumping again. She's not responding. She keeps going for what feels like an eternity until the ambulance turns up and whisks her away. Grace collapses back onto the grass, exhausted.

'Grace, are you okay?'

She's still out of breath. 'Yeah, I just oooooh.' She clutches the sides of her stomach, her face contorting.

'Are you okay?

'Yeah, that was weird,' she says, shaking her head.

I help her up from the grass. 'I'm just really...oooooh.' She nearly tumbles back down onto the grass.

Jazz stares at me and then turns to Grace. 'Are you having fucking contractions right now?'

'No, I'm fine,' she laughs. 'Just probably wind or something.'

We make our way into the house and comfort Izzy. We're just calling Michael to collect her when Grace doubles over again in pain.

'Right, we're taking you to hospital,' I insist. 'And I'm calling Richard.'

# Chapter 38
## Poppy

Hours later, I let myself in at home and slump down onto the sofa. I'm beyond tired; my eyelids are heavy and my brain foggy. Turns out Grace is in labour, but luckily her waters haven't broken, and her cervix hasn't started to dilate. They've got her plugged up with something that is supposed to slow it all down, and they've given her steroids to build up the baby's lungs. They're keeping her in and hoping it will slow down or completely stop. She's only 33 weeks. It's far too early for the baby to be born.

Michael says the nutter has been sectioned into a mental health facility and won't be allowed out again until the court case. I just hope now Izzy can really get the help and security she needs.

'Pops, is that you?' Ryan shouts from upstairs.

'Yeah, it's me.'

'Will you help me up here?'

Ugh, doesn't he realise how bloody tired I am! It's...I look at my watch, okay so maybe it's only half ten at night, but I've been through it.

I drag myself off the sofa and trudge begrudgingly upstairs. I freeze on the stairs when I find him in the hallway attempting to pull the loft hatch down. Oh my god, he's going to find Linda!

'What are you doing?' I say, my voice wobbly as I rush over to him.

'I need to get my old hiking boots out of the loft.'

'I thought you threw them away?' I say, knowing full well that they're up there.

'I don't think I did.' He opens the hatch and pulls the ladder down.

Jesus, Poppy, think of something to stop him.

Grams walks out of her room. 'How is Grace?' She spots Ryan attempting to get into the loft. 'Ryan, what on earth are you doing? Get away from there right now.

'Yeah, have they stopped the labour?' Nicole asks, coming out of her room in silky pyjamas.

God, can we fit any more people into the hallway?

'Err...' it's hard to answer when you're worried your husband is just about to divorce you.

'She's okay,' I try to dismiss. 'Ryan, I don't think they're up there.'

He's got his foot on the ladder now.

He rolls his eyes. 'And I'm sure they are.' He's climbing the ladder now.

Grams looks at me in desperation. What the hell am I going to do? I need to shock him with something. Err...think Poppy. THINK!

'Jazz is pregnant,' I blurt out. Grams and Nicole's eyes bulge. I kind of forgot that they were here for a second. Should probably have kept that secret a *tad* longer.

'No way,' Ryan smiles, still on the ladder. 'That's great news.' Then he carries on climbing.

'Ryan, stop! They're not in there,' I insist.

His head is now in the loft.

I close my eyes and pray for a miracle. He's going to kill me. He might actually kill me with his own hiking boots.

He pokes his head back out holding his hiking boots. His face is impassive. What the hell is going on here? Maybe he's so angry he can't even react yet. In shock.

'Take these will you, babe?' he says handing over the clunky boots.

His head disappears back up the loft. I hold my breath. He leans back down.

'Babe,' he whispers. 'I don't want to panic you, but we've got someone sleeping in our loft. Go and call the police.'

'Oh my goodness!' Grams shrieks. 'I saw this once on America's Most Wanted. Waited until they were all asleep, and then slit their throats. I say we leave the house immediately and give them a chance to escape.'

Wait, so he knows someone's up there, but he hasn't seen who it is?

'Err, I really don't think we should bother the police. Probably nothing.'

'Well, I'm leaving if that's your attitude,' Nicole announces, flouncing away to her bedroom. Well, that's an easy way of making her leave.

'I'm serious, Poppy,' Ryan insists. 'Get my phone. I'll call them if you don't.'

'Why don't we just give them the chance to leave,' Grams interjects, smiling at me with desperate eyes. 'That'd be the nice thing to do.'

'Nice thing to do?' he shrieks. 'Are you both crazy?'

I gulp, waiting for my fate. How did I ever think I'd get away with this?

He shakes his head. 'No, you know what, I'm going up there.'

'No, Ryan, don't!' I try to hold onto his leg, but he's already up there.

I race up the ladder after him and climb into the loft. He's investigating the sleeping bag and sniffing around almost like a dog. Where the hell is she?

'Ryan, let's just go back down.'

'No, Poppy!' He looks at me doubtfully. 'Why aren't you worried about this?'

I avoid his gaze, knowing if I look into his eyes he'll just know I'm guilty of something.

'I just think you've got the wrong end of the stick. That's my sleeping bag.' I don't even believe myself.

'And the empty packets of food?' he demands, his brown eyes beyond suspicious now. 'Are they yours too?'

'Err...' My hands are clammy. I look down again, hoping he can't see me swallowing hard, trying to regain some composure.

'Whoever is here,' Ryan booms around the room, 'Come out now, or I'm calling the police.'

There's a shuffle in a corner behind our plastic crates of summer clothes. Oh god. This is it. This is the moment I'll be able to pinpoint where my marriage ended. Where I fucked up beyond repair.

Linda slowly emerges from behind it, a scared, sheepish expression on her face.

Ryan's in front of me so I can't see the reaction on his face, but I dread to imagine. Linda looks up every now and again and then back down at the floor. I still can't help but feel terrible for her.

There's a pregnant pause, which I use to hold my breath and imagine going back in time and not thinking I could get away with this.

Slowly, *so* bloody painfully slowly, Ryan turns round to me. He sighs, rubbing his temples. My insides churn so hard I fear I'll vomit.

'Poppy,' he says quietly, almost eerily quietly, *'please* tell me this has nothing to do with you.'

'Okay,' I nod, glad to stay silent.

'She was only trying to help me.' Damn it Linda; shut the fuck up! Can't she see she's incriminating me here?

Ryan walks calmly to me, his shaking hands holding onto the top of my shoulders. He locks eyes with mine, pleading me for information. A bolt of fear goes through me.

'Poppy, explain to me how you ever thought this was a good idea.' He basically growls it, his lip curling up in disgust.

'I...' my tongue is actually shaking from nerves so badly it's hard to form a sentence. I attempt to swallow it down. 'She was homeless. She had nowhere else to go.'

Hatred flashes in his eyes. 'That's what happens when you're a drug addict!' he shouts back, his voice booming through the loft. 'Get her the fuck out of my house NOW. And don't talk to me.'

'But...' I try to explain, try to rationalise it somehow.

'Don't Poppy.' He holds his hand up to hush me. 'Don't try and explain this. I really don't want to hear it.'

Jazz

*10<sup>th</sup> April*

I rang Meryl first thing this morning to apologise and explain everything I didn't doubt Ollie had told her. She told me to get my arse over to hers, and she'd make sure me and Ollie had the house to ourselves at lunchtime while she picked up Jemima and brought her back to my house. That's how the Chelsea house feels. My house. Not *our* house.

The minute I put the key in the door a sense of calm settles over me. How is it this place still feels more like home? I walk into the safari kitchen, and although it's ridiculous, it's right. My house might have the most designer fabulous furniture, but really it's soulless. This is really a home.

I've not long boiled the kettle when I hear the front door slam.

'Mum' Ollie calls. 'Dad said you needed me. What's wrong?' He stops dead when he sees me.

God, that look on his face. He looks so defeated; dark rings around his eyes like he didn't get much sleep last night. How is it that I've made him this miserable? An overwhelming urge to touch him takes over me.

Before I know what I'm doing, I run towards him and throw myself into his chest. He doesn't hesitate to wrap his arms around me. I've missed his warmth. It feels like forever since we've done this. Just held each other. Just been together.

'I'm sorry,' I whimper into his chest. 'It's all my fault.'

He sighs heavily, as if the whole weight of the world is on his shoulders. 'We should talk though.'

Oh God. He wants to talk. That doesn't sound good. Could he be dumping me? Is he finally sick of my shit? I could vomit from fear.

He leads me to the table by my hands and sits down next to me.

'First of all explain the guy in the towel.'

'Okay, he's my friend, Rupert. He popped in, and your charming daughter Jemima threw her spaghetti bolognaise all over him. It was all in his hair, so I offered for him to take a quick shower. Apparently the ever-efficient Lucine collected his clothes for the wash while he was in there. That woman's like a damn machine.'

'Okay,' he nods, quickly accepting that. 'Now, the baby.' He points to my stomach as if I don't know where it's currently residing.

'I'm keeping it. Although I'm scared shitless and really don't want it.'

'Why are you scared?' he asks, eyes narrowed.

'Because I might get post-natal depression again. And even if I don't, newborns are fucking hard. Plus, this time, I'll have Jemima and the thought of her missing out on my time breaks my heart.'

'Other people do it,' he smiles. 'We'll figure it out, I promise.'

'It's not just that,' I admit. 'I just don't want another baby. I don't want to go through everything again. But at the same time, the thought of an abortion makes me feel sick. I'm just so confused.'

'You'll have me this time, from the very beginning. Plus, now you're rich you can hire twenty nannies if you want.'

'Okay.' I throw myself into his arms again, needing the reassurance from his calm beating heart.

'But I hate Chelsea,' he blurts out quickly. 'I'm really sorry, Jazz, but I do. I hate being so far away from everyone. And I really do think you should think of the people in your life before you got this money. Me, Mum, Poppy. All of those other people are just add-ons. Plastic add-ons.'

He's right. He's so bloody right it's hard to admit.

'I agree,' I sigh. 'I'm sorry I just rushed ahead with everything, but I was so eager to get my old life back. I felt like with this money I could get back to the young party girl I was, but I think that has more to do with having Jemima than it does money.'

He nods.

'And I forgot that before Jemima I didn't have you. You might be a total pain in the arse, but you're my pain in the arse. You know?'

He smiles, lighting up his entire face, his eyes glistening in delight. God, he's a sexy fucker. No wonder he has the power to make me apologise.

'Okay,' he says on a sigh. 'I have to be honest too.' Shit, he's not finished? 'I hate you having this money. I feel totally less of a man every time you buy something. Like I'm your little bitch or something. I hate that.'

Could that really have been the main problem all along? He feels emasculated by me?

'I'm sorry, babe, but I can hardly just get rid of the money. We just need to find a way to make it work.'

'Well, we could start with selling the house in Chelsea.'

I nod. 'I know you're right. But...well I don't exactly want to live with your mother forever either.'

He chuckles. 'Trust me, neither do I.' He pulls me in further, so I'm back, pressed into his shirt.

'So what do we do? Look for a house round here?'

'I actually have an idea.' He stands up. 'Come on, get your coat.'

Five minutes and 2 miles later he pulls up to a field. Why the hell is he bringing me here? I step out of the car grimacing. He didn't tell me to bring wellies. I'm in my Valentino heels.

'Come on,' he smiles, enjoying my confusion.

He takes my hand and guides me into it, the mud squelching around my beautiful red studded heels.

'Eight acres,' he smiles. 'This land has just been put up for sale. We could buy it and build our own house, exactly the way we want it.'

Build a house? Why didn't I think of that?

'Wow,' is all I can say.

All of this land? 'How much is it?'

'It's up for two million.'

'Jesus! All of that land for two million when we've been living in a terrace.'

'You're finally starting to see things my way.'

I give his hand a squeeze. I suppose I finally am.

'There's enough room here to build us a kick arse house and still have loads of land.'

'Well, I was thinking...' He kicks some dirt with the heel of his foot. 'Would it be totally crazy to suggest we build something small for Mum and

Dad here too?'

I know I should be horrified, but strangely I'm not. Damn it, I need Meryl's help. And it's bloody lonely being by myself all day. I'll need the company.

'I think that's a great idea.'

He beams back at me. 'God, I love you.'

I grin back. 'Right back at you, sexy pants.'

'But...' he looks embarrassed to ask something.

'What?'

'I mean...can we afford this? I don't even know how much money you inherited and knowing you it could all be gone now anyway.'

I smile devilishly. 'Well, now I know you're not after me for my money I don't mind telling you. I got twenty million.'

His eyes double in size, almost bursting out of his head. 'You what? Jesus, why am I still working? To the Caribbean!'

# Chapter 39
## Poppy

*Thursday 14<sup>th</sup> April*

Ryan hasn't spoken to me since he found Linda. Not at all. He hasn't even given me eye contact. I've tried to explain my reasoning's, but each time he comes up with a reason to leave the room. It's like he can't even bear to be around me anymore. It's breaking my heart.

The only good thing about it is that Nicole moved back into her flat, claiming she didn't feel safe at ours anymore. Every cloud and all that.

He doesn't seem to have sussed on that Grams was in on it, and I'm happy not to incriminate her too. He needs someone he feels he can trust. She keeps begging me to let her confess, but I won't hear of it. She's here to relax and rejuvenate, not go through this emotional rollercoaster. Linda's moved into Grams' bungalow, and I'm still keeping a close eye on her, hoping she stays on the right track.

The good news is that she seems a lot stronger in herself lately. Teddy's just taken her back to his for dinner today. Those two are beyond adorable. She insists they're just friends, but I know she loves him to pieces. I wonder if old people are even interested in having a physical relationship or if companionship is enough?

I'm just changing her bed sheets when the door knocks. Ugh, who the hell could that be? I hope to God it's not Nicole having changed her mind and wanting to move back in.

I stomp towards the door, already in my pyjamas despite it only being 6.30pm and begrudgingly open the door. Two uniformed policemen face me.

Oh my God, what the hell are they doing here?

'Mrs Davis?'

'Err...yeah?'

'Can we come in?'

I stare at them completely nonplussed. I mean, I've never heard of random policemen turning up at people's houses and asking to come in without arresting them. I look over their uniform again. Are they even real policemen? This could all be a scam. As soon as I let them in they could hit me over the head with a vase and steal everything. My mumma didn't raise no fool!

'Can I see some ID please?' I ask defiantly, hand on my hip.

'Of course,' one of them says, still not smiling. He reaches into his pocket and produces an ID card.

I look it over studiously, but realistically I have no idea what I'm looking for. I look up at them to see if they're sweating. Any signs of nervousness really. Hmm, they seem to be holding it together quite well. But still, I'd rather find out on my doorstep.

'Are you questioning me or something? Because if so I'd rather you tell me a bit about it before I let you into my house.'

'Nothing like that, I'm afraid.' He looks to his colleague. 'Unfortunately, it's a lot more sensitive like that. Not something to just blurt out on the doorstep.'

Okay, now I'm worried. I stand back to let them through, seeming unable to utter a single word. A cold sense of dread makes its way over me, starting from my toes and ending around my neck like a rope, strangling me.

I follow them into the sitting room and sit down across from them. I wonder what the protocol for this is. Should I offer them a cup of tea? They look to one another, anxious expressions marring their faces. What the hell is happening?

One clears his throat. 'I'm afraid that we're here to inform you that Mr Ryan Davis has been involved in a motorcycle accident.'

It feels like someone's punched me in the stomach. I stare back at them, open-mouthed, through blurry eyes. Are they...are they telling me Ryan is *dead?* That can't be it. It just can't be. I refuse to believe it, even for a second. To believe it would be to give up and I refuse to give up on him.

'What...what happened?' I just about manage to get out, my voice hoarse.

'A driver didn't see him. We were called to the scene.'

'Tell me he's not dead,' I plead, tears falling down my cheeks. If he is, it's game over for me. It doesn't matter who else is left, if Ryan is gone, I might as well be dead too.

'He's in intensive care. We'll drive you there now. We didn't want to risk telling you over the phone and you driving in a traumatised state.'

Okay, so he's alive. That's something. Although intensive care really doesn't sound like he's out of the woods yet. My shocked body is guided out of the house by them and before I know it we're on our way. I glance out of the window at the falling rain. I can't believe this has happened to me. To Ryan. When I think of him hurt, I physically ache, my heart weeping for him. My God what if he dies still angry with me?

The door suddenly opens, and I realise we're here already. I follow them like a zombie into the hospital and towards the intensive care unit. They explain for me that I'm Ryan's wife. I feel strangely detached from it all. Like I'm watching a movie with someone else going through it.

A female doctor guides me into a private room. Oh my God, please don't tell me he is dead. Surely they reserve these private rooms for breaking the bad news, right?

'Is he dead?' I blurt out on a sob. 'Please don't drag it out, just tell me! I need to know.'

She puts her hands up in what I can only imagine she thinks is a calming motion.

'Your husband isn't dead, Mrs Davis. But he was unconscious when he came in. He's got a broken arm and a fractured pelvis. He's in surgery at the moment.'

'Surgery? Surgery for what?'

'For his fractured pelvis.'

Am I wrong in thinking a fracture isn't as bad as a break?

'We're using plates and screws which will be screwed into his bones. It will hold his bones together while the fracture heals.'

Oh my god, he's basically being turned into a tin man.

'Okay,' I nod, my mind reeling from all of this information. 'But...he's going to be okay, right?'

She purses her lips, her face serious. 'We think he'll be fine. He's in for a long recovery time though. He'll need bed rest for a long time.'

'Okay.'

'Feel free to wait in here until he's out of surgery. As soon as he's come round I'll come and get you.'

I thank her before falling into the uncomfortable green chair. I text Teddy to let him know something's happened and please get Grams to stay at his. I don't want to give her a heart attack with what's really happened.

I yawn loudly. What is it about getting devastating news that always makes me feel so bone crushingly tired? I use my bag as a pillow and stretch my legs out onto the other chairs. Hopefully, when I wake up, I'll see that it's all been a dream.

I'm woken up by someone shaking me by the shoulders.

'Unicorn!' I shout with a snort still in dreamland.

The silence wakes me up fully. The doctor is staring down at me with a bemused look on her face.

'Mrs Davis, he's out of surgery. You can see him now.'

'Oh thank God.' I quickly wipe my drool away and follow her through the hospital into a room on a ward.

Ryan's in the bed, his arm in plaster, looking barely coherent.

'Oh my God, babe,' I cry, rushing over to him. I press my face into his shoulder and inhale his scent. The scent I never thought I'd smell again. He actually smells quite sweaty, but it's still the best thing I've ever smelt. 'Are you okay?'

'Yeah,' he croaks. 'It's not as bad as it looks.'

Is he serious right now?

'Yeah right! You look awful!'

'Thanks,' he attempts a smile but stops when it looks like he's in pain.

'Are you on enough pain medication?' I look around for someone. 'Nurse! We need more pain meds over here!'

'Sssh!' he hisses. 'I'm fine, Pops, really.'

How can he be so flippant about this? He's just had major surgery? He could have bloody died, and he's all *I'm fine Pops*. Like *I'm* over-reacting.

'Ryan they said you were knocked unconscious off your bike. You could have been killed. I thought I was going to find you dead!'

He nods, the edges of his mouth creeping into a smile. 'But I wasn't. It's just a broken arm and fractured pelvis.'

'Just nothing, Ryan!' I scream, completely losing it. 'You could have been killed. You could have left me all alone, forever. There's nothing *'just'* about it!'

He finally seems to realise how upset I am; his eyelids drooped.

'Okay, babe, hush,' he tries to soothe. 'I'm here.'

I hadn't realised I'd started crying.

'I don't care that we've been arguing. Promise me, *promise*, that you'll never drive that motorbike again.'

He smiles weakly. 'Okay. I promise.'

# Chapter 40
## Poppy

*Friday 29<sup>th</sup> April*

Ollie and I help Ryan into the house. It takes so long to do anything with him now. We're only bringing him home after two weeks in hospital, but I'm already seriously considering taking Jazz up on her offer of a carer. We settle him down in the sitting room.

'My baby is home!' Grams shouts from the kitchen, running in. 'Thank goodness!' She strokes his hair back as she places small kisses all over his face.

'Enough, Grams!' he laughs, shooing her away.

'Thanks, Ols,' I say at the door. 'I have no idea how I'm going to cope for the next few months.'

He smiles kindly. 'You will, Pops. You're the most capable person I know. Only you would turn your house into a health drop-in centre.'

I smile back gratefully. 'Whatever you think, I'm cracking open a bottle of wine tonight to get through it.'

The truth is that I'm stupidly scared. Scared of the responsibility of looking after him and making sure he doesn't get hurt further. Let's be honest, with my track record, I could end up falling over him and breaking his hip completely off or something. I really don't trust myself. But it's not like I have any choice. I have to just get on with it.

I wave out of the door while Ollie backs his car out and drives off home. Him and Jazz are renting a mansion in St Albans at the moment while the sale of their new land goes through.

I go into the kitchen and pour myself a large glass of cold white wine. I take a deep breath before bringing it into the sitting room. He looks so cute in that chair, pillows propping him up.

'Well, I'm off to bed now I know my baby is okay,' Grams smiles, winking at me. She obviously knows we need time together.

I sit down on the sofa next to him. 'Are you comfortable?'

He smiles back at me. 'So glad to be home.' He takes my free hand and squeezes it.

'I'm so glad you're home too. All that back and forth to the hospital was a bitch.' I smile to let him know I'm only half joking.

'I know. I'm sorry.' He gives me his puppy dog eyes, like he even needs to placate me. 'You know we need to talk about my Mum at some point.'

Oh god. We've been skirting around it since the accident, all so pleased he's alive.

'I'm so sorry,' I admit with a heavy sigh. 'The total truth is that she turned up at our wedding. She didn't disrupt it; I bumped into her in the toilets, and she asked me to send her some pictures. From then on I've been emailing her.'

He closes his eyes and takes a deep breath, obviously attempting to calm himself down.

'You realise how upsetting that is for me, right?'

I nod. 'I know it was a total betrayal of your trust, but...well, you have to realise that she's still your Mum, Ryan. Regardless of how she's let you down, she still gave birth to you. If it weren't for her stupid decisions, I wouldn't have you. And besides, she never asked for anything in return. Ever.'

'Apart from somewhere to live,' he says sarcastically.

'No! Teddy found her on the street and forced her to come and stay here. Look, she had a flat and a job. She was doing well, but she got fired and then got evicted.'

'How tragic,' he drools sarcastically. Realisation goes through his features. 'Wait, Teddy brought her here. Does that mean Grams knew about this?'

Oh shit. I thought we'd got away with her not being in the doghouse.

'Ryan, they found her on the *streets*. Living rough. How could we have just turned her away?'

He relents slightly. 'You mean she didn't try to contact you before that for help?'

I shake my head. 'That's what I'm trying to tell you. She was too ashamed to ask for help.'

He looks down at his lap. 'How awful is that? My own mother living on the streets because she was too scared of me.'

Well, this is a turn-up for the books. I never thought he'd blame himself.

'It wasn't like that. She lied to you. I totally understand why you wanted to cut her out.'

'But you couldn't.' He smiles shyly. 'See, that's why I love you, Poppy. There's so much good in you. You can't help but want to save the world. I mean, look at our house. You turned it into a woman's refuge.'

I hang my head in shame. 'I'm sorry.'

'No, *I'm* sorry. For making you scared to tell me.'

Maybe this whole accident has given him a new perspective on life.

'The good news is that I've been giving her random drug tests I bought in Boots, and they're coming back clean.'

'Really?' He looks hopeful, and that's all I want. Some hope that he might want to rekindle some kind of relationship with her.

'Really,' I nod.

'God, it's good to be home and clear the air,' he says breathing a sigh of relief. 'I feel so much better already. But...' he grins cheekily, 'the nurses were always quicker with bringing me tea.'

Oh shit. I completely forgot to make him one. Here I am holding my wine, and I've not even boiled the kettle.

'Sorry, babe. Coming up.' I place the wine down and walk into the kitchen, filling up the kettle.

Something's niggling at me. I know it's because I'm about to drink wine without absolutely knowing I'm not pregnant. Not that there's any chance, what with him being in hospital for weeks and us not speaking to each other before that, but I normally wait until I have my period. Some kind of confirmation. I shouldn't even bother doing a test, but...well, the thought of the possibility and me drinking despite it, makes me feel ill.

I run upstairs and quickly pee on a stick from the cabinet. There's no point even telling Ryan. The amount of these I've done, I really should have taken out shares in Boots. I'd be a bloody millionaire by now.

I go back downstairs, make his tea and bring it into him.

'So...' he starts with a wry smile. 'Are we going to talk about the elephant in the room?'

I frown at him, confused. 'Huh?'

He points over himself. 'The fractured pelvis. You realise this means we can't have sex for months, right?'

I nod. 'Yeah, I know. Why's that an issue?'

He sighs heavily. 'Because you know that means we can't be trying for a baby in that time. I know you'll be pissed at all of those wasted months.'

I can't pretend I haven't thought about it. Of course I have. The minute the doctors explained it to me I couldn't believe I hadn't thought of it sooner. But strangely I'm kind of glad. I feel drained by the whole thing. The constant sex, just for the possibility of conceiving and not for the fun was killing me. I feel mentally and physically exhausted from it. And I can't help but think we're not meant to get pregnant right now. Some bigger force, call it God or Mother Nature, has decided that now is not the right time to have a baby and I'm strangely okay with that.

'I'm not actually,' I admit. 'Nearly losing you made me realise that I've become too obsessed with it all. It's affected our relationship, and I just want to get back to us being us.'

'Really?' he looks so relieved. 'Don't get me wrong, I want a baby, but I can't help but agree with you.'

'Good,' I nod, pecking a quick kiss on his lips. 'I've started to think lately that it might not be the end of the world if we can't have kids. We can have amazing holidays together instead.' I may have been looking up holidays to Barbados to take my mind off everything.

He unleashes the full devastating effect of his brown eyes on me as if trying to communicate something crucial.

'Pops, I don't need fancy holidays or even children if it's not meant to be. I just want *you*. You're enough.'

I can't help but let the smile explode onto my face. 'You're enough for me too.'

'Good,' he grins. 'Now shut up so we can watch the rest of EastEnders.'

We have the most amazing evening just chatting and laughing. Almost like we're getting to know each other again. It's so nice not to have the pressure on our shoulders.

I pull the sofa bed out and make it cosy. Then I transfer him into it and empty his wee bucket. That's right, we don't have a downstairs bathroom and its way too early days to even attempt the stairs.

I tuck him in and kiss him goodnight, making sure his mobile phone is close enough to him. We've agreed it's easier if he sleeps down here alone. I don't trust myself not to accidently roll over and crush him. It's happened before. I kiss him goodnight and go up to bed.

God, I'm shattered, and this is only the first night. I'm glad I ditched the wine and had a cup of tea with him instead. It would have been way harder being a bit pissed. I go into the bathroom and take out a face wipe. I'm far too tired to do all that cleansing, toning, and moisturising lark. I sit down and have a pee, my eyelids already shutting from the urge to sleep.

That's when I spot the pregnancy test I did earlier. Oops, well I totally forgot about that. I pick it up and go to throw it in the bin when I see something weird. Is that...two lines? I pull it closer, so I can take a good look. Oh my God, there are two lines. What the hell? That means...I'm pregnant. No, I can't be pregnant. I can't be, can I?

Wait, I remember reading once online that if you leave a pregnancy test too long, you can get a false positive. It's obviously just that. Not that it doesn't start butterflies fluttering around in my stomach at the mere possibility. I dive into my room and take out the six remaining pregnancy tests I have left.

I use the bottle of water I kept by the bed last night to drink loads of water from the sink. Then I'm squatting and pissing on them all like a fucked up pregnancy test Wolverine. I place them all on the side and start the stopwatch on my phone. It's only three minutes. I can totally wait three minutes, no big deal. Okay, no I can't. I'm just staring at the tests.

I force myself to look in the mirror and contemplate the shape of my eyebrows. I should really pluck more of my left eyebrow or less of the right. Maybe I should get some of that eyebrow filling powder or gel. They seem to be all the rage these days.

I'm pretty sure I'm getting my hopes up anyway. I mean; I feel completely the same as normal. I don't have any of the symptoms that I'm forever looking for. Do I? I suppose I have been peeing slightly more, but not enough to warrant any suspicion. And I've been getting cramps in my legs just before bed, but I've never seen that listed as a pregnancy symptom.

Okay, that's all the waiting I can handle. It might only be one minute fifty-two seconds, but I have to look. I glance back at the tests. Two lines. All I can see are two lines on every single test. Shit the bed. I'm really pregnant.

I bound down the stairs and rush into the sitting room, flicking the light on. Ryan lifts his head, his eyes groggy.

'Pops?' he asks in confusion, blinking as if the light is blinding him.

I jump on the bottom of the sofa bed. 'Guess what?'

'Aagh!' he shouts, bending his head back down in agony. Oh shit, I suppose I forgot about the whole pelvis thing. But, I mean, can you blame me? I'm beyond excited here!

'Sorry, babe!' I hover my hands over him as if I suddenly have Reiki and can heal him. Who knows, maybe I now have some insane pregnancy healing power or something? It's definitely worth a shot. 'Only, I have the most *amazing* news!'

He yawns. Actually yawns, like I'm going to tell him some boring celebrity gossip or something. I've only woken him to tell him about a celebrity divorce a few times. And okay when Madonna fell at the Brits. You know; big news kind of stuff.

I wait a second and try to remember this feeling of pure bliss. I could actually burst from happiness.

'I'm pregnant.' I can't help but grin like the Cheshire cat who got the cream.

He stares back at me as if I'm trying to crack some ridiculous joke. 'Huh?'

'I know! I'm shocked too, but it's real. I did six bloody tests.' Goose pimples run up and down my back.

'Oh my god.' His eyes start welling up making me feel like blubbing too. Must be my hormones. My pregnancy hormones! I never thought I'd be able to say that.

'Our dreams have just come true babe. We're having a baby.'

## 19<sup>th</sup> December

As I stare down into my son's big green eyes, I feel more blessed than I have my entire life. I can't believe that Ryan and I made him. Made his tiny little fingers, his long little fingernails, and his little frog toes.

'We did it, Pops,' Ryan smiles, kissing me on my forehead.

It might have been the longest and most painful thing I've ever encountered, but the minute he was placed on my chest, it was love at first sight.

'I still can't believe it. We have a son. The only grandson in the family. Dad is going to be so chuffed.'

He gazes at both of us in awe. 'What shall we call him?'

We've had a few names floating around but not decided on one yet. I look down at his wrinkled face. I just know what he looks like immediately.

'I think he's a Ralph. What do you think?'

He grins. 'I was going to say the same thing. Ralph Douglas Davis.'

I love it. He sounds like a reporter from the forties.

I nod. 'Ralphy while he's a baby.' I'm already irrationally scared of him growing up and leaving me.

Ryan leans over me and plants a kiss on my forehead. 'I love you so much, Pops.'

I grin up at him. 'I love you too. But I probably love him more. Is that bad?'

He laughs. 'I'm pretty sure I can fight for your affections with my favourite little man.'

There's commotion outside of our door. What's going on out there? The door bursts open and Jazz walks in.

'I told you, I AM family,' she shouts at the nurse. She continues walking in, carrying my beautiful niece Beatrice; Jemima and Ollie trailing behind her. Her face lights up when she spots us. 'Oh my god!'

'It's a boy,' Ryan grins. He scoops up Jemima. 'Jem Jem I'd like you to meet your cousin Ralph.'

'He's squishy,' she giggles looking down at him.

She's adjusted so well to having a new baby sister. Jazz has too, even though she'll tell you it's hell. She actually started a blog called Crappy Mummy when she was pregnant. I think it was more to take her mind off the stressful building work going on in the plot of land they bought. Plus, with so much money she went through a bit of a weird time where she questioned what she was doing with her life. Now she's got over one million subscribers. Her posts are bloody hilarious and seem to have resonated with every other crappy mummy out there. She's still refusing to get a nanny, but Mum helps her out loads. That woman's going to be busy.

Their house is now built, and it is *beyond* stunning. It's a five bedroomed, six bathrooms house with a cinema room, games room, swimming pool and sauna. She never needs to leave the house again.

It was such a big plot of land that Mum and Dad have a smaller house next to them. I say smaller, it's still bigger than their previous three-bed semi and full of all the latest mod cons. As far as I can tell he's over his mid-life crisis. He stopped driving his motorbike after Ryan's accident and thankfully took out the earring. Although he's still talking about getting all of the grandkids names tattooed down his back, God bless him.

She's even built a house for Grams and Teddy. She was insistent on her having her own space away from us, and it kind of made sense for them to live together. Most of Teddy's family has moved out of London so this way they get to look after each other while still feeling that independence. We also have a carer go in three times a day to check on them and make sure they're eating well. We all know it's only going to get harder as they get older. Jazz also made sure alarms are all over the place so they can press it if one of them is hurt.

They've even kept a plot of the land in case me and Ryan change our mind and want to live there. At the moment, we're more than happy with our house around the corner.

'Beatrice, meet Ralphy.'

They're barely three months apart so are bound to be best friends.

'Ralphy's going to protect you when you're both older,' Ollie says to his girls. 'If any boys try any funny business.'

He'll be protecting a lot more than them. Grace and Richard welcomed Ava Amelia the day after I found out I was pregnant.

'Funny business?' Jemima asks. 'Like telling jokes? I love jokes.'

'Err...sort of,' Jazz grins. She turns back to me. 'You know you have the entire family in the waiting room, right?'

'Oh God. Give us a few more minutes before sending them in okay? I don't want to scare him straight away.'

'Okay,' Jazz says before leaning in closer to my ear. 'Julie's brought Ryan's mum and she's asking if she can come in too.'

Oh, crap. Julie seems to have got her Mum sorted again, which I never saw coming. I was sure she was done with her, but when she found out that she was clean, she stepped in. She's now settled in a council flat and working a part time job in a post office. Not that Ryan has relented. He agreed to me see her and send her emails, but he still maintained to both me and Julie, that he wasn't interested in any form of relationship.

'Ryan.' I look down at Ralph sleeping peacefully in my arms. He's about to experience his first awkward conversation. 'Jazz says your mum's here. Do you think we could let her see Ralph?' I scrunch my face up while I wait for his no.

He stares at me for a long time. Ollie visibly cringes and takes Jemima out.

'Okay,' he says finally with a nod.

My eyes nearly bulge out of my head. He said yes? Wow.

Jazz nods like a maniac, backing out of the room like she's scared of frightening a rare bird.

I turn to him. 'You don't have to if you don't want to you know.' I don't want him to feel pressured.

'It's fine.' But his body language tells a different story. He's stiff, cracking his knuckles as we wait.

The door opens, and Julie walks in shielding a scared and trembling Linda. She must be terrified Ryan's going to launch for her.

'Oh my goodness, guys!' Julie says when she spots him in my arms. 'He's so precious! And I love the name.'

Ryan looks down at Linda, who's not looking at Ralph. She's staring straight at Ryan with watery eyes. She launches herself at him, wrapping her arms tightly around his body. Ryan stays completely still but doesn't try to remove her.

She pulls back to look at him. 'I know I have absolutely no right, but I'm so proud of you. You're going to make an amazing father.'

'Am I?' he scoffs. 'It's not like I had a normal upbringing to draw experience from.'

She smiles sadly. 'Ryan, I'm so sorry. I know you might not ever forgive me, but I just want to say that if you ever are, I'll be here. Drug-free and ready to have any kind of relationship you're willing to give me.'

God, she's so sweet.

He looks down at Ralph. 'I just...when I look at Ralph I can't ever imagine hurting him. And you did. You left me time after time to go and get a fix. That's not what a parent's programmed to do.'

'Ryan, you have to realise that I was ill. Addicted. Nothing or nobody could stop me. I tried even harder with Julie, but I still didn't succeed. I regret so much, but I can't take any of it back, no matter how much I want it. I can only beg for some kind of forgiveness. Please think about it.'

He nods solemnly.

She looks over to Ralph. Her face crumples up in emotion, tears swimming in her eyes.

'He's beautiful, Poppy. Well done.'

'Do you want to hold him?' I ask. I feel Ryan tense beside me.

'Oh, no thanks. He looks more than happy with his mummy right now. I just wanted a quick peep. Now, I better get out of here before your mother finds out I saw him before her. She'd likely hurt me.'

'Probably stab you in the face,' I laugh.

We wave goodbye to them and brace ourselves for the inevitable entrance of everyone. Mum and Dad are going to be so pleased I gave them a grandson. Auntie Beryl will be here with sneezing Simon, who are still going strong. Izzy's out of the priory after a four-month stay. Luckily Michael has been amazing and worked with her therapists to ensure she's got a safe and loving home to come home to. She's eating well and has that spark back in her eyes. He even got her Mum to stay with them for her first few weeks. She's back working, and I think just knowing that his ex-wife is now in a mental hospital for the next twelve years helps.

Nicole had a baby boy around the same time as Grace and called him Alfie. Her and Grace have remained close friends, and I plan to have a cuppa with them soon so the babies can play together. Who would ever have thought that I'd be having tea with Nicole and Grace? Having a baby sure does put petty things into perspective.

'Are you ready?' Ryan asks, stroking my sweaty hair off my forehead.

I look up into his gorgeous brown eyes. 'As long as I have you I'm ready for anything.'

THE END

*Thank you so much for reading and I hope you enjoyed it! I would truly appreciate you leaving a quick review on Amazon. If you'd like to reach out to me my links are below:*

www.laurabarnardbooks.co.uk
www.facebook.com/laurabarnardbooks
https://twitter.com/BarnardLaura

## *Also by Laura Barnard*

The Debt & the Doormat
The Baby & the Bride
Tequila & Tea Bags
Dopey Women
Sex, Snow & Mistletoe

# Acknowledgements

Thanks first and foremost to my family and friends. Without you all being crazy I would honestly have no new material! Special thanks to my long suffering husband Simon who is always on hand as a sounding board, tea maker, house cleaner and all round life saver. Also my cheerleaders; my Mum Lorraine McCarthy and my auntie Mad Brown. Without you giving out my cards to EVERYONE you meet I'd probably have half my sales.

Big hugs to my friends Clare Pinkstone, Julie Wills and Sarah-Jane Bookham that beta read for me and didn't tell me to go away and re-write the whole thing.

Thanks to Claire Allmendinger from Bare Naked Words Editing – easiest and most fun edit I've ever had. Feel like I've also gained a friend. Formatting made this book so pretty thanks to Leigh Stone's mad skills.

Smoochy kisses to Natalie Townsen for being the fastest and most efficient proof-reader ever. You know I love you!

Enormous thanks goes to Kaprii and Lorraine from Two Ordinary Girls & Their Books who organised my cover reveal and release day blitz. So much hard work goes on behind the scenes that people don't realise and without them I would have lost my mind.

Love to my author family that I look forward to partying with at every singing we attend.

Big shout out to every single blogger, author and reader that has shared cover reveals, posted links and helped share the word. Without you us Indie

.thors would be nowhere in this world and a day doesn't go past that I'm not appreciative.

Lightning Source UK Ltd.
Milton Keynes UK
UKOW06f0801070416

271756UK00016B/317/P